THE PARADISE GENERATION

SANNA THOMPSON

umop apisdn press

The Paradise Generation

first published in 2024 by

umop apisdn press
Pōneke Wellington,
Aotearoa New Zealand
www.sannathompson.com

A catalogue record for this book is available from the
National Library of New Zealand Te Puna Mātauranga o Aotearoa

Cover design by Getcovers

ISBN 978-1-0670373-0-7 (paperback)
ISBN 978-1-0670373-1-4 (ebook)

Typeset in EB Garamond with Barlow Condensed Semibold, in New Zealand English.

1st edition 2024

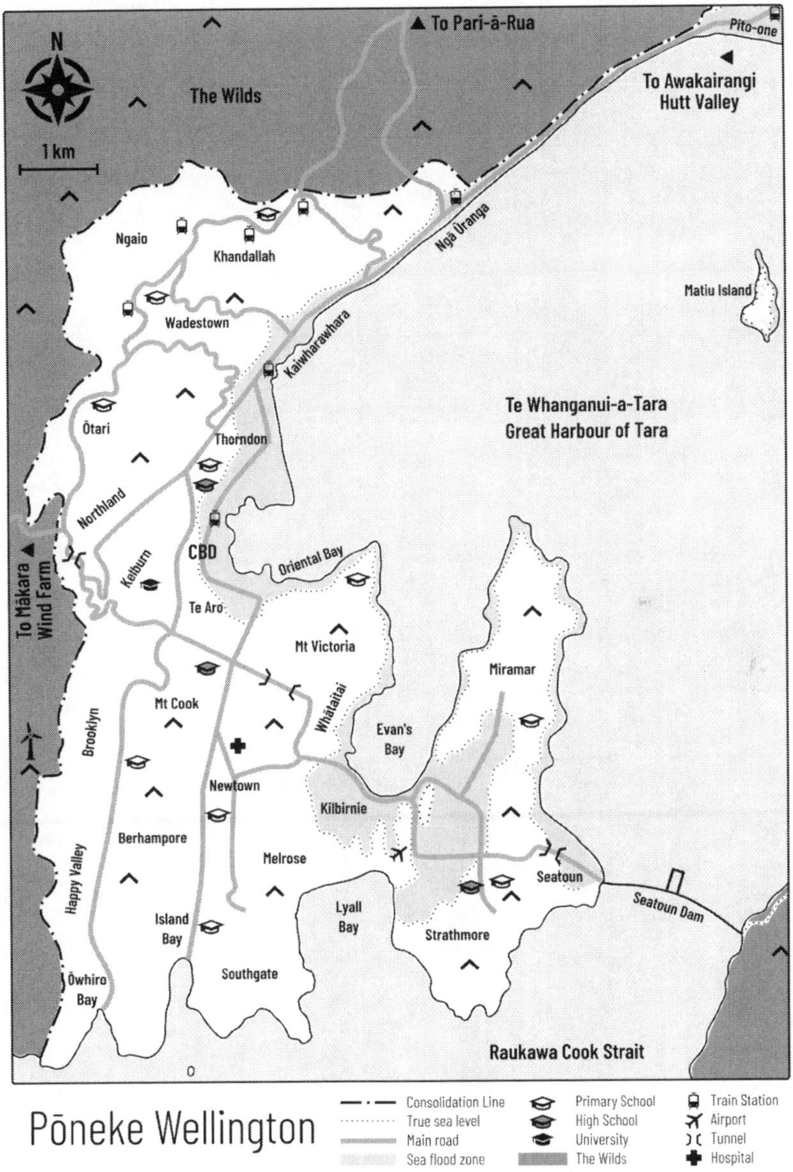

Pōneke Wellington

1

Gen-en

I PROBABLY SHOULD NOT have been at the hospital at three in the morning. Three a.m. is not *technically* visiting hours, but there was no way Mum would let me go twice in one week (even if I faked sick), and she doesn't notice I'm gone at three in the morning. Plus I couldn't sleep, so what else was I going to do?

"Morning, Kieran." The duty nurse had his feet up on the desk, face glowing in the light of his tablet.

"Hey. Any chance...?"

"Oh, I dunno about that." He tapped his tablet against his chin and raised his eyebrows. "How much you gonna give me?"

"Come on, dude... Pretty please? Sugar on top?"

"Bit late for you to be out."

"Jimmy..."

He grinned and motioned for my wrist. I held it out so he could code my chip with a door pass.

"You don't know anything about Joshi algorithms, do you?" I asked.

"I'm not doing your homework for you."

"You'd be more like a tutor than a cheating assistant."

He ignored me. "All done."

I sighed and swiped a few mints from the bowl on the desk. "Fine. Thanks."

"No problem. You want a lollipop too?"

I couldn't tell if he was teasing, but who passes up a free lollipop at three o'clock in the morning? "Sure," I said, walking backwards towards the long-term wards, hands held open to catch.

He snorted, rummaged in the desk and threw me two.

Lucas was on the second floor. I took the stairs two at a time, saluted the half-asleep nurse at her station and followed the corridors to his room. His door was open but his windows were on dark mode. I moved around the bed by memory, swiped up the window opacity so a little light shone in, and took the bedside chair.

"Hey, cuz," I whispered. "You awake?"

Nope. That was the problem with three a.m. visits. I touched his hand and he stirred, blinked, murmured something that might have been "hey Kieran! What's up?" but probably wasn't. He hadn't spoken in four years.

I sighed, dropped my bag and scuffed off my shoes, pulled the other chair close enough to put my feet up, settled both cushions behind me and unwrapped the first lollipop. "Yeah, same old... Couldn't sleep. Thought I'd come keep you company, maybe soak up some genius. I gotta hand in something for IT in seven hours, and I don't think what I've got is gonna cut it."

Lucas had been crazy good at IT. He'd been good at pretty much everything, or at least it seemed like it when I was twelve. His sister moved across the Pacific to Seattle that year for a Match, and his parents went too to help her settle in, so he stayed with us for a few months. Sometimes I wonder what would have happened if he hadn't stayed with us, if I hadn't nagged him to take me on adventures.

He should have been at uni by now.

"My brain's not working," I went on. "You know when you try to concentrate, but then you're just thinking 'gotta concentrate', or you can't stop thinking of stuff you're trying not to think of? So I thought maybe if I came over, it'd be like 'hey! Lucas is all good', and I can stop thinking about you lying here all by yourself, and maybe I can concentrate on Joshi algorithms. Or, you know, sleep."

They say talking to people can help them recover, so that's what I'd been trying to do every week for the last four years. So far it hadn't worked. Maybe it was just something they told friends and family to stop them going crazy.

"You know what would be amazing? If you could, like, hook up to a tablet and explain Joshi algorithms to me. Or maybe upload your brain to the cloud." I crunched the lollipop into tiny pieces and twisted the stick between my teeth. "Though I guess if you were in the cloud, then they'd be complaining about you taking up valuable server space. Shit, you can't win, can you?"

I pulled out my tablet and made another heroic attempt at the Joshi assignment, but my brain wasn't working any better here so it ended up back in my bag while I updated Lucas on the latest VR releases (a New Zealand doco about extinct giant moa in ancient forests, which I was pretty sure they'd filmed in our local green belt, and cave diving in Mexico).

I was describing the perilous abseil into a sink hole when the lights pulsed on, red. I stopped midsentence. In all my visits, they'd never gone red. Blue, yeah, for an earthquake last year, and I'd had time to duck under a table before the shaking started. There'd been a siren and announcement, too, but there was no announcement now.

On, off, on, off, like a heartbeat. I went to the door. The corridor was deserted, but I could hear the nurse's strained voice, something about emergency exits.

"You know what's going on?" I whispered to Lucas. "Anything like this happened before?"

The fire door at the end of the corridor slammed shut, way faster than a heavy roller door should move. I swore, grabbed Lucas's door and shut it, which meant I could only look out through the wire mesh glass. There was nothing to see in the corridor, anyway, just that pulsing red light. I kept looking. Fire doors meant fire, right? But where was the fire alarm?

The PA chimed, and a male voice came on. "All patients, please remain in your rooms. Repeat: stay in your rooms. We'll give you further advice as the situation changes."

"Great," I muttered, uneasy. "I gotta leave before six, or Mum's gonna notice..."

Lucas didn't answer, but his eyes were open now. He didn't look that worried. But then, he never did.

I checked the door for a lock. There wasn't one, at least not from this side. Hooray. I pulled out my phone and checked the Pōneke Wellington alerts page, but there wasn't anything there. Maybe it took a while to register an alert, or maybe this whatever-it-was wasn't big enough...? I'd barely thought that when a blue-and-red glow hit the glass. No siren. The cops had arrived, yet there was nothing on the alerts.

Something hit the floor above us, hard, like a dropped bowling ball. A muffled shout, then running feet. Slamming doors. I sucked in a breath, my heart stuttering into a new rhythm. What was on the third floor? It must exist, but the stairs just kept going up to the fourth floor, past a blank landing. I'd asked someone once and they said it was private staff offices, but you'd still have a door for those, right?

"Ah..." I said. "Do you think we should jump out the window?"

Obviously that wasn't happening. I pulled a chair over to the door and wedged it under the handle like they did in movies, kind of hoping I was being stupid. If the PA guy would tell us what was going on, I wouldn't have to–

A door down the corridor yawned open. A red-lit face peered around the corner. I half-choked on my tongue and pressed against the wall. All the people on this floor were supposed to be like Lucas – maybe they could feed themselves with supervision, do the physio that kept their muscles in good shape, but there was no way they were peering round corners with that kind of wild focus in their eyes.

Maybe it was a nurse.

But I knew all the nurses, or I thought I did. Okay, maybe I didn't actually remember their names a lot of the time, but still, I was pretty sure I could pick them out five doors down a darkened corridor with red flashing–

Okay, fine. It was a nurse. It was a nurse. No need to get freaked out–

Running feet, a dark shape sprinting past, hair flying out, hitting the exit doors with a bang.

"Oookay," I muttered. "We're good, right Lucas? We can just wait right here and all the scary people will go right past us and then they're not our problem any more. So we'll just wait... here..."

Now the alarm started up, shrieking in time to the red pulse. The shape must have opened one of the emergency exits. I clamped my hands over my ears and turned to see Lucas straining to sit up, eyes wide, mouth moving soundlessly.

I wasn't even supposed to be here.

I tried to pull Lucas's bottom drawer open with my elbow, hunching my shoulder against my ear and using my hand when the drawer refused to budge. His noise-cancelling headphones took a bit of fumbling with the case, but eventually I stuck them over his ears, pressed the on button, and he stopped looking so stressed. I pulled him out of bed and into a crouch behind it, wishing he had a second pair of noise-cancelling headphones. At least he wasn't hooked up to any tubes or wires. Did the "stay in your room" advice still hold? Alarms meant evacuate – but I didn't really want to follow whoever had run out the fire escape–

Tasers cracked. Then a gunshot. I swore and dragged Lucas lower. He fell the last bit, almost hitting his head, but I managed to get him sitting there in his hospital PJs. If the police were using guns, this was serious. Unless the dark shape had a gun? I pulled out my phone, hand shaking, and checked the alerts again. Still nothing.

Cold seeped out of the lino. I pressed my hands back over my ears.

The exit doors clanged like someone was shoving metal together. In the low points of the shrieking alarm, I could hear someone swearing over and over again. Then the alarm cut out. I guess we weren't supposed to evacuate after all.

The someone gave one last curse. Silence.

The red lights continued to pulse.

I pulled my hands from my ears and took a shaky breath, made myself peek up over the edge of Lucas's bed.

I didn't have to wait long before the dark shape appeared again, slower, limping. I saw its face this time – hollowed cheeks, dark eyebrows, checkerboard tattoo at her temple.

I sucked in a breath and froze. Definitely not a nurse. The checkerboard tattoo gave it away – Gen-en.

She passed. I didn't think she'd seen me.

It was the first time I'd seen a Gen-en in real life. Eighty years ago, they were everywhere, but then they decided Earth would be better off without humans and tried to wipe us out. Cue the Great Plagues. After that, people realised genetically engineered humans were a bad idea. Like, an end of the world bad idea. There are still a few left, but they keep them locked up so they can't finish the genocide they started.

She – or really, it – looked nothing like the winged or sword-handed Gen-ens in games like Fight Xtreme or Conquesterra, or even the ones we studied in history, tall and willowy with luminescent skin, living examples of Gen-en "Perfection". She looked normal, apart from the tattoo and her wild eyes. It creeped me out, but I guess it wasn't surprising. The Nix Gen-ens bombings a few years ago had killed a bunch of Gen-ens and outed a bunch more, so if Gen-ens were hiding in plain sight, they must look like normal people.

This was probably one of the Gen-ens the terrorists outed. Even psychopathic super-beings must get sick sometimes. The hospital would have had at least one guard on it, you'd hope, so it must have killed them or knocked them out.

Which gave me and Lucas real good odds.

Our door was barricaded. Sort of. I just had to sit tight, stay unnoticed until whatever was going to happen happened, and with luck get home before someone noticed I wasn't in bed.

The Gen-en's footsteps faltered. I held my breath, wondering if it had superhearing and could count how many people were in each room. It groaned, swore again, and then there was a heavy thump, like it had fallen into a wall. A swish of clothes. Strained breathing, a moan.

I'd seen Gen-ens wounded in movies – I'd shot them myself in VR games – but it was way, *way* different having a wounded Gen-en one wall away in real life. I had an insane urge to go find a first aid kit, just to stop the sounds. A wounded Gen-en sounds a lot like a wounded human. I guess that's what makes them so dangerous – you can't help feeling sorry for them.

Something rattled the exit doors. A gasp, more swearing from the Gen-en, and then scuffling and footsteps. I crouched and closed my eyes, hoping it was the cops – it would be, right? – and that they'd just come in and fix things.

It was shuffling, dragging itself along the floor. A door handle squeaked, a latch clicked. Was it going back where it had come from? Or hiding in some patient's room? It could take them hostage. It could–

A shriek of twisted metal from the exit doors. The low moans sounded muffled, then quiet. Boots on the lino.

"No sign," a cop muttered.

I opened my mouth to tell them it was in one of the rooms, but nothing came out. The boots crept down the corridor. I squeezed my eyes shut and tried not to breathe.

Doors clicked open. At the fifth door–

The Gen-en gave a strangled yell. "I'll kill you all, you stupid f–"

The crack of tasers. The yelling cut off.

2
Grounded

Lucas and I hid for the next twenty minutes. I dragged the blanket off and pulled it over us, and Lucas fell asleep on my shoulder while I tried not to listen to the cops getting a gurney with a squeaky wheel, the thwump as they lifted the Gen-en on. They fetched a doctor, and argued whether they should take the Gen-en back up to Level 3.

"Realistically, there's no point," one of the cops said. She sounded like she was in charge. "Let's just get it out of here and wait for the ruling."

When the gurney had squeaked its way out of hearing, the red lights stopped pulsing. I checked my phone again, and finally there was an alert:

Pōneke Wellington Hospital – Gen-en escape from custody: contained.

Oh, of course they talked about it once they had everything under control.

A cop tried to open the door, then knocked when she realised my trick with the chair. I stood slowly, shifting Lucas to lean against the bed and trying to shake the cramp out of my leg. I limped over to check the ID she held up, then dragged away the chair.

"Hi," I said.

"Hi." She wasn't the one in charge – her voice was different. "Kieran, right?"

"Yeah."

"I'm Roi. Jimmy said you'd be here. You okay?"

I shrugged. "Still alive."

She patted my arm awkwardly. "That's the spirit. And your cousin?"

"Won't remember any of this anyway." She looked kind of thrown, but I was too tired and shell-shocked to play optimistic about Lucas. "Um... have you called my parents?"

"Your Dad's on his way."

So. No chance of sneaking in at six a.m., then.

They let me sit in Lucas's room with a blanket and hot tea until Dad arrived. Maybe there was something in the tea, or maybe I was just super tired, because I felt kind of numb, like everything was happening just out of reach behind thick glass.

"Kier?"

I jerked, managed not to spill my tea everywhere, and put the mug on the bedside table. "Hey, Dad."

He wrapped me in a tight hug, and I thought maybe I was forgiven, but no.

"Glad you're all right," he said, hands on my shoulders. "Now, what the hell are you doing here in the *middle of the night*?"

"What do you think I'm doing here?" He opened his mouth to make some stupid "there, there, it's going to be all right" kind of comment, but I cut him off. "Lucas is helping me with my homework."

—— · ——

Mum was waiting for us in the front window in her dressing gown, arms crossed, mouth like a squeezed lemon. I took my time putting my bike away, but there's only so long you can fake falling over spare bike parts and losing a shoe. Dad had already gone back to bed.

Eventually I stood in the front hall in my socks, trying not to make eye contact as Mum yelled at me in a whisper – Verity was still asleep upstairs. At least I didn't have an audience.

"They said this is a regular thing! They thought we knew about it!"

There was definitely some truth fudging going on. Jimmy knew I was there without my parents' permission. I hung my head and tried to look like I was sorry, but Mum hadn't properly yelled at me in years, and apparently that wasn't the best strategy anymore.

"Look at me!"

I looked up, trying to focus on the bridge of her nose instead of her eyes.

She took a deep breath and softened about half a percent. "Do you understand why we don't want you going to the hospital at all hours?"

"Yeah," I muttered. "Cos the doctors are doing the best they can, and me spending all my time there isn't healthy."

"And?"

"And… it's not my responsibility to fix Lucas." I'm good at counselling-speak. I've had some practice.

"Exactly. And why don't we want you outside after your curfew?"

"Um…" This one was harder. "I might drink and steal stuff and throw rocks at penguins?"

Apparently humour was also a bad strategy. Mum gave me a look.

"It's dangerous, Kieran."

"Tonight was a one in a million thing," I burst out. "Nothing has ever happened, *any* other time I've been there–"

"But now it has–"

"If it was properly dangerous, they'd make a city curfew, and I always follow the city curfew–"

"Just not *our* curfew."

"No!"

Uh oh. That was definitely the wrong thing to say.

Mum's eyes glinted like steel. "Why is the city curfew more important than our curfew?"

"Uh... they have auto-tasers?" I said weakly.

"And yet, if you'd followed *our* curfew, you wouldn't have been caught up in what happened at the hospital just now."

"It was fine," I lied.

"You could have– could have–" Mum squeezed her eyes shut and I suddenly saw the fear behind her anger.

"Hey, I'm fine, okay? I'm fine–" I reached out to touch her arm, but she shrugged me off, drawing up to her full height. I was still taller than her – just.

"You betrayed our trust, Kieran, and that has consequences. Your father and I have decided." My stomach sank. "You're not leaving the house except for school."

"But Lucas–"

She held up a hand. "The doctors are perfectly capable of looking after him–"

"There's only six weeks until his med review!" If he failed the med review, there'd be a court hearing to decide if he was worth all these resources. You got Allocated four years to recover and prove your contribution to society. After that...

I didn't want to think about a world without Lucas in it.

"Leave it to *the professionals*, Kieran. You have exams. Once exams are finished, we'll review. See how you've behaved, how much we feel we can trust you again. We'll be monitoring your phone location. And I'll see when Margaret can fit you in–"

"I don't need counselling!" I burst out. "You said I didn't have to do it anymore!"

Mum shook her head, brushing off my words. "The police said you should talk to someone about... what happened at the hospital. And I think it'd do you good to talk things over again. Sometimes, Kieran..." She paused, swallowed, and carried on. "Sometimes, you can't fix things. And you need to figure out how to get through that."

My mouth dropped open. How could she say that, so matter-of-fact?

She hadn't noticed, was still talking. "Margaret would love to see you again–"

"I have exams. I've got to study."

"If you've got time to sneak out in the middle of the night, you've got time to do counselling," Mum said. "Is that clear?"

I hesitated, but she was staring at me so hard I could feel my insides searing. "Yeah. Clear."

She nodded and went to make coffee, leaving me standing alone in the hall.

Four years ago

THE DOORBELL RINGS. I'M twelve, tossing a cricket ball at the ceiling in my room. Bang. Bang. I've been doing it for twenty-two minutes – I'm trying to see how long I can go before Dad tells me to stop. He's quiet today. Normally it doesn't take more than three minutes before he starts yelling.

My room is almost above the front door, and I can hear the door open with a click.

"Lucas!" Dad says, and I miss the ball on its way down. It thwacks me in the chest and rolls to the floor with a muffled thunk. The carpet's thick, but you can still hear the rimu floorboards underneath. "How've you been? Didn't expect you–"

I don't hear the rest of his sentence because I'm already off the bed and skidding down the stairs. Lucas's bike helmet is hanging from his wrist, his hands in the pockets of his jeans. His hair is all sweaty from the ride, and his nose is sunburnt. I'm sure he's taller.

I'm never gonna catch up.

"Yo, my man," Lucas says, interrupting Dad and holding out his fist. I bump his fist too hard cos I don't stop fast enough. "What you been up to?"

"Testing my patience." Dad turns to me. "So no dinner."

I can't tell if he's joking. "But you didn't give a warning." My voice sounds whiny and I wince. I don't want to be just some stupid kid in front of Lucas.

"I gave you plenty of warnings. Remember all those other times I've told you to stop leaving red marks on the ceiling?"

"Orange marks," I mutter. "It was a basketball." Basketballs don't actually leave marks, so I changed to a cricket ball. Louder, and this way I'm actually making the marks I'm getting told off for.

Lucas is biting his lip to hold back laughter. "How about I take him off your hands for a night, then?" He sounds as if he's only just thought of this. "We could go camping."

Lucas started taking me camping when he stayed with us last year. I try not to look too interested, in case Dad swings around to "if you really want to, then no". "Aww, yeah, I guess."

Lucas smiles his responsible-sixteen-year-old smile, and Dad caves in about two seconds. The weekend stretches out full of possibility, instead of thousands of red marks on my ceiling. Andrew's gone to visit his rellies for the weekend, Xiao's stuck in doing the chores he didn't do last week, and Wiremu's got his sister's wedding. Even Verity's got a soccer tournament, and Mum's gone to be supportive.

Ten minutes later, I've stuffed my rucksack with clothes and a sleeping bag and strapped the tent on the back of my bike. Lucas is filling a bag with food nicked from the kitchen, and since Dad never really knows what's there, he won't be able to tell we've only taken chips and chocolate. It's just past lunchtime and the sun is at its hottest. Dad throws a bottle of sunscreen at my head and stands with crossed arms as we slather it on.

"You know the drill," Dad tells Lucas, rubbing sunscreen into my cheek where I'd missed. I bat his hand away. "Stay on the trails inside

the Consolidation Line, keep your phone on and call straight away if you get into trouble. Back by sundown tomorrow."

"Of course, Uncle Martin," Lucas says, shaking Dad's hand. "No worries."

3
Arrivals

THEY MADE ME GO to school, because Dad had an Allocations meeting, Mum couldn't get out of lab work and apparently they couldn't trust me to stay home alone and sleep, even if I'd been so traumatised by the Gen-en Incident that I needed counselling. At least school meant I could give Andrew the rundown face-to-face, and possibly sleep in bio if Ms Haney wasn't paying attention.

Andrew moved straight to the important questions. "Was the Gen-en hot?"

"I didn't really notice, cos I was *terrified for my life*."

"Aw, come on dude, you can be terrified for your life and still tell if someone's hot."

We were in English, waiting for the bell. I took out my tablet and checked my Joshi algorithm assignment. It had not been magically finished by elves in the last four hours. "I saw her – *it* – for like three tenths of a second."

"Twice, you said."

I gave in. "Okay, the Gen-en was hot."

"Like in Conquesterra?"

"Yes. Like in Conquesterra." The moaning in agony bit had been pretty close. I forced back a shiver.

Andrew whistled. "Man, I woulda killed to be there."

"Yeah, *terrified for your life.*"

Andrew waved that away. "It's just like a movie. There you are, innocent bystander–"

"Hero, please."

"–innocent bystander hero, protecting Lucas from the evil soulless Gen-en–"

And then *she* walked past, and I stopped hearing Andrew's schemes for the next Great New Zealand Flick.

Maybe it was the sleep deprivation, but the whole world seemed to go into slow mo. She paused in a patch of sunlight, hair glinting, and spoke to Mr Martin. He nodded and waved her towards the front, where a row of newbies stood looking awkward and fidgety. She glided over like a dancer. If angels had descended from the ceiling strumming those tiny harps I would not have been surprised.

Our eyes caught. Maybe the Gen-en had been hot, in a psycho-killer-middle-of-the-night kind of way, but it had nothing on this girl. Dark hair, mouth quirked in something that wasn't quite a smile, bright blue eyes – *blue* – and curves rivalling all the members of my sister's favourite girl-band.

"It begins," Andrew said darkly, snapping me out of it. "One week until exams."

God, he was right. I'd been so caught up with Lucas I'd lost track of school stuff. The new girl was a correspondence kid, like all the others mumbling through their introductions. Corrie kids did online school most of the time, but came into the city to take end of year exams.

Was that blue natural? I'd never seen blue eyes in real life. She hooked a stray curl of inky hair behind her ear and stepped forward.

"Kia ora, I'm Mira Sorenssen. Yes, my eyes are blue. Get over it." A few titters. She gave a small smile and stuck her hands in her back pockets. "We moved up from Ōtepoti Dunedin in February. My dad's a turbine engineer so I've been on a wind farm compound the whole year. Very boring. I'm taking history, art, maths, English, chem and philosophy. Looking forward to getting to know you guys."

Had she glanced at me when she said that?

"She can play my love interest," I muttered to Andrew.

"Who?"

"Last girl."

He rolled his eyes and set his tablet to copy what Mr Martin was putting on the board. Mira found a chair next to Te Aroha and passed her wrist over her tablet to wake it up. When she glanced my way I couldn't help grinning, and her mouth twitched like she was trying not to smile.

Did she think I was funny, in a bad way? Staring too much? Or was it an actual smile? She'd turned back to the board now, concentrating on English. Maybe I should be concentrating too.

But sleep deprivation plus Lucas stress plus Gen-en flashbacks plus hot girl, plus my usual inability to concentrate, were making it tough. It didn't help that I kept catching her eye all through class, zings flashing between us.

When the bell rang, Mira took a while to pack up her stuff, chatting to Te Aroha. Andrew saw me watching and kicked my foot. "Go say hi."

"No sleep. I'll mess up."

He shrugged. "What's your excuse gonna be tomorrow?"

"Um..." He knew me too well. "I gotta concentrate on Lucas. Just until his review."

"She's gonna be gone in a few weeks and you'll be thinking 'what if' forever."

"I'm grounded, too," I muttered, ramming my water bottle into my bag. "So–"

And then she was standing right there.

"Hey. You're Kieran, right?"

Uh oh. Te Aroha had been talking about me. That could be good or bad. We'd gone out for a week two years ago and decided we were better as friends.

"Yeah?" I said, cleared my throat and tried again. "That's me."

"Apparently you're the guy to ask for directions to Brooklyn?"

"Sure. I mean, yeah, I live in Brooklyn. You... do you live in Brooklyn?"

She nodded. "Yep, me and my mum got a place there for the summer."

"Awesome."

I was so smooth. Why couldn't she just ask her phone for directions? Was this some kind of trick?

"So, uh, are you walking home after school?" Did she seem nervous too? Or was it just me?

"Yep. No. Sort of. I have a bike... but I can walk it?"

I was supposed to report in to Dad at half past three, so we'd have to power it up the hill. Maybe I could blame my tripping-over injury from this morning and make it later...

"Mind if I walk with you?"

"No, sure, sure..."

She smiled and hugged her tablet to her chest. Her blue eyes held mine like magnets. "Thanks, you're a lifesaver."

Andrew gave me a low-five once we were round the corner and on the way to IT, where I would hand in my half-an-assignment. "Got her number, dude?"

"It's not like that."

"Oh, I think it is my friend. I think it is."

—— · ——

Mr Sankaran kept us in after school, and by the time I got to the main gate I was ten minutes late. I'd already sent Dad a text complaining about my sore foot, so I had an extra half hour's grace. I'd napped in bio and slept through lunch, so I was kinda more awake than I'd been in English.

Mira was sitting on the wall, picking at a patch of moss. She smiled as I skidded round the gate on my bike, those blue eyes even more startling in the sunlight.

"I didn't know if you were going to come."

I tried to look pained. "Me, stand up a beautiful girl?" I'd almost done it, though, arguing with Andrew that she couldn't be into me when I'd barely talked to her, plus the Lucas thing.

She raised an eyebrow. "I don't appreciate being objectified or labelled."

That shut me up, but then I saw her mouth twitch and realised she was joking. "All right." I stuck my tongue between my teeth and considered. Maybe she didn't like me, maybe her phone was just broken. But even if that was the case, I wasn't really losing anything by attempting a better pickup line. Except my pride. "Me, stand up a smart, funny, amazingly talented person I'd like to get to know better so that I can go on for hours about her fascinating personality and all the ways she does not fit labels and cannot be objectified?"

I scored an approving look, and silently thanked Andrew for pushing me into this.

"So do you want the crazy steep route, the crazy steps route, or the longer relaxed route?"

She tilted her head and considered. "Relaxed, please."

"Got it."

We started along Taranaki Street, me pushing my bike, swapping small-talk.

"It's so nice to be back in a city," she said. "There's a total of *one* other teenager living on compound, and we don't get on since he stole my history notes. And I've got a law internship for the summer, so that'll be fun. I'm going to take history and law at university, and maybe politics. After that, I'm going to try and get a job in government, law-making, that sort of thing. I want to help people, I think. Sure, they say we're the Paradise Generation, but there's still tonnes of stuff that needs fixing, and I'm going to try." Her voice was strong and determined, but she glanced at me shyly at the same time. "Sorry for going on about such boring stuff..."

"No, no, it's not boring," I said quickly. "It's amazing you already have so much of your life planned out..." I had no idea what I wanted to do. It seemed too far away to think about, the year after next, when Lucas had just weeks until his review.

Mira laughed, and my pulse skipped. There didn't seem to be quite enough air. "Not much else to do out there except go hiking."

She liked hiking? I liked hiking. "Have you been up Mt Vic?" I asked as we turned onto Webb St. She shook her head. "It's one of my favourites. You get awesome views from up there, and it's an easy way to see how the city's laid out. There are loads of good tracks around Wellington, even inside the Consolidation Line."

"I'll put it on my list, maybe you could show me sometime," she said, eyes sparkling. Electricity sang through me – was that an invitation to a date? She did like me. I wasn't screwing this up. And then, "Have you been hiking out Mākara way?"

Lucas's face flashed into my mind, and then the Gen-en's, dropping me back to reality with a thud. I'd walked right into that. Of course she'd talk about Mākara – that's where the wind farm was. I twitched a shoulder and muttered something about staying inside the Consolidation Line, which she didn't question. I guess I no longer looked like someone who'd sneak outside the Line. She didn't know about my three a.m. adventures, though.

"Oh, it's beautiful, you should go if you get the chance. The beach is wild. Awesome in storms, when the salt spray whips up around you."

"Wild," I echoed. I took a deep breath. Just move the conversation. "There are some great beaches on the south coast too. Just follow Ōwhiro Bay Road from Brooklyn. When the tide's low you can walk all the way to Kilbirnie, but you gotta avoid the seals. I got chased once."

"Chased" was probably stretching the truth (the bull seal had lumbered up a rock and given me the evils) but I enjoyed the story anyway. Mira returned a story involving an overly-affectionate albatross, and I tried not to gaze at her too much – made it hard not to trip over my bike pedal. She was pretty and smart and had opinions about things like Allocations and Neo-Saharan dance music, ninja movies and courtroom dramas. She missed her old horse in Ōtepoti. She laughed at my jokes.

I traced the patterns of her face in my mind; the kink in her eyebrow when she was passionate about something (and she was passionate about a lot), the twitch of her mouth in the moment before she laughed, the angle she tilted her head when she was thinking. I wondered what it would be like to hold her face in my hands, brush my fingers through her hair, my lips across hers…

We almost walked straight past the fork in the road where I'd go one way and she'd go the other. I could hardly remember the actual climb up to Brooklyn, which I did every day and complained about almost as often. I checked my watch. Five minutes until I had to be home.

"You're that way." I pointed up one fork. "And I'm this way."

"Already?"

"Guess we'll just have to finish this conversation tomorrow." There was a funny feeling in my chest, like something warm and happy trying to get out.

She fished in her backpack, then grabbed my hand, setting off a tingle that zipped up my arm and tickled the hairs on my neck. She wrote her number on the back of my hand.

And I hadn't even asked for it.

4

Match

When I got home I reported to Dad in his workshop, standing near the door so I was clear of the welding sparks. He must have got some new orders at the Allocations meeting, because he was whistling.

"I'm home!" I yelled, and he stopped welding, tipped up his mask and gave me a thumbs up. Then he went back to welding. I could probably duck away to see Mira and he'd never know.

But she'd be long gone by now. And I had a Match to check.

Inside, Verity was on the couch looking angelic and watching a chirpy host cook chickpea wontons.

"Just me," I said, and she switched to a shot of a giant Gen-en, complete with glowing red eyes and tiger fangs, bringing down a scimitar on a purple-haired avatar. Conquesterra.

I looked away. It was really nothing like the Gen-en at the hospital.

"Yah!" Verity muttered, swiping and flicking her wrist to activate her laser guns. "Die, mutant scum!"

"You know, one day Mum's going to come home really quietly and you won't have time to change it to something wholesome."

The Gen-en let out a blood-curdling scream. "Give up!" it howled. "We are the inheritors of the Earth! Submit, slave!"

"Oh, shut up," Verity told it, stuck her tongue between her teeth, and ended the screaming with a few complicated hand movements. If only complicated hand movements worked in real life. She paused the game. "I asked the house server to switch channels when anyone comes in the front door. No chance of Mum sneaking up on me. And hey, big bro, what did you *do*? Why are Mum and Dad being all prison-guardy?"

"Eh," I said, swiping an apple from the kitchen. "Snuck out. Saw Lucas. Got caught."

"Oh," she said, and I could hear her uncertainty. She knew you were Not Supposed to Mention Lucas to Kieran.

"S'fine," I said, taking a big bite of apple as an excuse not to talk and climbing the stairs to my room. I couldn't do anything about Lucas. The Gen-en was all safe and locked up again, and wouldn't cut me into pieces with a scimitar. And I had a girl's number – a girl with dark hair and blue eyes that zinged electricity through me.

It's funny, that moment when anything is possible. You want to know what'll happen, but at the same time you want to make it last. Once you've checked a Match, or opened your exam results, or unwrapped a Christmas present, there's no going back to not knowing.

I had to do it some time, though. You can't go out with someone without checking your Match. I pulled out my tablet and saw Andrew was online.

Success ;-)

U got it?

Yup.

:-D What does it say?

I sat in the perfect position on my bed, took a deep breath, clutched the pounamu pendant my koro had left me, and pulled up the Match engine. Her number (ink smudged, but readable) was NZS-309-6907-MS, so I put it in along with my own – NZN-626-0032-KX. The database hummed and haaed before spitting out the results.

The bottom fell out of my stomach. Today was cursed.

Whats the match? Andrew's message blinked at me, but I couldn't stop staring at the numbers. Surely this couldn't be happening. I ran it again, just to make sure, but got the same result.

1.2% percentage match

Kieran?

I took a deep breath, my fingers poised over the keyboard. *It's too close.*

Percentage matches above 1% are forbidden. We probably shared a great-great-great-great grandmother from some village in Inner Mongolia, Poland or Polynesia, but it was enough – with the world population as small as it is, we have to keep the gene pool moving. So, Matching. If people know right from the beginning who they can fall in love with, bad combinations won't happen. Plus, we get stronger global ties and understanding across cultures. If you disagree with your result, well, the re-education workcamps will sort you out, and maybe even relocation (I've always thought Greece would be a nice place to live, but I don't think they let you choose where you go).

It's supposed to make it simpler in the long run.

It sucked.

I clicked through half-heartedly to the in-depth report, knowing it wouldn't make any difference. Everything here seemed all right.

Personality match was great, no adverse recessive matches, and our relationship was likely to last, based on previous similar Matches. No lethal gene matches. If there'd been one of those, it would have been easier to accept, but... it was just the percentage that made it illegal.

Another message from Andrew flickered in the corner of my screen. I'd almost forgotten he was there.

Sorry, man.

Nah, all good. No time for girlfriends anyway.

—— · ——

I lay staring at my ceiling for an hour, then tried to sit on the roof outside my window and found Dad had installed a tamper-proof latch (I know it was tamper-proof because I tried to screwdriver it open).

Great. Trapped inside with exam study, Verity and my parents. No Mira outside school hours, not that we could be anything more than friends. No Lucas, outside *any* hours. I tried not to let that suck me into a downward spiral, tried not to ruminate on how my house arrest might destroy any chance Lucas had to recover. See? I still remembered what Margaret taught me. Avoid ruminating.

It was for the best. Mira and I couldn't legally go out. I had my own problems to deal with, rather than chasing a forbidden girl. And anyway, she was way too smart for me. Way too worried about fixing the world. Sure, some things were kind of shit (like, say, our Match), but what could you do about that? You had to focus on stuff you *could* control, because trying to fix anything else would make you crazy.

Thanks Margaret, again.

Verity made dinner, attempting the chickpea wontons from the cooking show. They sort of worked. Dad told us all about his Allocations meeting. No one mentioned Lucas, Gen-ens or being grounded. I didn't say anything except "pass the sauce", and went back to my room as soon as Dad cleared the plates. I set up the most mindless game I could think of on my wall screen (2D alien shoot 'em up), and it was doing a good job numbing my thoughts when I heard breathing and shuffling feet outside my door.

Finally the person – sounded like Mum – knocked. I ignored it, keeping the pew! pew! going until she knocked again.

"Yeah?" I asked, annoyed when my voice wasn't as irritated as I wanted. "What do you want, Mum?"

"Kieran, I'm sorry about this morning."

I kept pew-pewing.

"May I come in?"

I made a sound that she could take either way. The door opened. I paused the game and dropped my hands.

"I know you think we're being unfair, but you see our point, right? If something had happened to you..."

"I want– I *need* to see Lucas. Please. Once a week, supervised, anything, just to–" I broke off. To what? Keep trying for a miracle? Say goodbye?

She shook her head, cradling her elbows like she didn't really want to be here having this conversation. "No. Maybe after exams–"

"That's three weeks away!" And three weeks before Lucas's med review. Before they decided if Lucas's life was worth the resources he used.

"*Only* three weeks away. Margaret can fit you in on Thursday, and I think that'll be helpful."

She wasn't even *trying* to listen. What was the point of speaking? I huffed and lifted my hands to unpause the game, but she didn't take the hint.

"Another thing." She swallowed, cleared her throat. "They just announced on the newscast. They're going to nix all the Gen-ens they have in custody."

I dropped my hands, relieved but also... shocked? Yeah, Gen-ens were dangerous, and keeping them locked up took resources – just like it took resources to look after Lucas. But people had been saying that for years and the authorities never actually did anything. Something about the Gen-ens providing useful information, spy stuff or medical stuff or whatever.

"*All* of them? Cos one..."

"Yes." Mum didn't meet my eyes. She scratched behind her ear; one of her hearing aids must be bothering her. "Too dangerous to keep alive, they said. So you– you don't have to worry about that one anymore. I thought you'd want to know."

This was a weird version of Mum. I'd never seen her hesitate like this, except maybe when I'd woken up in hospital and was asking about Lucas.

"Uh, thanks." I felt weird too. Gen-ens were the reason Mum never met her grandparents. Why most of her generation never met their grandparents. And if that Gen-en had seen me, it probably would have killed me. But seeing one up close like that...

I wondered what they used to nix them. That made me think of Lucas, and my stomach dropped.

Mum chewed on her bottom lip, then crossed the room and gave me a stiff hug. "Study hard, keep safe, okay?"

"Sure?" I said, muffled in her jersey. My throat felt tight.

She pulled away and began to say something. Then her eyes fell on my screwdriver, still at the window. "Kieran–"

"I just wanted to sit on the roof. I wasn't escaping, I swear. And anyway, Dad's done a master job. Not getting out that window any time soon."

Mum took a breath like she was going to start yelling again, but took another breath and managed not to. She pulled something from her pocket.

"I was going through some old boxes and thought you might be interested in this." She dropped a silver thing about the size of a squash ball on my desk. It made a metallic thunk, with a few rattles that suggested things loose inside. "It's a bit broken, sorry. It's old and it's been dropped a few times."

"What is it?"

"It's a holosphere. An old knick-knack–"

"Sounds thrilling."

Mum continued like she hadn't heard me. "It displays photos. You throw it up and it projects around you."

I could see why it was broken.

Mum shrugged and crossed her arms, avoiding my eyes. "Maybe you could do something more useful with that screwdriver and fix it. There are some old photos on it. You can put new ones on it too."

What was this, distract Kieran with random stuff and hope he'll forget...? The silver thing looked like an alien spacecraft come to beam up the toy soldiers on my desk. Despite myself, I leaned over and picked it up. It seemed perfectly smooth, but then I noticed a tiny etch on the circumference, barely felt under my thumb. The material looked like mirrored glass, but it wasn't warming in my hand the way a glass marble did. I could see my face reflected darkly, distorted. I tried twisting it open, but the pieces wouldn't move, so I put it back on my desk. "Thanks."

Mum looked like she was going to say something else, but didn't. "Good night," she said at last, and left.

5
Friends

I SLEPT IN AND barely made it to first period, sliding into the seat between Andrew and Xiao just as the bell rang. Then I noticed Mira two desks away, face bright, one eyebrow raised. I couldn't help smiling back at her. Andrew kicked me in the shin.

"Hi, I'm Andrew," Andrew said, as I clutched my leg and glared at him. "Kieran has something to tell you."

Mira's face fell. She knew a bad news introduction when she heard it. Xiao, in the desk between us, suddenly looked really interested in his tablet.

I pursed my lips and forced myself to stop rubbing my leg. "One point two," I said, trying to speak in code so Xiao wouldn't understand.

No chance, though – he muttered, "Tough luck, man."

"Oh." She looked like someone had kicked *her* in the shin.

"I can send you the report if you want..."

She shook her head slowly. "Nah, don't worry."

—— · ——

She was in different classes from me the rest of the day, so we didn't get to talk again and I could sort-of kind-of concentrate on revision. I was cycling up Brooklyn Road after school, head down, focused on the press of the pedals and key dates in the Green

Wars, when I saw her on the footpath opposite. I swerved across the centre line and screeched to a halt in the gutter on the wrong side of the road.

Mira halted, eyebrows raised. "Hey," she said. "Emergency stop?"

"Tyre's bust. Gotta walk from here. You mind?"

She shook her head, fighting not to smile.

I lifted the bike onto the footpath. We walked in humming, pressing silence past six fence posts.

"So I was thinking," I said, as Mira said, "Y'know…"

We stopped and grinned at each other. I waved my fingers from the handlebars for her to continue.

"I know we can't go out, but we could still be friends…?" She hesitated, and I wondered if it was because the idea of us being friends seemed as crazy to her as it did to me. We weren't meant to be friends. We were meant to be *something more*.

But our Match was too close.

"Sure."

We could do this. I just needed to see things differently. And this was the way to do it – get so used to her that I didn't get distracted when she was in the same room, every part of me alive to where she was, the way her hair flowed around her shoulders when it was down, or its intricate strands of black and brown and deep red when she had little braids like today… *Stop.*

"You seem pretty good at history," I said into the silence. She'd answered loads of Ms Cheng's questions. "Way ahead of me. Like."

I could feel my neck going red, but she shrugged.

"Everyone has different strengths," she said easily. "That's why I dropped languages as soon as they'd let me."

"Me too!" I said, though really I'd dropped Mandarin because the advanced stream was by correspondence, which would give me even less motivation to do work.

"What are you stuck on?"

"Um... most things. You were saying something today about Doncaster's Cure, how it shaped politics and international borders and stuff after the Plagues. I'd never thought of that before."

Mira shrugged. "I read a lot. But it's interesting, right? The Cure worked best on kids, not so well on adults. So at the end of the Plagues, there weren't enough adults left to properly run things or keep the internet going or nix all the Gen-ens."

She didn't notice my shiver.

"So, Consolidation Lines to help rewilding, and countries sharing laws, international agreements to fix internet disintegration. Allocations and the world genome database."

"Hmm," I said darkly.

"Yeah, I guess that one sucks for us. But at least it catches Gen-ens. Most of them, anyway."

We reached our fork in the road, and stood awkwardly until Mira gave me a hug.

"See ya, Kieran."

The way she said my name made a shiver run up my back. Her hair smelled like oranges. I squeezed back, maybe a little too long, and pulled away.

But my hands didn't leave her arms. Hardly knowing what I was doing, I reached up and moved a stray braid out of her face, gently hooking it behind her ear. My hand rested there, motionless, my fingers thrilling at the soft touch of the forbidden hair, feeling her warmth tingling through my hand.

Her lips parted, and I swayed down towards her, thinking of nothing but what those lips would feel like, soft and warm and close to me. There were butterflies in my chest, flitting happily around, and my head felt light as air.

And then my brain caught up.

I stopped. Her breath hitched, and I almost lost it then, just kept going, right in broad daylight on the side of the road, but she turned her face away.

"Shit," she murmured. "I didn't–"

"I'm sorry–"

"This friends thing is going really well, isn't it." She gave a breathless laugh.

"Um. Yeah."

She stepped back, disentangling from my suddenly-leaden arms, and stuck out her hand. I took it, numb. We shook. She turned and walked away.

"Shit," I muttered.

—— · ——

Mum kept trying to drag me into the conversation at dinner. "Have you emailed the GA to accept your internship?"

"Hmm?"

"Your internship," she repeated. Mum worked at the Genetics Authority doing farm animal gen-en (totally legal – animals don't go crazy like humans do). She'd pulled a few strings to get it for me, but "internship" probably meant "fetching coffee for old scientists" and having even less time to see Lucas, if I ever got ungrounded. Mira's law internship sounded way more exciting.

Verity saved me with a blow-by-blow account of her soccer game, and I was doing my best to make noises in the right places while imagining Mira and I hiking deep in the hills, her hair falling across her face, me pushing it back, drawing closer, searching her eyes...

"I'm sorry about that girl, Kieran."

I choked and dropped my fork. "Uh, what?"

"The girl you Matched with."

Seriously? Mum probably had access to that kind of information at the GA. Maybe even had ALERTS set up.

"Girl?" Dad asked.

Mum nodded. "They were too close. Pity. Did you like her?"

I swallowed my mouthful of rice as best I could, and nodded. Why the hell else would I have done a Match? And what business was it of hers? "She's all right, I suppose." I chewed on my fork. Now we were here, I may as well ask something that had been niggling at me. "Don't we share like 50% of our genes with bananas?"

Mum sighed. "Kieran..."

"I'm serious. How come we share 50% of our genes with bananas, but the legal match threshold is 1%?"

"So you want to date a banana, now," Verity said, grinning.

Mum shook her head. "The banana match is just about genes. For relationship Matching they look at all your DNA, including the non-coding parts."

"So how close is 1%, exactly? Fifth cousins? Sixth?"

"Ask your mentor when you do your internship."

"You might not be related at all," Dad said. "It could just be bad luck in the way the genes fall."

Mum sent Dad a displeased look, and he shrugged at her.

"Knowing the technicalities will make no difference to the result, Kieran," Mum said. "Best to just avoid her and–"

"Take cold showers," Dad advised.

I groaned and covered my face with a hand. "Please don't say things like that."

"–concentrate on other things," Mum continued. "Like your internship. Interning at the GA is an enormous opportunity, Kieran. It could be the beginning of a career for you."

I shook my head. "What if I fail bio? The GA will probably kick me out."

"You're not going to fail bio," Dad said patiently.

"I believe they only kick people out of internships for extreme misdemeanours," Mum said, sounding like she was quoting from a policy. She probably was. "It's really a great opportunity, Kier."

"I'll email," I muttered.

—— · ——

On Thursday, Ms Cheng was halfway into a spiel on the Green Wars and ecological collapse – and weren't we glad we were the Paradise Generation, and didn't have to live through wars or plagues or internet disintegration or rapid sea rise like the generations before us – when the school bell went off. Three short bursts and then a long wail. For a second I was back in the hospital, waiting for the Gen-en to break through my chair barricade. Mira's eyes were wide, like some of the other corrie kids, but everyone else was sighing or swearing and sliding under the tables. Ms Cheng got the lights.

"Terrorist alert," I explained, sliding off my chair and avoiding her eyes. It was the first time I'd spoken to her since our almost-kiss

– we'd been mostly ignoring each other, and it was almost working, but I could make an exception in an emergency.

I'm not exactly sure how getting under the tables would help us if there was a real terrorist, but hey, it's an excuse to slack off work. I resisted the urge to put my hands over my ears. The school bell wasn't as bone-vibrating as the hospital siren.

"Terrorist–?"

They must not get as many in Ōtepoti Dunedin. Sure, we didn't have to deal with plagues or rapid sea rise, just terrorists.

"Probably peevs," Xiao said helpfully.

Mira gave him a disapproving look. "You shouldn't call them peevs."

"Fine, Persons Voluntarily Abstaining From Society. They cross the Consolidation Line sometimes. Steal stuff off trains. They'll get rid of them, don't worry."

Mira slid under her table too, but didn't look happy about it. "What about those Gen-ens they're keeping somewhere? They must be more dangerous, right? Didn't one escape?"

"They caught it," I said, feeling Andrew's eyes bore into my back.

"But aren't there like a dozen of them? Should we have gas masks? Or– shit, a lead-lined escape room or something. I saw what they did in Cascadia a few years ago."

"It'll be peevs. They nixed all the Gen-ens they were keeping." My voice felt far away. I tried not to think of the Gen-en's gasp as the cops rattled the hospital doors. "Or it's a drill. Or a false alarm."

"Cards?" Andrew offered, pulling a well-thumbed pack out of his bag.

Xiao swivelled to face us. "I'm in."

“Sure,” I said, and Andrew started dealing.

“Mira?”

But she was tapping something into her phone, looking completely unimpressed, and hardly looked up. “Um... no. Next time.”

Andrew wiggled his eyebrows at me in a “thank god you avoided that one” sort of way. I gave him a stone-faced stare, unsure if I was disappointed or relieved, and scooped up my cards. When the alert was finally called off, Xiao had thrashed us in eight rounds and Mira had switched her attention to a history module on her tablet, mouth still pursed.

—— · ——

The session with Margaret went okay, though I kept imagining Mum or Dad or Verity listening outside my door. We talked about Gen-ens, and how you could be terrified by something and still feel kind of weird when it got nixed.

“Like, we studied the Better Human Manifesto in history. Those photos of bodies laid out after the Gas Attacks. We watched old videos of the Gen-en rallies, yelling and screaming, stringing people up. They did awful, horrible things. But then you see one in real life... and it’s still yelling and screaming, but it’s different, because it’s right there, you know?”

“Yes, it’s real to you,” Margaret said. “You felt compassion for it, which is completely natural. That compassion... it shows more about you than it shows about the Gen-en.”

“I s’pose.”

I thought about mentioning Mira, but decided against it. Margaret let me complain about being grounded for a while, and pointed out that I could get the nurses to send me updates on Lucas.

I knew what the updates would be. No change.

"Because I'm not there," I said.

"Perhaps," Margaret said. "But you see how that idea led to you spending hours and hours at the hospital?"

"I guess."

"Try and see these three weeks as time to take stock, reassess. Get through exams, and see how you feel. You might find it lifts some weight off you."

Sure.

Four years ago

We don't stay on the trails. We never stay on the trails. What's the fun in that, Lucas reckons, when there's so much more to explore?

If you're game to drag your bike through a bit of bush, you can get to some of the old suburban roads and it's easier going along there. Not great, with tree roots pushing through the asphalt and sixty years' worth of dead leaves, but better than straight bush. Today we go out towards Kaharore and Mākara, circling through the bush to avoid the Consolidation Line checkpoints. Lucas does something to our phones so it looks like we're still up in the hills near Brooklyn.

There are a few houses with faded quarantine paint across their doors, and we don't go anywhere near them. It's no fun coming face to face with skeletons. The road winds up and up, and when the bush flattens out you can see the whole Kaharore valley.

"Here, this one," Lucas says at last, hopping off his bike and wheeling towards a house that was probably nice, ages ago. "What do you reckon?"

"Yeah, awesome." I let my bike roll to a stop. "If the top floor's still there, it'll have a mean view."

"Camping" with Lucas actually means "staying in houses outside the Consolidation Line". Lucas is making a map of good "camping" houses, but he won't let me see it.

"Can't have you knowing all my secrets," he says, grinning.

I guess that's okay. He doesn't have to take me, after all, and he still does. Andrew's really jealous, cos his dad loves talking about the adventures he had outside the Consolidation Line as a kid. The stories always finish "but don't you sneak off! Not until you're big enough to fight the peevs!".

Lucas burst out laughing when I asked if he'd ever fought peevs. "Nah, don't worry about peevs. They don't come this far south, and if they do, I'll protect you."

Vines sprawl across the house's walls and cling to the roof, faded paint curling in the gaps. The driveway has a tī kōuka tree growing in it.

"Doesn't look like any windows are broken," Lucas says. Sometimes the weather has slowly worn away at them, or vandals have got here before us. "It's in great nick. Look! It's even got an old-school lock!"

I drop my bike and sasquatch-step my way to the front door to examine it. "How do you open these? You need a metal key, right?"

"Well," Lucas says with a grin, like he's about to let me in on something. "When you don't have a key, you pick it with wire. Like this." He brings two wires out of his pocket with a flourish, and digs around in his backpack for a small bottle of what looks like greyish dust. "Graphite," he explains, blowing some off his palm into the lock. Then he pushes the wires in and fiddles them around. It takes about two minutes, and then–

"Done!" Lucas says triumphantly. The hinges are rusted almost solid, but with some wiggling and swearing and running shoulder shoves, we're in.

The place smells old. Really old. Dust covers every surface, coats the carpet beneath our feet and puffs up in small clouds. The house gets a lot of sun so it isn't too damp. The curtains are drawn, and cast dim blue or green glows over the furniture. There are still cans in the kitchen cupboard, and jars of strawberry jam.

"Check it out!" Lucas whispers. He's shoved open a door off the kitchen, and a smudged square of light falls over concrete floor, bits of bird's nest and then the curve of a car. He pulls out a torch. Its beam slices up the darkness and glints on spider-webbed windows, dust and green paint.

With the help of a hammer and shears to clear away the weeds, we get the garage door screeching open. In daylight, the car's in pretty good condition. The electronic locks have given up, and when I pull a handle the door comes open easily, releasing a cloud of dust. I sneeze.

Lucas is standing with sunlight pouring on his shoulders, giving the car a calculating look. I climb into the driver's seat – I can barely see over the steering wheel – and hit the horn. It wheezes faintly.

"What do you reckon? Do you think we can get it up and running?" Lucas says.

"Seriously?"

"Seriously."

6

Exams

"You're kidding yourself, Kieran," Andrew told me Monday morning on our last week of classes, collecting me by the back of the shirt as he walked past. I'd been standing by the school's main door fiddling with my phone, but Mira and her friends were sitting on the steps outside.

"Oi!" I said. I straightened my shirt and my satchel, and punched Andrew in the arm. "What did you do that for?"

"As I said, you're kidding yourself."

"About what?" We turned a corner and I glanced back at the last moment to see Mira still talking to her friends, cheeks pinker than usual. Andrew nudged me and I reluctantly kept walking, feeling it in my gut as the walls came between us.

"Eyes front. You can't even look at Mira without falling for her. It's best if you just avoid her."

And I'd thought I was doing well. "We're just friends!" Andrew didn't need to know about our almost-kiss. "And she's in like five of my classes."

"It's three, Kieran. Learn to count. Give it up. I'm sure if you tried the Match search you could get an amazing Match. Prajna and I–"

“I don’t want to hear about Prajna and perfect Matches,” I muttered.

Andrew shrugged. “Well, it’s a lot better than any insane ideas you might be having.”

I pressed my wrist to my locker and it swung open with a shriek. It needed oil. We had PE today, so I offloaded my gear and stood staring at the plain grey metal.

“It’s just...” I said quietly. I didn’t talk about hard stuff with Andrew much, but when I did, his advice was almost as good as Margaret’s. I took the plunge. “When I’m with her, I’m not worrying about Lucas. Which... I feel bad about, but everyone’s always telling me to take my mind off Lucas, so... I know we can only be friends. *I know.* But when we talk, it’s like it’s just us two in the world. She’s so sure of things, you know? She wants to change things for the better, believes they *can* change, has everything planned out. I don’t know what I’m doing next month, let alone the rest of my life...”

“I don’t know what I’m doing next *week*,” Andrew said. “Seriously though, dude. I get you about– about Lucas.” He chewed on his lip, rolling words around in his mouth before saying them. “I know it must seem like some precipice, coming up ahead, nothing beyond. But I’ll be there after it, no matter what happens. Xiao too. And your parents, and Verity. And if you ever need someone to take your mind off things, you know I will try my absolute damnedest.”

I swallowed past the sudden lump in my throat. “Thanks. I know.”

"I have boundaries, though, I can't do everything Mira might." He began ticking boundaries off on his fingers. "No making eyes at each other in the hall. No holding hands. No kissing–"

I shoved him off-balance and he laughed.

"But of course you wouldn't be doing that with Mira anyway, because you could get shipped off to re-education workcamps in Waiouru or Alaska. I'm fine with hugs, though. Anytime you want a hug, just ask."

The bell went. "Thanks, man."

"Feel better?"

"I guess?" And I did. Sort of.

—— · ——

Exams sucked. I definitely screwed up the question on Joshi algorithms, and I sat staring at the genetics section in the bio exam for ten whole minutes, then wrote a totally unrelated rant about banana genomes.

Andrew came over after our last exam, and we made deluxe icecream sundaes and played Conquesterra. Verity was at soccer practice and Dad was on a business trip in Awakairangi Hutt, so we had the house to ourselves.

"Weren't you going to that Link party tonight?" I asked as the time ticked closer to six. "Gonna go see Praaaaaajna?" I tried to ignore the pang of jealousy in my gut.

"Yep," Andrew said, totally obliterating a Gen-en that had swooped out of the green-tinged clouds. "That's the plan."

"Shouldn't you be home, getting all handsomified?"

"Doesn't start until eight. I've got time."

"Famous last words."

I heard Mum's steps on the path and swiped some controls to switch the game to a racing game. The door clicked and then I heard Mum taking off her shoes, putting her bag down.

"Hey Ms Xu," Andrew said as Mum appeared in the doorway. Mum liked Andrew – I think she saw him as Kieran's Responsible Friend, stopping me thinking too much about Lucas or unsanctioned activities like crossing the Consolidation Line, stuff that everyone was doing anyway. Andrew was the only friend I'd been allowed over while I was grounded, and that was technically just for studying.

"Kia ora Andrew. Post exams celebration, I see? How did they go?"

"Meh," I said, but Andrew gave a proper answer with actual detail about the exam, adding more evidence to the Kieran's Responsible Friend thing.

"And I'm going to a Link party this evening to meet up with Prajna," Andrew went on.

"Oh, how lovely."

"I thought, since exams are over, maybe Kieran could come too?"

"What?" I said.

"Oh, I don't know..." Mum glanced at me. "Kieran's grounded."

"Yes, of course," Andrew said reasonably. "But he's done everything you said, right? Hasn't complained? Much?"

I thought that was pushing it, but Mum seemed to be considering it. She hadn't said no, at least. But did I really want to go? I used to love going to the Virtual Reality suites when I was little, stalking my way through ancient jungle with my pet baby

T-Rex or building sandcastles on Mars. But Link parties were really formal – despite the skintight VR suits. And I'd be Andrew and Prajna's third wheel.

On the other hand, it would be getting out of this house, and I really, really wanted to get out of the house for something that wasn't school-related. And maybe this could be step one to getting to go see Lucas, prove I could be trusted. Best to keep quiet and look like the perfect son.

"And he's studied really hard and probably aced his exams–"

That was definitely pushing it too far.

"–and it's the beginning of summer, and I thought it might take his mind off things. You know?"

Mum was wavering. She *had* said she'd review after exams.

"It's all supervised and it finishes at eleven, so he won't be home late, and he'll meet lots of interesting people, expand his horizons..."

"Alcohol?"

"Only if you're over eighteen," Andrew said promptly. "They're very strict."

"Hmm."

"Please?" I asked. "I'll come home straight after–"

"If you go, I'll be picking you up straight after."

"Yeah, of course!"

"And I want your phone on at all times, location shared, and in your pocket. If we call, you have to pick up."

I nodded a couple of times. "Definitely."

"All right. I'll call your parents, Andrew, to confirm the details."

"Sure, thanks, Ms Xu. You won't regret it."

“What if I don’t want to go?” I hissed at Andrew, once Mum was out of hearing upstairs.

“You’re welcome,” Andrew said. “Come on, Prajna’s not getting there till nine, and I suck at small-talk with people I don’t know. It works, right? I get someone to talk to until Prajna gets there, you get out of prison. There’ll be loads of girls there, I promise. Girls who’ll be a good Match for you. And you can stop obsessing over Mira.”

“I am *not* obsessing over–” I waved that away, because I couldn’t come up with proper proof and maybe he had a point. I kept catching her gaze before exams, drawn like a magnet, breath catching. Then I guess we both realised nothing could happen, and the energy turned awkward, like when you twist magnets around the wrong way. “You think those girls will be by themselves, just waiting for me to ask them to dance? Not travelling around in packs?”

“Aw, don’t be so dramatic.”

“You know I’m right. And once Prajna gets there, you’ll be off in the corner with her and I’ll be left looking stupid all by myself.”

“You’ll meet someone, dude. And Prajna and I will hang around until you do.”

I chewed my lip. Getting to go out would be amazing, but still… “What if Xiao came too? Then I wouldn’t be stuck talking to randoms the whole time.”

“He’s working. And come on, don’t tell me you suck at small-talk. You live for random conversations with strangers.”

“I suck at small-talk.”

Andrew sighed and shook me by the shoulders. “You’re coming, dude. No arguing.”

7
Party

Mum kept moaning about the state of my hair, so I slicked it down with water and ran a comb through it, knowing it'd only get messed up on the way down the hill. I refused to wear anything nicer than my holey jeans and an old T-shirt. You took them off for the VR suit anyway, so what was the point?

I stuck my bike in the rack and found Andrew waiting at the main doors. He was wearing a hei tiki I hadn't seen before, the pounamu beautifully carved, flecks of grey caught in the green stone. He'd buttoned his shirt all formal, and the hei tiki stood out proud against the white shirt.

"Wow, handsome as," I said, feeling a pang of something I couldn't name. Andrew's Māori great grandparents had lived through the Plagues and been able to pass on not just pounamu but also stories, the history of his ancestors. I had the pounamu from my koro, but none of the history. His parents died when he was six – like so many others in the Lost Generation – so even if he'd lived long enough to pass things on to me, the stories were gone.

"Yep. Truth. Did you do *anything*?"

"I brushed my hair."

"Doesn't look like it."

"I brushed it twice. Once with a comb, once with the wind."

"Uh huh, sure." He paused. "You all good?"

I swallowed. "Yeah. Let's get this over with."

Andrew slung an arm around my shoulders and squeezed, leading me in the doors. "Youuuu will enjoooy it."

"You need to work on your hypnotism."

I felt better once I'd slithered into a VR suit and pulled on the VR helmet, getting the buzz of anticipation I always felt before a sim. We still had a few minutes to mill around in the blank suite with everyone else before they switched the VR on, visors up and looking embarrassed. The suit has to hug your body, and if you squint it looks like everyone's naked. There was a line for the outfit mod room, so I was glad I'd picked out my clothes before I came.

My helmet buzzed and I lowered the visor. The room came alive with people and music and sparkly lights, and I winced as the voices and band cut into my ears. Someone had left the helmet's sound up way too high. I sorted it, checked my clothes (black trousers, dark blue shirt, silver tie, silver shoes) and turned to see how Andrew's hei tiki had scanned through. It wasn't bad, actually. Sometimes the algorithm tries to smooth out stuff it thinks is "blemishes", but the stone's grey flecks and translucence had come through pretty well.

I'd been in this sim before. In one direction there was a sunset from some beach in Thailand, which later in the night would turn to deepest blue sprinkled with stars. Facing the beach was the long bar, with eight different bartenders colour-coded for their city. You had to choose the right bar guy or girl to get a real drink or snack, but if you just wanted to look cool with a VR martini or something, any one would do. The other two walls had benches along them, and colour-coded chairs sat around tables at one end. The other end was for dancing, and the first few dancers were jigging along to the jazz band.

Wispy curtains separated the main area from the deck. You could sit on the benches and see a full 180 degrees of the beach, but you couldn't go any further or you'd hit the wall. I actually quite enjoyed hitting the wall out there – it was right behind the benches, so you could lean against thin air.

"Do you see her?" Andrew asked anxiously, twisting his thumbs around in some weird solo version of pea-knuckle war. There had to be over five hundred people here, if I'd seen the stats properly.

"Didn't you say she was coming at nine?" I asked.

"Yeah..." Andrew said. "But maybe she's early."

"Prajna? Early?" I put my hands on his shoulders and steered him towards the bar. "Come on, you promised me a good time."

We got ginger beers and stood leaning against the bar, Andrew turning to check each new arrival. It was very difficult to hold a conversation with him like this, so I was almost glad when Prajna showed up. She looked stunning – not as hot as Mira, of course – but beautiful all the same. Her dress was green silk with gold bits all over it, and she had bangles all up and down her arms that jingled as she ran over.

"I'm so sorry I couldn't come earlier!" She flung her arms around Andrew, her hands disappearing into his back with a fuzzy white light as the haptics gave up. "Whoops, too tight." She adjusted so they looked like a proper solid couple and not some freaky ghost couple. Long-distance relationships were tough.

Andrew grinned, patting her back until she drew away, a sickening sort of happy look on his face. "I've been looking forward to this all week." Did *I* look like that when Mira was around? No wonder Andrew dragged me away from her. No one who looked like that could be in charge of walking in a straight line.

Prajna was returning Andrew's happy look. "You look wonderful!"

Andrew blushed. "Thanks, you too."

"I love your necklace. Pounamu, right?"

"Yeah, a hei tiki. It's been passed down through my grandmother's family for generations."

"Does it have a story?"

"'Course!"

Andrew launched into the whakapapa of his hei tiki and I turned away to get myself another drink, wishing they'd give me something stronger than ginger beer. Mira kept flashing into my head. The bartender, a skinny guy with slick dark hair, smiled at me.

"Feeling left out?"

I shrugged and turned my empty bottle in my hand. "I knew it was gonna be like this."

The bartender grinned and nodded towards the dance floor. "Lots of single girls around tonight, looking for a nice guy to talk to. Lots of guys too, if you're more into that."

I sighed. First time properly out of the house in weeks. Five hundred people from eight different cities, dancing and laughing. I could be meeting all these people, and I was just picturing Mira. "I think I'd rather just hang around here. You're from Sydney, right?" He had a sky blue shirt, which usually meant Sydney unless it clashed with another city.

"Yees," he said, putting on a broad Australian accent. Someone called him over to pour a drink, and I looked for the bartender dressed in black and gold, the Pōneke Wellington colours. She was way down the other end of the bar, and I couldn't be bothered moving.

"Not too busy from Sydney tonight." The Sydney bartender was back. "There's a footie game on, so I guess a lot of people have gone to that. Greg, by the way." We shook hands. "You just got dumped, didn't you."

I stared at him. "How do you figure that?"

He counted things off on his fingers. "Listless, dragged along by best friend to a Link party, searching through the crowd for a missing face." He shrugged. "I'm a bartender. We have to take courses in counselling, you know."

"Really?" I asked, then realised he was joking. "All right, I guess I've kind of been dumped. But we were never actually going out, so I dunno if it counts."

Someone wanted a mojito, and Greg began to construct it with slick pours and shakes as I told him the whole story. He put some mint in the top of the glass and handed it over. "That's bad, man. I feel for you."

This was way better than talking to Lucas. Guilt stabbed my gut. No, I'd have Lucas alive and well and talking over Greg any day.

"Any advice?"

Greg shrugged. "Everyone's different. My mate, he went bush for a month and came back good as new."

That wasn't an option. My parents would kill me.

"Had another friend who used to go chat up guys at parties like this, you know, no strings. Can't get up to much mischief at a Link party. And another one who ate a crap-load of icecream and cried for a week and got over it. My sister's friend's cousin, though... They had a story a bit like yours. They tried to keep it on the down-low but they got found out. Did a stint at Waiouru, then got sent to some boat in the middle of the Pacific. Sea plastic extraction. Their girlfriend got exiled to Iceland. Which sounds amazing, I've always wanted to go, but... it's Iceland, and she's probably not doing the fun jobs."

Yikes. I turned to stare at Andrew and Prajna. "Look at them. They've been together two years."

"Good on 'em. How'd they meet?"

"Match dating. They're just about guaranteed to end up together – perfect personality match, no bad recessive matches." Andrew didn't have the best genes. He had to watch what he ate, his dad was already on heart medication at age forty, and his eyesight was terrible without his contacts. That's sort of how we became friends in the first place – the first week of primary school, some older kids stole his glasses. I knew how Mum was with her hearing aids, always keeping them hidden, but Andrew couldn't do the same with his glasses and he was too young for contacts. I challenged the older kids to a fight, skinny fists up in front of my chin, and I would have fought them, too, probably got myself bloody knuckles and a black eye. But they thought I was so hilarious they couldn't stop laughing, and gave his glasses back.

It wasn't something Andrew talked about, but I got the feeling he was always trying to make up for his genetic disadvantages. He was Responsible Andrew, always-there-for-you Andrew, and he'd been determined to even things out with a good Match. Prajna was probably the best thing that ever happened to him.

I banged my head slowly on the bar. "I can't stop thinking about her. How do I stop thinking about her? I don't want to go to Iceland."

Greg pushed me upright. "No concussions on my bar, please. Here, on the house." He produced a VR beer from under the bar.

"It's fake," I said, slowly tipping the bottle so the liquid poured out and vanished.

"Works fine as a prop. Go, get out there. Maybe you'll find someone better than your wonder-girl. Talk to someone other than the bartender at least. Enjoy yourse–"

I was giving him a desperate look, so I had a close-up view when he disappeared.

I spun around to see people staring at each other, a few staggering to regain their balance and blinking at the nothingness that had once been their dance partner. The jazz band stuttered into silence. Muttering filled the room.

Andrew and Prajna had been slow dancing, and came up from each others' shoulders in a daze. I left the new drink on the bar and went over to them.

"Sydney's gone."

"Everyone from Sydney?" Andrew asked. I nodded. "Sheesh. I hope they're all right."

"It's probably just a problem with the connection," Prajna said, but she sounded worried. "If I disappear, it's not on purpose. And goodbye in advance. I had a lovely night."

Andrew shushed her with two fingers on her lips. "You're not going to disappear. They'll tell us what's happening soon."

I heard the words "terrorist" and "bomb" travelling through the crowd. It was almost never a terrorist, despite all the alerts. It had been a few years since anyone was killed in Australia or New Zealand, though cutting connections would be a terrorist kind of thing – chaos.

"Xiao!"

"What?" I followed Andrew's wide eyes to see Xiao coming in the door, wearing a black and gold uniform and looking sheepish. "Isn't he supposed to be at work?"

"That's what he told me," Andrew said. "Do you think..."

"Excuse me, ladies and gentlemen!" Xiao called. His voice was being amplified. "I'd like to apologise to you all for the glitch in the network tonight, and assure you that Sydney will be back online as soon as possible. There's no need to worry, it's just a, ah, technical problem due to a technician's error." His voice was confident until the last sentence, when his face started to go red. "Thank you. We wish you a very enjoyable night."

The band started up again and Xiao turned to go, but Andrew and I yelled and waved and he came over.

"I can't stay long." He pulled on his hair. "I gotta be back in the control room."

"You work *here*?" Andrew asked incredulously. "Why didn't you tell us? I thought you were just doing stuff for your dad at the shop."

Xiao shrugged. "I'm doing a trial shift for the night. If I pass, I'll do my internship here. I didn't tell you guys in case I didn't get it, and, you know." He sighed. "I'm pretty sure I'm not going to get it now, though. Not after I cut Sydney off."

I burst out laughing, but stopped when I saw Xiao's pained expression. "It was you? Classic. And here we all thought it was terrorists."

"Shut up," Xiao said. "Just wait until you're doing your internship and you make your first huge mistake."

"What happened?" Prajna asked. "I mean, is it like a big red button that says "do not press" and you pressed it?"

"No, I was trying to make something better. Showing off what I could do with programming and stuff. But I, er, made a mistake. They're fixing it now."

"You know, Xiao, there probably aren't that many people who could destroy a VR connection," Andrew said. "They might see it as a positive. You know, not afraid to try things out, push the boundaries."

"Yeah, yeah, yeah," Xiao muttered, but he brightened. "Look, I'll see you guys later. I gotta go back and face the music. Nice to see you, Prajna."

The Sydney outage gave me a conversation starter, especially as my friend was the cause of it, and I had a good time the rest of the night.

"Did you meet anyone interesting?" Andrew asked as we were waiting for Mum to arrive at eleven. I shrugged. I'd talked to lots of people, but the spark was missing. "Did you at least have fun?"

"Yeah, guess so. I can't believe all that with Xiao." I couldn't help snickering. "Do you reckon he's in or out?"

"I hope he's in. Wouldn't it be awesome if he interned there? We could get him to run any simulation we want."

"Skydiving the pyramids," I said promptly. I had a store of most-wanted sims I could call on without really thinking about it. "Dodging through Saturn's rings in a space fighter."

"I'd take Prajna in a hot air balloon around Machu Picchu," Andrew said.

"Sop."

Not that I was much better. I was already trying to think of somewhere I could take Mira that could top Machu Picchu.

Which probably wasn't helping with the whole forget-the-love-of-my-life thing.

8

Experiments

Mum didn't say much on the bus home, though she did listen while I gave a really boring rundown of the party. Dad was watching a cop show, but switched it off when Mum herded me into the living room.

"Good party?" he asked. "No dramas?"

"Yeah, great," I said brightly. I wasn't sure if Xiao's mistake would count against me, and hadn't mentioned it.

"We've discussed it," Mum said slowly, queen of the dramatic pause. "And you've kept your word. Studied hard, come straight home."

"Your window latch is still intact," Dad added.

"So we'll relax the rules a little."

"I can go out?"

"If you *stick to curfew* and tell us where you're going and who you're going with," Dad said.

"Okay. Yes. Yes."

"Keep your phone location on," Mum said. "At all times. And talk to Margaret once a week."

"Yes. Thank you."

"And if you break any rules, we'll be back to house arrest," Dad said.

I nodded. "And... what about Lucas? How often can I see him?

Mum chewed her lip before answering. "Twice a week."

"Or maybe three times?" I hazarded. "Saturdays, Tuesdays, Thursdays?" There weren't that many of them left.

She gave me a long look. "Okay, three. But if you're going tomorrow I'll come with–"

I must have looked horrified, because Dad interrupted.

"No, let him go by himself. The nurses will look after him. And there won't be any Gen-en interruptions this time, will there?"

She didn't look convinced.

"Andrew might come with me," I said. Responsible Friend to the rescue. "I'll ask him. And I'll talk to Margaret afterwards, I promise."

That seemed to do it. She nodded, and gave me a tonne of rules about phones and check-ins and time to be home.

She didn't say anything about what I could and could not take with me.

—— · ——

Even though I hadn't been allowed to actually *see* Lucas, I'd tried to use my non-studying time for research, trawling the net for miracle cures. There were stories of people talking after years because they'd been given some pill with mysterious side effects, or heard their favourite piece of music, or been surrounded by family telling stories. Not that I could really surround Lucas with family telling stories this afternoon, seeing as his parents only came out from Awakairangi Hutt every few months and his sister was in Cascadia. There was just me, and Andrew if he agreed.

I called him and explained my plans, and that Mum was only letting me go if he came too.

"So is this likely to end with us getting thrown out of the hospital?" Andrew asked.

"Unlikely. Don't want to get grounded again. I haven't been able to get any of the weird pills they talk about on the net, so we can't get arrested for those, and everything else... well, the nurses all love me."

"I'm not sure that'll make a difference to the cops."

"Hey, didn't you used to have a guinea pig?"

"Yes," he said warily. "We still have a guinea pig."

"Can you bring it?"

There was a long pause. "Exactly what do you need Sir Munchalot for?"

"Saving Lucas's life. Obviously."

It was weird being back at the hospital. I kept expecting the lights to pulse, the siren to go off, and I was glad Andrew was there. I'd timed our arrival so Lucas was just back from his morning exercycle session, when he's usually most alert.

Sir Munchalot seemed dazed when we put him on a towel on Lucas's lap. He sat blinking for at least a minute while I stood sentry at the door, and then made a break for freedom. Andrew grabbed him and turned him back towards Lucas, then gave him half a carrot. Sir Munchalot's whiskers quivered. He took it in two little hands and began gnawing.

Lucas made no sign he'd noticed the small fat rodent on his lap.

"What do you reckon would happen if we put Sir Munchalot down the back of Lucas's pyjamas?" I asked.

"You cannot be serious."

"Desperate times..." But the chances of Sir Munchalot getting squished were probably too high. Lucas had been staring out the window since we arrived, and I took his chin and gently turned him to face me. His eyes were blank, even when I stared into both of his.

We went down my list. Nothing made a difference – not his favourite music, or the Christmas album his mum played every year, or the old video of Lucas and his sister building sandcastles at Oriental Bay. The handshake electric shock made him jump and the smelling salts made him sneeze, but nothing more. I put Mum's holosphere thing in his hands along with a screwdriver, thinking maybe it would draw him out, but no.

Andrew pointed out that we were trying short-term, snap out of it things, and maybe it would happen slower than that.

"I've been trying for almost four years. We're doing all the stupid snap-out-of-it things now, which I know probably won't work."

Andrew bit his lip. "Sorry. That was dumb."

I took a deep breath. "We've still got Verity's cookies and his Dad's aftershave and the Blue Stilton to go. I'm not sure about the tequila, because maybe he'll choke, but we can do the faith healing stuff too." I paused. "I dunno if you have to believe in faith healing to do it."

"I think you do, yeah."

"Only thing missing is true love's kiss," said a voice from the doorway. I spun to see one of the younger nurses, Lauren, with a tray of food. Whoops. Should have checked meal times today. "What's the guinea pig for?"

"Small cute animals are proven to aid recovery from traumatic brain injury," I said. Well, there had been one case involving kittens.

"Right. You'd better put him back in his box before someone else sees him." Lauren put the food on a side table and carefully lifted Sir Munchalot off Lucas's head.

"Do you think the kiss needs to be from your true love?" Andrew asked, watching as Lauren settled Sir Munchalot into his box with some celery.

"It's just in stories, Andrew."

"I guess you'd need to have some sort of chemistry," said Lauren. "And no, I am not kissing Lucas to see what happens."

"Not your type?" Andrew asked.

Lauren gave him a withering look. "Well, first, he's my patient and it's unethical. Second, would you really want some random stranger making out with you in your sleep? And don't you say yes."

Andrew shrugged. "But maybe Lucas does know you. Maybe he can hear everything we say and he's been in love with you for years. In which case, yeah, I don't think he'd mind."

"The chances are slim," Lauren said, washing her hands at the sink.

"What about a girlfriend? Is there an old girlfriend we could recruit? Or a boyfriend?"

I shook my head. "I don't think he had a girlfriend. He never mentioned one."

Lauren set Lucas up with lunch and started his fork moving towards the macaroni, then up to his mouth. Once you did it a few times, he'd feed himself.

"What's next on the list?" she asked.

We tried the aftershave and the cookies, and the Stilton and tequila when Lauren left. Andrew attempted faith healing, which he reckoned he was better equipped for since he actually went to temple sometimes. It didn't work.

"There's still three weeks to go," Andrew said as we unlocked our bikes, heading home to meet Mum's curfew. "Anything can happen in three weeks."

Four years ago

Lucas likes to come over Friday afternoon, work on the car next morning, then meet his Pōneke friends the rest of the weekend. The car needs a few replacement parts, and I find most of them in my dad's workshop. I don't think he'll miss them, but I do my best to cover my tracks. New tyres are the last thing to find, and Lucas reckons he can get some but won't say how. It's probably dodgy so I don't ask.

He says he'll come one Friday, but then something comes up and it'll have to be Saturday. When he arrives he's three hours late, sweat dripping into his eyes, and he doesn't meet my eyes.

"So?" I ask. "Did you manage to get tyres?"

He swigs water before he answers. "Yeah. I stashed them in the valley, we can get them on the way. Just gotta check in with your parents and then we're good to go."

His voice is strangely flat. My bag's already packed and waiting by the door, but apparently checking in means more than just shouting "see ya!". Lucas wants to know where Mum is, and then he wants carrots and sends me into the garden to pull a few up.

When I return, Mum's in the kitchen, tablet against her chest. She looks pale, and neither Lucas nor Mum say anything as I wash the carrots and stuff them in our food bag. Their eyes watch me. I don't know whether I should be angry or worried. But we're going, aren't we?

Once we're on the road, four beautiful black tyres balanced on our bikes, I try bringing it up.

"What was all that about?"

"All what?"

"You and Mum."

Lucas glances at me, eyes sharp. "Did you hear?"

"From the garden? *Sure, Lucas, I heard from the garden. Mum's the one with the cyborg hearing aids, not me." Whoops. Mum doesn't like people to know she needs hearing aids, and I can't remember if Lucas already knows.*

But he doesn't blink. If anything, he seems more relaxed. He shrugs. "Just saying hi."

It's really, really hard to ask why he had to do it in private. So I don't ask.

The car's sitting just as we left it, the battery still fully charged. We toss our things in the back, I jack it up and Lucas fiddles about changing the tyres, muttering that it looked so easy on the instruction vid. At last he sits back on his heels and grins. "I think it's ready."

When the car starts, it rolls forward with barely a shudder. Way better than the other few times we've tried. Lucas is going slow – like me, he's only ever driven in games – but we're moving. Lucas jabs a thumb at the off-road button just to be safe, and we turn onto the road.

The speedo shows ten, twenty, thirty kilometres an hour on the straight stretches. The bush speeds past and my seat's juddering as we careen over branches and flatten small trees. I let out a whoop.

Lucas is laughing low and breathless. "I never thought I'd actually get to drive one of these." And then, after we've been driving a while, making for the rumoured beach at Mākara, "You want a go?"

This is why Lucas is awesome. He doesn't mention that I'm only twelve and, even when everyone drove cars, would have been too young. He doesn't ever treat me like I'm some kind of second-class citizen because of my age.

He gets out and I monkey into the driver's seat. The car's still running so I'm worried it'll shoot forward, but Lucas tells me the handbrake is locked and the car won't move without my say-so.

"Ease down gently on the accelerator," he says, taking the passenger seat and releasing the handbrake.

I ease down and the car rolls slowly forward, then faster as I press more. I lift my foot and we slow. I am in control of this car. Even crawling like this, my heart's thumping like crazy. I take a deep breath, stare out the windscreen, and bring us up to speed.

Lucas pulls some biscuits out of the food bag, but he doesn't touch the carrots.

Mākara Road turns off to the right. It would have been narrow even when people lived out here, but now it's just a strip of black asphalt between two armies of trees, only used to get out to the wind farm. At first I slow and drive carefully, but the sun's past the hills now and its light doesn't reach far through the tunnel of trees. I don't want to be stuck on this road in the dark, and the driving isn't hard at all, once you get used to it. I press down on the accelerator.

The road winds back and forth. I catch glimpses of a stream to our right. We pass an old sign but it's so overgrown with moss and dirt that you can't see what it says.

And then... something beeps, and dials light up all over the dashboard. "Error," says a cool female voice, and the wheel locks in my hands.

"Luc–"

"Shit," he says, clutching at his seatbelt and grabbing the wheel with one hand. "Foot off the accel–"

"It IS off the accelerator!" I yell, and I'm pressing down on the brake as hard as I can but we're still going so fast and a corner's coming up and oh-shit-oh-shit–

Lucas yanks on the handbrake but it makes no difference.

There's nothing ahead, just trees and dead trees and open air and it's coming up so fast–

Then we're falling and trees are hitting the windscreen, breaking through. The glass shatters in tiny glinting pieces and green leaves slap bloody streaks across my face and my arms are up to cover my eyes but they're not helping.

A tree hits Lucas's side of the car and Lucas isn't shouting anymore and then we hit ground, the car crumpling in the front, my head knocking hard against the window, but Lucas, Lucas has blood pouring out of his head and his eyes are closed and I don't even know if he's breathing.

The wheels are still turning, their faint hum breaking through the silence of the forest. Soon the night birds will start their calls again, the wind will rustle through the trees, and I will be alone in this dark forest, trapped in this car with Lucas, motionless, as the car runs and runs and finally, around three a.m. according to the glowing digits of the cracked dashboard clock, runs out of power and stops.

They won't find us until morning.

9

Interns

Monday was the first day of my Genetics Authority internship. It was raining, and Mum made me take the bus, so I wouldn't turn up "like a drowned rat".

"I'm too handsome to ever look like a drowned rat," I told her, but still here I was sitting next to her on the bus, trying to look like I didn't know her. I'd stuck my bike in the bus bike rack and we'd managed to grab seats, but the bus was bursting and I could smell wet dog.

"Have you made any progress with that holosphere?" she asked as we turned onto Lambton Quay. The wind spattered rain onto the windows.

"What?" I said. "Oh. Not really..." Apart from showing it to Lucas, I'd taken it apart and stared at it. "Maybe I could ask Dad–"

"Oh no, you don't need to do that," she said quickly. "I'm sure you can do it. Come talk to me when you've figured it out."

We dodged between awnings, hoods up, and made it to the Genetics Authority building without getting soaked. I locked my bike in the bike park and followed Mum into the foyer, past the receptionist to some heavy wooden doors. Mum held her wrist to the reader, then pushed through.

A long corridor stretched out double height, art dotting the walls. The carpet was a violent shade of red. More corridors yawned off to either side and a wide staircase spiralled up at the far end. Mum was already well down the corridor, peeling off her coat.

"Your orientation will be on the second floor," she said. "Come on, you've only got five minutes."

I tore my gaze from an abstract painting that moved and shimmered and caught up to her on the stairs.

"If there's anything you're not sure about, you can ask me tonight. You'll be fine." I wasn't sure if she was reassuring me or herself. "Do you want me to stay and help you settle in?"

"No!"

She turned and raised an eyebrow. "No goodbye kiss?"

Okay, she was teasing me now.

I hoped.

I found the orientation room easily. A few people slouched in revolving chairs, and a man wrote on a wall screen. I took a chair, hanging my damp jacket over the back of it and resisting the urge to swing back and forth. Mum had made me wear a shirt, but the man was wearing a T-shirt with "BIOLOGY RULES" on the back.

A quiet girl in my class, Mei Li, turned up with another girl I didn't recognise, both looking nervous. I nodded at Mei Li. My stomach was already feeling empty and I wished I'd had more than a quick piece of toast for breakfast. We all found our own way to fidget, and finally the man turned, nodded to us, and closed the doors.

"Tēnā koutou katoa," he said, clapping his hands together. "I guess you're all really excited to hear what you're doing this summer?"

We nodded, knowing there was no other option.

"Great! I'm Mark. First, I want you to look over the rules I've sent to your tablets, and then we'll get you to your assigned staff members."

The rules included things like "everything at the GA is private and confidential, and you must never ever ever tell anyone anything, including what kind of coffee we use". Once we'd all clicked the "agree" button, he began to read off our staff assignments alphabetically. Mei Li Chen got Dorothy Hatcher, room 612. She looked like she might throw up before she made it to level six.

I was used to being last, so almost didn't notice when Mark called Warren Zeiss ahead of me. Had he forgotten me? Should have been hard, with only six of us. But he put his tablet away and gave me a buddy-buddy grin. "Got something a bit special for you. He's requested you."

"What?" I said. "Who's requested me?"

He just zipped his lips and led me to the stairs. "It's a bit of a climb."

The steps went on and on. And on. Finally we reached a large metal number ten. The stairs changed into maintenance stairs and continued on up, but Mark led me into the level ten corridor. At least I wouldn't be working in maintenance.

Right at the end of the corridor was a blue door with a silver nameplate. *Professor Emeritus Edward Doncaster.* Doncaster? This wasn't *the* Doncaster?

But Mark knocked, and a gravelly voice replied.

"Come in!"

—— · ——

Mark pushed the door open and ushered me inside. He bowed to an old man about the height and weight of Verity, who was poring over some piece of electronic equipment and took no notice of the bow. I wondered how he stood the Wellington wind, and if he ever got blown away. I'd imagined him so much bigger than he actually was.

"This is Kieran Xu," Mark said.

"Sec, sec," Doncaster muttered, staring intently at some flickering red numbers. "Ahh, there we are."

He still didn't look up, though, so I took the time to goggle the room. One half was insanely tidy, with pale blue lino and sparkling stainless steel benches with chemistry sets, shiny instruments and tablets. I couldn't see a speck of dust, anywhere, and I have pretty good eyes.

The other half of the room was a mess. There was a desk with paper strewn all over it – he must have special permission to use that much paper – so much that it spilled to the floor. There were bookshelves with little mechanical toys ticking away and the occasional book sitting by itself. The rest of the books were in piles on the floor, so many that they looked like an obstacle course. I didn't think I'd ever seen so many books outside the public library's glass cases. Squeezed into one corner were three comfy chairs and a coffee table holding more papers and something that looked like a live frog.

It *was* a live frog.

The end wall was entirely glass. You could see out across the harbour, the misty rain brushing against the sea and Matiu Island sitting darkly amidst the waves. On a good day, the view would be incredible.

"So," said the man who was the closest New Zealand had to a national god. "This is young Kieran, is it?" He shuffled forward at a speed previously unknown in shuffledom, and took me by the shoulders. I tried not to shrink back as he peered into each of my eyes and looked me up and down like some sort of lab specimen. "Very good, Mark. Thank you, that will be all."

Mark gave me an encouraging smile in answer to my man-drowning expression, and left the two of us alone. This wasn't what I'd expected. Edward Doncaster spun me around a few times, then stepped back, sighing in satisfaction.

"Yes, you'll do nicely."

I took a long breath and stood there as he went back to his flickery machine, humming something that sounded suspiciously like a Delaney Jackson song I'd heard last week. I did some quick maths to figure out how old he was. One-hundred-and-twelve. He didn't look one-hundred-and-twelve. I guess being a national hero has its privileges, maybe extra rejuv treatments Allocated for heroic behaviour.

Doncaster's Cure had stopped the Great Plagues. He'd gone into politics after that, been involved in rebuilding the internet after its disintegration, but retired a few years before I was born. I'd seen him on newscasts sometimes, shaking hands with important people. Mum hadn't mentioned he was still working, let alone that he was still working *in her building*.

Professor Doncaster waved his arm impatiently for me to approach, and I realised I was supposed to follow him.

"Look, see here?" He stabbed a finger at the lines of letters on the screen in front of him. "This is your DNA. Category-A. Very nice." He stood back so I could see the screen, smiling proudly down at all the Ts and Gs and As and Cs. "Lovely mix there, you know. Couldn't have been better if it'd been genetically engineered. Not that it was of course. That's illegal." He winked at me and pressed a button, making the code zoom away into the distance.

This was my entry in the genome database.

I wondered if I could fiddle with it so Mira and I had a lower percentage match. And what did Category-A mean?

The long string of letters was divided into genes, with labels like HCL3 – hair. It still didn't make that much sense to me, but it was kinda cool to know that it was *me* on that screen.

"So you like biology?" Professor Doncaster demanded.

"Oh," I glanced at him to see what the right answer was. He wouldn't check my exam marks, right? "Sure."

He nodded. "As I thought. Anyone who knows what they're talking about is into biology. Biology helps us understand ourselves, our world, and change it for the better." He'd taken on a far-away look and clasped his hands together. "Every few summers I get an intern to help me with the paperwork, the databases and the chemistry. You'll learn about biology and genetics, and I'll learn about you hip young things today."

I coughed to cover a laugh.

"Today is just an intro, and I'm in the middle of some complex calculations, so maybe you'd like to wander the office until it's lunch time?"

"Sure." So I got an amazing view, cruisy work, the possibility of maybe maybe amending things in the genome database, *and* bragging rights about working for Edward Doncaster? This was turning out better than I'd thought.

"Oh, and I should say. You'll have access to classified information and as such may be a target, so it's best you don't disclose who you work for. Not even to the other interns or your mother."

I felt goosebumps. "A target?"

His mouth stretched into the wrinkles of his cheeks as he grinned, teeth fossilised in their gums. "You know, terrorists and such. Not to worry, it's just a precaution. It's never happened in the twenty years I've been taking interns, and it's not likely to."

I swallowed. Okay, terrorists did sometimes blow things up, but mostly they lived in news land. Like Gen-ens had before that night in the hospital. It wasn't nice to be reminded that terrorists didn't always stick to news land.

Doncaster showed me what I'd thought was a complicated piece of chemistry equipment, but turned out to be a coffee machine, then went back to his screen. He kept launching into snippets of life story, though, and I made encouraging noises as I wandered, staring out the window and flicking through books. Most of them were dry old textbooks, though I found a few with interesting pictures. Some were in pretty bad shape, with dirt stains and pages ripped out. A chemistry set made loud popping noises and spat green fire at one point, and Doncaster tipped over his chair rushing to fix it. I hoped none of the previous interns had suffered serious burns.

At twelve, Mark took me to see my "official" boss, a small bald man with an easy smile and an office down the corridor, Professor Friedrich Naidu.

"Any questions you'd like to ask?" Mark said as we shook hands.

Questions? What could I say if people asked me about what I was doing? What if they interrogated me on how Professor Naidu took his tea? I stumbled my way through some questions I hoped were vaguely intelligent, then Mark took me to lunch with the other interns. I swapped contact details with a few people, but it was hard to make conversation when I wasn't supposed to talk about what I was actually doing here. Why had Doncaster decided I'd be a good intern? My Category-A genome, whatever that meant?

Who knew.

10
Kiss

Xiao's parents were away that weekend, so he was throwing a party. I was pretty sure my parents would not let me go if they knew it was a proper party, but Mum surprised me.

"Yeah, Andrew's mum mentioned that," she said when I described a gaming tournament and pizza, leaving out how many people Xiao had invited. "Sounds fun."

"I can go?" I said, not quite believing her.

"Normal rules," she said. "Phone location on, home by eleven, no drinking. But you know that."

"'Course," I said. "And um... no catch?"

"Go enjoy yourself."

I guess actually sticking to the rules had its upsides.

Xiao was taking orders for pizza when Andrew and I turned up. The common room in his apartment building was covered in long streamers, and music pumped from a mean set of speakers. We drifted over to a games console where Ana Grey and Harris Patel were battling it out with lightsabers that hummed and crackle-clashed together. Andrew had been kinda quiet, but he took a turn with the lightsaber and completely destroyed Brendan Mbeke.

Pizza came in huge stacks and more people arrived, not just people from our class but people from Year Eleven and Year Thirteen. I made Andrew go and fill plates for us while I talked to Leilani about her shop internship, which sounded extremely boring. So far Doncaster had made me read a paper on how the same gene could affect lots of different things, and feed his frog, so maybe my internship wasn't much better. I *had* figured out the coffee machine, though, and found out that no, I couldn't make changes to the genome database – it was locked. I'd spent one morning collecting a book from his house in Mt Victoria, so it wasn't all stuffy office work, either.

I told Leilani Professor Naidu was letting me gen-en a giant moa, but I don't think she believed me. She went to talk to Mei Li after that, maybe to check my story.

Andrew dumped a plate of triple cheese in my lap and handed me a lurid purple drink. I screwed up my nose, but it didn't smell too bad and I took a sip. It didn't taste too bad either.

"There's more where that came from," Andrew said. "There's a gigantic bowl of punch you could swim laps in."

"No thanks," I said. "I'd be purple for weeks."

He poked his bright purple tongue out at me.

The area in front of the speakers had turned into a dance floor, and a few girls were twisting and shimmying in the spinning lights, eyes closed and hands thrown up. I wondered if Mira was coming. Was this her sort of thing? Te Aroha was talking to Brendan by the punch, and Mira had sat with her during exams so maybe they'd come together. Not that I should really be thinking about Mira, but–

"I'm going to dance with Leilani," Andrew said. I stared at him. Not *dance*, dance *with Leilani*.

"What?"

"I said–"

"Yeah, I heard what you said. What about Prajna?"

He shrugged and pushed himself off the squidgy sofa we'd taken. I pulled him back.

"Hey, what do you mean, *shrug*? What happened with Prajna?"

Andrew sighed. "She broke up with me."

"*What?*"

Andrew and Prajna were forever. Andrew and Prajna's love could not be conquered by seas wide nor time difference of eight and a half hours.

"She–" he broke off and stared at the ceiling, and I realised with horror that he was trying not to cry. How had I missed this? What kind of a best friend was I, mooning over a girl I couldn't have when Andrew had lost his perfect Match?

"When? Why?" I sputtered.

"I–" Andrew began, took a deep breath, and lowered his voice so I could hardly hear him over the music. "You won't tell anyone, right?"

"About Prajna?"

"No, what– what I'm going to tell you now."

I swallowed. "Of course. If you don't want to tell me, it's fine–"

"No, I want to tell you."

He was probably trying to convince himself. He glanced around to make sure no one was close enough to hear over the pumping music.

"I can't have kids."

I sucked in a breath. "What?"

He just stared at his hands twisted in his lap. I scrambled for words, but couldn't find anything that sounded right or might help. Just sitting there open-mouthed wasn't really helping, either. I remembered the other week, when he said he'd do his damnedest to take my mind off Lucas. He was so much better at this than I was.

"Hey, I'm sorry dude," I said at last. "That's rough. I mean, not that you'd want kids right now but– man. Sheesh." I thought about clapping him on the shoulder or something to show I was there for him, but that seemed cheesy. "And Prajna..."

He shrugged. "I think if it was up to her, maybe she'd have stayed with me, but... you know her parents. They want grandkids."

"I'm sure, like, when you want to think about having kids or whatever, they might have found ways to fix it. Medicine can do pretty amazing things. Or you could always adopt..."

"Doesn't help me get back with Prajna now, though."

I nodded. "Yeah, I suppose not. God, I'm sorry, Andrew."

There was a long pause as Andrew stared at the dance floor. I put my arm around his shoulders and gave him half a hug.

"She could have told them she was messaging someone else," he said finally. "I could have set up a fake account."

"That was never going to end well," I told him, and caught sight of Mira just coming through the door. She was wearing a short blue shimmery dress, her eyes done up with smokey makeup that made their colour stand out even more. No. Andrew. Focus on Andrew. "Secret relationships? Get real." I grabbed his hoodie and tugged him back and forth so his head wobbled. "Come on. If you want to dance with Leilani, dance with Leilani."

He didn't move.

"Or, don't dance with Leilani. Rebounds are a bad idea anyway. But dancing is a good idea." I pulled him up and pushed him towards the dance floor.

I didn't recognise some people – probably gatecrashers from other Pōneke schools or even out in Awakairangi Hutt. Xiao was dancing with a choppy-haired boy I'd never seen before, and a tall girl with long dark hair was battling lightsabers with Te Aroha. I wondered if any of them had known Lucas, four years ago, but they were probably too young.

We joined a circle of dancers and Andrew settled into his trademark shuffle, and after a few songs almost seemed to be enjoying himself. I sculled down my purple punch and managed to forget about Lucas. This was fun. I felt good. Warm and relaxed and ... oh. I stared suspiciously into my cup, and then at the punch bowl.

"The drink is spiked," I yelled to Andrew.

"Did you only just realise this?"

I punched him in the arm and tried to think how many cups I'd had. Three? Four? Possibly. Did I really care? I just had to make sure I was sober before eleven, which was in... three and a half hours. Or at least, sober enough to *pretend* to be sober when I got home. Unless Dad had a breathalyser somewhere. Did he have a breathalyser? No. I was fine. But how many had Andrew had? Was he likely to go comatose after drinking away his sorrows? Would I have to carry him home?

I watched his balance, and decided he was only tipsy. As long as he didn't have too many more.

I danced with a few girls, had another glass of purple punch and halted, dazed, as the world started to spin. I'd had wine and beer with dinner before, but not as much as this. Things were definitely starting to go blurry around the edges.

Xiao was still dancing with the boy with choppy hair. I tapped him on the shoulder, muttered the Prajna news and asked him to keep an eye on Andrew, then told Andrew I was going out for air.

"You gonna be okay?" I said.

He rolled his eyes and kept dancing.

—— · ——

I'd been to Xiao's apartment loads of times, and I managed to navigate my way out onto the balcony even with the room swaying. The air was cool on my face, smelling faintly of sea salt, and the sun was sinking slowly over the hills, throwing orange light across the city. I hadn't realised how close the air was inside the building.

"Hey," said a voice. I turned and found Mira looking back at me. She was leaning against the railing at the other end of the balcony. I glanced around. There was no one else out here.

"Hey," I answered. We stared at each other. I hadn't seen her since our history exam.

"How have you been?"

"Fine. How are you?"

She shrugged. "Fine. Exams are over."

"Yeah."

This was not the way I'd hoped our conversation would go.

She nodded towards the dance floor. "I think your friend likes my friend."

I twisted around to see. “Who, Xiao? And the boy with the hair?” They were bobbing along to a techno pop remix, doing way-too-dramatic moves and grinning at each other.

“Yeah. His name’s Enzo.”

“Is he from the Hutt?”

She looked down. “Nah. I met him out Mākara way, don’t know him that well. They look good together, right?”

I took a few steps and leant beside her on the railing, totally aware of the whole twenty centimetres of space between my arm and hers. The air hummed between us.

“Yeah. Hardout moves.” I tapped my fingers on the balcony glass. “How’s your internship? Law, right?”

“You remembered.” She smiled at me. Our eyes locked. God, her lips were so close, if I just... No. My head was fuzzy. Kissing her was a stupid thing to do.

It seemed like she had a similar thought, because she cleared her throat and looked away. “My mentor’s really awesome. I went to court on Friday, they were trying a woman for Allocations fraud. And you know what it was over?”

“What?”

“Coconut water. She had five thousand litres of it! When Ms Riley asked what it was for, she said you could get a DIY rejuv if you bathed in it for six weeks.”

“You’re kidding. Does it actually work?”

Mira shook her head. “Nup. Looked it up. All that coconut water thieving for nothing. She was young, too, wasn’t like she needed it.”

“Andrew’s interning at Allocations. Wonder if he could get me anything.”

She shoved my arm. “If you get sent to court, I’d have to watch you sentenced to a workcamp and that would suck.”

“Oh, it would suck for you watching, and not me getting sentenced?” I shoved her back. “Anyway, what makes you think I’d get caught?”

She laughed. “And what would you overallocate yourself, then? Those choc mint fudge bars you like?”

How did she know I liked mint choc fudge bars? Okay, maybe I’d been using them as my sugar-soaked-anti-brain-freeze before exams, but… she’d noticed. She’d been looking at me, like I’d been looking at her.

“Huh, yeah, you got me.” If I was overallocating, I’d overallocate Lucas another four years, another ten. But way to bring the mood down. “In fact, I have right here…” I brought a mint choc fudge bar out of my pocket, something I’d taken to the hospital today and forgotten about. “Want some?”

“Magic!” she said. “Ooh, yes please. Gotta see what the fuss is about.”

I broke it into pieces and let her choose. Her fingers brushed mine.

“I might be a little drunk,” she said. “But I think this is the best thing I have ever tasted.”

“Well, even if it’s cos you’re drunk, it’s a good assessment.” The “ss” didn’t come out quite right.

She grinned at me, showing purplish teeth. “You’re kinda drunk too.”

“Not as much as I was five minutes ago! And not as drunk as some people in there.”

She took another piece of fudge bar, and I took the last one, screwed up the paper and shoved it in my pocket.

"So how's your internship? You're at the Genetics Authority, right?"

"Yeah," I said, suddenly worried I would say something and spill the Doncaster secret. Though really, who cared? Did I really think Mira would pass it on to terrorists? She was the kind of girl who could keep her mouth shut. Probably. "Um, it's good. Sort of. Maybe kind of boring. I've got to feed a frog. And read stuff about biology. No exciting coconut water stories."

"Pity," Mira said. "And you don't get to rewrite the Matching rules, do you?"

I choked. She went bright red.

"Damn, didn't actually mean to say that out loud. It was a joke. Forget it."

"No," I said. "Um, no. Can't rewrite any rules."

"Ah well." She pushed off the railing and spun to face me, only swaying a little. She held out her hand. "Come over here, you can see the sunset better."

I could have hesitated, but I didn't. If Mira was holding out her hand, I was going to take it. She pulled me over to the corner of the balcony where you could see the very last of the sun glowing behind the hills. The first stars were appearing above us. It was quieter away from the doors.

"You said there were some good tracks up in the hills," she said, nodding towards them. "Do you go much?"

"Some," I said. Since Lucas's accident, I'd been on a few hikes and bike rides with Dad and Verity, all inside the Consolidation Line, and once outside it on a school trip. That was a year ago, three years after the accident, and I'd thought it'd be okay. The whole class there, chaperones galore, first aiders, two security guards just in case (though we were far enough south that even the most paranoid parents didn't mind signing the permission slips). I hadn't expected the tightness in my chest, the way my heart stuttered, my breath caught, not long after crossing the Consolidation Line. I'd faked a sore foot and sat on a log for a few minutes, drinking water and trying to psych myself up. I did it, but it was hard. "I used to go a lot, camp out there. But... you know. School. Time."

She nodded, though it was a pretty weak excuse. "Camping's fun."

"Yeah. Did you do it much in Dunedin?"

"Some."

We stared up at the glow of light on the hills for a while, and then,

"Do you want to go camping, sometime?" Mira asked.

There was way more meaning under her words than just camping. I pushed off the railing and stared at her. The wind ruffled her hair and mine, was cool on my face, but the world seemed to have shifted, and it was only partly the alcohol.

"Um," I said. Swallowed. "What did you have in mind?"

She didn't answer. Her eyes were reflecting the last reds and pinks of the sunset. I looked down, feeling my heart pound, remembering that afternoon on the roadside. I should go back in. There was nothing to stop us...

I took a step towards her, thought about it for a second, and then decided that I could, I would, control myself. Lucas, for instance, was a reason I would control myself. He only had two weeks until his review, and I should be spending as much time as I could getting him ready for it. Andrew was another. How could I think about being with someone when Andrew was inside, trying to forget Prajna? I turned determinedly in the direction of the door, but then she had her hand on my shoulder, turning me round, and her lips were on mine.

I could taste purple punch on her tongue, and wondered if this was taking advantage, but I was pretty sure she wasn't any more drunk than I was. We shouldn't do this... But... I put my arms around her and pushed her back into the corner of the balcony, where we definitely wouldn't be seen through the glass doors.

"I was wondering if you weren't that into me," I muttered, trying to talk in between kisses. She pulled my head closer. "And I thought we weren't going to do this. We could get in a lot of trouble. Re-education workcamps. Relocation."

"I don't care if it's illegal," Mira breathed. "I've been thinking about it, and I don't care. It's a stupid rule."

"Law," I muttered. "It's a law. Aren't you doing law?"

"Yeah. Lots of stupid laws around." Her fingers were tangling in my hair. She turned my head so she could whisper in my ear between light kisses along my cheekbone. "Maybe we can get it changed... or find a loophole. People in the cases I'm reading always seem to find a loophole."

It was hard to think properly. "You'd do that... for me?"

She blew a breath across my skin and I shivered. "You really *listen* when I ramble on. You look at me... like I matter."

"You *do* matter."

"Not to anyone else–" She drew back and shook her head, squeezing her eyes shut briefly. "No, forget that. I looked up our report – our Match ticks all the boxes apart from the percentage. So I checked the genealogy, couldn't find anything over six generations. Our ancestors weren't even in the same *countries*."

"It's not just about... about genealogy," I said. "It's still a law."

"Laws have loopholes. And we have this– this connection, right?" She put her hand on my chest, over my heart. It thundered beneath her palm. "You feel it?"

"Oh yeah," I said, catching her lips in mine. I could hear her heartbeat too, could feel it running through me. "Like... lightning. Like... a future."

To hell with the law. It was supposed to stop us before we fell for someone this hard. My hands roved her back, her shimmery dress silky under my fingers, and we kissed deeper, pressing closer until the warm space between us had dissolved into nothing. My body hummed. Her fingertips sketched fiery paths across my shoulders, up the nape of my neck, down my spine. My shirt shifted, the fabric rough against my skin. This was happening. It was actually happening. I brushed my lips at the base of her throat, where her pulse flickered and jumped.

"All right," I said at last, tracing my way up her jaw. "So we'll just have to keep it a secret until we find this loophole. Easy." I watched as her eyelids flickered closed. Was it that I had no self-control, or that I didn't actually want to use my self-control? She was right, though. How could feeling like this be wrong?

I ran my hand back through her hair, lifting it off her neck and smiling as she shivered. My head was spinning and the lights were coming on below, bright streaks in the twilight. I closed my eyes and leaned close, and her lips met mine once more and it was like stars exploding and waves rushing past me and falling off a cliff, all at once.

The noise inside the apartment had been growing louder, but I only noticed when people started yelling and shouting.

"Cops!"

11
Seagull

I PULLED BACK, BREATHING hard and light-headed. Mira stared up at me, her eyes wide, and I took a few steps before realising the cops couldn't be here for us. How would they have found out? We'd only been out here ten minutes, tops.

"One of the neighbours must have complained about the noise," I said. "And there's alcohol... Shit. They've probably done a Pulse to see who's here." The police weren't allowed to do Pulses much – mapping the locations of everyone's chips wasn't really "upholding the privacy and rights of decent free citizens" – but you got the feeling they took every chance they could. And catching underage drinkers was probably enough reason.

Mira's eyes were huge, the pupils black. "Are they going to arrest people?"

I twitched a shoulder. It wasn't about us. It couldn't be. "They just want to dock privileges or points or something–"

Someone in the apartment screamed.

It wasn't a girly omigod scream, either. It was a full-out god-help-me scream that shot scritching fingers of ice up my spine.

Shock was cutting through the alcohol haze. This was just underage drinking. This didn't deserve a scream like that. Mira started towards the scream, but I grabbed her arm. "We gotta get out of here."

She rounded on me. "What are they doing to them?"

"I don't know. Mira, it's the police, for god's sake. If they're going to arrest people, we can't stop them. We should get as far away as we can. There's a fire escape." I peered over the balcony. "Somewhere. There!"

"Enzo's still in there! Your friends! I'm doing a law internship, I should-"

"No, Mira, please!" It came out sounding more desperate than I meant.

Someone shot out onto the balcony. I gasped, but it was only Wiremu.

"Fire escape, right?" he hissed, and Mira pointed at the railing. "Thanks! You first?"

She shook her head and Wiremu was over the railing and gone.

"Please, Mira." If she wouldn't come with me, I was going to stay with her. Arrests and all.

Another yell, a boy's voice this time. It wasn't Andrew, I told myself. It didn't sound like Xiao.

"There's nothing we can do."

"Okay," she said at last, eyes wide. She clutched tighter to my arm and began to clamber over the railing. We were three storeys up, and the ground prowled restlessly below. Mira was over the side in no time, and I took a deep breath and put my leg over, striving not to look down.

The rungs ran out a way above the ground, and I had to jump the last few metres. Pain shuddered through my feet and knees, and I gritted my teeth. My hands still felt like they were clutching metal.

Faint reflections of red and blue light spun on a shut-up coffee stall at the end of the alley. The cops would be parked out there, dealing to whoever had screamed.

I hoped that kept them busy. Then I hoped that didn't make me a bad person, but was pretty sure it did.

Mira was waiting at the waterfront end of the alley. I ducked down to kiss her, knowing it was stupid, knowing the police were less than two hundred metres away and anyone could be walking by, but it was dark and adrenaline and alcohol coursed through my blood and I really couldn't think straight.

Mira met my kiss at first, but pulled away when the music from the apartment cut out. I saw what she was thinking.

"We can't do anything to help, Mira. If we try, we'll just get caught, and what's the point in that? They're probably just trying to scare people-"

"I'll go back alone," she said, voice breathless. "I should-"

I grabbed her as she started back down the alley. "You're drunk. I'm drunk. If they're arresting people for that, I don't want to be one of them. I don't want *you* to be one of them."

"They can't– It's not right," Mira said, voice stronger now. She pulled her arm away and rubbed it. "Ow."

"Sorry."

A figure appeared at the city end of the alley, a baton in one hand.

"Come on," I muttered to Mira. "*Please*. You can do lawyery stuff tomorrow if you really want. Right now we need to lie low."

She let me take her hand and lead her through the shadows to the wharf. It was a beautiful night, and people were out walking along the wharf or sitting on the rocks, arms around each other.

Stretched-faint blue and red lights cast our shadows ahead, and I forced myself not to walk any faster.

"What about the seagull playground?" Mira muttered. "Police officers wouldn't climb all the way up there?"

She was right. If they'd Pulsed us, they wouldn't try too hard to round us up. Picking us off in the open, maybe, but not climbing multi-level playgrounds built for eight-year-olds.

"Okay. Let's go."

It didn't take long to climb up. We settled against the cold metal, staring up at the stars. Mira drew my arm around her and held it with twined hands.

"Do you think they've arrested people? The people who screamed?"

I pulled out my phone. I could message Xiao... but if the police had his phone they'd get the message and I didn't know what they'd do with it. "Maybe they just wanted to scare people. No one was doing anything *that* illegal."

"Is there anything on your feeds about it?" She took the phone from my hand and scrolled through my latest updates. No one was saying much, but there was an anonymous post that just said "uh oh".

"I guess anyone who was there is still running or trying not to show they were there."

Mira handed me back the phone. "Or they've been arrested. I should have gone back."

"No, you shouldn't. You could have been arrested."

There was a long pause. Then, "I've never been arrested."

"Um?" I pulled back to stare at her. "It's not like it's something to be proud of."

Her eyes flickered. "Depends what you're arrested for."

"Being arrested for underage drinking is not something to be proud of."

"Okay, okay." She sounded like she agreed this time, and she squeezed my hand. "Don't worry, Kieran, I won't get myself arrested for something petty."

"That's really not comforting."

She turned her face up to kiss me, and I lost myself in her mouth for a while.

"So I guess we're doing this?" she breathed against my lips.

I nodded, trying not to let the air get between us.

"There's something..." she whispered. "I need to tell you."

"What." I didn't want to open my eyes. My fingers traced the line of her shoulder, down her arm to clasp her hand tight and not let go.

"Kieran." She pulled away, breath hitching. "I need to say this before we go any further. Just because otherwise... I'm not coming into this right."

"Yeah?"

"I– you know how I said I don't have any siblings."

"Yes." It was rare to meet an only child – most parents had the two they were allowed, or three if they had special permission.

"That wasn't completely true."

She was staring through the bars at the dark office buildings. I squeezed her hand, as much to tell her to keep going as to say I didn't mind she'd lied.

"I had a sister. She died last year."

"I– I'm sorry." My thoughts flew to Lucas. I could be in the same position as Mira next month. Lucas was my cousin, not my sister, but still.

She hadn't moved, but her pulse was jumping in her wrist. I couldn't stop myself asking the next question. "How?"

"She had a rare disease. They couldn't save her. I mean, they could tell us she had a seventeen percent chance of surviving the year, they could tell us which gene was responsible and what had triggered it, but they couldn't–" She squeezed her eyes shut. "–frigging save her." Her voice had gone quiet and jagged. "Sorry. I'm drunk. Shouldn't really be having this conversation drunk. But you need to know."

"Doctors suck. I know it doesn't mean enough, but ... I'm sorry."

She took a deep breath and opened her eyes. "No talking. Not yet. I haven't finished."

She rushed the next words.

"We were twins. Identical. Same genes. I might get what she had."

I felt like I was falling. I didn't think it was the punch.

"What?"

She began to repeat herself, but I shook my head. Without meaning to I was already pulling away, my hand leaving hers, and barbed wire coiled in my throat. Look at me, already abandoning her. She'd said "might". It wasn't certain.

Could I handle two people dying on me?

I felt her eyes on me, reached out and squeezed her hand. She squeezed back. I could hear her breath going in and out, with just a little too much control to be natural.

What if it were me? What if I was the one who might die, and she said she couldn't handle it? It'd be like Lucas's parents, who came to see him every few months and stayed for ten minutes. I understood it in some horrible way, they were protecting themselves by staying out in the Hutt and trying to forget they had a son, but... it was *Lucas*. How could they just leave him to stare at hospital walls all day?

The metal seagull creaked in the wind. Mira was sitting here beside me, alive with her hand in mine.

It was hard to imagine her lying in a hospital bed, heart slowing until its beat skipped... stuttered... was silent.

"Maybe–" I whispered. "Maybe they'll figure it out. Maybe the doctors–"

She laughed, and it was harsh. "They had over a year to figure out what was wrong with Melanie. They just kept filling her full of medicine that stopped her fainting – sometimes. But it didn't do anything to stop her dying."

"They're a year up on where they were before, then." I hoped I was making it better, not worse. "If you started now, got the doctors to do studies–"

"No." She smiled sadly. "I don't think I'm sick yet. A while back, I thought maybe I was, but it was probably just stress. They'd have nothing to study. And even if I did get sick–God. I don't want to spend my last year shut up in some hospital being experimented on. They won't fix me, and what's the point of wasting my last months?"

"If it's not wasted..."

She shivered. "It might not happen, anyway. Whatever gene's to blame might never turn on, and then I wouldn't have to worry about it. I could just be the lucky twin." Her voice was bitter. "Not the dead one."

I was sitting awkwardly, and the air was cold where Mira had been. Say she was going to die, say there was nothing that could stop it, would I stay with her? Could I?

It wasn't really making a decision, but wanting to have her close again. I edged towards her. She met me halfway, and though our touch stopped the chill, we didn't fit like we had before.

"What do you think happens ... after?" I asked. "Do you believe in souls? Something that continues on?"

She shrugged. "I don't know. I guess souls or something must exist, because Gen-ens are missing them. Souls must be made of something we can't replicate, or come from somewhere and go somewhere. Hopefully somewhere nice." She shifted and I moved my arm to get more comfortable. "Melanie said she'd come back to see me, if she could, but I've never felt her so I guess she's somewhere else. Or not."

Her voice cracked and without thinking my arms were encircling her and her face was buried in my shoulder.

"I think we have souls that keep living in some way," I said slowly. "If people just die and that's it... I don't know. I like thinking there might be something more, you know?"

"Yeah," she sniffled.

"You can't ever really know the answer to this stuff. You just have to figure out what makes the most sense. What means you can live your life without going crazy."

"Yeah." She seemed to shake herself and eased away, though our shoulders still touched and our hands interlinked. "Given that I might not be around much longer–"

"Don't be stupid," I cut in. She ignored me.

"–you still, um, want to do this? Whatever it is?"

"Yeah," I said, surprising myself. It was all instinct, but now I'd said it I knew it was right. "Yes."

"Why? What if there is no– no loophole? What if I get what Melanie had? What if–"

I kissed her to stop her words. "Because you make me feel like there is hope. That problems can be fixed. And if they can't..." I swallowed. "You can keep going."

She was quiet, leaning her head against mine.

"And you?" I asked. "I might mess up your plans. Your future you're so sure of."

She shrugged. "I think... you can make all the plans in the world, but if something comes along and you don't recognise what– what a chance you have, if you don't grab it with both hands because you're too worried about some far-off plan that might not even happen, then what's the point?"

"And... I'm that something?"

She nudged me. "I think so. Anyway, who's to say you won't make my plans come out better, if you're a part of them?"

"You haven't known me very long." She didn't know how totally I could mess things up.

"But I've got a feeling." She brushed down her dress and flashed me a watery grin. "So we just need to not get caught."

12

Dam

I WAS HOME BEFORE eleven, and sober enough to pass Dad's inspection. Despite my fears, the next morning there was nothing on my account about points docked or allocations withdrawn. Maybe they hadn't done a Pulse. We'd got away with it, as long as Mum and Dad didn't find out.

My head hurt. I ate three oranges and gulped down half a litre of water, which sort of helped. Reliving the evening with Mira (minus the police) sort of helped too.

There was a short newspost about unchipped teenagers being arrested at a private party in the city. That explained the police, but there were no real details – how many teenagers, where they'd come from, how the police had known, what had been done with them. They weren't city kids, because all of us were chipped, so they had to be peevs.

Maybe some of the gatecrashers had been peevs? Peevs were usually a lot dirtier and more crazy-looking, though, at least on newscasts.

I messaged Xiao and Andrew with single question marks, and got an immediate "ok, u?" from Andrew, and a message from Xiao fifteen minutes later with a squiggle face, which probably meant he was grounded and couldn't message more. He was okay, then. Not arrested, like I'd been thinking half the night.

Later in the afternoon I got an anonymous message: "Seagulls don't tell tales". I set up my own anon account and sent a message back, "Purple teeth do, though".

You got a talk?? Her message came back immediately.

I said it was juice

If we were doing this, we needed to get creative about meeting up. *You free tomorrow after work?*

Sure

Meet me at the city side of the Mt Vic tunnel, 5.30. I thought about adding "COME ALONE", but maybe that was too obvious and not quite a joke.

Done

—— · ——

When I rolled to a stop outside the Mt Vic tunnel, Mira was leaning on her bike wearing a slick blue corporate shirt, hair escaping a bun. Her bottom half didn't match: black bike shorts and neon cycling shoes, the proper ones that locked into the pedals.

"How was your day, Judge Mira Sorenssen?

"Most excellent. How was yours?"

"Pretty good." Sort of. I was still reading biology papers. At least maybe next year I wouldn't fail bio. This morning Doncaster had taken one look at my crisp green shirt and gelled hair and asked if I was going on a date, so that had been awkward. Even if this date hadn't been against the rules, there was no way I was going to discuss my love-life with a hundred-and-twelve year old. I'd made up something about a family gathering.

"Where are we going?" She ran fingers over her hair, smoothing it down. I put a hand out to stop her – I liked it better dancing in eddies – but stopped myself. We were out in the open, with buses and cyclists passing. She was looking into the blackness of the tunnel and the bus silhouetted against the bright dot of the other end, cheeks pink and eyes alive.

I wanted to kiss her. Really, really wanted to kiss her. My fingers and toes were tingling with it, and the air between us crackled.

Her eyes caught mine and swallowed them up. Her gaze dropped to my lips.

I shook my head and looked away. "It's a secret. Come on, we've got a way to ride." I pushed off without waiting for her, trying not to think about how no one would see us in the dark tunnel and maybe I *could* kiss her. Before getting run over by a bus.

I was out the other side before Mira caught up. The cyclists thinned out past Kilbirnie Park – no one lives on Kilbirnie Flat because it's close to sea level, and if the dam's breached there'll be a four metre wave coming through. Her eyes were bright, dancing when we swapped glances. Maybe it was because we'd finally decided to give *us* a go, or maybe because she'd told me about her sister. She knew I was with her anyway.

Mira had been to court again today, and even got to talk to some people in the cells. Her mentor sounded awesome. She asked what my mentor was like (grouchy), and what I was doing. I had to strip my answers of anything that pointed in Doncaster's direction, hoping Mira wouldn't notice my vagueness.

But at least I'd timed things right, and as we approached the airport the six o'clock from Auckland was floating down, swaying in the wind. We watched it land, holding our breaths as the hover skimmed the runway, bounced and settled properly to the tarmac.

"That looks fun," Mira said, pushing the hair from her eyes.

"Yeah, wish I could go on one. You didn't get a hover to Pōneke?"

She shook her head. "They wouldn't allocate us a flight. Just for important people, I guess."

The hover was still shuddering (with relief?) as it taxied to the terminal. We rode through Miramar, through the tunnel to Seatoun, and down Ludlum Street to the Seatoun Dam. The harbour was calm, for once, lapping against the stony beach and the ten-metre wall of the dam. The ramp to the top of the dam was steep, so we got off halfway and walked our bikes.

There used to be a public roadway across the dam to Pencarrow, but they closed it during Consolidation, when everyone moved into Wellington City or out to Awakairangi and no one needed to go there. The fence spanning the roadway was humming softly, and the only gate was for authorised personnel.

"Beautiful," Mira whispered, staring out at Raukawa Cook Strait.

"It's better on the other side of the fence." I marched my bike up to the gate.

Mira's wheels turned on the gravel.

"Uh, Kieran? What are you doing?"

I held my wrist to the reader and the gate beeped twice and swung open. Mira's eyes were wide.

"How...?"

I grinned. "Come on, we have to get through quick before the gate closes."

She swung off her bike and wheeled it forward, eyeing the sign promising prosecution and/or death. "Are you sure…?"

"Yeah, it's fine. Dad knows the head engineer. They won't mind, as long as we don't touch anything. Come *on*."

The gate was beginning to beep, warning it would soon swing shut. Mira gathered herself and passed through, and I followed.

The dam stretched away, running from Seatoun's craggy rocks to curve into the Pencarrow foreshore on the far coast, the shipping lock about halfway across. When I was a kid and obsessed with ships, Dad and I would spend hours out here. The best was when ships left the harbour, bobbing in the long enclosure as the water frothed and sputtered in, lifting the ship to sea level.

The sun touched the scrubby shoulders of the Ōrongorongo Range with golden light. Te Whanganui-a-Tara – the Great Harbour of Tara – spread to our left, frilly waves pushed around by the wind, and beyond that the Tararua and Remutaka Ranges in layers of green and brown and dusky blue.

"Wow," Mira breathed, walking her bike slowly forward so she could see past the empty control booth. I grinned and followed her.

"Try the upper path. It's the best view and there aren't many cameras."

"Cameras?"

"That's the only downside. They keep it all secure because of the ship locks. But we're just two friends going for a walk." She didn't look that convinced. "Don't worry, I've been in the camera control room. I know where the blind spots are."

We slogged up the steep path to the top walkway, a few metres above sea level. Wellington City is about four metres below normal high tide level, which is actually quite a lot if you think about it. Lots of buildings have markings showing the high tide mark, and you aren't allowed to have schools or accommodation below the line.

Not that the dam or the dykes would cave in, or anything – they're made of some sort of rubbery, earthquake-resistant stuff – but it was better to be ared.

The high wind was exhilarating and I Ieaned into it, pitting my strength against the elements. Mira's hair had fully escaped the bun and the wind was whipping it in wild streaks left and right. A strand caught her lips as she turned and yelled something, eyes alive. A loop of spray flung up and disappeared in the wind.

Mira waited for me to come alongside so she could shout in my ear. "It's beautiful! I'm getting salt all over my work clothes, though. Gonna have to tell my mum I got caught by a crazy lady with a water gun."

"Argh, sorry, I didn't think of that." Personally, I was out here on a bike ride with Xiao (Mum talked to Andrew's mum too much, so he wasn't a good alibi).

We reached a spot where the view was as good as you were going to get, halfway between the Seatoun coast and the lock. I checked they hadn't added any cameras, dropped my bike and swung Mira around to kiss her. She shrieked but didn't seem to mind, wrapping both arms around my neck.

My heart was hammering when we came up for air. It had only been two days since I'd last done that, but it seemed like months.

The wind was leeching away the day's heat and I was glad of Mira's warmth. We leaned against the sea wall, arms around each other, and I pointed out the Kaikōura Ranges against the sky. She'd been to the Southern Alps, and she tried to describe the feeling of snow beneath your feet as you climbed above the tree line. I've done snow-shoeing in VR, but ice is one of the things it can't quite get right. However much the haptics and the air-conditioning and the vid try to convince you it's real, some part of you knows it's not.

I pulled away, keeping hold of Mira's hand and searching around in my bag. She crouched beside me, taking advantage of the sea wall's shelter to finger-comb her hair.

"Somewhere in here," I muttered. "I have... Ah ha!"

I brought out the garlic bread, falafel, salad, lollies and strawberries I'd picked up from the supermarket. I'd used some of Verity's food Allocation points to get enough for the picnic, but she never reached her quota and no one would notice.

"What's that silver thing?" Mira asked, pointing at the holosphere. I'd had it in my bag since the visit to Lucas.

"Something my mum gave me. It's supposed to show pictures, but it's broken. I've been trying to fix it." Or at least, planning to try.

"Hmm. I think I know someone who could help you."

"Got a techie geek friend?"

"Yep. Techie as."

The garlic bread was still hot in its heat bag, the rich smell wafting out.

"Man, that looks amazing. This is Best Boyfriend material, you know."

"What's the prize?"

"There is no prize. It's just the smugness factor." She narrowed her eyes at me. "I don't think you need any help with that, though, judging by your face."

"Hey!"

"And considering you're going to be the next big-shot genius genetics Nobel Prize winner."

There was a pause that went on too long, and I forced a laugh. "Yeah, I can see that happening."

She blinked and pulled away. "Sorry, did I say something wrong?"

Maybe that laugh had been too bitter.

"It's stupid, I guess." I stared at the concrete, trying to find the right words. "Just, I so obviously am not Nobel Prize material. If I fail bio D–" I caught myself. "The GA might kick me out or–"

"Kieran, you're not going to fail bio–"

"Sure, so people generally pass when they only answer half the questions and go on about bananas."

She rolled her eyes. "Come on, I'm sure you answered more than that. And you're smart–"

"Me, smart?" I laughed hoarsely. "I haven't got an A since I was twelve. I haven't got a B in, what, two years?" I'd forgotten I'd only known her for a few weeks – she had no idea what my marks were. My stomach went into freefall. Now she knew, would she decide I wasn't good enough for her? "Forget it. You wouldn't understand, you've probably never got a B in your life–"

"Excuse me?"

"–and I'm sorry if I don't measure up to what you thought–"

"Kieran! Look at me!"

When I took too long, she grabbed my chin and turned it. Our gazes held for a few seconds, magnetised, and then she pressed her lips to mine. Everything melted away but us.

She drew back for breath. "Maybe I get a few good marks, but I also say stupid things and I'm terrible at languages, you would not believe... My point is, I don't care. It doesn't matter to me. I – I just want to be able to see you and talk to you and kiss you and have adventures with you. Be together." She squeezed her eyes shut. "It sounds so cheesy, you know? Like one of those bad movies. But it's true."

I stared at her. She was talking about me. And she was serious.

"You're not having second thoughts yourself...?"

"No, no, no," I said hurriedly. "Not at all."

She let out a breath. "Good. And you know, there are lots of ways to be smart. It's not just about marks. *I* think you're smart."

"Er, thanks..." I didn't know how she'd got that impression.

She picked out two strawberries, giving one to me and settling against my side. "We don't have to talk about it if you don't want to, but... what happened when you were twelve?"

I stiffened.

"I mean, you said you got A's before that. Did school just get harder?"

She didn't know about Lucas. Of course she didn't. I hadn't told her.

I opened my mouth, and shut it again. The silence lengthened.

"It doesn't matter, really," Mira said. "Sorry, I'm always too curious for my own good."

I pulled my arm out from behind her. She straightened, her brow creasing as she watched me.

She should know. If we were going to do this properly, she had to know. She'd told me about her sister.

I hardly even mentioned Lucas to Andrew, let alone anyone else. And I didn't think I'd ever told this story in full.

"When I was twelve," I said at last, "I was in a car crash. Near Mākara." I pulled up my hair to show the thin scar along my hairline, hearing the whump and crunch of car versus tree, the shower of crystallised glass. Seeing the chaos of green and brown in the sharp-shadowed light. "I got a bad concussion and a few stitches, spent a week or so in hospital. My cousin Lucas was in the car too. He wasn't so lucky. He lived, but... he never really woke up. He's in the long-term ward at Wellington Hospital."

"Oh." Mira glanced down. "I'm sorry."

The ranges were darkening in the twilight, layers of deeper blue against the slate sky. "He's okay, physically. Not on life support or anything. But... we weren't supposed to be out there." I swallowed, seeing Lucas's blank eyes.

"Go on."

I shook my head to clear it. "We found this car, fixed it up. I– I was driving. Went too fast, overloaded the ancient computer." I swallowed. "We were ages away from help. After the crash... things don't stay in my head the way they used to. It's hard to concentrate. I don't get A's anymore."

Mira scuffed her fingers along the asphalt, tumbling tiny stones. "You were twelve. Four years ago..."

I knew what she was getting at. Everyone knew the four year rule, had some relation who'd come up against it. "Four years exactly, next Friday."

"So..." she said. "Lucas is up for review?"

I nodded, not trusting myself to speak.

"Do you think he'll get through?"

I didn't say anything. It was answer enough.

13

Conversations

It was annoying, having to weave white lies when anyone asked about my internship. I felt I should have told Mira who I was working for. And I kind of wanted to tell Verity, so she'd shut up about me being frog boy. Okay, I fed a frog, but it was *Edward Doncaster's* frog.

When exam marks came out, Doncaster didn't seem to know or care. I'd failed one unit in bio, and a few units in history and IT, but done okay in maths, English and tech.

"Hey, at least you got enough credits to pass Year Twelve," Dad said, and gave me a box of choc mint fudge bars.

If Doncaster wasn't worried about marks (and he would have seen my existing marks when I applied), how did he choose people? Why had he "requested" me? Maybe he knew Mum and thought she was good, but of course I couldn't ask her.

Maybe he'd heard how good I was at smiling and nodding. He liked to have an audience, and it didn't seem to matter if I was interested or not – he still spieled on about historical events he'd lived through, or laws he'd had a hand in writing. Earlier in the week he'd been going on about population carrying capacity and the Malthusian trap, which would have been helpful for my history exam.

"You know, Kieran, we're a Goldilocks population now. Not too big, not too small. We don't intrude as much on nature as we did when I was your age. No famine, no war. Seventy-five million people in the world means there's enough to go around, and enough left over for nature to recover. But we've still got to tread carefully, replace our population, not grow it. If everyone follows the rules, Mother Earth will flourish and we need never be at the brink of extinction again."

Today he was focused on Allocations, and I wondered if he knew about Lucas and was trying to make a point.

"Allocations are important, Kieran."

"Yeah, I know, my friend Andrew's interning at Allocations." I tried to keep my voice light. There was more to Allocations than Allocating years to live, after all – food, energy, travel.

"They mean everyone gets enough. No materialism, no greed. We don't need very much to be happy, just to value what we have. If you make a good Match, you may get a little more at first, but there's enough to go around, and people must be rewarded for making a good Match."

I expected him to ask me why, but he just stared out at the harbour. It was a clear day, only a few small clouds zipping across the sky and throwing shadows on the water. Some brave boatie was out skimming the waves.

"Did you ever think about finding a Match?" I asked.

He rubbed his hand across the grey stubble on his chin. "I suppose I did, once. There was someone. Amy. She died in the last Plague."

I kept forgetting how old he was. "Oh."

"Karma, I suppose," he muttered, lost in space again.

I blinked at him. "Karma?" Was he talking about pollution or consumerism or whatever? Some people thought karma or God had acted through the Gen-ens, but I'd never thought Emeritus Professor Doncaster would be one of them. He'd stopped the Plagues, saved humanity from "karma".

A timer on the bench beeped and he shuffled over to transfer a red liquid from a beaker to a test tube.

If you wanted a proper conversation with Doncaster, not silence or a monologue, you just had to keep talking. "Karma like, humans were destroying the Earth so they got what they deserved? Or there *is* that evil environmentalists conspiracy theory." Evil environmentalists were way more scientific than karma.

Doncaster laughed and spilled a splash of liquid onto the stainless steel bench. Smoke rose from the spot. "I enjoy our chats, Kieran. They make life more interesting."

"So you don't think it was evil environmentalists?"

He raised an eyebrow and set the beaker on the benchtop, then held the test tube at eye-level and tapped it. "Highly doubtful. They'd need to be geniuses in bioengineering to make plagues with that kind of virulence, to balance the incubation period, infectiousness, mortality, get around all the safeguards from earlier pandemics... Best and brightest."

I moved the frog and picked up a book, flicking through to see the pictures. There weren't many and the type was miniscule. "Yeah, so a genetically-engineered brain." Along with the whole soulless lack of morals thing. I thought of the Gen-en from the hospital, screaming it'd kill everyone.

"True. How are those searches coming along?"

I dropped the book and went back to my screen.

Doncaster's interest of the hour was a particular type of short-sightedness that he was sure was associated with a resistance to cancer, meaning that some of the Matching guidelines might be changed. Short-sightedness was a trait to be avoided, but if the gene reduced the risk of cancer, maybe there were ways to harness it.

I typed in the sequence and the location of the gene, then searched for all the matches. The result list grew and grew and grew, starting with people in Pōneke and Awakarangi and then moving out to cover the whole of Aotearoa New Zealand, then Oceania, Asia, the World.

There were a lot of people. Lucky my trusty search could show me more detail about histories of cancer and things like–

Huh. Andrew's name jumped out. He wore contact lenses. I glanced across the rest of his entry, and saw an F.

An F?

Andrew had a Category-F genome?

I hadn't checked out any of my friends' genomes. It seemed ... icky, somehow. An invasion of their privacy. Okay, yeah, I'd invaded my teachers' privacy and the privacy of some celebrities, but that didn't really seem real. This was Andrew. This was my *friend.*

I squeezed my eyes shut and clicked through to the detail. One eye open. I skimmed the words, trying to treat them lightly in my mind, but they still seared there.

At the bottom of the page: *Right to procreate: denied.*

It wasn't that Andrew physically couldn't have children. It was that the authorities wouldn't *let* him have children.

My phone buzzed and I pulled it out, paranoia telling me it was Andrew, messaging to ask about his genome category. But no, he didn't know, he didn't know any of it, and it was Mira's alias account.

We good for tomorrow?

Yep, I answered, and wondered what gene category Mira was, but couldn't bring myself to look.

Should I tell Andrew? What difference would it make? There wasn't anything he could do about it. There wasn't anything *I* could do about it, either – I couldn't change the database. And what would I say, sorry, your genes aren't great, so they don't want you in the gene pool? I thought the whole point of Matching was to match up people with complementary genomes, so bad genes didn't matter so much.

Guess it was just another thing to add to my don't-tell list.

14
Adventure

I WENT TO SEE Lucas early Saturday morning, then met Mira at the bottom of Aro Street, the holosphere in my bag. She hadn't told me where her techie friend lived, but she'd promised a good bike ride so I was guessing the Hutt.

Mira was leaning against her bike in the shade of a tree, wearing slim cut-off jeans, a windbreaker and her neon yellow shoes. It had rained in the night and the green leaves popped against dark wood. The sky was washed clean of clouds. Mira smiled when she saw me and swung a leg over her bike. "Sleep in?"

"Nah, up for hours. Went to see Lucas."

"Oh." We set off down Willis Street and she looked sideways at me. "How is he?"

I shrugged. "Same as ever."

She nodded, and changed the subject. I'd been worried she might be all awkward, but she seemed to know to let things be, I guess from her sister.

By the time we reached the Railway Station the morning's tension was lifting from my shoulders. Mira filled me in on her Friday (more cell visits), and I told her about the towers of books in "Naidu's" office.

The harbour was almost still enough to reflect the hills across the water, patches of wind shifting across its surface. At the Ngā Ūranga Gorge turnoff, Mira veered left. I slowed.

"Um..." I drew in a steadying breath. "Your friend lives out *here*? Are we going outside the Consolidation Line?"

She stopped and waited for me to wheel up beside her. "Maaybe. You should probably turn your phone signal off. Just in case."

We were, weren't we. My chest was tight, my palms sweaty on the handlebars. I didn't want her to see me fall apart.

But I'd got through it on the school excursion. I could get through it now. Last weekend I'd climbed down the side of an apartment building and evaded the police. Before that, I'd escaped a Gen-en. This should be a piece of cake – I'd slipped out of the city for the first time when I was nine, after all.

I took a deep breath and deadened the signal on my phone, wishing I knew Lucas's decoy-signal trick and hoping my parents wouldn't decide to see where I was. "I gotta be back before five, or I'll be super-grounded again."

"No problem. And, uh, again?"

"Oh, right." I hadn't told her the Gen-en story. We set off up the Gorge and I described my night visits to see Lucas. "I was getting away with it, but then that Gen-en escaped."

"Wait, the one in the– oh shit, the one in the hospital."

"Yep," I said. "I saw her. She ran past Lucas's room."

Mira swerved, neck craned and eyes wide.

"Road!" I said. She righted herself and focused forward.

"God, you're not joking, are you?"

I shook my head, pleased at her reaction. "She was on the floor above us. There was this big bang, and an alarm. I didn't realise what it was at first, but then there were gunshots and I saw the tattoo when she went past the door."

"Holy shit. Did it see you?"

"Didn't seem like it. I pulled Lucas down beside the bed so you couldn't see us from the door."

She was shaking her head, face drained of colour except for two pink spots in her cheeks. "If it had seen you... you'd be dead."

"I dunno." Yeah, the Gen-en had been yelling abuse, but she hadn't been going room-by-room massacring patients. "It was hurt. Probably couldn't have done much damage. And there was stuff I could throw at it, hold it off if I needed to."

Mira nodded, looking mildly impressed.

I was back in Lucas's room, the red light pulsing, the siren, the Gen-en's moans through the wall. "It was pretty horrible. Knowing the cops were sneaking up on it, and it couldn't move."

"What, you feeling sorry for it? They don't have feelings, you know."

I shrugged, thinking of what I'd told Margaret. Maybe I was. But the Gen-en was dead now. With all the others. "Nah. Hey, um, what about the checkpoints?" They were around the next bend. They didn't exactly keep you in, but they noted if you left and you were supposed to have a good reason. Lucas and I had always bypassed them by going round the back trails.

"We're not going as far as that," Mira said, and turned off onto a steep once-was-street on our right. "This will take us around."

"So... we're staying inside the Consolidation Line?"

She shot me a raised eyebrow. "'Course not."

"And..." No, I wasn't going to mention auto-tasers. If she knew this path, she knew there weren't any auto-tasers, and I already looked like a wuss, feeling sorry for Gen-ens.

She halted and twisted back. "Come on, where's your sense of adventure?"

Yeah, where was my sense of adventure? I didn't used to be like this.

No one was going to die just because I crossed the Consolidation Line.

"Race you," I said, pushed hard to pass her, pushed everything out of my mind.

—— · ——

The old road joined up to a bigger one near the top of the hill. We were outside the Line now, out where things had been left to rot. Trees grew through cracks in the road and the skeletal remains of houses stared through thick mānuka, broken windows clutching at frames and grimy with dirt. Some houses had fallen in completely, their roofs blankets of grass and rogue pansies. I didn't see any that would make good camping houses – too exposed to southerly winds and rain. A length of faded tape had tangled around a tree and was flapping half-heartedly in the wind. Plastic, maybe, from before the ban. I caught an end and it came off in my hand, greyish black spelling out the first five letters of "quarantine".

"Where are we going?" I asked again. I was doing all right, with only one stop for water and a minor freak-out. I didn't think Mira had noticed. "This goes on for miles. Is it a shortcut to the Hutt?" Hopefully.

"You'll see."

"You know where you're going, right?"

"'Course."

We left our bikes beside a stream that was eating away at a road, changed our cycling soles and followed the water up through the trees. We had to wade at some places where the trees grew too close to the bank, but mostly it was easy going, hopping between stepping stones and up tiny waterfalls. A pīwakawaka eyed us, decided we were non-threatening and displayed its fan tail proudly, little chest puffed out.

It was getting more and more likely that Mira's friend did not live in Awakairangi Hutt.

"Here," Mira said after ten minutes or so, pulling me away from the stream to follow a faint winding path. It had been formed by treading feet, many of them, the moss and old leaves worn through to the damp clay.

"Uh, Mira?" I said, finally brave enough to bring it up. I'd been thinking maybe she'd inexplicably made friends with one lone peev, not a group of them. A village of them. "You didn't say–"

I didn't get to finish my sentence, because a guy dressed in worn camo appeared on the path ahead.

I gasped so fast I choked, and flung my arms out in front of Mira. How had I not heard him? How had I not seen him? How soon was he going to kill us?

"Stay back!" I yelled.

It took me a second to realise that Mira was laughing. Of course. Of course I didn't need to protect her from, what, a friend? A *peev* friend. She gently pushed down the arm I was using to protect her.

"Your face," she chortled.

My heart was still thumping in my chest. Mira pushed past me and hugged the guy.

"This is Kieran, my boyfriend," she said, waving a hand at me. The thrill the word "boyfriend" should have had was kind of overpowered by the shock still thrumming through me.

"I'm Nīkau," the guy said, mouth twitching. At least he had the decency not to laugh. He was tall, with dark curly hair and a nose like a Greek statue. He was probably in his early thirties, and he had this calm confidence that was reassuring and then worrying. Why was I reassured? I shouldn't be reassured. This guy looked like he could squish me flat without breaking a sweat.

He put out his hand for me to shake and I took it, hoping my hand wasn't as sweaty as I thought it was.

"I'm the chief medic at Horokiwi. Well, the only medic. And part-time sentry."

"Kieran," I said, realising too late that Mira had already told him my name. "Part-time really surprised boyfriend."

He did laugh at that, even though it was a terrible joke. My scattered braincells were slowly coming together. Horokiwi. I'd never heard of it.

Nīkau had to be a peev, but he didn't look like one. He obviously washed more than twice a year, and he looked as sane as any city person. Maybe the boy with choppy hair at Xiao's party *had* been a peev.

"My shift's almost finished, I'll show you in. What brings you?" Nīkau asked, turning and leading the way down the narrow track. Mira followed close behind, and I trailed behind her.

"Kieran's got a gadget he's trying to fix, I thought Elspeth could take a look at it. And I wanted to introduce Kieran to you guys."

As Nīkau moved, his untucked shirt shifted across a hard edge just above his waist.

He had a gun.

But he hadn't used it on us, I repeated to myself. He was a sentry, and maybe there were other peev groups he had to defend himself from. Mira trusted him.

"Any update on Enzo?" Nīkau asked, pulling aside some ferns so they wouldn't whack us in the face.

"He's doing okay," Mira said. "They're feeding him. He's got a hearing next week, and my boss thinks it'll go well. Raymi, though..."

Nīkau shook his head. "You know it's complicated, Mira. Raymi's not one of us. And Enzo chose..." He swallowed. "He made his choice, he'll get a chip, and looks like he's not in any danger–"

"But Raymi is!"

Nīkau sighed. "Take it up with Jake. Come on, I'm hungry. You hungry?" And he strode ahead of us, leaving me a chance to talk to Mira.

"How– how did you find these– these people?" I whispered. "And who's Enzo? And Raymi?"

"Remember my friend at Xiao's party? The one dancing with Xiao?"

"Yeah?"

"That was Enzo. He got arrested." She was staring at her feet. "If we'd stayed–"

I was beginning to figure things out. "We couldn't have made a difference, though, right? The police must have targeted them, if we'd got in the way..."

"Yeah..." she said. "I know. And I've been able to talk to him, because of my internship. He wanted to live in the city, see? So he–he got arrested on purpose. If I'd been arrested... it would have just messed things up."

"And Raymi?"

"She helped him get into the city. She didn't know what he was planning. And she's twenty, so the best she can hope for is lifetime workcamp. That's if they can't connect her to any "terrorist" stuff..." She gave the word "terrorist" heavy air quotes.

"And... might they connect her to terrorist stuff?"

She shrugged, her blue eyes dark. "Who knows what they can cook up."

15

Horokiwi

I DIDN'T REALISE WE'D arrived at Horokiwi until we were almost inside it. I'd pictured some sheds, maybe a few shacks.

At first it just looked like forest, with kids chasing each other through the trees, shrieking. But then I realised what I'd thought were trees – actually, no, they were trees, I'd been right the first time – were being used as the posts for houses, and low living walls of woven fern fronds wound about them. A few looked like traditional Māori whare.

Between the buildings the underbrush had been cleared away to form clearings cast in dappled light. An old guy with a worn T-shirt and headphones was chopping wood. He nodded to us as Nīkau led us to the kitchen, a building set half into the ground and open to the air at one end.

Savoury smells curled between the tables and benches. A woman with spiky red hair was stirring a huge pot at the far end, but her attention was more on a battered paper book. Something in Chinese that looked like a spy novel – maybe she'd found it in an abandoned house?

She looked up as we entered. "Mira! How's the big city? Haven't seen you in a while. Nice shoes. Who's this?"

"Kieran, Ruby. Ruby, my boyfriend Kieran." She pulled a huge block of dark chocolate out of her bag. "Here, thought you might like this."

"Amazing! You're the best, Mira."

Mira pulled me down on a bench while Nīkau talked to Ruby. I seemed to be getting pushed and pulled everywhere, probably because of shock. How did you act around people you'd always imagined as cavemen, when it was becoming more and more obvious that they weren't?

"Nīkau and Ruby left the city when they were twenty-two," Mira said. "They're too close a Match, like us."

I looked at them with new eyes. Yeah, I could see how they were together, now, the way Nīkau stood closer to her than you would to a friend, the squeeze Ruby gave his arm before grabbing some bowls and ladling something from the humongous pot.

"So they came out here?"

Mira nodded. The thought hung between us, and I felt my heart grasp at it, but... leaving my whole life behind? Leaving Lucas? Assuming Lucas was still...

Maybe once Lucas was better. It was an option, right? One year until I finished school and had to decide what to do with the rest of my life. I could be a Person Voluntarily Abstaining From Society, run away with Mira, be free of all the city's rules. We wouldn't need a loophole. I'd only been with Mira for a week, but already it felt right, true, like it would all be worth it if we could be together...

Ruby dropped something in front of me and I jumped. She nodded approvingly.

"Gazing at his lady-love like there's nothing else in the world. Yep, keep this one, Mira."

Heat rushed up my neck, but Ruby had already moved on.

"This still needs to simmer, but you must be starved after climbing that hill, so..."

Steam curled from the bowl, spicy, with hints of kūmara, pumpkin, and herbs I couldn't name. Verity would probably know what they were.

Nīkau swung his leg over the bench and sat beside me with his own bowl. "I'm sure it'll be edible, Rube. Elspeth will be in soon, she's just finishing up with the generator."

I took a tentative spoonful. It was probably the best stew I'd ever tasted.

Ruby told us how she'd met Nīkau, fallen in love, left the city. Nīkau added a word here and there. Ruby wanted to know our story, too, and listened closely, nodding and making me feel like she actually cared, giving advice, telling funny stories about times she and Nīkau had almost been caught. Even our escape over Xiao's balcony seemed sort of funny, looking back on it.

People began to trickle in, and Ruby literally put her chef hat on and left to serve lunch. Nīkau took on the task of introductions. Some people seemed genuinely interested in me, but after ten minutes I was saying the same things over and over again. *How did Mira and I meet? Did I like it in the city? What did I want to do when I left school? Did I have any siblings?*

It was coming up sixty years since Consolidation, and I guessed that would have been when a lot of peev villages started. Imagine, losing almost everyone you knew to Plagues, then refusing to join the cities to consolidate resources. Those people had to have been either very determined or very stupid.

The blur of new faces was broken by a woman with blue hair, who plunked a full bowl between me and Nīkau and shook my hand with both of her grease-stained ones.

"Sorry about the dirt," she said, picking at a black line at the edge of her nail and making no difference at all. "I think it's sunk into my pores. I've been repairing the generator all morning. Elspeth," she added as an after-thought. "Nīkau said you were looking for me?"

"Yeah, Kieran's got a gadget thing." Mira waved at me. I stuck a spoonful of stew in my mouth and fished out the holosphere. "It's supposed to show pictures, but it's broken."

Elspeth made appreciative noises and took it, turning it round. "Haven't seen one of these since I was a kid. I'll take a look after lunch, might have some parts... or could print some." She placed it in the middle of the table. "How's Enzo doing?"

"Okay. He's optimistic. They're treating him fine."

"Good," Elspeth said, but there was a quaver in her voice. "I told him too many stories about growing up there. Made it sound like the paradise it's supposed to be."

Nīkau put his hand on her shoulder and squeezed. "You're not the only one who told him stories."

"So they'll let him stay in Wellington?" I asked. Maybe I'd see him at school next year. It was a strange thought. In less than an hour, peevs had gone from cavemen to a guy who might sit through one of Mr Yates's endless assemblies.

Elspeth nodded. "It's his choice. He's a minor."

"Still young enough to mould into a *model citizen.*" The words were spoken with such acid that I coughed out a breath.

"Mikale, we have guests," Elspeth sighed, and the man who'd spoken shrugged and swivelled back to his stew.

A massive guy ducked through the doorway, dark ponytail streaked with grey. Mira half-rose in her seat, saw him get caught in a conversation, and sat down again. "That's Jake," she said. "He's one of the leaders. Him and Adelaide."

Jake had the heavy look of a man who'd been young and fit not long ago, his shoulders broad beneath his leather jacket. He was one of those people with a presence, something you can't quite put your finger on, but where you know you'll shut up as soon as they open their mouth. He filled a bowl with stew and came to sit beside Mira, the bench creaking. This close, you could see the hollows beneath his eyes. He was followed by a pixie-like, light-skinned woman who looked like she'd walked straight out of an American movie from a century ago; dark hair, perfect cheekbones and a pursed mouth.

The woman put her hand out for me to shake. Her eyes were soul-piercing, her grip like iron. "Adelaide. Welcome."

"Kieran."

"What's happening with Raymi?" Mira asked.

"Oh, no hello?" Jake said, taking a spoonful of stew and chewing.

"Hello. Nīkau says you're not doing a rescue."

"That's correct."

"But–"

"It's too big a risk. If Raymi's people want to get her out, that's up to them. They've got a lot more experience in that type of thing, anyway."

"Are they doing anything?"

Jake shrugged. “They haven’t been in contact.”

“But you told them where she is, right?”

“We did. They thanked us for the information.”

Mira grimaced. “I could help them. How do I get hold of them?”

Adelaide shook her head. “You’ve already done a lot, Mira. So much. You should keep your head down, not draw attention. If people found out what you were doing–”

“But–”

“You could put us in danger, too,” Jake said. “The city doesn’t bother us because we don’t bother them. But if we’re brainwashing impressionable young minds...”

“I am not an impressionable young mind,” Mira said sourly.

“It’s how they’ll see it,” Elspeth said, scraping the last of her stew from her bowl. “Come on, Kieran, want a tour? Then I’ll see what we can do for your holosphere.”

Elspeth showed me the main hall, the produce garden, the chickens and weka (carefully separated, because the weka bully the chickens), the stream with its swimming hole, the waste processing system. She was a good tour guide, and when I showed interest in the generator she really lit up, hands weaving patterns in the air as she explained how it could run on sunlight, wind or muscle-power. I recognised the muscle power component: they had one of my dad’s pedal-to-power converters, which turned a bicycle into a power source. I wondered if they’d stolen it, and didn’t mention my dad made them.

Mira got dragged off to play hide-and-seek with some six-year-olds, and Elspeth ended at her house, a smallish woven hut that reminded me of Doncaster’s office – one half of the room was covered in pieces of machinery and electronics, while the other had a chair and a sofa and a coffee table, and a shimmery curtain sectioning off what must be her bedroom. The floor was wooden, polished smooth with use.

"Where's your holosphere?"

I handed it over. She figured out the trick to open it a lot quicker than I had – twist carefully the wrong way, and the two halves unscrewed. Inside was a mess of circuitry, a set of miniature holo-projectors, and a memory card. The metal casing was transparent from the inside, allowing the holo-projectors to shine out.

"Not too much work. How are you at this stuff?"

I shrugged. "I'm all right. My dad taught me how to solder."

She peered closer at the mess and nodded. "I reckon you can fix it yourself. See here, just need to reattach this, and swap out that gyro for a new one, it's all corroded. I'll draw you a diagram. I think the projectors should still work? If not, you should be able to get standard replacements in the city. Not sure about the gyro, though. It's an old design..." She tapped a finger against her chin and went to the tech wall. "Somewhere..." she muttered, pulling out drawers and peering at shelves. "I keep thinking I'll get some sort of system going, but I never do. Ah, got it!"

She held up a tiny chip that must have been a gyro and handed it to me.

"Thanks, Elspeth."

"No problem. Come back out if you have any trouble."

"Off! I said off!" Mira was struggling at the door, two kids hanging off one arm and one kid off the other. The kids ignored her. "I'll tell the taniwha to get you!"

"She's not kidding," Elspeth said. "She's friends with the one in the Korokoro Stream."

The kids shrieked and vanished.

"Did you find Tomas?" Elspeth asked Mira as I put the holosphere back together, extra gyro inside.

Mira nodded. "I gave him Enzo's letter. He didn't say much."

"Yeah." Elspeth shook her head. "He's not been well since Enzo left. Now it's just him, no Pania, no one."

"He has you guys," Mira said, but she looked uncertain. "And Enzo will come visit, once everything's settled down."

"It'll be dangerous for him," Elspeth said. "More dangerous than for you. They'll be watching him. But hey." She squeezed Mira's shoulder. "It's not something you can help. What else have you been up to this week?"

Mira swallowed and shot me a smile. "Well, Kieran took me out on the Seatoun Dam on Wednesday–"

"You got onto the harbour dam?" Elspeth said, turning to stare at me. "I thought that was all closed off to the public."

I grinned and waved my chipped wrist. "Not if you have connections. My dad knows the head engineer."

"The view's amazing," Mira said. "And just standing up there, right on the edge of the sea as it crashes below you, pretty incredible."

"Glad you liked it," I said, bumping her with my shoulder. She bumped me back and smiled, clearer this time.

Elspeth grinned at us. "You two are so cute."

"Shut up," I said.

16

Perfection

"So HOW DID YOU run into them?" I asked Mira, once we were back on the cracked road to the city.

Mira bit her lip and stared at the asphalt. "It was after my sister died." I almost didn't hear her over the air whistling past my ears. "I wasn't doing very well. I stopped going to school because everyone stared at me, and I felt sick every time I went to class." She glanced across at me. "We were in a lot of the same classes, see? And being there without her..."

I nodded. It was probably like my fear of leaving the city. Which was actually okay, at the moment. I'd managed to get through the whole day outside the Consolidation Line.

"My parents weren't doing great either. Mum couldn't look at me the same, and Dad spent so much time at work I hardly saw him. Then in February he transferred up to Mākara, so we came with him."

"Change of scene."

"Yeah."

"Did it help?"

"Sorta. I started correspondence school, and no one knew about Melanie, so I could forget it sometimes." She swallowed. "And then of course I'd feel all guilty, you know?"

"Yep." Too well.

"Dad still worked insane hours, but we were all on compound so at least we had dinner together. Mum was kind of... absent? Still is, a lot of the time. Like, she's there, but she doesn't really listen or–" She gave a hollow laugh. "Melanie's gone, but I'm– I'm still here. She's still got one daughter. But it's like she doesn't– she *can't* really care."

"I'm sure she does–"

Mira swerved her bike towards mine. "You've never met her. You're just saying that because that's what parents are supposed to do."

I guess I was. I mean, look at Lucas's parents. "I'm sorry."

"Anyway, I'd go bush whenever I could. Never got grounded." She flashed a smile my way. "I think I partly hoped my parents *would* ground me, show they cared enough. But green is good for the soul, too. I guess I felt... alive again, when I was out there."

"I should thank the bush, then." I took a deep breath and yelled, "Thanks, bush!"

The bush didn't answer. Mira laughed, and it was real this time like I'd hoped. "Dork."

I shrugged. "Needed to be done. So lots of time in the bush... I guess that means you came across the peevs."

"Outsiders. They don't like 'peevs'. But yeah, I ran into Adelaide. She actually pulled a gun on me."

"She *what?*"

Mira grinned. "Pulled a gun. I had to stick my hands up in the air and everything."

On second thought, Adelaide did seem that kind of person. Something about her eyes and bone-crushing handshake.

"How did you get out of that one?"

"Talked fast. Looked young and non-dangerous. Luckily their group isn't the murdery type, though they warned me against going further north."

The wind didn't reach into this valley, and the sun flashed through the trees with bursts of heat. The sunscreen I'd put on this morning would have worn off by now.

"Right. Don't go further north, just in case." I said, imagining peevs more along the lines of what we saw on the newscasts. Maybe they'd been the ones behind the Nix Gen-ens bombings. "They're... different from what I expected. They brush their hair and everything."

"Yeah, unlike some people." Mira swerved her bike towards mine and I almost ran into a tī kōuka tree trying to avoid her. I braked, lost my balance and fell into the grass.

"That wasn't fair!" But it was hard to be angry when she was laughing so hard, even if it was me she was laughing at. She squealed as I dragged her down.

"Look, I'll do your hair for you," she said, still laughing. She combed her fingers through my hair, then messed it up. "Stylish."

"Just because you spend an hour in front of the mirror every morning."

"I do not!"

"Mirror Mira! Mira, Mira on the wall, who's the fairest one of all?"

She slapped me on the hand.

I kissed her.

All my previous girlfriends (well, all three) had steadily become less interesting the longer I went out with them. In the back of my mind I'd always guessed the same thing would happen with Mira, and then our illegal relationship wouldn't be a problem because it was over. But that really wasn't happening. I didn't want it to happen.

"Have you thought about becoming a p– an Outsider?" I asked a little later.

She was leaning over me, the sun glowing through her hair. "I have. Nearly went through with it, too. I was pretty angry about Melanie. The government makes out like everything's perfect, if we follow the rules and do what we're told nothing bad will happen. The Paradise Generation and all that. But... the government can't control everything. They just make you think they can. I mean, they obviously made a mistake with my parents' Match."

"Yeah, they're still revising the guidelines," I said, thinking of the stuff I was doing for Doncaster. They might even have changed because of Melanie's death. "Wait. If they hadn't made a mistake, your parents wouldn't have got together. You wouldn't have been born."

She rolled back onto the grass. "True."

"Well, that's a pretty sucky world, if you're not in it."

A snort. "Thanks. I've thought about it, you know. Like, is my life only worth living if I'm perfect and healthy? That's what Matching is about, isn't it? Making a perfect healthy population so we don't have annoying sick people taking up valuable hospital beds and doctors' time."

No one had ever put it quite like that, but... "I guess you're right." I felt uncomfortable. Gen-ens had been all about Perfection – it was one of the reasons for nixing them. And what I'd seen on

Andrew's file yesterday... there had to be a good reason for it, right? It couldn't just be that he wore contacts and needed to watch his weight and had a higher risk of heart disease. "Is it really about being perfect? I mean, there's perfect... and there's healthy..."

"Who decides what's healthy? We can't genetically engineer our way to a perfect healthy population, because exhibit A, your crazed Gen-en, and we can't stop people having kids or kill them off, because we're not neo-Nazis."

She was wrong – the GA *did* stop people having kids. But what was the point in telling her that? We couldn't change it. She might tell Andrew, and I didn't want to get him hurt.

"But we *can* try and stop people like me ever being born by Matching people," she continued. "Simple, right?"

I coughed. "I guess this is why you weren't that worried about our Match."

"Yeah. Once I'd checked we weren't second cousins or anything."

It hurt my brain. Of course you didn't want people to die young. That was awful, like Lucas– not that Lucas was going to– But stopping people dying young was a good thing, right?

Until it meant Mira wouldn't exist.

"So you think Matching should stop?"

She sighed. "I dunno. Maybe people should just have the choice, you know? Go see what their Match is if they're worried. Decide if a risk is worth it."

"And what if their kids have terrible lives?"

"No one's going to tell me my life is terrible," she said fiercely. "That's something I decide for myself, not some Matching rules committee. Melanie's life wasn't terrible, until the last year or so.

And even then…" Her voice cracked. "She was kind of amazing. She said at least she'd had fifteen good years to experience the world and be my sister. Better than nothing."

She was staring up at the sky through the trees, eyes glittery. I leaned over and kissed her on the forehead. Brushed her hair out of her face. She closed her eyes and leaned her face against my palm.

"Why didn't you stay out here, then, away from the city rules?"

The corner of her mouth lifted. "I asked Adelaide if I could join Horokiwi, but she said I should wait until I was older to decide. Think about how I could do good from inside the cities, change things." She opened her eyes and kissed me quick. "And I'm kind of glad I didn't, now, because I never would have met you."

"Awww." I smiled back. "That's me, your knight in shining armour, making your life less terrible, one day at a time."

She punched me on the arm.

"Ow. Okay, you make my life less terrible too. Thanks for not joining the Outsiders just yet."

"You're welcome."

17
D-Day

I WAS BACK HOME with five minutes to spare, and my parents obviously hadn't tried to check my location because they weren't waiting with handcuffs. At dinner I reported back on my ride out to Awakairangi Hutt with my new friend "Mitchell", then spent the next few hours in my room, reading all I could on peevs. No, not peevs, *Outsiders* (though that search term didn't show anything useful). There wasn't much, and most of it was from the cities' point of view, worrying about PVAFS incursions or listing terrorist attacks. The Nix Gen-ens bombings were there, dated when I was in hospital after the accident. By the time I'd recovered, it was old news, and I didn't know much about them.

I clicked on the link and scrolled through the images – fast – and skimmed the story. A PVAFS group had hacked an old database of suspected Gen-ens, and instead of bringing it to the authorities' attention, they'd planted five bombs in Gen-en houses and workplaces, shot three more in the street, and released a manifesto with the names of ten others they couldn't kill directly. The three shooters were arrested after a chase, and they found two more accomplices in a raid the week after. All five PVAFS got re-education and relocation, which meant they probably ended up in some workcamp halfway round the world. The ten Gen-ens were arrested and detained indefinitely. That "indefinitely" had ended a month ago, after the Gen-en failed to escape the hospital.

Her face flashed through my mind again. What had her life been like, before the Outsiders exposed her? Did the shop assistants see that crazy glint in her eyes when she got groceries? Had she killed anyone, like that serial killer Gen-en they caught in Cascadia twenty years ago?

Elspeth and Nīkau hadn't mentioned anyone at Horokiwi getting arrested, but I hadn't asked. It didn't seem like it was the same group, though. If it even *was* an Outsider group, and there wasn't some conspiracy. I understood Mira's annoyance at the terrorist alert, now – she knew Outsiders, and knew they were good people. At least, the Horokiwi group was.

My eyes blurred from skimming a screen too long. I put my tablet away and went to get a glass of water.

Mum and Dad were putting the dishes away, speaking low beneath the slide of china and clink of forks. I was halfway down the stairs when I heard Lucas's name, and the tightness in Mum's voice. They were talking about me.

I sat carefully, hoping this was not one of the squeaky steps, and closed my eyes so I could focus on what I was hearing. Their words swam up to me through the silent house, and I hardly dared breathe.

"–he used to be so, I don't know, sharp," Mum was saying, but she wasn't talking about Lucas. "Actually curious about the world. Top in his class. Now it seems like Lucas is the only thing he cares about..."

There were another few clinks into the cutlery drawer and then Dad spoke.

"He still thinks it was his fault."

"He was twelve! Lucas shouldn't have dragged him into his stupid schemes. It's on Lucas, not him."

"I'm sure that doesn't change how it feels."

"I want–" Her voice caught. "I want him to be the way he used to be. This wasn't how I imagined him at sixteen. Sneaking out – maybe – but sneaking out to see his friends, a nice girlfriend, not his delinquent cousin in the hospital!"

"You didn't think Lucas was delinquent when he stayed with us."

"That was before he crashed a car with our son in it."

Lucas hadn't crashed the car, I wanted to say. *I'd* crashed the car.

There was a long pause, and I checked my escape route. But then Dad began again.

"It will work out, Leah. Just like it did when he started school and you were worried he wasn't making friends, or when he didn't get on with his teacher in year four. And when you were pregnant, we thought he–"

"Please don't remind me of that."

Thought he *what*?

"I'm just saying. He's healthy. He's a good kid, mostly. Maybe the med review will help him move on."

My fists clenched. They were treating it like it was a done deal, like nothing could be changed. And I'd thought Dad was on my side, that he understood what I was trying to do.

It was hard to breathe. There was still a chance, wasn't there? But less of a chance if everyone just gave up on him.

I wasn't going to give up on him. I refused.

"And I think the GA will be good. Give him some direction."

"Yes, but it isn't *his* direction, is it? He's only doing it because I pushed him into it. There's no spark there." She clicked her tongue and a cupboard door opened and closed. "He changed so much after the accident. He has no drive. Just... just Lucas."

I opened my eyes and stared at the wallpaper. What would she think if she knew about Mira? Was that enough drive?

"Give it time. See how he is, after Lucas has passed on..."

The world tilted. Dad had said the words. He'd actually said them. I squeezed my eyes shut and wished I could do the same with my ears.

"What if it makes it worse?"

I eased myself up against the wall, ready to move away.

"We'll be there for him. He just needs closure."

"He needs to find something else to live for. And I don't know how to help him find it."

A kiss. I imagined Dad kissing the top of Mum's head, like he often did. "Maybe he'll find it himself. He's got his internship, his friends. Just one week until the med review, ten days until court, and we'll help him get through it."

One week. One week to prove Lucas was getting better.

Even though he wasn't.

——— · ———

I met Mira again Wednesday evening, in the bush between our houses. Night creatures hummed about us – rustles and the cry of a ruru quite close that made us jump. We'd barely kissed hello when she said she was helping with Raymi's escape.

"What?" I yelped.

"It's not looking good for her. She'll be charged and shipped off any day now. Do you want to help?"

All my muscles tensed. My heart beat painfully. "I– I don't know if I have time," I said in a rush, and could feel her disappointment in the silence. "I mean... with Lucas and all, and the GA, and..." I trailed off. Okay, I was a coward. And maybe I shouldn't have made myself such a hero when I told my Gen-en story. Now she thought I was all gung-ho. "And you have a reason for being there, don't you? You're a law intern. I'd just get in the way."

She shrugged and looked away. Starlight caught in her hair. "It's okay. It's your choice."

I remembered what Mikale had said, about model citizens. I wanted to say yes, yes, I'd help, but my mouth wouldn't obey.

"Um... when is it happening?"

"Friday evening, after work. When everyone's at the pub, pretty much."

"Ah." I couldn't go anyway. I had no idea what I'd be doing Friday evening. I couldn't think that far ahead. "Lucas's med review is Friday."

"Oh. Hope it goes well."

"Hope the escape goes well too." I swallowed. "Please, *please*, be careful. Is it with Raymi's people?"

"Yeah." She cut her eyes at me, her shoulders tense. "It's what I want to do, and they need me, so I should, right?"

There was almost a plea in her voice, and I wondered if she was trying to convince herself as well as me.

"I–" If I said no, maybe Raymi wouldn't get out. Maybe she'd be sentenced to life in a workcamp for terrorism. "If you want to do it, do it. Just be careful. I can't lose you."

—— . ——

I spent all Thursday evening at the hospital, and Mum didn't even comment when I got home at half past nine. She watched me sideways over her muesli on Friday morning, and Dad presented me with a packed lunch. Apparently they weren't going to bring it up.

"Can I go see Lucas today?" I asked as Mum took away the breakfast dishes.

"Kieran, we agreed–" she began sharply, but broke off. "I know what day it is. And I don't think it's good for you. Anyway, don't you have work?"

I did. Jimmy the nurse said the med review was booked for four p.m., so maybe I could leave work early. Mum and Dad didn't have to know. They'd probably find out, though...

But what did that matter? If they grounded me for months, I'd still know I'd done what I could. And maybe, just maybe, I could convince the doctors...

Doncaster didn't seem to care when I asked to leave early. "Sure, sure. Just finish off those searches."

I could get to the hospital in twenty minutes, so I planned to leave at half past three. And then at two-forty-five I got a message from Jimmy.

They're running ahead of time. Three p.m. now.

My stomach swooped and the fear hit me in a wave from my scalp to my toes. Everything seemed super-sharp, hyper-dimensional.

I'd thought I could deal, thought I could be all calm and grown-up, but it hadn't really hit me until now. They were reviewing him. Giving medical opinions. In fifteen minutes.

I coughed and glanced at Doncaster, engrossed in some urgent paper. The air pressure had dropped, the ground had shifted. He must notice I was at the edge of a chasm. But no, of course not. This was Doncaster we were talking about.

I made my hand move, dragged the search findings to the right folder so the task was at least semi-finished, and told Doncaster I was going. He grunted, and didn't look up.

At the bike rack I had to lean against the wall and suck in deep breaths, trying to convince my body it was calm and stop my legs shaking. How was it that my mind could be completely rational, could tell me that I needed to get on that bike and ride, and still my body felt these waves of terror?

The deep breathing wasn't working. My hands shook. Another deep breath, a swallow against my dry throat. I forced my mouth into a smile, felt it stretch my cheeks until it was almost real, telling my body that yes, everything was fine. I clamped down on my fear, let my breath out slow, and settled my shoulders. My mind was skipping back to the speed and the thump and the crunch of glass, to Lucas's bloody face in the car, but I pushed it all away. I got on my bike and started pedalling.

I'd already tried everything I could think of to bring Lucas back. Maybe he'd had a miraculous recovery overnight; but Lucas had had four whole years to get better, and he hadn't. The doctors would decide he wasn't ever going to get better.

Words kept repeating in my head. He's going to die. They're going to kill him. He's dead already.

No, he wasn't dead already. He was still there, at least in body, and I could see him.

I was going to see him.

I slammed my bike into the hospital bike rack and half-tripped on the way past reception. It wasn't Lauren at the desk, thank god. The doors opened at my chip-swipe (visiting hours) and I leapt up the stairs. In seconds I was outside his closed door.

I peeked through the window. Three people in white coats and two in nurse's scrubs, all gathered around Lucas's bed, their voices drifting under the door. He was sitting up, but I couldn't see his face. Should I go in?

One of the doctors turned towards me, and I ducked back, leaning against the light blue wall and trying not to look like I was eavesdropping. The Gen-en had slid down the wall two doors away. They'd cleared away the blood, but I still felt I could see it.

"...pupil responds to light, patient blinks, but no other behavioural response," came a woman's voice. It sounded like Dr Wu.

Styluses tapping. There was a soft snick, and Lucas grunted.

"Withdrawal from pain. No move to self-care, though. Lack of high level cognitive processing."

"Has he ever recognised friends or family?" A man's voice this time. Maybe Dr Brown?

"No. He doesn't follow them with his eyes, or act differently when they're around."

Lucas didn't act differently when I was around?

"He feeds himself." That was definitely Lauren. I wondered if she'd report what I'd been doing with Andrew.

"Automatic processes, learned motor skills."

"Yes."

There was a pause.

"There's no one home, though."

Another pause.

"No." Lauren.

A white heat rose in me. They had to do more, look closer, look harder, until they found Lucas. MRIs, trial drugs, blood transfusions, brain transfer to robot... My hand was on the door handle, turning.

"You can't," I was saying, "you can't. You can't just leave him there for four years and then kill him. You haven't done enough. There's still time, and how is he hurting anyone just lying there?" They all turned to stare, except for Lucas.

"We have limited resources," Dr Brown said, his eyes soft. Like when you look at a two-year-old with a scraped knee. "You know this, Kieran. Everyone gets four years. If a patient can't contribute to society or to the lives of their friends and families at the end of that time, the most humane thing to do for everyone is to let them go."

"To kill them," I spat. "To kill them when you never tried hard enough to *fix* them."

"We tried–"

"You didn't, you *didn't*," I choked out. "You DIDN'T try." Now I was shouting. "He's not better, so how could you have tried? We're the *Paradise Generation*. It's not fucking supposed to happen this way!"

I scrubbed at my eyes and pushed Dr Wu and Lauren out of the way, and then I was at Lucas's bedside, clutching at his arms.

"Wake up, Luc, wake up, wake up, wake *up*." I dimly felt people trying to pull me away, but now I was shaking him, and his head was rocking forward and back and he wasn't waking up. "Lucas!

Come on, Lucas, wake up! Please, Lucas, please, please don't do this to me, come back, Lucas–"

"Get him off! Get him out of here!" someone was yelling, and "Get the guard!" and "Sedative!". I kept shaking Lucas and shaking the clutching hands off.

"Please, Lucas, please–"

Hands peeling away my fingers one by one, arms around my chest, pulling me back. I struggled, getting a punch in someone's eye and another in a gut, but they still had me and they were still dragging me away from Lucas. Lucas, who was sitting there, eyes still staring at nothing, as Lauren checked him over.

The fight drained out of me. Numbness spread like a warm blanket over my soul, and my thoughts floated apart. Sedative. Someone must have stuck me with something. And it didn't matter, not really, because now I was floating, the sprinkled holes of the ceiling slowly turning above me.

18

Decision

"Kieran?" It was Lauren. Wasn't she checking Lucas? Maybe she'd finished. Time was moving strangely.

"Yes?"

"How do you feel?"

"Warm," I mumbled.

"That's good. We've called your mother, she'll be here to take you home soon."

This seemed worrying, but the feeling was so deep down and I was so warm and floaty that I let the thought drift away.

—— · ——

"Kieran." Another voice, more commanding. The scary doctor, the one who swept the halls once a month with doctors and nurses darting behind. "We think it best if you stay away from the hospital for now. Just until things are more settled." He laid his hand on my arm. "If you do try to enter, you'll be stopped at reception. The inner doors have been coded against your chip. We'll review in a few weeks."

"Lucas," I muttered, his meaning pushing through. "I need to see him before..."

"You'll be able to see him," the scary doctor said. "Just not right now. Not when you're under such pressure."

—— · ——

Mum was there, lips pressed white.

"We had to sedate him," one of the nurses was saying. "Apologies for that, but he was going to hurt himself and his cousin."

"I understand, I do." Mum clamped a hand on my shoulder. "I'll take him home and put him to bed."

"It'll wear off in a few hours. He can still walk, he just needs a bit of supervision."

Mum had my backpack over her shoulder. It looked strange on top of her business suit. She got me standing and switched her death-grip to my forearm, then escorted me out the door, down the stairs, past reception and into the bright light of the evening. I squinted and shaded my eyes.

"Don't you ever do that again," Mum muttered as we crossed to the bus stop.

"My bike..." I tried to twist out of her grip, but she held fast.

"Verity can get it tomorrow. You're staying in this weekend."

"But my bike..."

She stopped abruptly and swung me into something between a hug and suffocation. "Kieran, don't worry about your bike. Lucas isn't your responsibility. You shouldn't be here."

"I–" She was acting very strangely, and I couldn't quite grasp why. "I don't–"

"You've got to accept it," she said, her breath against my hair. "Lucas has not been Lucas for a very long time. He's not coming back."

I tried to get out of her arms but she wouldn't let me and I didn't have the strength. Instead I slumped against her, and she rubbed circles into my back like she used to when I had a bad dream.

Maybe I'd wake up soon.

—— · ——

The weekend passed. I wasn't allowed visitors. I couldn't leave the house. But Mum kept bringing me food, and asking me about my internship and anything else she could think of that wasn't Lucas-related. The numbness had worn off, though I still felt weird. Out of it. Dad sat me in front of a soccer game with Verity, but I couldn't follow it. I tried chatting with Mira through our aliases, but my fingers kept getting dyslexic and mashing buttons until the tablet asked if I needed accessibility options enabled. Raymi's escape had gone perfectly to plan and it wasn't in the news, so at least something had gone right on Friday.

I talked to Margaret on Monday evening. It didn't help.

—— · ——

Wednesday was sunny. The weather didn't care that Lucas's fate was being sealed. Mum didn't say anything when I asked Dad to come to court with me, not even that I shouldn't skip work. I'd been the one to put him in the hospital. I would be there with him right until the end.

I hadn't seen Aunty Pascale since Christmas. She'd always been thin, but now she looked like she'd been living on crackers and water for the last six months. Her makeup couldn't disguise the dark hollows of her eyes or her sharp cheekbones. Uncle Jeremy had his arm permanently attached to her shoulders, but I wasn't sure if it was to comfort her or hold himself up.

They had a special room at the High Court for medical decisions. It had recycled rimu panelling, like the valuable wood would make up for the terrible decisions they made. The seats were blue-dyed leather and didn't have enough stuffing.

Lucas's older sister Fiarenza had come home from Cascadia for the hearing, braving the long flight and two weeks of managed isolation. She hovered near her mum's arm looking out of place. The rest of the court room was scattered with lawyers and doctors and people who didn't know anything about Lucas and didn't care. And the judge, of course.

"All stand."

It takes a long time to decide whether to kill someone. The doctors gave their opinions. The lawyers argued about the exact definition of the words "physically and mentally fit", and whether Lucas would ever be described in those words. The judge nodded and took notes in what I imagined was very precise handwriting, brow furrowed.

It didn't seem real. How could it be real? I wondered what twelve-year-old me would think if he was suddenly put in this court room, listening to strangers debate the pros and cons of his favourite cousin's death. Listening and knowing it was his own fault.

I looked away from the people in their smart suits, up towards the small gallery. No one should have been up there.

But someone was.

I straightened. Oval face, dark hair. I couldn't see the colour of her eyes from here, but I knew they were blue.

Mira met my gaze and gave a small, sad smile. "Kia kaha," she mouthed. Stay strong.

It was hard. Fiarenza was sitting beside me, breath ragged. Aunty Pascale stared straight ahead, unseeing, and Uncle Jeremy held Fiarenza's hand, his eyes watery. I leaned into Dad, not caring that Mira would see.

Three hours, and it was done. I didn't understand why it had taken so long – why not just say "euthanise" in the first ten minutes and be done with it? But no, you had to be sure you were doing the right thing, that this was best for society and for the individual, for the family and friends, be sure that the patient would never again be a "valuable" member of society. You had to convince yourself you were doing good.

The thirty-first of December. That was the date they'd set. And then no more Lucas.

—— · ——

I spent the rest of the day staring at the ceiling of my room. Faint red marks dotted it from my cricket ball days, and a spider was constructing a web in one corner. Around eight there was a knock on my door. I must have made some sort of acknowledgement, because it opened a crack and Verity's head came through.

"You didn't come down for dinner."

I didn't think that needed an answer. Verity pushed her way further into my room, holding a tray.

"I brought you some. Thai chicken curry. I made it myself."

She put it on the bed and the smell drifted towards me. I didn't trust myself to speak, but nodded at her. She stood shifting her weight and taking breaths as if she'd say something, but in the end didn't say anything.

"Verity."

She paused in the doorway and looked back. I took a deep breath.

"Thanks."

"You're welcome."

Dad had unlocked my window latch so I took my dinner onto the roof, sitting precariously on the corrugated iron. The metal was still warm from the sun, but the wind took the heat and left me shivering. I didn't care. What was shivering compared to what Lucas had gone through? To what he would go through just two weeks from now?

The Thai chicken was good and just spicy enough to sear my throat. I scraped the plate clean and shoved the tray back through my window. The sky was full dark now, and the stars were out by the thousand, sparkling in the crisp night. I stared out over the harbour, wondering how many other people were responsible for someone's death.

A stone skittered on the roof. Then another, and a whispered "Kieran!".

I edged forward. A figure stood in the garden below, near a narrow path that ran into the bush. A path that, I realised, also ran near Mira's house. "Mira?"

"Yeah. Is there a way up?"

I pointed at the plum tree that hangs a branch over a corner of the roof, and she headed towards it. After some cussing, she was dropping onto the roof and making her careful way towards me, crouching with one hand trailing and the other stretched out.

"You shouldn't be here."

She shrugged and eased down beside me. "It doesn't matter. What does anything matter at the moment?"

We sat like that, side by side, staring over the trees and the street lights glowing and dimming as people moved through the city. The moon rose, silvering the world's edges.

Lucas would never see this.

I took a shuddering breath and held it, struggling to hold back tears. Mira put her arm around me and pulled me to her, stroking my hair. I leaned in, trying not to think, focusing just on the warmth between us, but then she took a breath as if to say something. I pulled away.

"Don't say it's all right," I choked out. "It's not all right."

"It's not all right. It's horrible."

"It's my fault," I said. "He's going to die because of me."

Mira shook her head and pulled me in once more. "There are so many ifs. You can blame anything – your parents for letting you go, Lucas for starting the car project, the roadworkers for not making the road safe enough, school for not warning you about the dangers of ancient cars, time. The sun for setting too early. Need to get Māui in there, right? Slow it down with giant ropes and patu."

I snorted through tears, imagining the mythical hero wandering through downtown Pōneke with a club made from his grandmother's jawbone. Laughing made it easier to cry, somehow, and I couldn't stop the next sob. Mira pulled me closer, her fingers teasing at my hair.

"The doctors for failing to cure him. The scientists for spending too much time on space travel and not enough on fixing brain damage." She swallowed, and I knew she was thinking of her sister. "His parents for giving up on him–"

"They didn't give up on him," I said. Mira was silent. "I mean, they didn't come so much these last years because it's far, and ... and it was just so hard to see him like that, not getting better. Ever."

"You still went," Mira said quietly. "Even though it was hard."

"I *had* to," I choked. "Don't you see? It's *my fault*. I had to try–"

Mira pushed me away and held my shoulders, making me look at her. Her face looked ghostly in the moonlight, blurry through my tears.

"It was not your fault. You can't go around throwing blame anywhere else, either. It happened through a long line of actions and luck, and you did all you could to fix it."

"But I didn't." I could have done more. What, I didn't know, but I could have done *something*.

"You did, okay? Would Lucas want you to beat yourself up? Grieve him, learn from it, know he'll always be watching over you. Do something amazing with your life, celebrate it like Lucas wasn't able to." Her eyes bored into mine, and I realised she was crying too, soundlessly, the tears leaving trails down her face. "You owe it to him more than you owe him your guilt."

I didn't think my voice would work properly. I just put my arms around her and we stayed like that, sharing our heat beneath the stars.

19
Tasers

The world continued, as I guess it does. I went to the GA on Thursday and Friday. Andrew came over on Saturday and we played games all day. I did not mention genome categories. He did not mention Lucas, except for saying he was sorry and hugging me when I answered the door.

"Just keep going," Dad said on Sunday afternoon when I wouldn't get out of bed. "It helps."

So I tried. I caught up with Xiao, asked how his VR internship was going. I had another session with Margaret. I met Mira on Monday, and after work Tuesday too, when we got so caught up in talking (and other things) that I didn't get home until almost eleven, just on the edge of curfew. Dad was sitting in front of the muted newscast, asleep.

Something caught my eye. A familiar face. It was Elspeth from Horokiwi, but she looked way different from when I'd met her. Her hair was dirty, matted, and her skin sickly pale.

PVAFS dies in hospital after auto-taser malfunction ran the banner beneath her picture. *Suspected of terrorist plot.*

I choked back a laugh. Elspeth? Terrorism? And how could they suspect you of terrorism and talk about an auto-taser "malfunction"?

The full meaning of the words hit me. Elspeth was dead. It didn't matter what she'd been suspected of.

She was dead.

Same as Lucas would be, come New Year.

I sank to my knees. The presenters moved on to a story about revised chocolate allocations due to bad weather somewhere.

I'd seen Elspeth a few weeks ago. I'd promised to show her the holosphere, once I fixed it. How, in a few weeks, could she go from healthy and happy to dead?

Dad woke with a grunt at midnight, turned sleepily and jumped at the sight of me. "Kieran? What are you doing?"

"Just watching something." The screen was showing some old movie, and I had no idea what was happening even though I'd been staring at it for an hour. Dad levered himself up and gave me a long look.

"Are you all right?"

I couldn't tell him I'd been outside the Line and met peevs, and now one of them was a suspected terrorist, and she was dead, actually dead, they'd killed her...

My knees were numb. I rose jerkily to my feet. "Yeah. Just tired."

Dad coughed. "If you ever want to talk about ... about Lucas ... or about anything, really ... you know I'm here, right?"

"I know."

"And if it's too off-putting, me being your dad and all, there's Margaret–"

"It's fine, Dad. I'm fine." My eyes were still fixed on the screen and didn't want to move. Dad stood and collected me in his arms, patting my head to lay against his shoulder. I breathed in the smell of him – bike grease, fresh air, the hint of aftershave. It was my childhood. Back before people got hurt, before they died, before "terrorists" were people I knew.

Dad went to bed, but I couldn't sleep. I wanted to talk to Mira, but she might not have heard yet and I didn't want to be the one to wake her and tell her.

I fished the holosphere out of my drawer and fetched Dad's little touchpoint from the shed, stubbing my toe in the dark. I took the holosphere apart, unscrewing and screwing and welding until all the dead pieces were replaced. The holosphere didn't have any wireless connectivity, so I connected it to my tablet with a cord and three adapters, praying it would work.

It did. Thirty files showed up, though half of them were corrupted. Which wasn't surprising, considering how old the thing was. There were a few informational things: two globes of the world with different sea levels, some famous people I recognised and some I didn't, names above their heads. Maybe a set of history flash-cards? The rest of the pictures looked like holiday snaps, from the warped 2D previews – blue sky and cricket on a black sand beach, a group of kids chasing each other. None of the kids looked like Mum or Uncle Jeremy. A boy and girl about my age standing in the waves with their arms around each other, the boy holding the camera and grinning, the girl about to throw a handful of water at him. The same couple, smiling in a street packed with people, more people than I'd ever seen. Cities like that didn't exist any more.

It hit me that this sphere wasn't Mum's. She probably didn't even know what was on here. It belonged to someone who was long dead, someone who'd probably died in the Plagues. Dead, all these people.

Just like Elspeth. Just like Lucas in a little over a week.

—— · ——

I got about half an hour's sleep, and that half hour was filled with tasers and hospital beds, rising seas and Gen-ens whose clothes melted from terrorist to police officer to civilian and back again. Dad had to literally pull me out of bed, convince me work would make me feel better, and force muesli bars and orange juice down my throat. Mum had already left, so I couldn't ask about the holosphere.

I had a short message from Mira.

She was just going to see her family for Christmas.

Shit.

I'm so sorry, I messaged back. It felt like I was apologising for the whole city. Auto-tasers weren't supposed to kill people. Malfunction or not.

I got to work just on time, pulled a crease out of my T-shirt and tried to look awake as I passed the receptionist. I hadn't looked in the mirror this morning – I knew I'd see a shadow-eyed zombie looking back. My hair probably stuck up in a thousand directions.

Doncaster was often too engrossed in his work to hear a knock. I'd stood there for ten minutes once before someone walked past and told me to go right in. So today I didn't bother knocking and just pushed open the door.

Something was different. There was always an unusual smell in Doncaster's office, a cross between cleaning chemicals, coffee and some weird odour that might be frog. Today it had another tone to it ... sweet and sickly.

Doncaster sprawled in the chair facing the window, a bottle hanging loosely from his hand. I paused. Was he dead? Asleep? His face was turned away and I couldn't tell.

I set my bag carefully on the floor, took a deep breath, and tip-toed between the piles of books so I could see him properly, hopefully without him noticing me.

There was no chance of that.

His gaze was fixed somewhere beyond the window, glazed and blank. A bead of saliva quivered at the corner of his mouth. The remains of a night's drinking were scattered about – empty beer bottles, a small bottle of whiskey, a few crushed potato chips. The large bottle in his hand was vodka, about three centimetres left in the bottom.

I backed away, thinking I'd rather not be here, but I nudged a pile of books. It began to totter. I spun and tried to right the leaning tower, but just knocked against another pile. The books crashed into a heap of skewed spines.

Doncaster turned. His eyes didn't quite focus, and I almost took another step back before remembering the rest of the books.

"Boy?" He shook his bottle vaguely at me. "Closer."

I stayed where I was.

"Boy!"

"It's Kieran, Professor." I shuffled a couple of millimetres forward, which seemed to satisfy him. He grunted and turned back to the window. The wind was up, turning the waves into shifting white lace.

"You see all this?"

I nodded, but he wasn't watching me. He repeated the question.

"Yes," I said.

"Wouldn't have been possible. Had to be done." He took a swig from the bottle, and stared dubiously down the neck. "For the good of the planet, our survival. Happiness. Yes, boy, that's what it comes down to. Happiness. Paradise Generation."

"Uh, yeah." I wondered if he'd notice if I left. What were you supposed to do, stay and wrestle away the bottle? Leave quietly and never mention it again? Go and tell someone? Who?

"Years, I worked on it. Logical, really. Can't break eggs without making... uh... can't make an omelette without..."

I looked around for more bottles. I couldn't see any, but that didn't mean they weren't there. He probably had a liquor stash somewhere. I turned very carefully and began to edge through the teetering towers of ancient biology textbooks.

"It's not enough to cut back the population. You have to make sure everyone works together, understands each other. Erase the differences so people stop killing each other. Make us all one people, all the same."

"Yeah." I had no idea what he was talking about. I found the cupboard, underneath a lab bench and held ajar by an empty chip packet. There were two more bottles of vodka in there, and a large bottle of whisky. I took them out one at a time and placed them on the floor, careful not to make any clinking sounds.

"Matching makes sense on a whole range of levels, you know."

A gulping noise as he took another swig.

"Strengthens the gene pool. Helps people forget their roots, their differences. And it worked, didn't it? There's no racism. No one kills people over religion anymore... perfect solution, don't you see? Boy?"

If I kept him talking, maybe he wouldn't notice where I was. "Yeah, of course." What could I do with the bottles?

"Couldn't have been done any other way."

"No."

Doncaster's bottle thunked against his chair.

"It was the right thing to do. The right thing." He was mumbling now. I moved the alcohol into a cupboard full of bottles labelled POISON, because even drunk he probably wouldn't go near those.

"Boy?" He twisted his head and tried to get up, but ended up just falling back into the chair with a burp.

"Here."

He sighed and shifted. "And anyone who says otherwise... I did right."

"Of course." Now I just had to leave as quietly as I could, tell someone, maybe Mark the intern wrangler, and get out of here.

"But so many dead. Patrick. Amy. My poor Amy. My fault." He gave a sob, and liquid swished as he brought the bottle to his lips. My chest clenched, the words touching an answering guilt inside me. They still hadn't let me see Lucas. But what was he talking about? If anything, he'd saved everyone from the Plagues. "It *had* to be done. And now this Elspeth woman..."

I paused, my hand on the door handle. He was only rambling. It didn't make any sense.

Or maybe I didn't want it to make any sense.

My heart skipped as I began to piece things together.

"What about the Elspeth woman?"

I caught a glint of something in his eye. He'd swallowed back the sobs, but his tears pooled. Edward Doncaster, international hero, saviour of the world, crying. It had to be the alcohol, right? That's all it was.

"Example. Had to be an example. If they opt out, they must understand they're out. Can't come back. Or society crumbles."

"I don't understand."

"No," he said sadly, drew the bottle to his mouth but seemed to forget about it halfway. "You wouldn't. People shouldn't have to understand what we do for them. What we protect them from. Who we kill for them."

My stomach dropped. Maybe it hadn't been an auto-taser.

"They were *meant* to kill her?"

He didn't answer. His hand shook, the bottle clinking, and he didn't answer.

I felt like I was going to be sick. I pushed down on the door handle, eased it open and pulled the door shut behind me. I stared down the hallway at the luxury carpet, the oil paintings, the gold lettering on the doors. And I put one foot in front of the other and made it outside.

It couldn't be true. It was a malfunction, that's what the news said. Regrettable. Unlucky. I thought of Elspeth's quick smile, the way her hands wove patterns in the air as she talked.

No one would ever see that again.

20
Trigger

I CLIMBED THE SEAGULL playground on the waterfront and sat in the top. The night I'd been here with Mira had been still, the stars sprinkled above us and the sea a low murmur. I'd been here with Lucas, too, many times. We'd spent whole days wandering around the waterfront, hiding from Fiarenza up here or trying to rollerblade down the slides. Now the wind whistled through the bars and waves slapped against the rocks. I lay on the salt-pitted metal and stared up at the roof, caught between turning things over and trying to put my mind on freeze.

Lucas would be dead in a week, because the authorities said you couldn't be un-useful for more than four years. Elspeth was already dead, because the authorities thought Outsiders should never be allowed back in and killed anyone who tried.

And Doncaster – the guy who'd made up half our rules – thought Elspeth had to die, so he was as much to blame as whoever had pulled the trigger. Okay, maybe not *quite* as much. Though if the person who pulled the trigger had been acting on orders, how were they more to blame than the ones who'd given the orders, or who'd sat in a room discussing whether or not to kill a woman in cold blood?

With my eyes closed and the wind cutting through me, the rest of Doncaster's words floated back.

"It's not enough to cut back the population."

"So many dead."

And last, but not least, *"My fault"*.

His words pieced together, casting every other conversation in a new light. The world had been bad, everyone knew it. Green Wars. Nature brought to the edge of collapse. Hatred because people looked different, or believed something different from you. Doncaster reckoned only the best and brightest could have thought up the Plagues. So... no one but Edward Doncaster. And he'd been the one to find a cure. What if he'd known how to cure it all along, had waited until enough people died before he told anyone?

Nine and a half billion people dead.

It added up. No matter how much I hoped it wouldn't, it did.

I pulled out my phone and tapped search terms into it, trying to find any hint that Doncaster had done it. Or hadn't done it. There was nothing. But couldn't that mean something in itself? There were tonnes of conspiracy theories. Why wouldn't one of them involve Doncaster dreaming up his own plague – or plagues – and then taking all the credit for the cure? Maybe they were censoring it.

I cleared my browser history and squeezed my eyes shut. Doncaster, rogue geneticist. Doncaster, genocidal maniac. And the last Plague had killed Amy – wasn't that his own Match?

It was cold, and I only had a T-shirt. I began to shiver. A kid poked his head up from below and we stared at each other, then he backed away down the ladder. I checked my watch, my cold limbs protesting. Almost one o'clock. I'd been here three hours.

Should I go back? I couldn't face it. He might be more sober by now, or maybe asleep, and there was nothing I could do if he was asleep. I didn't want to talk to him, anyway. I didn't want to talk to anyone. I just wanted to think, to figure things out, to find all the reasons that it might not be true.

There weren't many. We trusted him. He was a hero. A conspiracy this big could never have gone unnoticed.

But what if it had? What if everyone who'd noticed was killed or bribed or brainwashed? Doncaster wasn't part of the authorities anymore. Maybe they'd found out and had "retired" him, but hadn't thought it important to tell everyone else.

It hurt my head.

So say he'd engineered a Plague, or all of them. Then he'd cured it, and used his hero status to guide the world by his own ideas. He was right about the racism and religion thing, because those didn't really divide people anymore. Everyone had united against the Gen-ens. And against the Outsiders.

I guess the hate wasn't really gone, it had just... shifted.

And if Doncaster had engineered the Plagues that destroyed the old world, killed billions of people, that meant the Gen-ens... didn't. If Doncaster did it, the Gen-ens weren't responsible, but they got nixed – *killed* – anyway.

I tried to figure out how I felt about that. Even without the Plagues, the Gen-ens had done some pretty terrible things. That footage of the Gas Attacks, with the hundreds of dead sprawled where they fell, bodies layered one on top of another, humped shapes murky through the mists. And there was the Better Human

Manifesto. The Gen-en James How, eyes alight as it spouted its crap about the right of the Gen-ens to inherit the Earth, and the proper place of "naturals" as slaves. I'd seen the Gen-en in the hospital screaming it'd kill everyone, and even if I maybe kind of felt something for it when she got shot, it was still promising death.

Gen-ens didn't have souls, essences, whatever you wanted to call it. They didn't have that strange spark that made a person a person. They didn't value human life like we did.

Maybe they hadn't let the Plagues loose, but they'd done an awful lot of other stuff. Were scapegoats scapegoats if they deserved to be punished for other things?

But... what could you do about it now? Revealing Doncaster as some evil supervillain wouldn't bring back the people who'd died. It wouldn't have any effect on Lucas's sentence. Maybe it would stop Gen-ens being killed now, but was that even a good thing? It wouldn't make much difference to the Outsiders, just because society was built on a *total lie*.

And how would you go about telling people in the first place? I was sixteen. No one would believe me, and if what I thought was true, the authorities probably had ways of shutting me up that I didn't like to think about.

And really, I could be completely wrong about all this.

—— · ——

We had a half-hearted attempt at Christmas dinner on the twenty-fifth, but Lucas's family didn't make the trip in from Awakairangi Hutt and it was just me, Mum, Dad and Verity. I missed the Christmases when we were younger, back when Fiarenza still lived in New Zealand and all four of us kids would play Creeping Up in the garden or melt into the trees and make the adults come collect us. The mountains of pavlova and berries and roast kūmara and rice salad and green salad and melon and lamb and mint sauce and stuffing… Whoever allocated Christmas food obviously ignored all the guidelines on moderating consumption.

The food was like ash in my mouth and I barely heard the conversation. Verity had spent hours beating egg whites and I expected daggers when I refused her pavlova, but she just shrugged. My parents thought I was still grieving for Lucas, and I was, but I also couldn't stop thinking about Elspeth and Plagues.

I met Mira later on the bush path, with the moon turning the leaves silver. It was the first time we'd seen each other since Elspeth's death, and she shook against my shoulder, tears soaking into my t-shirt. I held her tight, kissed her hair. For the first time in days I felt steady, like I knew what I was supposed to do. I couldn't fix my own shit, but I could be there for her.

"I brought you something," she whispered, wiping a hand across her face and bringing out a stone pendant on waxed black string, one arm holding me close. "It's for more than just, you know, Christmas. I made it."

"Wow, Mira," I breathed, turning it into the light and making out the swirls of waves and koru.

"I want you to think, every time you wear it, that waves might wear away at the shore, but there's always new life as well. Creation and destruction. Circle of life." She looked down and her fingers clutched at my t-shirt. "All that shit. I know it doesn't help with Lucas, or with– with Elspeth, but…"

"It's beautiful," I said, and swallowed. I wasn't going to cry. I'd gone almost a week with no tears, and I wasn't going to cry. "I'm sorry, I didn't–"

"It's fine." She shook her head. "You've had a lot going on."

A lot going on. Ha. Lucas would be dead in a few days, they'd killed Elspeth, my boss was probably a mass murderer, going out with my girlfriend would get me arrested...

"Hey, hey," Mira said. "Look at me. You'll get through this. I'm telling you, you will. We both will."

I swallowed, throat burning. She didn't know the whole story. And I couldn't tell her.

21

Confession

I SAT IN THE plum tree with my tablet all day on Boxing Day, trying to read the books I'd got for Christmas but mostly running through all the things I had no control over. By the afternoon, my stomach roiled and cold sweat shivered across my shoulders.

So I started making a list of things I could get control over. I could make sure I said goodbye properly to Lucas. We could hold a memorial for Elspeth. I could spend as much time with Mira as I could, under the radar. And I could ask Doncaster about the Plagues. What was he going to do, kill me? He was a hundred-and-twelve. And anyway, he seemed to like me.

Doncaster worked Saturdays – said he enjoyed the quiet – so he'd probably be in at the GA tomorrow, pottering around, setting small fires on bench-tops. Just waiting for me to ask him what the hell he'd done.

The next morning I grabbed a few kūmara left over from Christmas dinner and spun down to the GA, nearly taking out a few kids playing soccer on the way. I stashed the bike and considered my t-shirt, sweat-stained more from nerves than exercise. To hell with it. I was still presentable, unlike Doncaster earlier in the week. And if he wasn't here, it wouldn't matter.

His door was ajar. I peered round it. Doncaster was standing at a lab bench, just like a normal day. Just like a normal, non-genocidal person.

"Um, Professor?"

He turned and waved me over. Once I was staring into a microscope and cursing myself for not having the guts to speak, he cleared his throat.

"Look, Kieran, I'm sorry about Wednesday. It was a hard day, after that poor woman... It won't happen again."

I nodded, still with my eyes glued to what seemed to be a hyperactive blood cell. "Of course. You, um, don't need to mention it."

He gave a great sigh. "Oh, I know, but I thought I would. Just, you know, things can get out of hand. You say things you don't mean..." I could feel his eyes on my back. Did he remember his words, or was he just making sure he hadn't given anything away?

"Like admitting you set loose Plagues that killed ninety-three percent of humanity?" I said before I could stop myself.

Doncaster sucked in a breath. There was a long pause.

"Yes, I suppose like that," he said at last. Then, "Damn. Did I actually say that?"

The blood cell did a somersault. "Not exactly... But it wasn't hard to figure out."

His hand came down on my shoulder and I spun around, throwing him off and backing away. He sighed.

"Kieran, I'm not going to hurt you. I'm sure we can come to some sort of understanding."

"So you did do it?" I asked, my voice hoarse. Doncaster shrugged, but a muscle jumped in his jaw. I'd rattled him. He began threading his way through the stacks of books to his armchair.

"Maybe we could sit down and have a little chat. Do you think?"

I stayed where I was. "Why did you do it?"

Doncaster settled himself and nodded to the window; the city sparkled in the sun, and people drifted along the waterfront in twos and threes. A rollerblader spun around a corner and out of sight. "I believe the ends justify the means. If the world had continued the way it was going, we'd have none of this. Just an overpopulated, smoking, dead world hanging alone in space."

"You can't know that."

"You can't know any different. You're of the Paradise Generation. You'll never know what it was like to share this planet with so many teeming billions, with people who only wanted a better deal than the next person. People who fought and killed over stupid, petty things. Who didn't see the ways we were all the same, only the differences. They wanted us to produce more and more, consume more and more. There's only so much that Earth can take. We couldn't keep growing indefinitely, and moving onto space stations was only ever a short-term option. I saved Earth, Kieran. Me. You have me to thank for your life. Do you understand?"

I stared at the floor, clenching and unclenching my fists.

"So the Gen-ens didn't do any of it."

"Oh, they did a lot," Doncaster said. He was leaning back in his chair, one leg crossed casually over the other like he wasn't at all worried, but I had more of his attention than I'd ever had before.

The muscle in his jaw was still jumping. "The Olympics Massacre, the Gas–"

"I know, I know. But they didn't massacre *most of humanity*, did they?"

"They might have done, with time." He was watching me carefully.

"If you hadn't got them all killed."

Doncaster shook his head. "I didn't point the finger at them. They were just the most likely suspects."

"Because they have no souls?"

"Come now, don't be unscientific. You'll have seen James How's speeches. He actually *promised* to wipe out humanity."

I swallowed, seeing James How yelling into a microphone that Gen-ens were the next step in evolution, that humans could no longer disrespect them, that Gen-ens would inherit the Earth.

Doncaster had said "he". Not "it".

"You killed billions of people. Stood by while the survivors killed the Gen-ens. And now you just stand by while they kill Outsiders like Elspeth, who never did anything wrong."

Doncaster raised his eyebrows. "Oh, you knew her, did you? I wondered. I'm sorry these things have to be done–"

"*Have* to be done? Why?"

He just shook his head. "You're young, Kieran. Our society balances on the edge of chaos. We have to hold tight to its structure, or we'll lose thousands of years of progress. The cities are the guardians of human knowledge, and we must guard against those who want to overthrow them."

"Elspeth didn't want to overthrow the city. She only wanted to see her family. At *Christmas*. And you killed her."

"I didn't kill her." He looked almost horrified. "I didn't give the order. Maybe I had some hand in the policy, way back, but what happened was nothing to do with me."

"Policy?" I repeated. They had a policy that told them to kill people.

Sadness crept into his eyes and I didn't know if it was real or fake. "She'd already made her choice. It's a hard line, but it cannot be crossed. Once she'd decided she wanted no part of the cities, she couldn't come back, not for anything. Otherwise how can we keep control? Keep the cities the paradises they are?"

"You're insane." I began to back towards the door. "If people knew about this–"

He raised his voice over mine. "Kieran. You've been spending a lot of time with a certain girl recently. Mira Sorenssen."

I froze. "How do you know about that?"

You could almost see his tension lessen. He waved a hand at a console in the corner, knowing he'd played a trump card. "That's a Pulse device."

Shit. "You need a warrant to use that." But he was Edward Doncaster, wasn't he? Of course he was above the law. "And I'm not a criminal or a lost person."

"Well, you and Mira did get a little lost, did you not? All the way out past Ngā Ūranga."

"We were on a bike trek."

"Interesting place to go on a bike trek. And why would you want to avoid the checkpoints? You know that's a very bad thing to do, Kieran. Checkpoints are for your own safety."

He knew about Horokiwi, I could see it in his eyes, in the way his lip curled. I took a deep breath and crossed my arms, hoping I looked tough.

"So what?"

He shrugged. "Sit down, Kieran. You're now part of a very small, very exclusive group that I have worked very, very hard to keep small and exclusive. This kind of thing doesn't work if more than a handful of people know. That's where PRISM went wrong, where the Tuskegee experiment went wrong. And there's something I could help you with."

"What the hell do you think would make me–"

"Girlfriends. Or one girlfriend in particular."

I opened my mouth, stared at him, and closed it again. "What about girlfriends?"

"Sit down and I'll tell you."

So I sat, hating myself the entire time. Doncaster gave a serene smile and leant even further back in his chair.

"You and Mira Sorenssen have a percentage match of 1.2%. In other ways, though, you're a perfect Match. Excellent genomes, complementary pairings for a few bad genes, personalities and chemistry well-suited. You know, the percentage match limit is just an arbitrary line to increase population mixing, based on a thousand key genes."

My heart was in my throat. Mum had said it was the whole genome. Had she been wrong about how they calculated it? Was it less important than everyone made out?

"It's a relic, really," Doncaster continued. "Meaningless. I could shave a few tenths of a percent off. You'd be legal."

Legal. The word echoed in my head, blood coursing through my veins like liquid light. This was our loophole. We wouldn't have to sneak around anymore. We could do what normal couples did – meet up for coffee in an actual café, go to the VR suites and wander around Rome or Machu Picchu.

And in return ... in return I'd say nothing about this to anyone. Ever.

I ran my tongue around my teeth, pressing against each one in turn. It was a trade. Ignore the fact Doncaster had killed *billions of people* and blamed it on Gen-ens.

I could ignore what I knew, and have Mira. I could forget what I knew, and get one thing I wanted, even if everything else had gone to shit. Lucas was dead. Even if they didn't kill him, I knew he wouldn't ever be the person I knew. There wasn't anyone inside his head anymore. It was all just muscle memory; eating, exercycling, staring out the window.

The Plagues were in the past. Those people were dead and there was nothing I could do to change that. Doncaster was batshit crazy, but he hadn't done anything bad recently. He wasn't with the authorities anymore, so he didn't really have much power. He hadn't been directly involved with Elspeth's murder. He said. And he was actually being quite nice about all this. He probably wouldn't do any more damage, would he?

I thought about what the world could have been like if he hadn't released the Plagues. We hadn't had any real wars in the last sixty or so years, but it had been pretty bad in the fifties and sixties. There were too many people, too few resources, and nature was in steep decline. Climate refugees, poverty, war. We had nearly seventy-five million people on the planet at the moment. I tried to imagine a hundred times the number, more than a hundred times.

I stared out the window. Maybe we would have found another way. We could have colonised the Moon, Mars, be on our way to Alpha Centauri by now. Maybe we'd have built floating cities above the ones the sea had drowned. We could have claimed the deserts and Antarctica, restricted population growth much like now, built towers hundreds of metres into the air. It would have been like in old movies, sparkling cities reaching to the sky.

But it hadn't happened like that. And the world was mostly good like this. Not much disease or poverty. Some people didn't like it, like the Outsiders, and I could understand that. Maybe there were lots of rules, and maybe people like Doncaster could track me, but if you got right down to it I could be happy. Lucas would want me to be happy. I had my family and friends. I could have Mira.

If I told people the truth, we'd lose our national hero. The whole country, the whole world, might lose faith in the society we'd created. When your guiding principles are written by a murderer of billions, can you still follow them? Everything would be questioned, even the good stuff. There would be riots, coups. Wars. And that was all if they believed me.

Maybe it was better to leave it as it was.

Doncaster was watching me.

I met his eyes and gripped the arm of the chair. "So how do we do this?"

22
Legal

MIRA WAS STILL IN her pyjamas when I hammered on her door.

"What–" she said, eyes wide, and jumped outside, holding the front door to. "What are you doing here?"

"I've got some news."

"You shouldn't be here," she hissed. "My mum's just inside, she could–"

"It doesn't matter anymore."

"What? What's your news?"

"We're legal."

Her mouth sagged and the door swung slowly open behind her. "Uh, what? Is this–"

"It's all sorted. I fixed it. I found our loophole."

She stared at me. "How?"

I wasn't completely sure what was going to come out my mouth. There were two ways I could go: lie and say I'd figured out how to hack the database, or tell a little tiny bit of the truth.

"The guy I'm working for fixed it for us. The percentage match limit is just arbitrary, see, so–"

"You mean you *told* him about us?"

Damn, I'd forgotten about that. "Well, he guessed. He kinda, well, has access to a Pulse device, and he noticed we were together a lot."

"That's illegal."

I chewed my lip. "Come on, Mir. Every silver lining has its cloud."

She stared at me, but then her lip twitched. "Give me ten minutes to get dressed. I'll meet you at the gate."

I hung around her garden wall, picking at the moss until she reappeared. She stepped away when I tried to kiss her.

"Wait, Kier. Just tell me what happened."

I gave her a highly-edited rundown as we walked.

"So he just did it? Just mentioned that we looked like we were going out, and offered to fix it for us?"

I stared at a piece of chewing gum stuck to the footpath. "Well, he likes me."

"But... aren't you just another one of his 'little machines that provide feedback at the push of a button'?"

Maybe I'd gone a bit overboard complaining about my internship. "Well, he's a nice guy underneath it all. He has quirks, but everyone has quirks." One of those quirks was thinking that genocide was a good thing. I shut the thought out. I was not going to think that way. This was karma coming round for me, giving and taking. I'd lose Lucas, but I'd gain Mira. And maybe, maybe that could make things better.

"Fine, he can be quirky," Mira conceded. "But what about everyone else? People know we're an illegal Match. We can't just say 'all fixed!'."

I shook my head. "We can say it was a false positive. Or negative or something. We've both got ... um, quality genomes." I didn't like thinking about genome categories. "And no bad recessive matches. We're good."

She was silent for a long time. We were walking towards Ōwhiro Bay, the walls of the valley rising like shadows on either side of us. By the time we reached the old abandoned houses of Happy Valley, I could bear it no more.

"So, what do you say?" A horrible thought hit me. "It wasn't just that I was forbidden, right? Am I boring now it's legal?"

She swung round and punched me on the arm. "Don't be stupid. Of course I still like you. It's just ... a lot to get my head around. I mean, it seems kind of dodgy."

I grabbed her hand and pulled her to a stop. Took a breath. "Mira. This is what I've wanted since I first saw you. I know it's not perfect, but nothing really is. You've got to take the good with the bad and hope everything works out okay in the end. And it *will*, I know it. We don't have to hide things anymore, or be afraid someone will find out. We can just be another couple, out on a date."

"There are no strings attached, right?" Mira said. "We don't have to give up our firstborn or anything like that?" She reddened. "Well, if we have kids..."

"Nope. No Rumpelstiltskin stuff."

Well, not really.

—— · ——

Mira's mum was out that night at a show. I combed my hair after dinner, put on a clean shirt, and went to confront my parents.

They were watching a movie in the living room, Verity lying on the floor beside them with half an eye on the movie and the rest on her phone.

"So..." I said.

Dad paused the movie, one eyebrow raised.

"You look nice," Mum said. "What do you want?"

"Can I go visit Mira?"

"Mira?" Dad asked. "Who's Mira?"

"Is she your giiiirrrrlfriend?" Verity asked from the floor, grinning widely.

Mum's brows were drawn together. "That name's familiar... She's not the girl you Matched with last month?"

I nodded, realised I was twisting my hands together and stuck them behind my back. "Yeah. We ran the Match again, just to be sure, and it came up fine. No issues." No issues at all.

"Whoo! Kieran's got a girlfriend," Verity said, relishing the words. She turned back to her phone. I hoped she wasn't posting it all over her socials.

"Congrats," Dad said, exchanging glances with Mum. It looked like they were trying to hide their smiles. "I guess that sounds fine, as long as you're back by eleven. Where does she live?"

This was easier than I'd thought. I gave them Mira's address, and grabbed my bike from the shed.

For the first time, I took the main road to her house. Out in the open. Legit. No more secrets.

For this at least.

The moon was bright. I'd uploaded some photos and a few of the paintings Mira liked to the holosphere, which I hoped was romantic and not weird stalkery, but left the old photos on there.

She'd be interested in the history. I knocked on her door, hearing the sound echo around the house and shifting from foot to foot. Finally I heard footsteps on the stairs, the light flicked on and Mira's face appeared at the window.

"Who is it?"

"It's me, stupid."

She grinned and opened the door. I darted down to catch her lips and she giggled and hooked her arms around my neck, dragging me inside.

"What you got?" she said, once a swirling breeze reminded us the door was wide open. I closed it and showed her my bag of choc mint fudge bars, pizza and popcorn.

"I thought we could watch that new Hans Chung movie? Supposed to be good."

"Excellent idea."

"And..." I pulled the holosphere out of my hoodie's pocket, wrapped in tissue paper. "For you. Belated Christmas present."

She took it curiously, pulling at the harakeke ribbon. "It's not... It is! You got it working!"

"'Course." I swallowed, my throat suddenly sharp. "Had to do Elspeth justice. Throw it up."

She did, only high enough to get a glimpse of Van Gogh's Starry Night projected around us, our shadows intermingling with swirls of light and deepest indigo. "Whoa!" She let out a shaky laugh. "Scared I'll break it again."

"Then I'll just fix it again."

The next picture was a view from the dam, a clear day with Awakairangi Hutt and Horokiwi to my left, Raukawa Cook Strait to my right, the colours of the Pencarrow coast playing across

Mira's face. For a second we were in our own bubble of light, thrown back into our picnic on the dam, and then Mira caught the holosphere once again.

"Thank you. I love it."

The pizza took barely ten minutes to heat, and we set ourselves up in the living room with the movie, pizza, popcorn, fudge bars and a little bottle of champagne Mira found in the cupboard.

"Mum hates champagne," she said. "So really we're doing her a service."

The champagne was tart and fizzy on my tongue and didn't really go with the pizza, but it felt appropriate. We were legal now. Mira curled up against me, pulling my arm around her and lacing her fingers through mine. Some way into the movie and some time after the popcorn ran out, she turned her head up to kiss me. I shifted to make it less awkward, and she shifted, and soon she was lying on top of me on the couch, my hand in her hair, hers tracing circles on my shoulder, trailing fire in the wake of her fingertips, and the movie became nothing more than background noise.

Our legs entangled. I touched her hip, stroked up her spine beneath her T-shirt. "Is this okay?" I whispered. Her skin was so soft.

"It's good," she whispered back. "How's this?" She kissed the corner of my mouth, then my jaw, my neck, and I dug my fingers into her back.

"Don't stop. This is the best I've felt in days."

She giggled. "No problemo." She kissed my collar bone, the hollow below my Adam's apple, my other collar bone, but then she pulled back. "Kieran, um."

"Yeah?"

"I'm not sure how to say this, but..." She stared down at me, eyes glinting. "You're not using... this... as a– like a rebound, or a crutch, or whatever, for what happened to Lucas?"

The bottom dropped out of my stomach.

"No, I–"

Was I?

I shook my head. This was unrelated. Completely unrelated. "No." I said, definite. "This has nothing to do with that. This is because... because I can't stop thinking about you. Your hair..." I ran my hand through it. "Your lips." I skimmed them beneath my thumb and her lips curved into a smile. "Your eyes. Your body. The way we fit together. I think you are the most amazing, wonderful, awesome person in the entire universe. And hot. Also very hot. Am I allowed to say that? Not objectifying you?"

"I'm okay with it," she said, smirking. "This time." Then she sobered quickly, searching my eyes. "I think– you seem– I don't know, if you want to stop, or talk about Lucas, just say the word, and we can–"

"I'm fine. I don't want to stop."

She stared into my eyes like she could uncover all my secrets. Her blue eyes had tiny threads of silver running through them, and a fiery ring of gold around the pupil I hadn't noticed before. She blew out a breath. "Well, if that's how you feel."

And we were back to kissing.

The movie continued on, but it hardly registered. We had hours before Mira's mum was due home. I didn't think I was quite ready to go *all* the way – especially with Mira's Lucas question so fresh – but that didn't mean I wanted to stop. Mira slowly unbuttoned my shirt, running her hand over my chest so I shivered. She pulled off her own top and we were skin to skin, breaths catching, hands roaming...

"What about our trips to Horokiwi?" Mira said suddenly, her hand going still. I broke off from kissing her neck and tried to slow my heartrate. "If your boss knew we were together a lot, he must have known we were going out there."

"Does it matter?"

She pulled back, frowning. "Yes. Yes, it does."

I sighed. "Yeah, he knew."

Her brow furrowed. I wanted to smooth it out with my fingers, and maybe reach inside her head and stop her brain churning out these thoughts.

"Does he know about the Outsiders? That we were going to see them?"

I remembered the curl of his lip when he talked about them, people who actually *chose* to live outside his perfect society. "Yeah. He– he didn't object."

She sat up so she was straddling my hips, staring intently at me. I shifted, fixing my gaze on the movie so I wouldn't have to meet her eyes. "You're kidding, right?"

"Well, he did say we should never go out there again."

She whacked me.

"Ow!"

"No strings attached, you said!"

"It was– it was more like advice! Not like an order. And we're lucky he didn't report us."

"Lucky?" Mira said, incredulous. She climbed off me and stood, arms crossed tightly around herself. "It sounds like we owe him.

He doesn't report us, he makes our Match legal. What does he want in return?"

"God, can't you just leave it? You always have to think through everything." I grabbed my shirt from the floor and pulled it on, began to do up the buttons. The first couple took a few goes, because my fingers kept slipping. I almost ripped one off in frustration.

"What did he want? What did you do?"

"Nothing," I muttered, doing battle with my third button. "Absolutely nothing."

"It doesn't seem like nothing." She grabbed my wrist and held it, even when I twisted my hand to try and free it. "I think I love you, Kieran." I stilled and turned my face towards her. "But something's bothering you. Something is wrong about this whole thing."

"Please, Mira, let it go."

"No."

I turned to look at her, at her blue eyes, her brow creased in concern, her hair falling across her face, and then I kissed her again, quickly. She wasn't going to let it go.

"I found out something," I said against her lips.

"What?" Another kiss.

"You can't tell anyone."

I thought about Doncaster's warning, that I might be in danger if people knew who I worked for. But this was Mira. She knew the Horokiwi Outsiders, but I trusted her not to tell them, and they were nice people. Well, except Nīkau and Adelaide carried guns... But they probably needed them, outside the city.

As for the Plagues thing, it was the same for Mira as it was for me. Say something, and be ignored or laughed at or maybe destroy society (probably not, though). Say nothing, and be together.

"Swear you won't tell," I said. "Please, Mira."

She looked wary. "Why?"

"Cos it could be dangerous if you tell. For both of us."

A long pause. But then she nodded. "I swear. Cross my heart and hope to die."

I spoke in a rush. "My boss is Edward Doncaster. Yeah, *that* Edward Doncaster. He engineered the Plague viruses."

She'd stiffened. "What?"

"Look – I don't want to say it again. I don't even want to think it again."

But she was backing away, her eyes wide.

"He killed everyone? And he told you this?"

I shook my head. "I figured it out on my own."

She was quiet for a very long time. I tried to count my breaths to stop my thoughts.

"He made the Match legal in exchange for you keeping quiet."

"He didn't say it straight out like that, but... yes."

"Shit," she said, throwing back her head and staring up at the ceiling. I could see the pulse in her throat. "Shit."

"Mira..."

She grabbed her T-shirt and pulled it back on. "Get out."

"What?"

"Get *out*."

"Why?"

She took a deep breath and pointed to the door, still staring at the ceiling. Her eyes glistened. "I can't do this. I can't just accept a–

a bribe to keep quiet about a man who murdered nine and a half billion people. And if you can, I don't think I can stand to look at you. Get out."

My bones felt turned to powder, strength leaking from my muscles. I wrapped my arms around me, sure the room was suddenly colder. "You're not... you're not going to tell anyone, are you?"

She looked at me then, her eyes hard. "Is that all you can think about? No, I'm not going to tell anyone. I don't have the proof, I didn't figure it out myself. But you should."

"It wouldn't matter. No one would believe me," I muttered.

"So why did he bribe you to keep quiet, then? Out."

I took a deep breath and picked up my hoodie. I could only find one sock, but didn't want to risk Mira's wrath by looking for it. My shoes were in the hall.

Mira slammed the door as soon as I was outside, hitting the backs of my heels.

23

Darkness

Everything was quiet outside, still. The stars shone down from a cloudless sky. The weather people had predicted pouring rain, lashing wind, thunder rumbling through bloated clouds, but they were wrong as usual. I would have preferred the pouring rain.

My shoes wouldn't fit my feet, and I realised I was shoving the left one onto my right foot. I didn't bother to do up the laces, just pushed them inside my shoes.

Can't think, can't think, don't think.

I stumbled along the bush path, trying not to bang into trees in the dark and failing badly. My arms were getting scraped raw and I fumbled with my hoodie, then tried not to get even more lacerated as I fell sideways into a gorse bush. Lucky me, managing to find the only gorse bush in the entire Consolidation zone that hadn't been ripped out or poisoned.

Why couldn't she understand? We were free to do what we wanted now. It wouldn't make a difference if I told anyone about Doncaster. Those people were already dead, Doncaster was ancient and would probably die soon and the world was quite happy not knowing. Better for society to stay quiet.

And Elspeth?

I stamped down on that thought.

I pulled myself out of the gorse bush. It was barely ten p.m. Verity would still be awake and probably ready to wolf-whistle at me when I came through the door.

The house was lit up. I stood staring at it for a while, numb, mind blank. Mira didn't want me. Everything I'd done, everything I'd risked, was for nothing.

I couldn't go home.

My bike was leaning against the wall in the shed. I wheeled it out, wincing as the gears clicked and the tyres whispered against the gravel. Out on the road I hooked a leg over the bar and freewheeled down the hill, my heart pounding as the darkness swallowed me, dim street lights flickering and fading as I sped past. I sucked in thick gasps of air and cycled through silent streets, shop windows empty and staring. Mind blank. Blank so I couldn't think about where I was going, where I'd come from. What I'd done. What other people had done.

Past the wharves. Past the stadium, the ferry terminal. The sea beside me, calm, constant.

I stopped just before Ngā Ūranga Gorge, dropped my bike and sat on a rock right by the water. Salt spray washed my face and I stared into the sea.

Nothing I did could change anything, so what was the point in trying? I couldn't have Mira, I'd already lost Lucas. I'd tried and failed and now I may as well just sit back and wait for life to screw me over again.

I could dive in.

Swim out and out until my arms cramped, my legs stopped moving, until the cold water began to leech away my body heat. Maybe I'd meet Lucas, in whatever came after.

I bit my lip hard and stood, made myself walk away from the water. I got back on the bike, turned off my phone signal and began the trek up Ngā Ūranga Gorge. I wanted to talk to someone, and Andrew didn't even know I'd had a shot with Mira. It hadn't seemed cool to tell him, with Prajna's rejection still fresh. The Outsiders knew, though. And they also knew Mira. Maybe they could even give me advice on how to get her back.

My watch told me it was nearing eleven, but Ruby might still be up. There were no streetlights out here, but the stars gave a sprinkling of light and the moon provided the rest. A few clouds drifted across it as I turned onto the track, but I remembered the way.

—— · ——

Nīkau was on guard. I didn't notice him until he popped up beside me, feet silent on the dirt. How did he do that?

"What are you doing out here this time of night, Kieran?"

I stopped and glanced up the track towards the village. I could just make out a few lights through the trees.

"I– I wanted to talk to..." It seemed weird to admit I wanted to talk to Ruby, his wife. "To you, maybe." Nīkau didn't really seem like the talkative type, and he looked doubtful.

"To me?"

"Yeah." I stared at the ground and swallowed. "Mira and I had a fight."

"Oh." He leaned against a tree and folded his arms. "Big one?"

"I think it's over. Like, completely."

"What did you fight about?"

I shook my head. There was a tree at my back and I slid down it to sit on the ground. "It was nothing."

"Doesn't sound like nothing."

I closed my eyes. What could I say?

"Well, maybe this makes things easier. You don't have to decide whether to leave the city, if your relationship is worth–"

"That's just it," I forced out. "We didn't have to make that decision."

"But you said you were illegal."

"We were. Now we're not." I rubbed my hands into my eyes. "That's what the fight was about."

"I see." He didn't sound like he saw at all.

I took a deep breath and dragged myself to my feet. "Got any of that chocolate left over from last time?"

"You're optimistic," Nīkau muttered. "Best we got is berries."

Ruby gave me berry tarts and beer and let me rant about crazy girls. Nīkau drifted off to where Jake and a few others were gathered around a fire. I recognised Adelaide's face lit garish orange by the firelight. She was poking at the fire with a stick. Nīkau sat down and another guy took his place as guard.

I finished off the last of my beer and laid my head on the rough wooden table.

"What's the worst thing someone can do, do you reckon, Ruby? Like, something that would make you never want to see them again."

She was washing pots, and quiet for a while.

"Killing someone who didn't deserve it. In cold blood."

Well, I hadn't done that.

"Why, Kieran?"

I turned my head away and focused on the crickets and the whisper of the trees. Maybe I could just live out here. I wouldn't have to see Mira again. It would be easier for me and she'd be happy.

Voices raised around the fire. The wind ruffled the hair against my neck and I heard the first drops of rain.

"What are they talking about?"

Ruby harrumphed. "Elspeth."

I glanced at her. Her back was all tense and she was scrubbing at a pot as if it was covered in concrete.

"What's wrong with that?"

She shook her hair out of her face. "They've been at it for days. They're trying to decide if they should do something about her death. If it was accidental or what, and if it even matters if it's accidental."

"Oh." I knew it wasn't accidental. I cleared my throat. "I'm sorry. It's horrible."

Jake clomped over in his combat boots and grabbed a carrot out of the cool chest.

"Kieran," he said. Crunch, went the carrot. "Hear you and Mira split up. Pity."

"I'm sorry about Elspeth," I said. "She–" What could you say? My pity-fest seemed stupid in comparison, even though my heart still felt like it was eating out my chest. "I liked her."

"Yeah," Jake said. "We all did."

I tried not to think of Doncaster. I hoped nothing showed on my face.

"What are you going to do?" I spun a twig between my fingers and stared at Jake's chin, trying to read his expression without looking like I was doing it. Jake glared at Ruby. The twig snapped.

"Show them they shouldn't mess with us."

"Come on, Jake, you haven't decided yet, right?" Ruby said.

Jake ignored her. He turned to go back to the meeting, but I grabbed his arm. His muscles were iron. "What does that mean? My family's in Wellington, and Mira–"

"Don't you understand? There are people like you, who live in cities and swan out here when you want an adventure. There are people like us, who can't live with the restrictions or made a mistake a long time ago and are forced to survive out here. When you're hungry, you flash your chip and you get food. When we're hungry, we have to hunt or find or steal it. I can live with that. Sometimes it's not so bad.

"But when Elspeth wanted to enter the city to see her family – for *Christmas* – they shot her. We have to make a stand, or things will never change."

"It could have been an accident..." I said, but my voice was unsure even to my ears. "What's the point in making waves? They'll come after you."

He sucked in a breath, face reddening, but caught a look from Ruby. He shrugged like someone had stuck him with an electric probe. "Maybe enough people will hear about it. Maybe it won't be censored out and others will take a stand. You don't even know the half of your world, kid."

The carrot top flew into the grass like some kind of cruise missile, and he returned to the meeting, one more anonymous silhouette around the fire.

—— · ——

Ruby was still doing war with the pot. She didn't look up as I went into the trees, circling closer to the meeting. Jake obviously wanted me to stay out of it, but I had to know what they were planning. Then maybe I could persuade them to stop. Or if that didn't work, maybe I could call Andrew, Xiao, my family, and warn them. I could warn Mira.

They were speaking softly now, almost too quietly to hear over the snaps and pops of the fire. I edged closer, staying in the shadows and pulling my hoodie around my face. If I stopped them, maybe Mira would want me again. Maybe what I'd done wouldn't be so bad.

Words caught in the air. Sea. Chip locks. Surveillance. Nothing concrete enough for me to go on. I took out my phone, flicked on the signal and held it tight, ready to step out into the light if I thought I could stop them.

"*Liberate Pōneke Wellington won't help us,*" someone said. "*They say it's too risky, too many consequences. We've got the bomb, but we don't have the experience or the skills to do it ourselves.*"

Shit. A bomb. Okay, but it sounded like they weren't ready–

"*I do.*" A woman's voice.

Okay, a bomb they were ready to use. Maybe I was in a little over my head. Weren't these supposed to be the non-murdery Outsiders? I scrolled through my phone for Andrew, but paused. I didn't know the details, couldn't warn him to stay away from anywhere...

A raindrop hit my hand. The sky was pitch, the air electric.

"*Maybe you do, Adelaide, but we still don't have...*"

The wind shifted, carrying the sound away from me. I took one more step. Two more.

Crack.

I'd stepped on a dry branch. I froze as every head around the fire turned. They couldn't see, right? They'd been staring into the fire, for god's sake. They wouldn't–

A silhouette stood and grew larger. I turned and ran, but it was dark and I didn't know my footing and the guy was much faster than me. He rugby-tackled me to the ground, my phone flying. The breath punched out of me. My attacker ripped back my hood.

"You."

He dragged me upright and pulled me to the fire where everyone was on their feet now. I twisted around to see his face. He looked familiar, and adrenaline brought his name out of the depths of my brain. Mikale.

"I thought there was something weird about you," he muttered into my ear. And then, aloud, "He was spying. Hood up, sneaky as anything." He had his hands tight around both my upper arms, and didn't move a muscle when I tried to get out of the hold.

Jake came forward and yanked my chin up. "True? Were you eavesdropping?"

"No, I–"

Mikale let go of one of my arms just long enough to slap me.

"Search him," Jake muttered.

Mikale went to get my phone, which was glowing like a beacon in the midst of the trees, while Tomas – Enzo's dad – held me and rifled through my pockets. Excuses flickered through my head. I'd just been taking a leak, I thought I saw a kiwi–

Mikale was back, flicking through my phone. Ice stole over me. Doncaster was in there.

"Come on, I wasn't spying! There's nothing in there you'd care about–" I broke off as Mikale held the phone for Jake to see. "Shit."

Tomas shoved me backwards. I expected to fall right to the ground, but someone had stuck a chair behind me and I landed with a thump.

"Why would Edward Doncaster be in your call history?" Jake asked.

"Um," I said, flailing for a reason. "You know I'm an intern at the GA. One of my friends snuck into Doncaster's office and called me on a dare–"

"He's lying," Ruby said. She'd come up behind Jake and was wiping her hands on her jeans, looking disappointed. "Look at his eyes."

She'd turned on me this fast?

Mikale punched me in the stomach.

"I'm not lying!" I gasped. "I swear!"

Jake had my phone now. "Looks like you called Doncaster too. Why is that?"

"I told you, my friend called me, I called back for– for a prank!"

"You are lying," Jake said, squatting so we were eye to eye. "Doncaster's phone would only work for Doncaster. It's a pretty basic security measure.

"The only people Doncaster would call would be those he trusts. Friends, family, colleagues, or, what did you say, interns?"

I stared at the ground, biting my cheek so hard I could taste blood.

"Are you a spy, Kieran? Intern to Edward Doncaster by day, spy by night?"

"No!"

"The evidence counts against you."

Heavy drops began to fall, splashing into my hair and running into my eyes.

Jake glanced at the sky. "Looks like a good storm. Come on."

They dragged me to the dining hall. By the time we got there, I was covered in mud from the knees down and my hoodie was soaked through.

Tomas was doing something on a tablet. "Yep, records say he's interning for some Friedrich guy, but that guy happens to have an office on the same floor as Doncaster."

"Interesting." Jake slumped down in his own chair and stared at me. I saw Adelaide out of the corner of my eye, lightly running her fingers over a matte-black gun. I tried not to look at her. "So what do you do for Friedrich?"

I kept my mouth pressed shut. No one knew I was out here. They wouldn't search for my phone signal for another few hours, and by then the peevs would have turned it off. The police could track me if they needed to, but unless Doncaster was doing one of his random illegal Pulses, they wouldn't get authorisation for another twenty-four hours. By which time I might be dead, the way things were going.

"Emails back and forth between Doncaster and Kieran..." Tomas said. "Sure looks like they know each other."

"Mikale, didn't you say you had some pliers somewhere?" Jake called, and the reply came with the sound of metal clacking together.

Breathing was like sucking air through a straw. Even though I hadn't actually done anything to them, the circumstances looked bad.

What did I have to lose? Apart from my fingernails.

"Okay, fine, I work for Doncaster–"

Mikale was right in front of me, forcing my chin up. "How much have you told your master, you little shit?"

"Nothing!" I yelped. "I swear! I had no idea about you guys when I came out here last time! I didn't even know where Mira was taking me! And I've never spied on you, there's no way I'd do that."

"Mikale," Jake muttered, and Mikale backed off. "How do you explain lurking in the forest just now?"

"I was just trying to figure out what you're doing, so I could warn my friends–" My throat was all tight. I coughed to clear it. "My family."

"And what about Elspeth?" Jake said. "Was her death an accident?"

"How would I know?" I asked, but my voice shook. Awesome liar, I was.

"Look at Jake when you're talking to him," Adelaide said sharply. Her nails dug into my wrist, and I dragged my gaze to meet Jake's, then wished I hadn't. His face had gone hard, and there was barely a trace of the calm, careful man I'd met a few weeks ago. Now he was just a very big guy looking at me like he wanted to punch me through a brick wall.

"I think you know a lot more than you're letting on. Did they target her?"

"Yes," I muttered.

Ruby drew in a sharp breath.

I tried to steady myself, to summon whatever self-assurance I could fake. "Because they don't want pe– Outsiders to mess up society."

"Mess–?" Jake repeated, incredulous. "And it's official? Not just trigger-happy guards or auto-taser malfunctions?"

"It's official. Doncaster helped write the policy. What– what does it matter?"

Mikale scoffed and turned away.

"It matters," Jake said, "because you knew. You knew he did it, you worked for him, and you didn't say anything."

"Only since Wednesday, though, I swear–"

Someone grabbed my hand, twisting it so I bit my lip trying not to cry out. My leg skittered on the ground as I tried to stay in my chair.

Jake leaned forward. "Kieran ... that is your name, right? ... even if you weren't spying on us, the fact you knew what happened to Elspeth and kept quiet is unforgivable. You put yourself right up there with the authorities who exile us and kill us if we try to see our families. Who fake terrorist alerts to make sure their citizens hate us."

Fake terrorist alerts? That explained why Mira was so dismissive of them. He was right in my face now, breath hot against my skin. I could smell the casserole he'd had for dinner. I tried not to breathe too deeply or too fast. Tried not to shrink back from him.

"I thought you chose to live this way," I muttered, unable to help myself. "To free yourselves from the rules and regulations of the cities. The cities didn't exile you."

Jake laughed. It wasn't a nice laugh. "They make it damn near impossible for some of us to stay, though. I should be in some re-education workcamp in Waiouru. Nīkau has medical stories you wouldn't believe."

"What about Enzo? He must think the cities are better than out here. He's doing fine, Mira says. I'll see him at school next year."

Tomas spoke up. "He'll be in state care until he's eighteen. I probably won't see him for years. They may even drug him to make sure he stays under control."

"Drug–?"

"He can solve our problem," Mikale said, spinning a pair of pliers idly around his fingers. "He has access to the dam. I heard him tell Elspeth."

"Oh," Jake said, and considered me. "Well, that could be useful."

24
Hostage

THEY HAD A CAR. Somehow, these crazy peevs had found a car and got it to work, the same way Lucas and I had done it, I guess. They argued for a while, and then stuffed me in the back with my hands tied in front of me. It was getting on towards one in the morning.

Adelaide drove extremely slowly along the snaking cracked road, headlights on full beam, windscreen wipers swishing. I was wedged between Nīkau and Mikale and the car seemed to get smaller and smaller with every bump.

It was still raining fitfully, hammering us and then relaxing into mist. I twisted my hands, trying to get some blood running through them, and testing the strength of the knots at the same time. Mikale glared when he felt me move.

Even if I could get my hands untied, there was still no way I was going to get out of this car without their help.

Every so often the headlights would flash on a house I thought I knew from biking around Awakairangi Hutt, or a set of play equipment, skeletal in the harsh light. We were probably somewhere near Pito-one.

The harbour opened up to the right, wide and dark. I could hear its dull roar over the lighter patter of rain on the car and the buffeting wind. The water would be freezing cold, spray flying up as the wind caught it. I hoped I wouldn't be pushed into it.

—— · ——

Just as the tingling from my fingers got unbearable, we stopped. I tried to see out the windows, but Adelaide turned the headlights off, leaving only the dull glow of the instruments. The ghostly light didn't help my nerves.

She twisted in her seat to stare at me. "You ready, Kieran?"

"Ready for what?"

"To go out into that." She nodded at the storm, still in full swing. The sky was pressing down on us. A flash of lightning lit up cliffs to our left, and on the right a long wall led out across the torn sea. The Seatoun Dam. We were on the Pencarrow side, with Wellington City across the water. Mira and I had picnicked out there just weeks ago.

"Oh shit," I muttered. "What are we doing here? What do you need me for?"

"You're a smart boy," Adelaide said. "You figure it out." Mikale and Nīkau manhandled me out of the car. I nearly tripped with my hands tied, but they caught me and set me on my feet. Nīkau put my hands between his, frowned and loosened the rope a little, then left me to Mikale.

It took approximately ten seconds for me to get soaked again. My hoodie and jeans stuck to me and I wanted to put my hood up, but I couldn't do it with Mikale holding my arms. Nīkau was doing something in the boot of the car, and emerged with a silver briefcase.

"You guys can't be serious," I said, eyeing it. I'd only ever seen them in movies, but I was pretty sure I knew what it was. "There's no way I'm gonna help you blow up the dam."

"See? You can figure things out for yourself," Adelaide said, voice raised over the storm and the slap of waves. She had a gun in her right hand, and spun it expertly. "And you don't really have a choice about what you do at the moment, do you? You wasted your choice when you chose to lie to us about Elspeth."

Despite the regular terrorist alerts, there hadn't been an actual attack in almost four years, not since the Nix Gen-ens bombings. That had, at least, exposed the Gen-ens hidden in our midst. This would be an attack on a massive scale, flooding Te Whanganui-a-Tara, tidal waves sweeping into the city, no upsides. And I was the key to it.

Mikale transferred his grip to my shoulder and spun me around, digging his fingers in when I almost fell. He began to push me towards the chain link fence.

I took two steps and lashed out with my foot, twisting under his hand and trying to shake him off. He stumbled and I threw myself into the darkness, shoes skidding on gravel, somehow keeping upright.

There was a shot, and loud swearing floated through the wind and rain. It would only be warning shots, right? They needed me alive.

I tried to run faster, but my balance was off with my hands tied in front of me. Adelaide had a torch and I could see my shadow spotlit against the silver raindrops, but I had no idea where I was running to. Where did this road go? Were there places to hide?

My foot hit a crack in the pavement and I went flying, hands and forearms skidding against the ground and jeans ripping. I tried to push myself up, ignoring the raw pain of my bloody hands, but I hadn't taken a step before someone tackled me to the ground.

"Let me go!" I screamed. "I won't do it! Help! Help me!"

"Who's gonna hear you way out here?" Mikale said in my ear. "Stop screeching like a baby and do what you're told."

He dragged me back to Adelaide and Nīkau. I jerked my shoulders, but it was mostly just for show. What was I going to do even if I did get free? The car wouldn't start for me so I couldn't steal that, and no one lived this side of the dam anymore. The nearest people were in Waiwhetū, at least two hours' sprint away.

We reached the fence and found the gate. Nīkau got out some sort of device.

"Nīkau, please, come on, you can't let them do this. What about Enzo? He's there, he's in the city!" No response. I tried again. He'd been quiet when they were plotting back in Horokiwi, maybe he was just going along with it because he had to. "You're a nurse, right? Didn't you have to take that hypocritical oath or something?"

"Hippocratic oath. Though the hypocritical oath is probably a better word for it, considering what they count as 'do no harm'." He fiddled with his device and nodded. "Cameras are on repeat. Don't touch the fence, it's electrified."

Mikale grabbed my bound hands and tried to shove them against the reader. I threw myself backwards, landed in the mud, turned and tried to run again, but Nīkau handed the bomb case to Adelaide and jumped after me. They held me while Mikale forced my hands up to the plate, knocking me on the head so I saw stars.

There was a beep and a soft click as the gate unlocked. I swore as they shoved me in.

"So you weren't lying about that, at least," Adelaide said, obviously pleased. "Maybe you're not such a waste of space. Forward."

The dam stretched into the swirling rain. I twisted and tried to duck between the two men, but there was no hope of that. Mikale shoved me onto the upper path. My feet skidded on the concrete.

"You do realise we're being nice," Mikale said. "We don't actually need you. Or at least, not all of you. We just need your wrist, and the chip in it. So if you make too much trouble, we could just cut it off."

I stopped struggling. Normally you had to have a pulse to activate chips, but I didn't want them giving it a go anyway.

My lips were salty with sea spray, and the wind and rain made it hard to breathe. Everything looked the same – endless concrete, sea far below on one side, on the other threatening to overflow the path with every ponderous wave. It was almost a surprise when Mikale pulled me to a stop. We'd reached the lock.

I put up token resistance as they forced my wrist against another reader, but I wanted to stay in one piece.

We were on the main control pathway now, above the seaside lock gate. I was surprised my chip had let me in here – Dad's friend really had given me full access – but now there was nothing stopping these people from setting up bombs in the most vulnerable places.

A path led into the darkness towards the harbour and the other lock gate. Adelaide ran her torch over the control buildings and down to one of the massive gates. I flashed back to the afternoons with Dad, watching the lumbering gates ease open, the water gush through and a ship tug at its moorings as it rose.

"This is the weakest spot," she yelled. "I'll set one up here. Nīkau, take the harbour gate. And take Kieran in case there are more readers." She opened the briefcase and removed something, then handed it to Nīkau.

More shoving from Mikale. I took the path beside the lock. This was a maintenance path, and the only railings were hip-height and open. I wondered if I could push Mikale into the water, but then I'd still have to deal with Nīkau and I might fall in myself.

There weren't any more fences to get through. Nīkau set up his bomb above the harbour lock gate, and then we met Adelaide back at the seaward gate. We started the long walk back to the car.

"How are you going to set them off?" I asked, yelling to be heard over a burst of thunder. I hadn't seen any timers, and if there was an ignition device maybe I could steal it and throw it into the sea.

Adelaide snorted and I heard her pat something. "It's a proximity switch. Got the receiver right here. When we're a kilometre away or the receiver's destroyed, the bombs go off. If you want to steal it and run away, be my guest. But you'll have to stay within that kilometre radius if you want to stop the bombs."

Scrap that, then. The seawater would kill it or carry it away.

"What's the point? Just flood Wellington for the hell of it? You'll only get the low-lying bits, anyway." Please let everyone be safe above sea level like they were supposed to be.

"First off, it's a king tide and we're in the middle of a storm. Second, it's a statement. And third, what's on the low-lying bit? The Genetics Authority, the cops and the courts. They'll be destroyed, or at least accessible only by dinghy. And let's hope

Doncaster's in the GA, working into the early hours, and has to be rescued."

I halted. Mikale poked me in the back and I gritted my teeth and moved forward, focusing on the road coming in and out of view as the rain gusted across it.

We were still about twenty metres from the fence when the first bomb blew. It lit up the night in orange, catching the raindrops pelting to earth. I threw myself to the ground, landing heavily and looking back to see a huge ball of fire erupting from the harbourside lock gates, hazy through the rain. The whole dam shook, and then the sound reached us, a sound like the cannons on Anzac Day but louder, much louder.

I hunched my shoulders as the sound rolled around us, echoing off the hills, but Mikale was dragging me to my feet and pulling me, stumbling, to the final gate. He wrenched my hand up to the reader. My ears rang. Mikale pushed me through, but once the gate clanged shut the grip on my arm slackened. If I was going to get away, now was the time.

I wrenched backwards. Mikale grabbed at me but I twisted and yanked my arm from his grip. Gravel slid beneath my sodden shoes. I tried to get my balance back, but the world was unsteady, what with the wind and the rain and the echo of the bomb and my slightly-concussed head. I stumbled two half steps, twisted as Mikale came after me. Light lit the sky – not a bomb, just lightning – and I arched away from him, throwing my weight to the side, ready to roll and come up running like in movies, but there was a fence in the way.

A touch of chain-link metal. I thought for a second that maybe the charge had gone, maybe the electric fence wasn't electric anymore, but then a huge kick of energy threw me forward.

Everything went black.

25

Chip

I dreamt of Mira. Her lips on mine, urgent and rough, but then a great weight hit my chest, again and again. I opened my mouth to scream but choked and coughed. Rain stung my face, sharp stones dug into my back. I rolled to my side and managed to bring myself to my knees, shaking and gasping great long breaths through crushed ribs. The stones dug into my grazed hands. I couldn't get enough oxygen and I felt like I'd been stuck inside a coffee grinder for days.

"We need to go before they start looking for us," a woman said. Adelaide. The last few hours came back to me in a rush and I retched, then threw up. "Eww."

"Are we taking him or leaving him?" Mikale.

"Bring him," Nīkau said. "We can't leave him here in this condition. Not with the dam about to go."

"We could drag him up the hill a bit," Mikale suggested, but Adelaide cut him off.

"He's just been electrocuted, Mikale."

"It was his own fault."

Adelaide kept on, regardless. "That shock will have fried his chip. There's no good reason not to take him with us, and if we take him he can't blab to the authorities."

"Yeah," I managed, but wasn't completely sure what I was agreeing with. In the distance, a siren began a thin wail, falling in and out of hearing with the buffeting wind.

Mikale and Nīkau each took one of my shoulders and hauled me up. I was still shaking – couldn't seem to stop shaking – and my legs wouldn't hold me. My back burned and pain stabbed my right sole whenever it touched the ground. Mikale swore at me, and they half dragged, half carried me to the car.

Nīkau sat with me in the back, somehow managing to sit me straight and buckle me in. My breath was coming light and quick and shaky, and my whole body fizzed with excess energy. They didn't bother retying my hands. I doubted I'd be able to run. Adelaide put the car in gear and slammed on the accelerator, and we jounced across the stones and up the hill towards the cliffs. My back chafed, my ribs and head ached, my hands stung, my foot burned.

I coughed again and ran my tongue over chapped lips. "Wha–" I took a shaky breath. "Where are we going?"

"A safe house," Nīkau said.

His face lit up in a flash of orange light that hollowed out his eyes and leeched the colour from his skin, and then the sound of the second explosion hit us, rolled off the hills and hit us again. The light faded slowly. Adelaide pushed the car to its limits, pressing me back into the seat, and I imagined the dam behind us blown outwards, the rush of water pouring into the harbour. A tidal wave bearing outwards, hitting Matiu Island and circling to wash over the coastal strip of road and railway, the wharfs, Oriental Bay. The people in their houses above the beach, waking to the roar of water sweeping over the road and the boat sheds, the pine trees' needles hissing in the wind and swirling into the torrent.

I couldn't stop shaking.

"You should thank Nīkau for bothering to stop and give you CPR," Adelaide half-yelled above the wind and the rain and the stones skittering beneath the tyres. "You weren't breathing."

I remembered my dream about Mira and my face heated. I couldn't look at Nīkau. "Thanks."

Nobody said anything for ages. I shut my eyes and breathed in, out. My heart was beating slow and heavy in my chest, so slow I wondered if it might stop. I bit my lip and tasted iron.

We were going up, zigzagging back and forth. An old road led up to Pencarrow, so that must be where the safe house was. I opened my eyes once and saw the edge of the cliff yawning to my right, rain ripping past and scattering in circles. Adelaide was driving as far from the edge as she could, but it wasn't far enough. I squeezed my eyes shut and tried not to think about it.

The road levelled off. I'd biked up here with Dad and Verity, and remembered the old suburb spread before us. Some houses had almost disintegrated, exposed to the south winds and the sea, but in the valley some looked almost untouched. At one time, it had been someone's idea of the perfect suburb, with sculpted parks and little shops and curving streets set into the hillsides. The people who'd lived here had been major resource hoarders.

You could see none of it in the storm, though. My heart was beginning to beat more normally and I felt less sick, but my body was still shaking and I was lightheaded. I tried resting my head against the cool window, but the pitted road made it judder and knock.

At last we came to a stop.

I didn't open my eyes. Adelaide and Mikale got out. Nīkau undid my seatbelt and slid an arm behind my shoulders. I made a feeble attempt to push him off, but my muscles were rubber. Mikale grabbed me from the front, and between them they got me out into the wet air.

I slid to the ground.

"Stand up!" Mikale said.

"I– I can't," I muttered, and I was trying. Mikale swore and he and Nīkau carried me to a gaping black hole of a door. The door slammed and the storm's noise lessened. I keeled over onto dusty carpet. Adelaide held a bottle of water to my lips, and I managed a few mouthfuls.

"Are there any burns?" Nīkau asked. I took stock of my aches and pains, and separated burning from the general wrongness.

"My right foot. And my back."

Nīkau stripped off my shoes and shirt and rubbed cold salve over the burns. He cleaned the dirt out of the grazes on my hands, covered them with stinging salve, then stuck gauze on all the salve. He checked me for broken ribs, but apparently they were just bruised. They didn't feel just bruised. Adelaide and Mikale had disappeared, but I could hear them arguing.

"You're lucky it didn't kill you," Nīkau said at last.

"I'm lucky you didn't kill me. You probably killed a few people with your tsunami."

"Oh, so you've got morals now? I thought you didn't mind people being killed in cold blood."

I didn't answer. Nīkau put everything back in his first-aid kit and got to his feet, sighing.

"I can leave you here for the night, or I can move you to a bed. Which would you prefer?"

The dust was making my nose itch. "How well-preserved are the beds?"

"Very. People clean this house out once or twice a year, stock it up. Just in case."

The peevs were a lot more organised than anyone gave them credit for.

"Bed."

He carried me to a bedroom and settled a blanket over me. The salve had deadened the pain in my back, but I still had to lie on my front. The shaking had lessened while Nīkau doctored me, but it returned as I lay there in the dark.

No one knew where I was. Adelaide had said my chip was fried, so they couldn't Pulse for me. I hadn't told anyone where I was going, and Nīkau had looped the cameras so I wouldn't have been caught on them. They'd have a record of my chip opening the gates, but where would that get them?

Shit. If people had died... Without me, the peevs would never have been able to access the dam. They might have done something small, something that would make a statement but wouldn't destroy half the city.

Or they may have figured out a way to destroy the whole city.

Whichever it was, I was still stuck in an abandoned 'burb with crazy lunatics with no idea what they'd do with me.

They brought you here and patched you up, said one part of my brain. I could still hear muffled raised voices from another room, and it sounded like Nīkau had joined the argument.

But they're not very happy about it, another part said. Mikale had threatened to chop my arm off, and Adelaide was way too fond of her gun.

And the worst part was, I knew they had a point. I'd never betrayed them, hadn't had the chance to, but I'd accepted what Doncaster had done. I'd accepted his offer to make everything legit between Mira and me, ignored Elspeth's murder. Even before that, I'd accepted Andrew's status as a second-class citizen. I'd accepted all these things as the price we had to pay to keep the world the way it was.

—— · ——

The next thing I knew light was streaming in the window. I opened my eyes, but mashed them closed as the light split my head in two. My stomach clenched. I rolled and threw up over the floor.

All my muscles ached, my burns throbbed, my ribs caught at my breath and I was still shaking. If anything, I felt worse than I had the night before – cold and sweaty and exhausted. I wiped my mouth and opened my eyes for a fraction of a second to see if there was water nearby, but there wasn't and the effort made my head explode with pain. I moaned.

A cool hand touched my temple.

"Hey, Kieran." Nīkau. "Your temperature's up. How are you feeling?"

"Like hell," I mumbled.

"Hungry?"

The thought of food made me sick. "Eurch." I dragged in a deep breath and hugged myself, trying to stop the shaking. "Water? I'm parched."

I heard Nīkau crouch beside me. He had to be almost on top of the vomit, but didn't seem to care.

"Open your eyes."

"No." I turned my face into the pillow. "Too bright."

The curtains clicked as Nīkau pulled them along their rails. Manual curtains. Retro. The light grew dimmer.

"Open your eyes."

"Why?" I moaned.

"Do it!"

I turned back to him and opened my eyes. The room was still way too bright, even though the curtains were thick. Nīkau peered into my eyes and swore.

I closed them again. "What?"

He yelled for Adelaide. It took a while for her to answer, but then I heard bare feet padding on carpet. A wave of heat hit me and I wanted to throw off the blanket, but it hurt too much to move.

"What is it?"

"They've been drugging him. His pupils are dilated. He's gone into withdrawal."

"Drugging him? I thought he was Doncaster's little lap dog."

"Apparently Doncaster doesn't even trust his lap dogs."

"Drugging me?" I managed. "Who? Why?"

They ignored me.

"Well, at least now we know his chip's definitely dead. Can we move him?"

"I don't want to until he's come out of it."

"How long?"

"I don't know. Depends on the dose. Could be days. Maybe you guys should go, get out of the way before they realise they need to search out here. The shielding on the house won't fool them for long."

There was a silence.

"Could we leave him?"

"Up to you. I wouldn't want to leave him alone."

I wanted to say "leave me," but the words stuck in my throat. I didn't want to be here by myself, and even if the police were searching for us there was no telling how long they'd take to find this house. "Shielding" didn't sound good. "Water," I said instead.

"I'll get it," Nīkau said, and left the room. Adelaide stood beside the bed and I could feel her looking down at me.

"Maybe you're not such a suck-up to the authorities. But being drugged doesn't completely excuse your behaviour."

"I'm not drugged."

She laughed. "Not now, you're not. They were doping you. Making sure you followed the rules."

I snorted into my pillow, and winced as the movement cut into my head. "I didn't follow the rules. And what, they've been slipping stuff into my food? Come on."

"They don't dope your food, stupid. That little chip in your arm is a miniature chemical factory. It takes things from your blood, whips them into shiny new molecules."

"That's bull." They weren't drugging me. Adelaide must have given me something, or...

"Well, electric shock won't give you these symptoms. Your body just can't handle things without its dose of happy."

The shaking hit again, stronger. Adelaide yelled for Nīkau and rolled me onto my side, hovering as I thrashed.

Finally it stopped, and I was left gasping for breath. Nīkau held a glass of water to my lips and I gulped it down.

"They do it to people who might cause trouble," he said, wiping my mouth with a pillow case corner. "We think it's also a sort of punishment. Deactivate your chip, go into withdrawal. Repent, rechip, and all the symptoms go away. Thank god they never thought I was a troublemaker."

"But I'm not a troublemaker," I groaned. Why would they do this to me? "Except liking Mira, I've never done anything illegal. Well, nothing *that* illegal."

"So you actually do have feelings for Mira?" Adelaide said. I opened my eyes enough to glare at her.

"Of course! Did you– did you think it was all show?"

She barked out a laugh. "Pretty much."

"It wasn't." But there was no way I was going to convince her. "Look, leave me somewhere people can find me and I swear I won't say anything about you guys. Swear on my life. I can handle the withdrawal okay, it's not that bad." My migraine drove a point deep into my skull and I squeezed my eyes shut, totally destroying my argument.

"It's going to get worse," Nīkau said.

"Worse?"

"Hallucinations. Paranoia. More convulsions. Thirst. You can't be left alone."

"Great. Didn't you say it all stops if they put a chip back in me? I think I'd rather have a chip."

Mikale hissed from the doorway. "See? He *wants* to be one of them. Just like Enzo. He doesn't care about the cost. What the hell are we supposed to do now, wait with an invalid until the cops take us away?"

"I'll stay here if you two don't want to risk it," Nīkau said. "Maybe he'll talk more sense when it's over. And anyway, Mikale, I don't remember you dealing well when you lost your chip, and you *chose* to take it out."

They left me alone. I lost track of time, barely noticing when someone tipped my head back and put water to my lips. I dreamed of a wall of water bearing down on me, of lightning ripping the sky open like tissue paper, and Doncaster's eyes watching me by satellite, even though my chip was dead. My head was taken apart with a diamond-edged saw, and my stomach clenched and ached from throwing up. I didn't know how many hours passed, or how many days. I didn't care.

26
Awake

BIRDS SANG.

I groaned and put my hands over my ears. There was no way any living thing should be singing when I felt like– like–

Like what?

I opened my eyes. The thin bar of light under the heavy curtains didn't hurt my eyes. Or at least, the pain didn't make me want to throw up. This was progress.

Those stupid birds could still shut up, though.

The first thing I did was take a shower. I had to lean against the wall, but the dizzy spells weren't as bad and my stomach was sore from hunger instead of upset. My burnt back and foot were still tender, my ribs still ached, but I heal fast and it wasn't terrible. I gulped down some coppery shower water, stripped the gauze off my hands and watched my fingers grow wrinkly. I felt like I was washing away not just the dirt and sweat of the last few days, but the last of the drug as well.

Nīkau had left a spare set of clothes on a chair. I stood in front of the mirror and stared at myself. My eyes were sunken grey shadows, and my hair stuck up in wet spikes. The clothes could have fit an elephant, but at least they were clean. I ran my fingers through my hair, trying not to look like an escaped criminal. I parted it to the left, then to the right, then messed it all up again.

Now it reminded me of Mira.

Adelaide, Nīkau and Mikale were talking in low voices in the main room. I heard my name.

"Go, Kier," I muttered, took a deep breath, and pulled the door open.

The three of them were sitting around the table eating crackers. Nīkau came to check my temperature, then nodded.

"Just about back to normal. How do you feel?"

I could have made a list of all my aches and pains and burns, but shrugged instead. Nīkau waved towards a chair, but I hesitated. They'd kidnapped me, after all. Did I really want to sit with them, like nothing had happened? He raised an eyebrow when I didn't move, and held out a cracker.

I took it and sat.

Adelaide cleared her throat. "There've been ... developments ... while you've been out of it."

"What developments?"

"They think you're dead."

My mouth fell open and the cracker fell out. "Say what?"

Nīkau ran a hand through his hair, looking almost as tired as I did. "They know you went onto the dam, but they don't know you came off it. Your chip died between the explosions. The media is pretty evenly balanced between blaming Outsiders for kidnapping and murdering you, and blaming you for leading the bomb team yourself."

I was still stuck on the fact that everyone thought I was dead. "And you didn't think to say 'hey, everyone, he's here'?"

Adelaide glared. "We could have up and left, but we stayed to look after you. You think we'd let ourselves be arrested just because of their little misunderstanding?"

I rubbed at my eyes. "God, my parents. Verity. Mira." Did Mira even care? I felt a sharp pain in my chest. No, I would imagine she cared, even if she probably didn't. "Was anyone killed by the flood?"

"No," Nīkau said. The ban against living below sea-level had worked, then. "A few injuries and a heart attack, but I don't think that counts."

"Sure it doesn't. You know they're going to come after you now."

"They already are."

"Great," I muttered. "So how long have we got before I'm rescued and you guys are stuck in jail?"

Mikale shot me a vicious look and went to stare out the window.

"Maybe twenty-four hours, if we're lucky," Adelaide said. "So far they've relied on their sensors, but they'll come through on foot to make sure they haven't missed anything. We want to be out of here before then, and now you're up and about..."

I didn't feel that up and about. "So you guys are going to drag me back to Horokiwi."

"There's no one there," Adelaide said. "Abandoned, thanks to you."

"I didn't narc. I'm not a spy."

None of them answered. I put my head in my hands.

"Have you got any painkillers?"

"You got the last of them," Nīkau told me.

"We're moving out at dusk," Adelaide said. "If you want to come with us, fine."

Mikale scoffed.

"If you want to go back to the city, make your own way to the beach and take your chances. Who knows, maybe they'll go easy on you."

"Or there'll be a tragic accident. Or they'll pump you so full of drugs you end up a vegetable," Mikale said.

I froze. "Uh, what?" My brain was still foggy, but it felt sharper than it had in a long time. Years, even. "What did you say?"

"He's just trying to scare you," Nīkau said. "But yeah, it happens."

I stumbled back and my chair fell over with a crash. "What day is it?"

Adelaide sighed like she'd expected nothing more of me and went to make a cup of tea. It was Nīkau who answered.

"The thirtieth. Why?"

"Oh god." I was shaking again, and my legs wouldn't hold me. I sat on the floor, an upturned chair leg digging into my back. "I've got to get to the hospital."

I hauled myself upright and went for the door.

Nīkau grabbed me, grip tight on my bicep. "We can't go outside until it's dark."

"I've got to get to the hospital."

"Yeah, we heard that. Why?"

"Lucas." I twisted, turning desperate eyes on him. "My cousin is up to die tomorrow. I've got to save him."

"Whoa, what?" Adelaide said.

"I have to go!" I yelled, struggling from Nīkau's grip. Nīkau and Mikale joined forces to drag me to the floor, and then Mikale sat on me.

"Now," Nīkau said pleasantly, crouching down to my eye level. "Explain further."

I thrashed some more but it hurt my injuries too much and I was never going to get out from under rugby-built Mikale. "My cousin – Lucas – has been in a waking coma for four years. They're going to kill him tomorrow. Ten in the morning. We were in a car crash. They said it was a brain injury, but..."

"But you think he's been drugged?" Adelaide asked.

I nodded into the floor. Mikale let me sit up, but still held my arm in an iron grip.

I felt like crying.

"Why?"

"I–" Maybe it was just hope. But if there was a chance... "He used to spend tonnes of time outside the city. We'd find camping houses out there–"

Camping houses... or safe houses? And why had he been so weird, that last day?

I swallowed. "We found a car, did it up. Crashed it. I got through okay, he... didn't. But maybe they started drugging me then, and did him too. So I gotta go." I tried to ease my arm out of Mikale's grip. "I gotta save him."

"And how are you going to do that?" Mikale asked. "You can't just walk out with him."

"I can try. I can get friends to help."

"How are you going to get into the hospital in the first place?"

I closed my eyes. My brain was humming, thinking through all the connections, everything I could do to get Lucas out. I wasn't used to it moving so fast.

This would have been useful during exams.

"They let me in after hours. The nurses know me." I opened my eyes. "Are the nurses in on it? The doctors?"

"Some of the doctors," Nīkau said. "Not all. Not the nurses. Do you think they'd agree to care for patients for four years just so the authorities can kill them legally?"

"You were a nurse, weren't you," I said. He nodded. "Did you know?"

"I found out. I wasn't supposed to. That's why I left."

"There's a fire escape three doors down from Lucas's room. We can manage him down the ramp. We'll find somewhere and camp… I've got to get his chip out."

"Now you're thinking," Adelaide nodded, but it wasn't a very nice nod. "And what are you going to do when he's dying of withdrawal? If he's drugged, his dose'll be a lot higher than yours was, and much harder to survive."

Nīkau cleared his throat.

"They have an antidote."

"What?" Three voices at the same time.

Nīkau held up his hands, warding off the stares. "It's only for special circumstances. Sometimes they make deals with people. And it's incredibly hard to get hold of."

"But you *can* get hold of it," I said.

Nīkau stared at his hands.

"Yes."

27
Night

I'd hoped the Outsiders might have a motorboat stashed somewhere, but no. They had a double e-kayak. E-kayaking would still be faster than driving all the way round the harbour, though, and sneakier too.

"You sure you're up to this?" Nīkau asked, watching me lower myself into the front seat.

"I'm good."

"Let me know if you need a break, and I'll paddle on my own for a bit." To Adelaide's surprise and Mikale's disgust, Nīkau had volunteered to come with me, saying there was no way I'd make it on my own. He was also the only one who knew where to find the antidote.

"I said I'm good. And the jet will help, won't it?"

We pushed off.

I was not exactly *good*. My ribs ached, the burnt skin on my back and foot was too tight, my arms were stiff, the grazes on my hands were barely healed. But anger surged through me, fizzed in my veins, pushed me forward stroke by stroke by stroke. I'd never felt like this, not when I was twelve and still in control of my own brain, not when I found out what Doncaster had done. I understood people who planted bombs, who raved on the newscasts before they got tasered or dragged into vans.

The dark line of the dam cut off in jagged shapes, but out in the middle of the water it was still, like nothing had changed. I kept having to remind myself this was a stealth mission, keep my strokes less violent and more sly, save my energy. Ripples spread behind us, criss-crossing and glinting white, the underwater jet a soft whoosh.

We passed the point at Miramar and then Roseneath, narrowly missing the top of a lighthouse poking above the surface. The city lights glowed, flickered on water alongside the scattered silver moon.

Oriental Bay was gone, the sand under a few metres of salt water. We got to Waitangi Park around low-tide, and Nīkau steadied the kayak as I staggered out. I pulled myself up a half-drowned pōhutukawa tree to the footpath, and when I turned back he was just a black shape disappearing into the night. He'd kayak around to Evans Bay, and take a shortcut to the hospital from there.

Courtenay Place was knee-deep in water and deserted. None of the streetlights were working, but the moon was bright enough to see the tide mark on the buildings, just above the tops of the doors. Seaweed draped across park benches and tree branches lurked in the water to trip me up. Shit, maybe the water had even reached Xiao's building. It stood above sea level, but only just. I searched it out on the skyline and saw it, standing tall but windows dark.

Further up Taranaki Street it was drier. There were a few people out, and I pulled my borrowed baseball cap down, but no one glanced my way and a few even sped away. I'd expected more police around, but maybe I was in the wrong part of town.

I couldn't rescue Lucas on my own, and Nīkau would be busy stealing antidote. Andrew was the best bet for muscle, and he wouldn't give me away to anyone. I hoped.

I passed school, its windows hollow eyes in the night, cut a right and slogged up the hill to Andrew's house in Mt Cook. When I reached his window I was shaky, sweating through every pore and wishing I hadn't drunk all my water an hour ago.

Faint light glowed from behind the dark mode window. I tried to tap softly on the glass, but my hand shook and juddered it. Whoops.

There was a rustle of movement and the glass cleared to transparent. I blinked and shielded my face, the light stabbing my eyes. Even through the triple-glazing I heard a gasp, and as my eyes adjusted the shape in the window resolved into a person. But not the person I'd been expecting.

"*Mira*?"

—— · ——

Her eyes were hollowed and her face blank with shock, but otherwise she looked as amazing as ever. I smiled broadly, instinct, before I remembered our last conversation.

I don't think I can stand to look at you.

The echo of her slamming the front door behind me.

My fault.

If I'd told Doncaster screw it, the world needs to know, what would have happened? Mira would still be with me. She would have helped try to spread the word. I wouldn't have gone to the Outsiders, maybe they would never have figured out how to get onto the dam, and the city wouldn't be washed with the dregs of a king tide.

But I'd still be drugged. Lucas would still be dead tomorrow. And if we'd tried to say anything, the authorities would have silenced us somehow, in ways I didn't want to think about.

Now, I had hope. Anger. And if Lucas got out of this alive, I was going to do what I could to let the world know about Doncaster.

That was the decision Mira had wanted me to make, wasn't it? That no matter the futility, no matter if you thought you could never make a difference, you had to try.

Mira was still staring at me. Why was she here, of all places? I had a plan with Andrew, knew where I stood with him, I thought. With a little bit of convincing, he'd help. Mira, though...

She slowly pushed open the window and put out a hand. Mine lifted to meet hers, but she touched my arm instead, wrapped her hand around it, squeezed like she was making sure I was real.

Andrew loomed behind her. He blinked.

"Holy shit. Kier?"

"Surprise?" I said weakly. Mira took her hand away, the shock on her face beginning to turn. Was that a tear in the corner of her eye, or was I imagining what I wanted to see?

"You're alive."

"Yeah."

"We thought–" She broke off.

I'd thought I knew all her expressions, had memorised them, but this one was new. Confused? Angry? Hopeful? She squeezed her eyes shut, opened them again, and yes, those were definitely tears threatening to spill over.

Maybe she'd forgiven me.

Mira slapped me. Hard.

"Ow," I managed.

"That's for making us think you were dead," she told me in a hoarse whisper as I rubbed my cheek. "And for whatever the *hell* you did to get wrapped up in the *dam* attack. And for–"

"Hey, hey, not that he doesn't deserve it for *having a secret illegal girlfriend* and not telling me," Andrew said, carefully taking Mira's shoulders and shifting her away from the window. "Or for thinking *that* was a good idea from the start–"

"The percentage match is complete crap," I burst out.

"–whatever, I'm defending you dude – I think maybe we should let Lazarus in before we wake the neighbours, and give him a chance to explain himself before we jump to the corporal punishment."

He pushed the window further open and extended a strong hand to help me in, like when we were kids sneaking in after wandering the bush. When I was settled on the floor of his room (strangely tidy, I guess because Mira was here), he gave me a lung-squeezing bear hug and pointed me to his desk chair. The wall screen behind it was showing a freeze-frame from some cop show, a board scattered with red string and coloured squares.

"I'm so glad you're alive. Details. Now."

"Yeah," Mira said. "What the hell happened?"

My feet were very happy about sitting in the chair, especially the one that was still healing from the electric fence burn. I took a deep breath. "I'll tell you if you help me rescue Lucas. Tonight. Like, now."

"Now?" Andrew shot Mira a glance. "No offence, Kieran, but you look like a zombie after a Conquesterra campaign. Just, like, still in one piece. Maybe you take a breather. You can spare twenty minutes, can't you?" He passed me a glass of water from his bedside table and I sculled it, the water soothing my throat.

Could I spare twenty minutes? I didn't know. My blood was still fizzing, and the need to just keep going, keep going, keep going, thrummed through me, blocking out anything else. Nīkau would be coming ashore in Evans' Bay by now, dragging the kayak up what was left of the beach. Picking his way through the bush alongside the road up and over Mt Victoria, heading to the hospital.

"Kieran!"

"I'm meeting Nīkau behind the hospital at three-thirty," I said, almost tripping over my words. "With Lucas."

"Okay, so we've still got a few hours. Who's Nīkau?"

"I know him," Mira said. "So you've been with the Horokiwi Outsiders?"

"Yeah. They kidnapped me."

"They *what?*"

I told them the broad strokes of what led up to the dam attack, my words tripping over themselves. Mira had her arms crossed, her face darkening as I went on, while Andrew's eyes grew wider and wider.

"Okay," Andrew said at last. "So now you're a wanted terrorist, you thought maybe you'd go one better and rescue Lucas?"

"I mean, not quite, but yeah?"

He nodded. "And you want my help. Which means, if we're caught, it'll be jail or a re-education workcamp." He blew out a breath and nodded again. "Okay."

I didn't think I'd heard right. "What?"

"Okay. I know what Lucas means to you. I was kinda surprised you hadn't tried some hare-brained scheme before."

"Hare-brained? Excuse me? When have my schemes ever been hare-brained?"

"No comment."

"Yes, comment!"

He grinned. "You seem different. Like... you got your spark back, zombie looks aside. What's your plan?"

I took a deep breath, a rush of gratitude joining the roil of emotions inside me. He'd been my best friend since we were five, so I'd hoped he'd agree, but still – he'd risk jail or a re-education workcamp for me. Then guilt: I hadn't told him about his gene category, that the authorities were screwing with him.

But I could tell him later. After we'd got Lucas out. "I– thanks, man. If all goes well, you'll be back home by dawn. The plan is, we get in by sweet-talking the nurses–"

"You're supposed to be dead or a terrorist," Andrew pointed out.

"I'll sweet-talk the nurses," I repeated, louder. "And then we gotta get Lucas out the fire escape. Nīkau's meeting us outside, and then we'll escape into the bush."

"How are you going to deal with a semi-comatose guy?" Andrew asked.

"He won't be semi-comatose. I hope."

"What?"

I squeezed my eyes shut, then opened them again. And I told them what I'd been through *after* the dam attack.

"Drugs?" Mira said incredulously, speaking for the first time in a while. "They drug people?"

"It's not unbelievable, is it? I mean if you, um, don't want to get pregnant, you apply for contraceptives through the chip, don't you?"

Silence.

"You think maybe your accident... wasn't an accident?" Andrew'd caught on fast.

"I don't know. Maybe the accident was real, and they just took advantage of it. Maybe they planned the whole thing. It doesn't matter. I'm still getting him out."

"And what if it really is a brain injury?"

I couldn't answer.

"Okay," Andrew said after the long pause, clapping one of my shoulders on his way out of the room. "If you're going to sweet-talk the nurses, you'll need a shower. I'll get you a towel."

Mira and I were left alone. She'd scrunched herself in a chair in the corner, her hoodie sleeves pulled over her fists. I wondered if I'd given her the right details to prevent another slap.

"Not that I'm not glad to see you, but... what are you doing here?" I asked awkwardly.

She met my eyes. "I came to ask Andrew about you. I mean, best friend, sort-of-girlfriend, together we must be able to figure out what happened to you, right? Then we got a bit... carried away. My mum thinks I'm staying at Te Aroha's."

"Right." I scuffed my foot against the carpet. "What, um, was your theory?"

"Aliens," she said, straight-faced.

"Aliens," I repeated, pausing to give the idea its proper weight.

"Well, that was our first theory. The rest..." She gestured behind me, and I turned in the desk chair to see the wall screen. I realised the red string and coloured squares weren't from a cop show – they were Mira and Andrew's working.

"Wow," I said, taken aback. "Did you guess anything right?"

"Not even close."

Andrew reappeared with the towel and a pile of his clothes fresh from the laundry. "Here you go. Go wild with the shampoo, then we can get out of here."

I took them and crept down the hall to the bathroom to have the world's shortest shower. When I got out, the cuffs of the borrowed jeans rolled up and belt cinched tight, Andrew was ready with a backpack and three water bottles, wearing a black baseball cap that shadowed his face.

Three water bottles. One for Lucas? Unless...

Mira was standing at the window, one of Andrew's old sports caps on her head.

"You're coming?" I asked stupidly.

"Can't let you go and have all the fun."

"Does... this mean I'm forgiven?"

"No. Still deciding."

"Oh." I swallowed. "Right." I dumped the damp, salty-stiff safe house clothes in Andrew's laundry basket and followed them out the window.

"I've got clothes for Lucas, and food and water," Andrew said. "Your tsunami did something to the pipes, by the way, but I've got *connections* now at Allocations, so my parents shouldn't notice any emergency drinking water going missing."

"Um, is that fraud?" Mira asked in a low voice as we started down the hill. "Corruption? Hmm, no wait. Embezzling?"

"Shut up," Andrew said easily.

I felt steadier now than I had getting to Andrew's house. The break had done me good, not to mention the vote of confidence from Andrew and – more unbelievably – Mira. "What else has happened? Is Xiao all right?"

"His building got evacuated after the storm, the ground floor had some damage. He's staying with his aunty."

"Oh. Good. I guess. I mean at least he's not..."

"Yeah."

28
Rescue

IT WAS ALMOST THREE in the morning, and there was a ten o'clock curfew. I was lucky I hadn't been caught earlier. The curfew made it harder to get to the hospital, dodging street lights and taking the back streets, but we reached the hospital gates okay.

I paused, staring at the stark lights of the reception.

"You got your sweet-talk prepared, right?" Andrew asked. I shook my head. "Oh goody."

"Shut up."

Mira nudged me forward. "It'll be fine."

It felt like it was true. I could do this. I was good at talking, wasn't I? Even when drugged. I should be even better clear-headed. "Okay. Let's go."

The waiting room was empty, eerie. I recognised the nurse on reception, but didn't know her well. At least she hadn't been there for my meltdown. She looked up with a distant, professional smile that quickly froze.

Andrew and Mira hung back, ducking their heads away from the cameras. I walked right up to the desk and smiled at the nurse. It only took a few seconds for her to twitch a reluctant smile in return.

"Look, I have no idea what you might have heard about me, but it's probably not true. You know me," I glanced at her name-tag, "Sue. You know I wouldn't do what they say I've done. And I'm obviously not dead, am I?"

She shook her head.

I sighed and looked as tragic as I could. It wasn't hard.

"Lucas–" my voice cracked. I swallowed and tried again, not sure how much of this was acting and how much was real. "It's Lucas's last night. You couldn't let me..."

"You want to see him?" the nurse said gently. I nodded, feeling my eyes burn.

"I promise I won't do anything stupid. I just want to..."

She stared at me, sizing me up, then nodded briskly. "You're a good boy. Give me your wrist."

"I– uh..." I cleared my throat. "I don't have a chip."

She stared at me like I'd cut off my own arm.

"Is there, um, any other way?" I shifted my weight to my other foot.

Sue sighed and gave me a long look, then turned to her screen. "I can open the doors manually. But only for fifteen minutes, you hear?" Then she glanced at me and her voice softened. "If you need longer, just give me a ring. All the handsets direct here."

I nodded. "Thank you. It's been a tough week."

"The less I know, the better. But be careful. I don't like seeing a nice boy like you in this kind of trouble."

I nodded. "I'll try." I glanced back at Andrew and Mira. "And, uh, my friends can come too? They won't be any trouble. They brought chocolate. Lucas's last taste of choc–" I broke off like it was too much for me, and hoped Sue wouldn't ask to search them.

“Oh, all right,” Sue said kindly. “Go on through.”

“Thank you so much, this really means the world–”

Andrew dragged me towards the ward doors. Mira was already there, one hand ready to push them open. Sue smiled and turned back to her screen.

“Good job,” Andrew muttered once we were through. “Now lead the way.”

How many times had I followed this path? More than a hundred. Five hundred? A thousand? I stared at the scuffs on the floor and followed the ghost of myself up the stairs and through the halls. Avoided looking at the place the Gen-en had slid down the wall.

Lucas was lying on his side, turned towards the window. As I came around the bed his eyes opened, and I jumped back.

But he wasn’t seeing me. It was just like every other time.

Mira nudged me and I kept going. It was almost three-thirty. We probably had ten minutes until the nurse thought to check on us, but Nīkau had warned he might set off a few alarms.

“Hey, Lucas,” I whispered, taking his left arm. “This won’t hurt. Yet.”

I pulled the de-chipper Nīkau had given me out of my pocket. It looked a bit like a bike bell. Andrew stared at it.

“Is that it?”

I shrugged. “So they tell me.” I felt up and down Lucas’s wrist for the tiny bump of the chip, but couldn’t find it at first. Lucas turned his head to look out the window and pulled his arm away. I swore under my breath, and wished my hands would keep steady.

The second brush over, I found it – right under the skin, a small hard thing that moved beneath my fingers.

"So you just press the button, and the chip's screwed?" Andrew whispered.

"I hope so." Nīkau said there was no way to tell whether the chip was dead, until it wouldn't work on a door or you started getting withdrawal from the drugs. With the really heavily-drugged cases, when the withdrawal set in, you had a few minutes to administer the antidote before cardiac arrest. A window between knowing the antidote was needed, and needed now, and death.

I pressed the button.

There was a click, and as Nīkau had promised, nothing happened. I pressed the button twice more to make sure.

Lucas was still staring out the dark window with a glazed expression.

Now came the hard part. I pulled back the covers. "Okay, everyone grab a sheet corner."

"Can't he walk?"

"It takes him ten minutes to get to the physio room down the hall. Andrew, you're strongest, so you take his bottom half and Mira and I will take the top."

Andrew sighed but began dragging the covers onto the floor. Mira took the opposite side of the bed from me, and I bunched the top left corner in my fist.

"One, two, three," Mira said, and we heaved on our corners. Lucas made a small grunt of surprise, but didn't take his eyes off the window.

I hoisted my sheet corner over my shoulder and we manoeuvred him carefully over the bed frame. The hallway was clear, and we shuffled towards the exit doors, then through to the emergency doors.

"Ready?"

Mira and Andrew nodded. I took a deep breath and leant on the emergency bar, pushing the door open as far as it would go.

Sirens wailed. We ran out the fire escape and careened down the ramp, turned the first corner, then the second. The last leg of the ramp didn't reach the ground, but began to lower as we approached. It was still a metre from the ground when I reached it, but we couldn't stop. Mira and I negotiated the drop without hitting Lucas's head, and Andrew had an easier job with his feet.

We sprinted towards the trees with Lucas swinging between us, and made it in what was probably a world record for three people carrying another in a makeshift hammock. The trees' shadows hid us from the hospital, but we had to get out of here fast.

"Nīkau!" I hissed, staring round into the darkness. My eyes still hadn't adjusted. "Nīkau!"

There was no answer.

"You're sure–" Mira began.

"Of course I'm sure this is the place!" I snapped. "Look, there's the sump. He said beside the sump."

"What the hell is a sump?" Andrew asked, panting. I ignored him. I couldn't call any louder, or everyone would know we were here.

I felt like I was going to be sick. Without the antidote, Lucas would die and all this would have been for nothing.

The sirens cut off. They must have figured out there wasn't any fire, that the fire door was open, that Lucas was gone. I swore.

And then there was a crashing shatter of glass.

"Kieran!" Nīkau bellowed, and something small and white flew into the night. "Kieran! Go!"

I couldn't move. Mira pushed her corner of the sheet into my hands, leaving me staggering, and sprinted towards the spot where the white had landed, her silhouette clear against the building. She bent down, still running, grabbed at it, turned and sprinted back.

I was still standing frozen. Nīkau was in there. Nīkau had broken a window to get me this antidote, and now he was probably being tasered or wrestled to the ground or shot.

"Come on, Kieran, he said go, we have to go," Mira said, sliding the small white thing into my pocket and pulling us into the trees.

—— · ——

We carried Lucas up into the bush behind the hospital, at the south end of Mt Vic. He was lighter than I expected, I guess from spending four years living off hospital food.

"How – long?" Andrew grunted. Maybe it wasn't just that Lucas was light – maybe Andrew was taking a lot of the weight so I wouldn't have to. Mira too – her face was red and white in splotches and she was puffing badly, but she kept going, and growled when I tried to take more of our side of the sheet. Moonlight shone down through the leaves.

"Not much further, we should get to the ridge," I managed, but Andrew shook his head.

"No, I mean – how long – until he starts – getting sick?"

I didn't know. The antidote was in my pocket, and my heart squeezed at the thought of Nīkau stuck back there, caught or tasered or dead... No, I couldn't think about that now. Nīkau would be all right. Wouldn't he?

I'd started feeling awful straight after my chip died, but that was probably the electrocution. Nīkau (no, don't think) had first noticed it the next morning, so at most six hours. Lucas had got a much stronger dose than me (if it was a dose, and not just plain old brain damage), so maybe it'd be faster. I'd always thought Nīkau would be here to do all the technical stuff, and I hadn't really listened when he explained.

"We just have to watch him," I said. Leaves crunched and slid beneath my feet. We reached the ridge line.

Lucas started convulsing.

"Lay him down!" Mira hissed.

I tried to do it gently, but he was thrashing so much we couldn't do anything gently. One of Lucas's legs jerked out of Andrew's grasp and kicked him in the stomach, but Andrew caught at a spindly branch and managed to right himself. Mira put her hands under Lucas's head to stop it hitting the ground as he moved.

"Now, Kieran," she yelled. "I'm pretty sure this is the right time!"

"Right," I muttered, fumbling with my pocket. My fingers closed around the drug pen, but slipped off. I clenched it like I'd clenched crayons back in kindergarten and drew it out. "Right. Pull back his shirt."

Andrew ripped at his buttons and Lucas's thrashing did the rest. I pulled the lid off the pen and stared at it. These were designed to be used by anyone, to be easy and obvious, but I'd never had to use one before. And this wasn't a normal drug. Nīkau had been so clear that this had to be done right.

"Here," Mira said, breathing hard."Give it to me."

"What?" I said. "Nīkau–"

"I know how to use them, all right?"

I remembered her sister and didn't ask how. I tossed her the pen.

She pressed it to Lucas's chest, around where his heart should be, and held it there. Almost immediately, his limbs stilled, and his breath came out in a long sigh. She kept holding the pen.

I bit at my lip. I hadn't been able to do it.

"He's – he's not ... dead?" I said, when Lucas had been still for way too long. Andrew and Mira shook their heads.

"He's breathing," Andrew said, rocking back on his heels. "Do we move him?"

I stared up and down the track and checked my watch. It was just past four o'clock, and the sky was greying towards dawn, lone birds calling in the darkness. Morning joggers would be here in the next hour or so, the early crazy ones. We had to move off the path. "Yes. Just like before?"

"You take his feet," Andrew said.

29
Clearing

We headed south, away from town, crossing a deserted Constable Street and heading back up into the bush. There was a clearing off the track, far enough that the trees hid us from view. We were the other side of the ridge now, and you could see Kilbirnie, the dark shadow of the sea flooding halfway across, glimmering in the moonlight. We laid Lucas on a patch of long grass, and put Andrew's spare hoodie over him to keep him warm.

He could wake up soon. He could be the Lucas from four years ago, sixteen-year-old Lucas.

I was older than he'd been when the car crashed.

"So what are you going to do now?" Mira said. When I didn't answer she glanced at Andrew. "Kier?"

"Nīkau... he was gonna take us up country," I muttered. "Find another Outsider group."

But Nīkau was gone. I swallowed. The police would know I was alive, that I'd broken into the hospital and stolen Lucas. Now I was a bomb accomplice and a kidnapper. A proper fugitive.

Mira eyed me. The truth was, I didn't know what to do. Wander up the coast, avoiding auto-tasers, hope we ran into friendly Outsiders? Go hide out in one of Lucas's camping houses until they stopped looking for us? Like they'd ever stop looking for us.

My eyes fell on Lucas.

"I want to do something," I said quietly. "I want to show everyone what they're doing. I want to stop them drugging people. I want to get Nīkau back."

If he was still alive.

Mira nodded, like maybe she respected me a bit more. "Yeah. I could talk to Jessica today, find out where Nīkau is, what kind of court options we have."

It took me a while to remember who Jessica was. The lawyer Mira interned with. I shook my head. "It's the courts who did this. It's the whole *system*. If we do it their way, nothing will ever change. We need to do something bigger."

She stared at me. "You're talking the Doncaster thing too."

"Yeah."

"So um... you're kind of sounding like a terrorist, you know that?" Andrew said. "You already blew up the dam, so now you're gonna move onto Parliament?"

"Of course I wouldn't blow up Parliament," I said, annoyed. "And I *didn't* blow up the dam, it wasn't–"

Mira laid a hand on my arm and I stopped, losing my train of thought. My arm tingled, her touch light. Maybe she...? But no. Focus. I dragged my attention from her hand to her words. "Not that I don't agree with you, but you're still getting over withdrawal and being electrocuted and you haven't slept since yesterday."

"I'm fine!"

"We do things properly, or not at all. And that means you need to sleep. Lucas needs to recover. Nīkau's either... dead... or they've got him in a cell. Things aren't going to change much in a few days."

She had a point.

"But... Kieran," Andrew began. "I know it's awful what they did to you and Lucas, but you don't need to go do something completely idiotic to stop them. Like Mira said, do it the proper way, through the courts, and then you don't need to be a fugitive."

"It's not just about me and Lucas." I glanced at Mira. Better start telling the truth sometime, right? "I've been working for Edward Doncaster."

"You *what*?" Andrew punched me in the arm. "Congrats, man. And you didn't *tell* me?"

"He started the Great Plagues. On purpose."

Andrew stared at me, mouth slack.

"And–" I took a deep breath. "They're stopping you having kids. There's nothing wrong with your, uh... it's just they do this genome category thing, and you..."

I trailed off. Andrew had gone white.

"I'm what, Kieran?"

"They think your genome is too low-quality." He'd always known his genes weren't great, but I guess it was different having the official word on it. Having that official word destroy his relationship with Prajna, cut off a future he could have had.

Mira shot to her feet. "But– the whole point of Matching is to stop bad genes meeting! So we don't have to rely on genetic engineering or– or stopping people having kids!"

"Apparently it's not enough. They want perfect." I'd almost told her that day, cycling back from Horokiwi. Had the drugs stopped me saying something? Or just my own stupid logic?

"Why don't people know about this?" Mira paced, fists clenching and unclenching. "Any of it?"

"Maybe some do. And they think it's an okay price to pay, like killing every Gen-en ever because people think they started the Plagues."

"Yeah, but Gen-ens are soulless maniacs–" Her brow furrowed and she turned to stare at me. "Okay, maybe that's just something they told us. Oh!" She patted at the pocket of her windbreaker and brought out my holosphere. "Where did you get all those pictures?"

Heat rose up my neck. "Oh, well, I was just looking through your socials and..."

"No, the other ones." She threw the holosphere at me, and the picture of the beach with the kids appeared, salt spray and waves.

"They were already on there. They looked historical, so I thought you might be interested–"

"Show more," Mira said, impatient. "There are some weird ones."

I threw it up again, Van Gogh's Almond Blossoms, and again, and this time there was a picture I'd never seen before. A woman with long hair, a baby wrapped in chequerboard red and grey in her lap. She wore a red and grey square stitched onto her shirt, and her expression was dark, anger caught and held beneath the surface. Her name was there – Carla Generi – just like the history flash-cards I'd scrolled through on my tablet. But this hadn't been one of them.

"Like that," Mira said as it fell back into my hand.

"That wasn't on there before. I checked all the files. Some of them were corrupted, though..."

"They're Gen-ens, right? They haven't got the tattoo, but their clothes..."

"Yeah, I guess."

I threw it up again. One of my photos appeared, and disappeared. I threw it again. A globe of the world. A Zephyr abstract. And then another unknown, this time a man midspeech on a stage, red and grey square on his shirt. The camera angle was haphazard, backs of heads taking up half the shot, like it had been taken by someone in the crowd.

"Hey, that's that guy…" I began.

"James How. Better Human Manifesto," Mira supplied. "But he looks younger. We always see him when he's in his thirties. He barely looked older than us there."

"Maybe it's from before they decided Gen-ens were evil." Mum couldn't have known what was on this. There was no way – the files were corrupted and the components dead. But… she'd given it to me after my encounter with the Gen-en. "Before the tattoos, before the Gas Attacks or anything else. Maybe they never show us this because they don't want us asking what *led up* to those attacks."

As I spoke, the sun shot a sharp streak of golden light above the Remutaka Ranges. We didn't have long until parents would be knocking on doors and finding Andrew and Mira gone.

"You guys have to go." I could figure out the holosphere later. "I'll stick here with Lucas. You have parents and work and lives. And you're chipped, if they do a Pulse–" I broke off, realising Andrew hadn't said anything in a while. I leaned over and nudged his foot. "Andrew. Are you all right?"

He took a deep shuddering breath and stared into the sky, blinking.

"Andrew?"

"I have a low quality genome."

"No! Well, according to their categories. But the categories don't mean anything, okay?"

Look at me, for example. I was Category-A. How was I so much better than Andrew?

He shivered and stared straight at me. "So what makes me a bad bet in the gene pool, then?"

It was a challenge.

"I don't want–"

"Tell me!"

Mira was watching me too. I wasn't going to get any help there. I took a deep breath and closed my eyes, thinking of the day I'd called up his records. The page swam up in my mind's eye, almost scaring me with its sharpness. I still wasn't used to my brain working properly.

"Three lethal-match recessives. Eyesight correction needed. Metabolism correction needed. Nutrition watch. Intelligence–" I swallowed. "One-oh-one. No Plague resist allele. Chance of heart disease–"

"Okay, stop."

I opened my eyes to find Andrew standing, staring into the distance. I stood too and put my hand on his arm, to show him I was there and I was his friend and all the things I couldn't say out loud, but he shrugged me off.

"Andrew... sorry, I–"

"Shut up. You– I– no." He plunged into the bush, hacking away at the undergrowth. It didn't look like he was going in the direction of home. I flopped down and put my hands over my face. Andrew, my best friend since we were five, who'd just helped rescue Lucas, might never speak to me again. And I wouldn't blame him. He'd stuck by me so long, but when it was my turn to stick by him, I'd done nothing.

Mira sat beside me. "He just needs some time. It must be hard to get used to the fact the government's screwed you over that much."

"Yeah, it is." I could still hear Andrew crashing away from us.

"And the fact that his best friend kept it from him."

My stomach turned. "Mira… I'm already feeling about as guilty as I could possibly get." I threw my hands down and stared up at the puffy clouds, lit in patches of dark and light by the low sun. "I – I suppose I could just say yeah, none of it was my fault, it was all the stupid drug's fault, but… I *did* do those things. I can't take back what I did, or change it, and not taking responsibility for it… that's as bad as doing it in the first place. So now I've got to make it right, and I'm trying, Mira, I'm really trying. So please don't go on at me."

"I–"

Lucas groaned. I shot up. His eyes weren't open but he was coming round.

Mira took a breath as if to say something, let it out, and began again. "I'll go find Andrew. Back in a few minutes."

"Yeah," I said, distracted. She brushed my shoulder as she left, following Andrew's trail of destruction into the bush.

30
Return

Lucas was definitely stirring. My chest fluttered, my brain speeding through things to say. Welcome back, long time no see, had a good sleep?

I slid over, eyes fixed on him. His hand moved feebly, then stilled. But somehow – I couldn't tell how, maybe his breathing or the pulse jumping in his neck – I knew he was awake.

"Hey," was all I could manage.

His eyes snapped open, wild, arms lashing out, and I skidded out of range, streaking grass stains on Andrew's jeans. "Hey, hey! It's Kieran!"

He fell back, squinting at me through the sunlight. "Kieran?" His voice was gravelly. "You're all grown up."

"Yeah."

Great speech, Kieran. Great speech.

"Where... where am I?"

"Near the hospital. The town green belt."

"Hospital..." He squeezed his eyes shut, put his hands to his face. "The hospital. The hospital... What..." He shook his head, opened his eyes, stared around at the trees. "I–"

"Yeah?" I said, when no more words came.

"I... feel like shit. You got water?"

I handed it over and helped him sit against a tree. He took long gulps, staring blearily at the bush. It took him a few minutes, but as I watched he grew more alert, blinking away the haze until he could focus properly on my face.

Four years since he'd done that. And I'd almost lost him completely. No coming back to life with a miracle antidote.

How many others were like him?

"What... happened?"

"I– I crashed the car." I could hardly say the words. "I'm sorry, I was driving and I–"

"What? No, Kieran, hey. Crashed?" He shook his head, swallowed, pressed his fingers to his forehead like he could force his brain to work.

And I could almost see the memories floating back to him. His hands shook very slightly, and he kept blinking into the light. I remembered what it had been like waking up after my withdrawal – my brain, suddenly working. I guessed it'd be like that for Lucas, but times a couple thousand.

"We..." he said at last. "Kaharore, right?"

"Yeah. On the Mākara road. And we... you..."

He stared into the trees. "The car malfunctioned. I shouldn't have let you drive."

"I–" I knew he shouldn't have. But I'd been the one with my hands on the wheel–

"No, Kieran. It's–" He shook his head again, rubbing his eyes. "Not your fault."

"But–"

"It's not your fault!"

His words sank into me like Margaret's or Mum's or Dad's never had. Even Mira's words hadn't hit me like this. I felt chills, an icy ocean wave taking away the littered pieces of guilt and dark thoughts. He clasped my arm, holding it tight.

"It's not your fault."

I nodded slowly, my eyes burning. Lucas was here, alive, talking. I'd got him out. I'd saved him.

"Hey, it's okay," he said, and I threw my arms around him. He felt frail. He patted me as I tried not to cry. "It's okay."

The birds were singing and calling and trilling now, into the silvery dawn light.

"We need to move soon," I said, my voice thick. "They'll be looking for us."

Lucas swallowed. "Oh. *Oh.* Catch me up. How long has it been?"

I cleared my aching throat, swiped my sleeve across my face, and told him about his med review, court, realising he might be drugged, the hospital escape. I wasn't sure I was making sense, or that Lucas was following.

"We're not chipped?" he asked, halfway through his third muesli bar from Andrew's backpack. "Good. That's good. Can't track us. Got a little extra time, maybe."

"We should still find somewhere safe before the sun's too high. They, um, think I helped blow up the Seatoun Dam."

His eyebrows raised. "Hold up, what?"

I went through the whole kidnapped-by-Outsiders, electrocution, withdrawal thing as quick as I could.

"The authorities drugged you too?"

"Yeah. Just enough to stop me asking questions, I guess." I took a deep breath and rubbed at the burn on my back, which was at the itchy stage. "There's something I have to know. Why did they target us? Was it random, or...?"

Lucas shook his head, avoiding my gaze. "I'm sorry."

Shit. He knew why. "Don't be. Why us?"

He shivered and pushed his long hair out of his eyes, grabbed a hank and stared at it. He'd never worn his hair long before. "I found out some stuff."

He didn't explain and I got impatient. "What stuff?"

"I hacked the AI that controls censoring. There's a tonne – a *shitload* – of stuff in the search-and-destroy list. Makes you wonder if internet disintegration was an accident. I didn't get much of a look at it, but things like rule exemptions for powerful people, letting kids die from diseases you can cure. The drugs they gave us, too." His eyes slid away from mine. "I guess they traced me. Maybe they made that car malfunction, or just took advantage of it. I don't know."

"So... like, a hit."

He gave a small smile. "Yeah. I guess."

"You made them scared enough they put a hit out on you."

"Or... anyone who steps out of line has to pay for it." There was guilt in his voice now. I'd spent four years blaming myself for the crash, and now he was going to do the same thing.

"Stop. It wasn't your fault either. If they wanted you dead, why didn't they just finish the job with the car crash? Why wait four years?"

He was quiet for a long time. "I think... they were trying to figure me out. This– this isn't the first time I've woken up."

"You woke– what do you mean? They'd have told us–"

Lucas shook his head. "*They* woke me up. Three times, I think?" He closed his eyes, his words starting slow but gaining speed as he spoke. "It was dark, each time. The first time, I had bandages… so it must have been not long after the crash. They asked me questions about what I wanted to do after school, top of my class in IT, made out like I was getting better. Seemed innocent. The doctors were kind. They told me I'd be going home soon."

I swore under my breath, his words triggering a memory I hadn't thought of in years. My time in hospital after the crash – I remembered the same thing, but for *me*. Doctors asking questions, promising I'd go home soon. And I had.

"But I think I gave the wrong answers," Lucas continued. "The next time, it seemed like it was winter, so maybe six months after the crash? A year and a half even. They asked me more questions, and this time it felt like they were trying to make me reveal who I'd been working with. I tried to give better answers, but no way in hell was I giving up my friends. The third time… well, that was basically an interrogation. They knew what I'd done, who I'd worked with, and they wanted to know if I'd consider working for them." He laughed dryly. "I spat in someone's face, I think. It's all kind of a blur. Then next thing, I'm waking up and you're here."

"God."

He shrugged. "But I'm out now, thanks to you. What's next?"

"Um. I'm sort of making it up as I go along."

That didn't seem to faze him. "There's a safe house in Southgate, we can crash there and figure out what to do."

Safe house. Not "camping house". "Your friends were Outsiders, right?"

A pause. Thoughts flashed behind his eyes, unreadable. "Yeah."

"Knew it." I wondered if his Outsider group knew Adelaide and Mikale and Nīkau. "So they got you because of that and the hacking. But what about me? Why would they do me too?"

He looked down, scrunching the muesli paper in his fist. "I guess cos you were with me. Maybe they drugged you to make sure you stayed in line." He gave a lop-sided smile. "Doesn't look like you did, though."

Full disclosure. I had to tell him everything, or it would all just get worse. And anyway, if I didn't tell him, Mira sure would.

I stared into the trees. "I've been working for Edward Doncaster. I found out he let the Great Plagues loose. I agreed to keep quiet."

"He– You *what*?"

I glanced back at him. His eyes, usually sleepy-lidded, were wide.

"I was drugged up at the time, but that's no excuse."

"You–" He swallowed and tried again. This didn't seem like the Lucas I'd known – he was too cautious, too guarded. Didn't he trust me? "You kept– Why did you agree?"

"It was a deal. I met a girl, but our Match was illegal. He offered to make it legal." I almost laughed. "Stupid, right?"

Another pause, and then he gave the ghost of a grin. "Oh, little cousin's growing up."

"Shut up." I felt warm inside. He was back, he was *here*, teasing me like he used to. Everything was going to be fine. "She got suspicious, though. I had to tell her and she, uh, dumped me. Then I got kidnapped..."

"What's that?" Lucas had seen the holosphere.

I tossed it to him, and it flashed a holiday pic of the strangers. "Mum gave it to me. It's got some old photos. Normal stuff and... pictures of Gen-ens."

He turned it over. "Do you know why she gave it to you?"

"No idea. I had this run-in with a Gen-en at the hospital, though, so maybe–"

Crashing branches, and Andrew and Mira reappeared. Lucas dropped the holosphere, pushed to his feet and swayed, fists up. His pyjama shirt hung open, his thin chest showing. He didn't look like he could take anyone, but the glint in his eye said he was going to try.

"It's all right, it's just my friends," I told him. "You remember Andrew? And this is, um, Mira."

"Ah. The girl with the strong convictions, right?"

"Uh." Mira shot me a funny look. "I guess I am."

"Good on you. Hey Andrew."

"Hey," Andrew said, arms crossed. He didn't look at me, directing his words at Lucas. "So what's the plan? We gonna invade Parliament on a hovercraft or something?"

Lucas raised an eyebrow. "You want to take on the cities?"

—— · ——

My watch said a quarter to six, but Mira and Andrew wouldn't leave until they knew our plans.

"If you want to do something, your best chance is tonight." Lucas was behind a tree, changing into clothes from Andrew's backpack. "Before they figure out what happened with me. And it's New Year's Eve, right? They can't just shut the whole city down. We can blend in with the New Year's crowds. I can hack into the network, with the right equipment, send out something on every channel, every popup. So what do you want to say?"

Mira was staring at me. I forced myself to meet her gaze, ignoring the hurt and hope tingling in my fingers and churning in my gut. Deep breath. "I could get Doncaster to confess. You send it out live, international broadcast."

Now they were all staring at me.

"Will he actually do that?" Andrew asked. "Or was that a joke?"

"You don't think I can do it?" I tried to summon up that drive I'd felt before, push through my exhaustion to the spark beneath. To the twelve-year-old boy who'd followed Lucas over the Consolidation Line. "Are you saying you don't believe in my super-powers of sweet-talk?"

Lucas snorted, emerging from behind the tree looking almost back to his old self in a pair of jeans and a dark hoodie.

"Sorry, but he's Edward Doncaster," Mira said. "You're not going to get a psychopathic national hero to admit he killed nine and a half billion people on international broadcast. It's not like he feels guilty about it–"

"But that's just it!" I was on my feet, digging my fingernails into my raw palms. "He *does* feel guilty! He goes on drunken benders and cries about his dead girlfriend and asks if it was all worth it. He wouldn't do that if he didn't feel guilty."

Lucas held up a hand. "Drunken benders?"

"Yep. I had to hide the vodka. It wasn't pretty."

"Xiao could get us into the VR suites..." Mira said slowly.

"They'd have what I need to hack into the network," Lucas nodded.

"So we just need to get Doncaster in there," I said. "And then we make him confess live. Cast doubt on everything. Cities and Outsiders. Matching. Stopping people having kids."

"Even if you could convince him to spill, no one's going to believe it," Andrew pointed out. "Especially if it comes through a VR camera. How hard would it be to just get Doncaster's face and paste it over the top of someone else confessing? That's what everyone's going to think."

You could almost see Lucas's thoughts ticking through possibilities. He shook his head. "It doesn't matter. We just need to plant the seed, and make sure it stays there."

"Extreme kidnapping with chance of death," Andrew said. "Well, I'm in."

"Are you crazy?" I burst out. Not one hour ago, he thought I'd betrayed him. And yeah, he was probably right. His eyes narrowed. "Sorry. It's just, you don't need to do this. Lucas and I are already fugitives, but you can get back to your normal life. We need Xiao for like, ten minutes, to get us into the VR control room. That's it."

Andrew shook his head. "Normal life? They screwed up my whole future. I can't go back and just accept my 'normal life' when I can do something about it. And I want to be there. I want to hear why he did it, why he thinks the government should decide who can have kids. He was there at the beginning, wasn't he? He was on the original committee that set all this up."

"If you're there, you'll be caught up in it, maybe arrested." I didn't have an exit strategy. Or at least, my exit strategy was convincing enough people the authorities were wrong, getting enough eyes on me that when we got caught, they'd let us off.

Andrew shrugged. "If it means what happened to me doesn't happen to anyone else... then I'm coming. You can use me as exhibit B if you want. Awesome guy, exemplary student, best friend ever, persecuted by the authorities. And," he gave a wistful smile, "maybe Prajna will see."

"I don't want you to–"

"You're not the boss of me, Kieran Xu."

"I–" But nervous laughter bubbled up inside me. "Okay, fine, come. And Andrew... I'm sorry I didn't tell you. Really, really sorry."

He shrugged. "I know. I can see. So let's just go and stick it to them."

I threw my arms around him, and he squeezed me back just as tight. When we drew back, Mira was standing looking expectant.

She'd already taken so many risks. Finding the Outsiders, helping get Raymi out of the city. What were the chances she was going to stay behind?

"I guess I can't convince you to watch from home?"

"No," Mira said. "We have to do it." She glanced at Andrew. "I'm not going to just sit back while you go off and start a revolution. This is a chance to change things, to set things right. And if you want to kidnap Doncaster and get him from his house to the VR suites, you're going to need as many people as you can get."

I tried one last time. "Are you sure. *Absolutely* sure."

"I'm sure. This is–" She swallowed. "This could be my one chance to do something that matters..."

Before she got what her sister had. My chest clenched and I wanted to ask her if she'd had any symptoms, but I couldn't in front of Andrew and Lucas. It was her secret to tell.

"Okay," I said. "Okay."

"Good," Mira said. "By the way, can I have the de-chipper?"

"What?"

"Just in case."

"Might be a good idea," Lucas said.

I reluctantly handed over the device. "Don't use it unless you really, really need to. Andrew, you get Xiao to come to the VR suites at eleven tonight. And talk to my parents. Tell them I'm okay and Lucas is okay, but–" This was going to be difficult. What if the police turned up at their door and they didn't act surprised that I was still alive? "Maybe wait a bit. Until after the police come?" My stomach twisted. I was a terrible son.

"Mira, um..." I didn't really feel I could tell her what to do. She was on the knife edge between girlfriend and as-soon-as-we-fix-this-I-never-want-to-see-you-again, and if I pushed too far, did something stupid, I could tip it the wrong way.

"Get on with it," she said. "What can I do?"

"Look up old–" I broke off. There was a low thunk, thunk, thunk coming from the direction of town, and it was getting louder under the morning birdsong.

"What is it?" Lucas rose to a shaky crouch.

"Do you guys hear that?"

"Hear what?" Mira asked, turning in the direction I was staring in.

"It's a helicopter." I grabbed my hoodie and the holosphere from the ground, the sum total of my belongings. "You guys have to go. And we have to find somewhere safer."

"I don't hear any– oh." Andrew stared at me. "They'll already know we're here. There's no point in us running."

I shook my head. "Andrew, stop it."

Mira paused with one arm in her jacket, her gaze flicking between us.

Andrew crossed his arms. "I'm staying here. Distracting them. You two don't have chips, so they don't know for sure you're here."

"You'll have to answer their questions," Lucas said quietly.

"I know. I can act clueless if I need to."

Mira pulled her other arm into her jacket and shrugged it on, winding her hair out from under the collar. "I'm staying too. And you've got no time to argue, Kieran, so go."

Andrew threw his backpack at me. It hit me in the stomach, but I caught it. "Go, stupid. They want to kill you both. They don't care about us."

The helicopter was definitely getting closer. Lucas was already at the edge of the clearing, a little steadier on his feet than before. "He's right, Kier."

It was happening too fast. We hadn't finished planning, hadn't made more than the bare bones of something. And what if they arrested Mira and Andrew? I shook my head to clear it, sucked in a shaking breath and swung the bag on my back. If I was still here when the helicopter arrived, there was no way they'd be able to talk their way out of this.

"I'll see you at Doncaster's house at ten," Mira said. "Good luck." Her blue eyes held mine for a second, longer, and then I tore them away.

"You too. I–" *I love you.*

And then we were running.

31
Hidden

LUCAS HAD ALWAYS BEEN good at moving through the bush without leaving a trail, but I could hear his coarse breathing up ahead and the rustles of his footfalls. I tried not to break the foliage, imagining the officers abseiling into the clearing, ignoring Andrew and Mira's protests and following our trail south.

We crested the brow of a hill and the thud of the chopper blades dropped. Lucas slipped on the steep ground, but managed to keep his balance.

"There's a – stream cutting – somewhere," he wheezed. He'd spent too long in that hospital, no matter the physio and daily exercycle sessions. "It'll hide us – infrared."

I felt like running, getting as far away as possible, but Lucas couldn't go on like this and he had a point about the infrared. "Sounds good."

The stream was too wide and lazy to cut much of a channel in the clay. Lucas stumbled in and turned upstream. I grabbed his arm and he hesitated, then leaned heavily on me. We waded until the banks narrowed and the trees drew closer overhead, stepping on the curves of muddy gravel that looked shallowest. I could still hear the blades of the chopper turning, turning, but the sound was removed, otherworldly. Here, the birds chirruped to each other and the stream's trickles seemed more real than any manhunt.

Lucas fell. I pulled at his arm and he staggered up, but this was as far as he was going to get. The banks were almost at head height now. This had to be far enough. I dragged his arm over my shoulders and half-carried him to the mud beneath an overhang.

Lucas leaned against the bank and stared up at the exposed tree roots. "Thanks, Kieran."

"Don't jinx it. We're not out of the woods yet."

"Ha," he returned dryly. "Ha."

And then we were silent, ears straining for any faint sound of people. My mind kept showing me things I really didn't want to see: Mira and Andrew failing to explain to the police what they were doing there, Mira kicking and punching as they dragged her into the helicopter, Andrew with a stick, swinging it like he had some hope against guns and tasers. Andrew limp on the ground, eyes blank and staring up at the cold blue sky. Mira fighting from the grasp of an officer in the helicopter, falling and dangling from one hand as her fingers slipped one ... by one.

"Kieran. Kieran!"

I opened my eyes. Lucas was shivering against me, and even his gaze seemed to flicker.

"I think they're gone."

"You think, or you know?" I whispered, still fighting against my imagination. The police skidding down the bank, their tasers flashing in leaf-filtered light, the thud of energy meeting skin...

"Can you hear anything?"

I strained my ears. No chopper. The birds in this valley were still singing, oblivious. "No."

"Then I think we're okay for now. And, ya know, I'm getting kinda cold sitting here in the mud..."

I levered myself up, trying not to groan at my stiff joints. Lucas was probably hurting a lot worse than I was. My clothes were sodden. Lucas clasped my arm and stood, teeth flashing as he bit his lip.

He couldn't stop shivering as we hiked out of the valley. I didn't know if it was the after-effects of the drug or the beginnings of hypothermia, but I pulled off my borrowed hoodie and made him put it on over Andrew's, then clutched at my elbows for warmth. The bush was cool, despite the sunlight cutting through the canopy. We stayed in the town green belt, past the skeletal remnants of the zoo, hugging the hills through Melrose and Houghton Valley, avoiding the streets of overgrown houses. We were still inside the Consolidation Line, but the bus didn't go up here and people preferred to live lower down the hills, closer to the city. I found more muesli bars in Andrew's backpack and a block of chocolate, but by ten o'clock I was feeling the effects of a long night with no sleep and too much adrenaline, not to mention the burns, scrapes, ribs and lingering withdrawal. We were stopping for rests more and more frequently. I didn't know how much longer we could hold it together.

At last we reached the house. It was below a ridge, staring out towards the city. It didn't look any less decrepit than its neighbours from the outside, but once Lucas jimmied the lock on the back door I could see this place was looked after. The floor was clean, and there was none of the usual damp you got in abandoned Pōneke houses. Lucas stumbled to a fat sofa and collapsed with a sigh. I clicked the door shut behind me.

The main floor was open plan, stairs leading up to a mezzanine. Peering through the front window's ancient net curtains, I could see far along the road in both directions, and north towards the city. Good sight lines. The screens didn't work when I rapped at them, but the cupboards in the kitchen overflowed with cans, huge bottles of water, and packets of pasta and rice. A few were past their use-bys but I wasn't going to complain. I split a can of fruit salad between two bowls and gave one to Lucas, fighting an urge to force it in faster as he spooned each tiny piece to his mouth.

"No chance you can fire up the net in here?" I asked as he started on his second cherry. I'd valiantly given him three. "The screens don't work."

He nodded. "There should be one upstairs that's connected. Always used to be." He glanced up, spoon hovering. "There won't be anything on the news about your friends, you know."

I pressed my fingers together and got to my feet. I didn't want to look at him. "I know." I hadn't known really. I'd hoped. "They might have talked their way out of it. Mira– we have aliases. She could have left me a message."

"You can't have an alias they don't know about. Even if she does leave a message, they'll know who sent it."

"Yeah, but she'll code it so they won't figure it out. And you can fix it so they don't know I've picked it up, right?"

"I think so. As long as they haven't changed things too much in four years." He set his bowl carefully down on the coffee table. "Kieran. Are you sure you want to do this? Not just find some place to chill out, maybe an Outsider settlement?"

"Are you saying you want to give up?"

He seemed to chew his words, then took a deep breath. "I mean you should get away. They want you, and they're not going to go easy on you if they catch you. Leave it up to–"

"They want you too, Lucas," I muttered. "Don't say I can't handle this."

"That's not what I–"

"I got you out of hospital, didn't I?" I said, suddenly angry. "I got through a city in lockdown and spirited you away, and now my friends might be in trouble. I have a chance to do something here, and you're not going to stop me."

Lucas slumped into the sofa. He looked pale and tired and – and *sad*. "I don't want to stop you. I think what you're trying to do is great. I–" He took a deep breath. "I just, I don't want to see you get hurt. You're still my kid cousin, and it kills me what they did to you. You should be away. Safe."

"No one else is safe," I muttered as he picked up our bowls and dumped them in the sink. He didn't turn and I was left speaking to the back of his head. "Why should I be? I'm the best chance we have of making a difference – I've got an in with Doncaster – and I'm going to use it. If it works, we won't have to worry about hiding away with Outsiders."

Lucas cleared his throat.

"Yeah," he said, very quietly.

——— · ———

Lucas brought the one working tablet downstairs. I sat in an armchair while he fiddled with it, tongue poking out as he dodged spy algorithms and circumvented firewalls. Or I guess that's what he was doing. He was taking longer about it than I liked, but I couldn't exactly complain. I couldn't do half of what he was doing, much less after four years in a coma and a few hours stumbling through the bush.

At last he nodded and passed it to me. "That should do it. There was some basic encryption on there, but I've improved it. They shouldn't be able to trace you."

"Can I access my messages?" I caught myself waving my wrist over the screen and stopped. My chip was not going to log me in. My chip was long dead.

"Already got them, from both your accounts. Bottom right hand corner. I haven't looked at them."

I flicked through. A few ads from groups that hadn't caught on I was legally dead and/or wanted for terrorism, and lots from friends and acquaintances. None of these were very direct – lots of "hope you're all right" and "where are you, man" instead of "why did you have to die".

There was nothing from Mira.

I tried not to throw the tablet down, but didn't really succeed. It skidded over the slick coffee table and Lucas sucked in a breath as it teetered on the edge before settling. I squeezed my eyes shut.

"We need to sleep," Lucas said. "Otherwise we're not going to be any use tonight."

"I don't know if there's going to be a tonight," I muttered. The light dimmed and I opened an eye to find him standing over me, arms crossed protectively over the tablet. "And shouldn't one of us stay on watch? Like in movies?"

I couldn't read his eyes. Had I ever been able to read them?

"What will we do if someone comes?" he said at last. "You think we should shoot them or something? That would really help our cause. If they find us, that's it. There's no getting away from it. So why stay up and watch if you can't do anything? Better to grab sleep while we can. There are beds upstairs. Come on."

I didn't move.

His voice softened. "Kieran. I'm sure your friends are fine. They're probably just spinning an amazing story for the police. Didn't Andrew once steal like half your birthday cake and convince your mum his dog ate it? He can spin a lie. Mira will send you a message in another few hours, and you can get all lovey-dovey with it. But in the meantime you need sleep. So come."

He got me upstairs and into one of the beds, shoes off and everything. This had been a kid's room, once upon a time. There were still glow stars stuck to the ceiling, which gave out a feeble light when Lucas drew the curtains, coughing at the dust.

"I should be putting you to bed, not the other way around," I said as he went out the door.

"I've had four years of sleep. I'm good."

"You're yawning."

He gritted his jaw and shook his head. "I'll sleep too. Night, Kieran. Or afternoon. Whatever."

He didn't wait for my answer, just pulled the door to. I sighed and listened to his steps move down the hall, and then into a bedroom. He was right. The best thing I could do now was recharge.

I was asleep as soon as I closed my eyes.

32

Message

THE CACKLE AND TWITTER of birds woke me. For a second I had no idea where I was, but then it all hit me. I was in a safe house in Southgate, and despite near misses in dream-land and reality, I wasn't dead yet. And Lucas had been right – I felt loads better for the sleep. But hungry. Extremely hungry.

I rolled off the bed and tiptoed down the hall, peeking into every room as I went. In one I found a bed with freshly rumpled covers, but no Lucas. Shit. Had they come and taken him, but not found me?

"Lucas?" I whispered, checking the bathroom. Maybe he was already awake, and downstairs.

But I couldn't hear anyone. There was a silence to the air that told me I was the only one here.

I crouched at the balcony by the stairs, peering through the bars at the kitchen below. Nothing had moved – a few packets of pasta were still on the bench, and my glass of water was sitting on the coffee table.

I closed my eyes and listened for a breath, a shifting in a chair, a footstep, but there was nothing. The sun had sunk behind the hill, and the room was dim.

My heart was going all out now, my breath quick and shallow. I told myself to calm down. I just had to get this over with, find Lucas, and keep going.

Or get caught.

I edged onto the first step, then the second and third, still crouching. Another two steps and I could see through the bars to the rest of the ground floor. Empty.

Lucas wasn't here.

I swore.

Maybe he'd just gone for a walk? I couldn't see any notes, but the tablet was on the coffee table. I pounced on it, but no reassuring message from Lucas. There was something from Mira.

All fine here, webs woven etc. We still on for tonight? We could meet in the same place we met before our sunset picnic. At the time we agreed. Hope you're well. XXXX

I stared at the four Xs. She was fine, things were happening tonight, though she'd changed the meeting point, and she'd signed off with four Xs. Was it just a way of signing off, or did it literally mean four kisses? She must have thought about the significance of it. She wouldn't just put four kisses if she didn't mean them, would she?

The door screeched. I almost dropped the tablet again and clutched it to my chest, ducking behind the sofa.

A click, and footsteps crossing the entrance tiles. Reality shrank. Sneakers. It could be Lucas. But then... it might not be.

Whoever it was, there was only one of them. And I could probably whack them over the head with the tablet (though then I'd lose all communication with Mira). I couldn't stay hidden behind this sofa forever.

I stood, tablet ready to throw.

Lucas jumped and swore. "God, Kieran, you trying to put me back in the hospital? You almost gave me a heart attack."

"Same to you." I hadn't realised I was so angry at him. "Where the hell did you go?"

He shrugged a strap off his shoulder and pulled a backpack around to show me. "Supplies. They have a store buried out the back."

"And you didn't leave a note?"

"I was only gone for ten minutes. You were sleeping like a baby."

I laid the tablet down and flexed my hands, trying to release the tension. "You scared me, man."

He dumped the backpack and grabbed me in a hug. I hesitated, then returned it. It was scary to feel how little muscle he had on him.

"Sorry," he muttered, and pulled back. "I'll leave a note next time."

"What supplies did you get?" I reached for the bag, but he turned me towards the kitchen instead.

"Just stuff. A phone. Some extra food. You want dinner?"

"You cooking it?"

"Sure."

Lucas liked cooking. Same genes as Verity, I guess. He whistled as he pulled pots from the cupboard while I sprawled in a chair. I couldn't reply to Mira's message without giving away that I'd seen it, so we'd just have to turn up and hope for the best. We threw ideas back and forth as Lucas stirred some pasta-based concoction. He tried to convince me once again to stay here, or head up the coast, but I wouldn't budge and he let it drop, frowning into the pot.

"At least let me figure out a better exit strategy than just 'we get caught'," he said at last.

"Go ahead. What have you got?"

"I'll check the blueprints, see what kind of backstage corridors they have. And we hope the police don't storm them."

It didn't seem quite real. I had to keep reminding myself that, in a few hours, we'd actually be *doing* the stuff we were brainstorming. And it would have consequences. There would be no going back, not after we'd kidnapped Doncaster and started the VR link. Even if Lucas's exit strategy actually worked, we'd be on the run.

But there wasn't anything I could go back to anyway.

—— · ——

I hadn't realised how lucky we'd been with the moon the night before. Tonight it was covered by clouds, and most of the time you couldn't even see its faint ghostly glow. I didn't think my eyes would acclimatise, but they did. The lights from the CBD reflected dimly against the clouds, and the silent trees were shades of charcoal. My burns and ribs felt much better after the sleep. Lucas's breath came heavy, but he didn't need to rest as much as he had this morning and we made good progress along the ridge line towards the city.

At last we reached the road up Mt Vic. We walked in the middle where the light was brightest, hopping over tree roots, potholes and gaping cracks. Fifteen minutes to get to the rendezvous at the tunnel.

Rendezvous. Ha. Like I thought I was in a spy movie.

Lucas stopped, staring up towards the faint outline of the triangle monument, and then back the way we'd come. "Somewhere around here there's a path..." he muttered, and went towards the trees on the left. "Can you see anything? It'd be faint, not used much."

We pulled at bushes for almost five minutes before we found anything that resembled a track, and even then we weren't sure it was right – it looked steeper than Lucas remembered. I handed myself from springy branch to springy branch, trying not to slap Lucas in the face as he followed. It was slow, but at last I found a chain-link fence blocking my way; a backyard, a dark house sitting just beyond. I jumped the fence, wincing at the creaks of the wire. It was New Year's Eve, and curfew wouldn't start until two a.m., but if anyone saw us they might recognise me from newscasts.

The garden was a tangle, but the house looked lived in and probably would be, this close to town. We crept around it to the road.

"I think ... we're north of the tunnel," Lucas said. "Isn't there an old school on the south side? And bush?"

"Yeah," I said. I'd checked the map before we left, and the old Pōneke Wellington East Girls was definitely marked to the south, with no houses all the way to the hospital. "Shit, unless we haven't gone past the hospital yet."

Lucas elbowed me and started south along the road. "We're well past the hospital. I saw its lights."

Fifteen minutes late. Twenty. I wanted to jog, but Lucas dragged me back. "Slow and steady doesn't get caught by cops."

And then we were above the tunnel.

"Wait." Lucas pulled me to a stop by the railing and peered over. I joined him, scanning the empty road beneath.

"Maybe they're in the tunnel?" I whispered.

"That would set off the lights," Lucas whispered back. "They might be late–"

He broke off as someone wandered out of the entrance. No lights. I squinted. It was hard to tell from above, but the walk was wrong for Andrew and the figure was too tall to be Mira.

Lucas began to move very slowly off the fence. Together we backed away into a garden.

"It's a trap, Kieran."

I shook my head. "Mira wouldn't..."

"She may not have had a choice. We don't know what happened after we left."

The plan was falling apart. We needed at least another person to help with Doncaster, and Xiao at the VR suites, and if our cover was blown... I swallowed hard. "Do we abort?"

"Not yet."

"But Mira has the de-chipper. Everything hinges on Doncaster not showing up in a Pulse! And how the hell are we going to get him to the VR suite and broadcast by ourselves?"

Lucas pulled me down a path beside a small apartment building. I stumbled, feet tangling in grass.

"If all else fails, we can cut Doncaster's chip out of his wrist. I'm pretty sure I can run the VR suite. How hard can it be?"

I didn't answer, remembering Xiao's adventures with Sydney.

Had Mira even written that message? Had she been waterboarded until she revealed her alias? Until she gave up the words that would get me to the rendezvous? How much of our plan did they know?

"The kisses!" I said, too loud, and froze with one leg on either side of a fence. Lucas hissed at me and I almost fell the rest of the way. "The kisses," I repeated, softer, as I picked myself up. Lucas's face was blank in the darkness. "They weren't kisses. They were crosses. As in, danger."

"So she was trying to warn you. Smart. If we're lucky, she managed to keep the rest of our plan secret."

I felt light. Maybe they had Mira, but she was fighting back, giving us time. I hoped Andrew was doing the same. And we'd make Doncaster confess, and the world would be horrified, and then she'd be so impressed we'd get back together and live happily ever after.

We stopped one more time for Lucas to regather his strength. I was still imagining our perfect future when we reached Doncaster's road, hopping the fences of orderly gardens. People definitely lived in these houses, and sometimes the windows glowed, but no one came out to investigate the dark shapes moving through their ferns and flowers.

Doncaster's house was right on the cliff edge. Good for throwing people down, I guess, or maybe it was just the view over Oriental Bay and out to the Hutt that attracted him. We crouched hidden in the blades of harakeke bushes until Lucas deemed it safe. The plan was to get through a window, avoiding the camera at the front door and bypassing the chip lock. We crept around the side of the house, eyes and ears alert for movement. Every window so far was shut tight, but there were tonnes of windows on the ground floor, one of them–

I froze. I didn't know why, but then I heard the soft breath around the corner, the shift of a foot. Someone was there.

33
Vanish

I HELD LUCAS BACK. Something... I closed my eyes, strained my ears and took another step, silent on the springy herb grass. I could almost imagine I heard a heart beat.

I don't know how, but I knew. I snapped my eyes open and rushed around the corner, into a collision with a karate chop to the neck.

"Ahh, jeez..." I staggered back into Lucas, who caught me but then couldn't hold my weight. We ended sprawled on the ground beneath my shadowy attacker.

"Oh no, I'm so sorry!" Mira said in an anguished whisper. "I thought it was the police or a guard or–"

"Just us," I said hoarsely, trying to get my throat back in working order. "So glad ... to see you. What happened? The tunnel..."

"They– they had security footage of us from our picnic at the dam. They told me what to say, where to meet up with you. I hoped if you got the message with the Xs you'd understand..."

"He understood," Lucas whispered, half laughing. I picked myself up off the ground and pulled him up. "Eventually."

"Do they know the rest of it?" I still couldn't quite meet Mira's eyes, but felt them pulling me in anyway. No matter if she was mad at me, I couldn't stop wanting to be where she was, see her quick smile with that flash of mischief, feel her hand warm in mine...

"No," she said. "I didn't tell them more. Neither did Andrew. They didn't even arrest us, just questioned us, and Andrew's mum showed up and reamed them out for holding us without charges. Maybe I should be interning with her too. They let us go home to sleep and wait for further questioning. But I still had the de-chipper so I fried my chip, went to Andrew's and he fried his too."

She took a deep breath. "We're probably going to get arrested. And I don't want to go to jail still mad at you. When I woke up this afternoon, I don't know what it was, but I knew–" Her voice caught. Her whisper was already low, but it got even lower. "You made mistakes, but you're trying to fix them. You're not holding back anymore. When I threw you out that night, I was so angry. You were just giving in, becoming part of the problem, and I didn't understand how you could... And then after the dam, when I thought you were out of your mind or– or *dead...*"

She held out her hand. I took it, and her hand squeezed mine tight, like a lifeline.

"And I wanted so badly to understand what had happened, how you'd become this person I barely knew... But this. *This* is you. Breaking Lucas out, trying to right things for Andrew, for Lucas, for all those people who died in the Plagues. I know you said you have to take responsibility for what you did, but just the fact that you even *said* that. You're the guy I– the guy I fell in love with, Kieran. I love you."

I could hardly breathe, and her eyes were so blue, open, staring into my soul, and I felt like the world had fallen away and it was just the two of us in the darkness, linked by our gaze. The words came easily, like they'd been waiting for days, weeks, to come forth. "I love you too."

We swayed together, breath and brush of lips, and it was starlight and electric connection. She'd forgiven me, for real. This was happening.

Lucas cleared his throat. "Come on, guys, breaking and entering doesn't do itself."

We drew back, my breath stuttering. Mira's eyes reflected the light of the clouds, and her smile was mischievous, full of hope and laughter.

"Right," I whispered, squeezing her hand. "Right. Time and place. At least now we have three people to carry Doncaster. Where's Andrew? Did he convince Xiao?"

"They should be at the VR suites. Do you guys have any water? I drank all mine."

I gave her my water bottle and she sculled the whole thing. "Thirsty, huh?"

She shrugged. "I guess police questioning does that."

We crept along the side of the house, checking each window, and found one of the back windows left open a crack. It was on a latch, but I wiggled it with Lucas's screwdriver and pulled the window wider. Simple. Mira gave me a boost and I slithered through the gap. From the stainless steel beneath my fingers and the tap digging into my arm, this was probably the kitchen.

"Okay?" Mira whispered.

I was half-in, half-out of the window, and while I didn't have my full weight on her hands she must be getting sick of holding me up.

"Yeah," I breathed, and shuffled forward until I could put my knee in the sink and ease onto the draining board, which was happily clear of plates and knives. Apparently Doncaster had his cleanfreak side in charge of the kitchen.

I hadn't noticed any motion sensors or cameras in the kitchen when I was last here, and there was no tell-tale beeping. Lucas handed me our backpacks and I set them beside a ceramic teddy bear jar. Didn't seem like Doncaster's taste. Maybe it was a present from some relative.

I swallowed. I didn't like to think of Doncaster with relatives.

I helped pull Lucas in, and led him to the foyer. The alarm started beeping softly. He swung open the alarm panel, and with a few quick swipes the panel welcomed us in. I opened my mouth to say something but he held up a hand, scanning the hall before fixing on a small cupboard above the alarm panel. Low humming came from it, almost below hearing.

The house server. Duh.

Lucas opened the cupboard and connected his phone to a port on the little humming box. Thirty seconds of intense focus, then he nodded.

"I've looped the cameras, turned off the motion sensors and muted all the mics so the server won't hear if Doncaster calls for help," he whispered. "Seemed like the least noticeable way of disabling the security system."

"You are a criminal genius." How had I never seen this side of him?

He shrugged, disconnecting and closing the door. "I try."

We tiptoed back to the kitchen. Mira was standing at the window, wide eyes glinting in the low light. We pulled her through, her feet scrabbling against weatherboards for a breath before she made it. She paused on the draining board while we listened for movement, but I couldn't hear anything.

"Right," Lucas said, sorting through his bag. "You know where his bedroom is?"

There was a terrific rumbling snore from directly above us.

I pointed up. "There. Just a guess."

I dropped my bag beside the back door. It'd be easier to carry Doncaster downstairs without it. Lucas kept his. Mira wound her hair around her ponytail to make a bun, then stood with her arms crossed, her breathing shallow. Oxygen seemed to be short.

"Up we go," I muttered. Better not to think, just do.

"Right. We don't want to wake him up," Lucas whispered as we crept up the stairs. "So try to keep quiet."

"I never would have thought of keeping quiet. Thanks, Lucas," I murmured.

"No problem."

Doncaster was still snoring. We followed the sound until we were standing just outside his door, staring at each other.

"How are we..." Mira breathed.

"Lucas has a way to knock him out," I whispered. "It's not just knocking him on the head, right Lucas?"

Lucas nodded and opened his backpack. He took out a wadded T-shirt and a medicine bottle.

"Hold this," he whispered, giving me the T-shirt. He unscrewed the bottle, then flipped it up on the T-shirt. I could feel the cool liquid seeping through the fabric, and very soon I could smell it.

"What is that stuff?" I gasped, covering my mouth and nose with my sleeve. I could only smell the barest sickly trace, but it was already making me light-headed.

"Knock-out cocktail." Lucas said, screwing the cap back on. He took the pad and held it at arm's length, and its reek washed towards me.

"Does it ever kill people?" Mira asked, voice muffled behind her sleeve.

"Almost never," Lucas said, but I caught the "I hope," under his breath. If Doncaster died, we'd never get anything out of him. Nīkau would be stuck wherever he was forever, and I would be an outlaw.

"Come on." He eased open the door.

A humped shape lay in the king-size bed, the glow of clouds filtering in the frosted window. The snoring had stopped. Lucas crept across the thick carpet, jerking his head for us to follow. He'd need help if anything went wrong. I swallowed my nerves and approached the bed.

Doncaster slept right in the middle, surrounded by miles of sheets and blankets. Lucas would have to climb right onto the bed to reach him. I got into position on the left side, ready to lunge and grab, and Mira stood on the right.

He seemed asleep. Breathing slow and even, a faint rattle on the in-breath.

Lucas put his free hand very carefully on the edge of the bed.

No movement.

"Wait!" I whispered.

Lucas halted, eyebrows raised.

I'd caught sight of Doncaster's watch – still on his wrist. Of course he'd wear it to bed. It was probably logging his heart rate to raise the alarm if he had a heart attack. Or, say, there were intruders in his room.

Lucas had taken out the house's security, but the watch would link directly to the cell network.

I indicated my wrist, and Lucas caught sight of the watch. His brow furrowed, then he dug in his bag and came out with a device that made me think of the de-chipper, just bigger. He pressed it on, mouthing "network blocker".

Hopefully that solved the problem.

Lucas tried his knee on the bed. He had to do this right the first time. If he woke–

Doncaster snorted. Lucas froze. The old man sighed, his bald head settling deeper into the pillow. He didn't seem any closer to consciousness and Lucas put his other knee on the bed. This time, Doncaster didn't move at all, and I let out my breath.

It was scary, really, how easy it was to sneak up on someone asleep. It made me hope no one ever tried to do it to me.

Lucas took another knee-step and was about to try a third when the old-man-lump reared up and yelled for help, blankets twisting and coming my way. I yelped and stumbled back. But he wasn't aiming for me. He was aiming for the bedside table.

I was still off-balance. In a second he'd knocked me sideways into the bed. Something cool and hard jabbed into my temple, and a wiry arm tightened around my neck, stopping me falling right onto the duvet.

Doncaster was holding a gun to my head.

So much for all our security precautions. The house server wasn't answering, but that didn't matter if he had a gun.

"Don't come any closer," he rasped. Mira had grabbed a textbook from the bedside table and looked ready to leap over and whack him. "I'll shoot him."

"Professor," I gasped. "It's me. It's Kieran."

His hand trembled, just the slightest movement, but I felt it before the gun came steady again.

"Kieran." He paused. "And I guess this here's your cousin. And your girl– Stop!"

Lucas had crept forward, but now he froze again, wadded T-shirt poised.

"What a short memory. I repeat: if you move, I'll shoot Kieran."

I swallowed, my Adam's apple bobbing painfully against Doncaster's arm. His hand had wavered. Maybe he could shoot somebody else, but me... He wouldn't do it. At least, I didn't *think* he would.

Could I bet my life on that?

"He won't," I choked out. "He likes me."

"Oh, you think so?" Doncaster screwed the barrel deeper into my head. I could hear the smile in his voice, but also the uncertainty. He didn't think he could shoot me, either.

"Come on, Lucas," I said, more sure of myself now. He wouldn't shoot me. He couldn't kill someone he knew at close range. He'd–

"Okay, then." Suddenly the hard press of the gun was gone. The lack of it was like a physical thing, but his armlock was still iron tight. "What about her?"

The gun pointed unwaveringly at Mira. She dropped the textbook. Lucas had been moving forward, but he stopped, eyes flicking to me.

"I'm a good shot. Maybe you were willing to gamble your own life, but are you willing to gamble hers?"

"Don't worry, Kier–" Mira began, but panic was rising in me like a wave.

Not Mira. He couldn't shoot Mira.

"Okay okay! Don't shoot her!" My words fell over each other, my pulse beating harsh and fast. "Don't shoot her. Please. I'll– I'll– do what you want. Just don't shoot her!"

I could feel him chuckle. "Young love. So reliable. Crick!"

It took me a second to realise he was addressing the house server. No answer came, and his breath hitched.

"We've cut all comms," Lucas said gently, his hands raised, placating. "If you come quietly..."

"You'll what, kill me later?"

"No killing anyone!" My voice came out strangled. "Professor, you granted our Match!"

"I did! Two top quality genomes, a perfect Match in all ways but that relic of a percentage match. And yet here you are, attacking me in my own home?"

Fair point.

"You only granted it because Kieran called you out," Mira said coldly, as if there wasn't a gun pointed straight at her head.

Doncaster lunged for the door, dragging me with him. Lucas leapt for Doncaster. He clapped him with the knock-out cocktail and the gun went off, hitting the wall. Fumes swept over me.

I was floating away, watching my body sink to its knees, still entangled in Doncaster's bony arm.

"Get Kieran!" Lucas's voice, and then Mira's arms were around me, pulling me into clearer air. Everything spun.

Lips on mine. I knew that, could respond to that. Mira's hands on my face, her kiss urgent, pulled me back into my body. She loved me, she'd forgiven me, she was kissing me...

"No, don't kiss him!" Lucas. "You'll just get half decked yourself!"

I pulled away, drawing in deep breaths. My brain was clearing.

"Slapping him might make a difference," Lucas suggested, and Mira's mouth twitched, though her eyes were worried. She tapped the side of my face and pulled me up. The room spun again, but she left me leaning on the wall and went to help Lucas.

"Heart's still beating," Lucas confirmed. They pulled back the bed clothes and laid Doncaster on the bottom sheet.

I put my hands against my head, closed my eyes, and took a few deep breaths. I could still taste the sickly sweetness at the back of my throat.

Mira de-chipped Doncaster, then we untucked the corners of the bottom sheet. I was really, really happy he wore pyjamas, even though they were thin cotton and looked like he'd bought them midway through the twenty-first century.

"Déjà vu," I muttered.

Lucas's eyebrows raised. "Yeah?"

"We did exactly this to you. Minus the drugs."

He grinned. "Much easier with people who are already unconscious."

"Here's hoping Doncaster's as light as he looks," Mira said, and on the count of three we lifted him.

He wasn't. And neither Lucas nor I were feeling that hot. By the time we got Doncaster to the door, Lucas was puffing and staggering, and Mira nudged him out of the way, taking that entire end of the sheet so it was just me and her. He made a feeble attempt to take it back, but ended up following us, holding the T-shirt over Doncaster's face.

Apart from a stumble on the landing, we managed to get to the hall without any major bruises.

"So, wheelbarrow next?" I asked, only half joking. We laid Doncaster on the floor. "Maybe he has transmission equipment here?"

Lucas shook his head, tapping at his phone. "He wouldn't have the equipment to hijack everything." He was sucking in deep breaths. He'd barely carried Doncaster a few metres before Mira'd taken over. How the hell were we going to do this? "My back-up can meet us here."

"Back-up? Who?"

"Just some friends. They're only five minutes' away." He shoved the phone back in his pocket. His breathing was slower now, controlled. Our eyes locked, and I was struck again by how little I knew him. His eyes weren't the eyes I remembered from our "camping" trips.

"Why are they only five minutes' away?" I asked, struggling to keep my voice even.

"I was hoping I could talk you out of this before we got to the VR suites, and we could take over."

"Get over yourself, Lucas," I hissed. "I'm not walking away. Not after what they did to you, what– what they did to me. The world is going to keep working this way unless we do something–"

"But *you* don't have to do it!" Lucas put his hands on my shoulders but I shrugged away.

Mira was looking between us, brow furrowed. Did she think I should run, too? Hadn't she wanted me to stand up and do something?

"Trust me, Kieran! Just– just–" He growled and turned away, slapping the wall.

"The police'll be pleased with the fingerprints on that." I tried to force a grin. It didn't work. It didn't matter, though, because Lucas didn't turn around to see it.

He took a deep breath. "If you leave now, go over the back fence, you can make it to those Outsiders you're friends with–"

"I am not friends with those Outsiders. They wanted to cut off my arm."

"Listen to me, Kieran."

"What about me?" Mira broke in.

"You should go too. But Kieran, please. If you keep doing this, shit is going to hit th–"

"Oh, so you can do it but I can't? I'm nearly seventeen, Lucas. I've lived more life than you have. Don't treat me like I'm a kid. You never did before..." My voice was choking but I couldn't stop it. For so long I'd dreamed about what it would be like when Lucas woke up, when everything was back the way it was, when we had awesome adventures and I could tell him everything.

He obviously hadn't been telling me everything, though. And he still wasn't.

34

Fly

Tapping. We all froze. My heart tried to jump out of my chest.

I turned very slowly towards the back door. Through the frosted glass stood a hazy shadow.

Lucas drew in a breath. "It'll just be my friends. If it were police, they'd burst in tasers blazing."

I let him past, arms crossed. He stepped over Doncaster, staying close to the wall so his shadow wouldn't be visible.

Lucas rapped out a soft pattern on the glass, and whoever was on the other side answered with a variation on the rhythm.

"It's okay," Lucas whispered, though I'm not sure if it was for our benefit or not, he said it so quietly. He turned the handle and pulled the door just wide enough for someone to slip inside.

"Lucas," came a girl's voice. I peered into the darkness, interested despite myself.

"Raymi," Lucas replied. There was a mix of something in his voice – an undercurrent of nerves. Hope, maybe. Or perhaps I was reading too much into it.

"Raymi?" Mira whispered incredulously.

"*The* Raymi?" I muttered. "Enzo's Raymi?"

The girl stepped further into the hallway. She was tall, that much had been obvious from her shadow, but she was also the same age as Lucas, with dark hair coiled around her head. Her bright, sharp eyes made me want to avoid her gaze even though she hadn't yet looked at me.

"Yep," Mira murmured.

Two others slipped in behind her.

"Where is he?" A guy, with an accent I couldn't place. Raymi's companions were men, one shouldering a hockey bag and the other with a grey beard that caught at the dim light.

"On the floor." Lucas pointed. They noticed us standing over Doncaster's unconscious form.

"Who're they?" Raymi asked. My stomach squeezed. Lucas hadn't even mentioned I might be here. He'd just assumed that I would go. "*Mira?*"

"Hi." Mira waved a hand.

Raymi turned her piercing gaze on me.

"Who's the guy?"

"Kieran," Lucas said after a long pause. "My cousin."

"Your–" Raymi began. Her face, previously about a four on the ten point scale of friendliness, had cooled to a one. "Oh. And you brought him *here*?"

"He knows Doncaster," Lucas sighed, rubbing a hand over his face. "He's the best one to get information out of him."

"Thanks for noticing that," I said acidly. "Nice to meet you, Raymi." I was going to be infinitely polite. I stepped over Doncaster and held out my hand, but she didn't take it and I was left pretending I'd just been stretching my arm.

"I'm Sione," said the man with the beard, nodding at me but showing no hint of a smile.

"Marcus," said the other, the one with the accent and the hockey bag. "I'm pretty sure I can get us a route down." He said rowt, not root. Maybe he was American. His voice sounded a bit American, but then it also sounded European and Kiwi.

"How?"

Everyone ignored me. Marcus crouched on the floor with a groan, checked Doncaster's pulse and lifted him a little on the sheet. Then he dropped Doncaster's head to the ground with a thump.

"This should do. The sheet will hold him."

"For what?" Mira asked.

"Marcus is a fly line expert," Sione said from the front room. He was standing at the window in the dark. "He's been all around the world, you know. We're lucky to have him."

I didn't want to admit I had no idea what a fly line was, and no one seemed to be paying me any attention, so I said nothing.

Marcus, Raymi and Sione tied Doncaster into his sheet with origami-like efficiency, and attached hooked bungy cords at his feet, waist and chest. The three of them worked like they'd done this a thousand times before.

"Do you think Raymi...?" Mira lowered her voice. "Was she Lucas's girlfriend?"

I shrugged. The tension between them could definitely be that. "I have no idea. Lucas never mentioned her. Ever."

Raymi and Sione took Doncaster and we followed them outside, keeping to the shadows until we left the road and veered into a park, climbing even higher. The scattered lights of the city winked through the trees. At last, in a clearing, Marcus reached into the hockey bag and pulled out the most ginormous gun I'd ever seen.

Lucas saw my look of alarm. "It's not for killing people. It's for shooting bolts at buildings."

Which is what Marcus did. He knelt and rested the bolt gun on a park bench, sighted along the barrel, and shot something into space. I could make out the hulk of the Embassy Theatre at the head of Courtenay Place, silhouetted against the scattered street lights, and the apartment building next to it. It was a long way. There was a high whining, whistling hum as the line spooled, and then a distant *thunk* as the bolt hit a wall on on the roof of the apartment building.

"Won't people have heard that?" I asked.

Marcus gave me a funny look. "Unlikely."

I was tempted to ask if it was safe, but that'd probably insult Marcus, and I didn't want to insult the man with my life in his hands.

I took a seat on the wall while Marcus performed some complicated knot work around the park bench, his hands quick and certain. Mira sat beside me, sipping from her water bottle.

"It's weird," she said abruptly. She lifted her hand as if to put it on mine, but dropped it again, so our little fingers were mirrored across empty space. "He said we had top quality genomes. A perfect Match. But I have the same genome as Melanie, and she died of a genetic disease. Shouldn't I be like Andrew, with a 'low quality' genome?"

Melanie's ghost seemed to hang between us.

"He was probably just talking crap, trying to throw us off." Something niggled at me, a memory from when I'd confronted Doncaster. "Complementary pairings for a few bad genes..."

"What?"

"Something he said, before he granted our Match. Maybe my genes cancel out yours."

We stared down at the city, the dark shapes of the buildings and the lights around the bars that were open above sea level, the wandering groups of party-goers. She shook her head. "That's... I don't know how I feel about that. So I'm not 'perfect', but it's acceptable if I'm Matched with you? What happens if we break up?"

My heart seized. I'd only just got her back, and she was talking about breaking up? "I'm sure you'll find someone else just as good," I returned, voice level.

"Hey." She moved her hand closer. Our fingers touched and I could feel the current between us. "Sorry. I don't want to break up. It's just... twisty tangled head-messing."

"Yeah."

And then Marcus was tugging on the string of death and proclaiming it ready. The conversation felt unfinished, but we went over.

"Um... how much will it hold?" I asked as Marcus made me a makeshift harness from bungy cords and bedsheets.

"It's spider silk," Sione told me. "It could hold an elephant."

"I'll go first," Marcus said. "So you don't need to worry your pretty head about it."

I wasn't sure I liked Lucas's friends.

Marcus had his own special sliding thing, and before I could think to ask him any more really important technical questions he was sliding down the line.

"I'll go with Doncaster," Sione said. "When I tug on the line three times, it means we're all set for you at the other end. Kieran goes after me. Then Mira, then Lucas, and Raymi last, after she's set the charge."

"The charge?"

"Just a small explosive, set to go off after Raymi makes it down," Lucas supplied, when no one else answered. "Then Marcus can reel back the remaining line and use it again."

"That's reassuring," I said, but Lucas had already wandered away. I tried to see the landing spot and make out Marcus's figure. It was impossible at this distance.

It should have made me feel better. If I couldn't see him, knowing where to look, the police probably couldn't see him either. And we'd get there a lot faster this way than with the wheelbarrow plan.

"See you down there." Sione settled Doncaster's origamied form and let go. The odd pair whizzed away into the darkness.

I stood and put my hand on the line, which was still humming with Sione and Doncaster's flight. I could do this. Marcus's quick and certain knotwork meant I would avoid quick and certain death. A few bungy cords and a bedsheet didn't seem safe or sane, but Marcus had promised this would work. Really.

The wind shifted, and whispered words floated my way.

"I didn't mean – we couldn't." Raymi's voice. "I'm sorry. I wanted to–"

"I was expendable," Lucas said flatly. "Even to you."

I stiffened. It was a private conversation, not meant for me, but all the same I turned so I could hear better, glancing at Mira. She was staring out over the city, oblivious. I wanted to know more about Raymi, about the girlfriend Lucas had never mentioned.

"I was sixteen, Lucas!" she hissed. "What did you expect me to do? You were stuck in hospital, and it was 'don't make waves, don't draw attention so close to D-Day', and then half our group was dead or captured! I couldn't have done it!"

What was D-Day?

"Kieran got me out," Lucas said. "He's sixteen."

There was a pause.

"Well, we all know about *Kieran*, don't we?"

What about me?

Lucas sighed. "Okay, forget about Kieran. How about Mira? She's as old as you were, and she helped get you out of the cells, didn't she?"

Three tugs on the line. Time for me to go. But...

"That was different. I was just some random, they weren't guarding me like they were you, they didn't drug me, they couldn't–"

"They weren't guarding me last night. It would have been nice to wake up and see my girlfriend's face before they killed me, you know?"

"There was nothing I could do, Lucas. I'm sorry. I'm glad you're alive. Can't that be enough?"

I glanced back at them, trying to be as casual as I could. Lucas was standing with his back to Raymi, arms crossed. Mira caught my hand and squeezed it.

"Your turn."

"See you down there."

She kissed me on the lips, then tapped my back twice like cops did on cars in cop shows. Sending suspects off to their date with the law.

I took a deep breath, closed my eyes, and let go.

—— · ——

The wind was in my eyes, dragging fingers through my hair, sucking past my ears so I could hear nothing but the howl of it. I turned my head to stop the noise and heard instead the high hum of the bungy cord against woven spider silk. I could feel the space yawning open beneath me, my legs hanging out with nothing to stop me falling but a bungy cord, a sheet and a wispy spider line.

I forced my eyes open. It was no good landing in a sprawl on the other side and breaking an ankle because I hadn't seen where I was going. It wouldn't improve my reputation with Lucas's friends, either.

Even in the darkness I could see the dark shadow of Mt Victoria sloping away to my left, and the houses clinging to the hillside below. I was more than halfway, coming up fast on the roof of the apartment building. Someone was there to catch me.

Closer, closer. I was going too fast. Had Marcus said anything about putting out your arms to slow down? I couldn't remember, but on second thought there was no way I was letting go of my sheet. My fingers hurt. Maybe I was clutching too tight. And it was coming, the first parapet was right beneath me and–

Suddenly I was running, my feet scraping and tumbling along the ground, trying to keep traction as momentum pulled me forward. Marcus was the dark shape waiting, and he grabbed me as I shot past, swinging me in an arc that sent my stomach sideways and spun my head but slowed me down pretty quick.

"Thanks," I muttered, disentangling myself. Marcus nodded, unhooked the bungy cords, tugged three times on the line and then ignored me completely. I sighed and sought strength in the dim glow of the clouds. Another few hours and then I wouldn't have to deal with these people.

Doncaster was lying to one side, apparently forgotten. I knelt beside him, reaching into the old man parcel and checking his pulse just in case he'd managed to die on the way down. His mouth was slack and his hands were crossed on his chest like an Ancient Egyptian mummy. No, his pulse was strong and steady, steadier than mine after that ride. He wasn't dying any time soon. The T-shirt still reeked.

Mira's feet scraped the roof behind me and she came over, staring down at Doncaster with a vaguely disgusted expression.

"Dick."

Soon all six of us – seven if you counted Doncaster, which I didn't – were on the roof, and it was on to the next leg. My legs were still shaky from the first go and my head felt light, buzzy, almost like I was drunk. Raymi and Lucas weren't looking at each other or talking.

Once we got to the VR suites, we had to get through the locked doors or round the party-goers, hack into the control room and convince Doncaster to talk. The last one would be my job. And I'd have to do it on live feed, which wouldn't be a problem at all. As if I didn't have enough adrenaline already.

"Your turn," Lucas said. I jumped. Sure enough, Marcus had already placed his bolt in the VR building and gone. The line negotiated a course between tall apartment buildings, skimming just a few metres from one on the left, and then further on another on the right. Sione and Doncaster were almost to the other side. Mira was waiting for me to go.

I steeled myself and attached my rig to the line, swung back for momentum and threw myself out over the void of the half-flooded Kent Terrace, trying not to think too much.

This time I could almost enjoy it. The wind wasn't too strong and as long as I ignored the fact that tiny pieces of line and ancient cotton were all that kept me from tumbling to my death, it was like a VR rollercoaster ride, or an extreme version of the flying foxes in Central Park. It was also my last breath of clean, fresh freedom before we entered the VR suites and there was no turning back.

I didn't know what would happen afterwards. Even with Lucas's escape plan I wasn't sure we could get away, because we were going to keep broadcasting until we had all we wanted or they broke the door down. Considering the size of the lie, the door-breaking would probably come first. Which would mean I'd be right in the middle of it when the police poured in, tasers drawn, and collected us to put in boxes.

I was hoping for the cell kind of box, not the six-foot-under kind.

I wished Mira was far away, then realised Lucas wished the same thing about me, and decided to stop wishing.

Bang.

I swore and twisted on the line, spinning as the roof of the VR building approached. Orange light threw sharp shadows across the rooftops.

Bang, bang, crack.

Blue light. And green.

Bang, crack.

I just had time to realise it was only fireworks, that it was midnight, the New Year, before I hit the roof at the wrong angle and scraped across the tarred surface, ripping Andrew's jeans but thankfully not my skin.

"Fireworks," I gasped as Marcus came to disentangle me. "Just fireworks."

He raised an unimpressed eyebrow.

There was no door on the roof, so we had to climb down the spider silk and get in from the ground. Marcus went first, cradling Doncaster as he abseiled down, then Sione and me. I'd abseiled at school camp, but not at night as a fugitive and not with a roof overhang that meant I only managed to touch the wall three times on my way down. At least we were above sea level here, and the ground was dry. My hands shook as I undid the makeshift harness. Mira was far better, touching the ground with perfect poise, her eyes shining and hair blown wispy.

Marcus had picked a good spot – around the back, away from the streetlights. I checked Doncaster – still alive – and stared at the dark façade. There were very few windows. No door on this side, either. We'd have to go around to the side entrance, and trust there weren't security lights or cameras.

"Where are Andrew and Xiao?" I asked Mira.

"They should be in Studio 2, waiting for us. Hopefully."

I chewed my lip. "I guess we try the side door?"

Mira was staring past me. Iron scraped against iron. "Or... I guess we could go through the manhole?"

I turned and saw Marcus already climbing inside.

"That goes into the building? And they're sure it's not flooded?" I asked Lucas, who shrugged.

"Looks fine. I told them we needed to get into the VR suites. They looked up the city plans. I guess they know what they're doing."

Yay for them.

35
Trap

It was dark down the manhole. Very dark. The tunnel wasn't, as I'd feared, a sewer, and the king tide must not have reached it, because the floor was dry. Even so, there was a kind of dampness to the air that made it a bit like breathing a dirt-flavoured milkshake. Marcus and Sione had managed to get Doncaster down here without seriously harming anyone, and now we were feeling our way along the condensation-slick walls.

"Right," Sione's whisper floated back from his position two people in front of me. "The wall of this tunnel is close to the wall of the basement for the suites. We just need to cut through it, and we're in."

He took something out of his bag, and there were a few clicks as he fiddled with the settings, then a brilliant beam of light shot out, blackening the concrete floor. He pressed the laser drill to the wall at about hip height, ramped up the voltage and drew it slowly down and around. It was like cutting through butter, and soon there was a singed black circle large enough to squeeze through. Sione swapped the drill for a small crowbar, dug his gloved fingers into the side of the circle that was no longer smoking, and levered the layers of wall out, laying them carefully on the floor to one side.

"I'll go first," Lucas said, crouching and pushing his backpack through before crawling after it. Swirls of echoed light from the laser still danced across my eyes. Mira went next, then Marcus and Sione edging Doncaster between them. Raymi waited for me to go, and it felt a bit like she was making sure I couldn't escape.

The room beyond was just as dark, but open, the ceiling low. I followed the sound of breathing and footsteps to the far wall.

"Kieran?" Lucas whispered, so low I almost couldn't catch his words.

"I'm here." I slid across to him.

"There's a door here, can you feel it?"

"Yes." The outline was bumpy under my hand.

"Is there anyone behind it?"

"How should I know?"

"I thought I could hear someone. You've got better ears than me."

"Shouldn't have listened to music so loud." I put my ear to the crack of the door and strained to hear a breath, or a shift of clothing, but there was nothing but a faint pound of bass. I pulled back and shook my head, before remembering that he couldn't see it. "I don't think there's anyone there."

"Good. In we go then."

The door creaked, and the hallway beyond was a little lighter, enough that we could see the shapes of each other. We followed Lucas past closed doors to a stairwell, and up it to the ground floor. The music from the main VR suite pulsed through the walls, and the silent flickering of lights as we passed through the empty corridors was eerie. Hundreds of people were partying just a few walls away, but we were six people (plus one unconscious maniac) creeping through the back ways. At last we stopped by a closed door with a large "Two" stencilled on it. Lucas tried the handle, but it was locked.

"Secret knock," Mira whispered. "Let me try."

She rapped out a pattern and waited. We sweated through a long pause and then the door opened, and Xiao was wrapping me in a hug that squeezed half the breath out of me.

"Don't die again," he said. "I can't take it."

"I'll try not to. Where's Andrew?"

Xiao pulled back, his face paling. "He's not with you?"

"No." My insides clenched. "Should he be?"

"I thought he was going to stay with you...?" Mira said.

Xiao shook his head. "He went up to meet you guys at Doncaster's house, help you get him down here. You didn't see him?"

We shook our heads. Xiao swore.

A hand squeezed my shoulder and I turned to see Lucas, his face grim.

"He could be fine. But we can't know. Wherever he is, the best thing is to keep going with the plan. We want to change things, right? If anything's... happened... to Andrew, we've got a better chance of fixing it if we expose the authorities. Okay?"

I nodded slowly, unable to speak. This was my fault. But I could fix it.

Lucas swung himself into a seat and started typing and swiping madly, scrolling through code and erasing the record of us in the corridors. Xiao, who'd never met Lucas even when we were kids, drank in the commands and codes over Lucas's shoulder, biting his lip so hard it was white.

Sione and Marcus dragged Doncaster into the VR studio and began to untie him. The room was well sound-proofed, and Xiao assured me that the party noise would be nil once we had the doors shut. We were going to use the production setup, where we wore discreet VR lenses and earpieces that we hoped Doncaster wouldn't notice. If he did, no big deal except we'd have less time to work with before the cops joined the party. Xiao pointed me to the props store when I asked, never taking his eyes off Lucas's screen.

"What are you looking for?" Mira asked, following me. Raymi was sitting sullenly on one of the swing chairs in the corner of the control room, and I could feel her eyes on me until the wall came between us. I shook her out of my mind and looked around at the shelves and cupboards and stacks of strangely-shaped objects. The light wasn't bright enough, so I clicked my fingers and said "brighter" until I could see what some of this junk was.

"Something that might convince Doncaster he's actually out in the bush," I said. "I don't expect him to move much, so something big enough for him to lie on will be fine. Moss or leaves would be good."

"Right." Mira rolled back her sleeves and set her jaw. "I'll take this side, you take that side."

I found a barrel of leaves that felt like real ones, though I wasn't sure what they were made of. There was a barrel of dirt beside it, and then another of fake snow. A few moments later Mira emerged from one of the stacks dragging a lumpy rolled-up mat, but she slapped at my hands when I tried to look and said I'd have to wait until we were in the studio.

Doncaster was displayed in all his pyjama-d glory on the bare floor when I rolled our barrels through the door, the origami sheet thrown in the corner. Lucas, Xiao and Raymi were in the control room through the glass, Lucas still working away with his tongue poking out the corner of his mouth. Marcus was staring down at Doncaster, his expression hard to read, and Sione was checking the emergency escape instructions, hands in his pockets.

Mira unrolled her mat next to Doncaster. It was a carpet of moss, tree roots and little ridges of dirt about three by three metres, plenty big enough to trick an old man. I opened my barrel of leaves and started to spread them around, but Mira took them away from me.

"Leave the set-dressing to the art student," she said. "Look, dirt goes first, okay? Then leaves. Dirt doesn't usually fall from the sky. Leaves do."

"Well, they don't fall from the actual *sky*," I began, but even I could tell she was doing a much better job than I was so I left her to it. Raymi came over to help her. I caught Sione smirking, but his face wiped of all expression as soon as he realised I was looking at him.

I sat down cross-legged, leaned against the wall and closed my eyes. Andrew would be fine. He'd probably just stopped to watch the fireworks, or his parents had caught him sneaking out and grounded him or...

But I couldn't think about that now. I had to focus on the next hour, think back through all the conversations I'd ever had with Doncaster. He'd organised the Plagues, or some of them at least. He'd killed his Match. What was her name?

The conversation came swimming back to me. I could hear Doncaster's voice in my head, see the bottle hanging from his hand as he slurred names. Patrick... and Amy. He'd killed Amy, and he'd loved her. I had to bring her into things, try to make him care about every person he'd sent to their death as much as he'd cared about her.

"Okay, we're ready," a muffled voice floated through from the control room. My eyes snapped open. A speaker crackled and Lucas's voice boomed into the room. "Sorry, we're ready guys."

Mira stood, wiping her hands on her jeans and looking proudly down at the leaf-strewn floor. There were ferns, curling their fronds in one corner, and a moss-covered stump to prop Doncaster against. If I was a bird in the middle of it all, I would be pretty confused. "Now we just need to get Sleeping Beauty on there," she said, nodding at Doncaster.

Marcus and Sione took care of that, and we had our final meeting in the control room.

"If anyone wants to back out now, go for it," Lucas said. He didn't look my way, but I knew he was talking directly to me. "Once you're on the feed, there's no going back. It's not a coward's way out to be back here behind the scenes, making sure it all goes smoothly like my buddy Xiao here, or out of the building entirely." Lucas and Xiao fist-bumped. I stared stonily at Lucas. He cleared his throat. "What I'm saying is, it's not too late. In a few minutes, it's going to be."

"I'm doing it," I said. "No one else knows him, and no one else has heard him confess. You guys are all just strangers to him. He doesn't care what you think. He probably doesn't care what I think, but I at least have a chance."

Marcus nodded. Raymi had her head tipped to one side and her eyes narrowed at me, and I couldn't figure out what she might be thinking. Did she approve of my speech, or did she think I was a stupid kid, like Lucas obviously did?

"I'm in," Mira said, taking my hand. "I want to be part of this."

Nobody else made a move to leave.

"Fine," Lucas said, brow creased. "Raymi, Marcus and Sione will be our getaway crew." He turned to look at Raymi. "But if you get a chance to get away and it's not looking good for us, take it. I don't want you getting caught if you don't have to be."

Raymi stared at the floor and nodded slowly.

"I'll give you one minute to get used to things before I start broadcasting," Xiao said. "Though if you manage to get him to confess in the first thirty seconds, I'm sure I can get it out with a bit of a delay."

"That's not going to happen," Raymi muttered.

"Come on, we can do this, people," Mira said, clapping her hands together. "Where are these special contact lenses I've heard so much about?"

I wished Andrew was here with us, putting on the slick professional VR gear. He'd probably explain the Allocations rules and bore us all, eyes shining. The bulky public VR helmets weren't pretty but they stood up to a lot of wear and tear, whereas these lenses and feather earpieces (that's what it said on the box) didn't. Xiao fitted us all then started on Doncaster, swearing impressively as he tried to get Doncaster's lenses and earpieces in. With a bit of help from Mira, they were finally in, and Xiao withdrew, taking the T-shirt soaked in knock-out cocktail.

We were alone with Doncaster. And a few seconds later, we were alone with Doncaster in a dark forest, the wind whispering through the trees and curling into my hair – the air conditioning was playing its part too. A ruru called from a valley over, and you could hear the sound echoing into the night.

"Wow," I whispered, impressed. I'd never been in this particular sim before – I could go out the door of my house and experience the real thing any time I wanted – but they must use this for tourists wanting to experience the Aotearoa New Zealand bush. The designers had done a pretty good job of it. Our clearing was a little bigger than the mat, and stars speckled the sky in a patch between the overarching trees. I could hear a stream chattering away to my right, and tiny blue lights shone through the trees. Glow worms.

"Um, Xiao? It's overcast," I said. Xiao muttered something and, just like that, the stars were replaced by the shadows of clouds, glowing faintly with reflected light. It wasn't quite as dark as it would be in real life, but hopefully Doncaster wouldn't notice that.

Lucas pulled a tiny bottle out of his pocket and unscrewed the cap. "Smelling salts."

He wafted them under Doncaster's nose.

36

Persuasion

DONCASTER JERKED HIS HEAD away from the bottle, but his eyes were still closed, his breath rattly. Lucas held the salts more firmly beneath his nose and this time the old man's eyes flew open. He slapped at the bottle, but Lucas had already taken a few quick steps back, glancing at me.

Doncaster's eyes were wide, darting. "Where am I?" he demanded.

I leaned over him and waited for his eyes to focus. It didn't take long. His nostrils flared.

"Kieran again."

I held out a hand to pull him up. "Me again."

Doncaster regarded my hand.

"It can't be comfortable lying there," I said flatly. "Sit up."

He chewed the edge of his lip, then took my hand so fast I almost jerked away. I pulled him up, surprised by how light he seemed now I didn't have to carry him all the way from Mount Victoria to the VR suites. His hand was dry and papery, and I dropped it as soon as I could, then squatted so I was level with him.

I could feel the weight of eyes staring at me – Mira, always Mira, Lucas, Lucas's friends, Xiao... and maybe a few hundred million or so more, if Xiao had linked into the feed already. I didn't want to think about them. I had to focus on Doncaster, on getting him to talk about what he'd done.

I could do this. This was a game, this was words and sweet-talking. This was pretending.

"Do you want to know what's been happening to me the last few days?" I began, like we were just chatting in his office. "You must be wondering how I went from intern to terrorist in a few hours."

Doncaster gave the barest twitch of an eyebrow to show that yes, indeed he might like to know how that had happened.

"You remember, a few days ago, I arrived at your office a little..." I tipped my head to one side. The pulse jumped in his neck. "...angry. I'd figured out what you did. I'd figured out you set loose the Great Plagues."

Beat. Let it sink in. Let all the people watching see the mask of his face, the set of his lips as he faced me.

"You didn't deny it. Instead you told me the Matching laws, the laws you helped make and the laws that prevent me from being with the girl I..." Come on, I could do this. "The girl I love. You told me those laws were relics, meaningless. You said you could change the record, make us legal, and you did. In return for my silence."

I smiled at Mira. She forced a tense smile in return.

"The girl I love had a problem with this. She told me it was over between us." I shifted focus back to Doncaster, whose eyes hadn't left me. "I wasn't thinking straight. The only people who'd known about us were Outsiders – PVAFS, peevs – and I went to see them. That wasn't the smartest move. They used me to blow up the dam." I held up my wrist. "Then I got electrocuted by the boundary fence, my chip short-circuited, and I found out the authorities have been drugging me for the past four years to stop me making *trouble*."

"What do you want?" Doncaster said quietly.

"I'd like to know if you think it was worth it, killing ninety-three percent of humanity so we can have this amazing Paradise. Where people are shot for trying to live outside the cities, are told they can't have kids, are drugged, and die because it's more convenient for the authorities." This was for Andrew, wherever he was. Please let him be okay. It was for Elspeth. For Lucas.

Doncaster closed his eyes. "I don't know what you think you're talking about, Kieran, but you've got it wrong. I never said I did any of that. I never said the Great Plagues were my creation."

Okay, I hadn't really expected this to be easy. But it would have been nice if it was.

Lucas shifted, rustling the leaf litter we'd so carefully arranged.

Doncaster's eyes snapped open, his attention drawn to Lucas. He swallowed, expression wary. "It's Lucas, correct?"

"How do you–" Lucas began.

"Oh, you're infamous," Doncaster said. "Youngest hacker we've caught in three decades. Does your cousin know what you did?"

Lucas opened his mouth but nothing came out.

"How many deaths are on your head?" Doncaster continued, but his eyes were back on me, watching to see my reaction.

Deaths?

"I never–" Lucas began heatedly, but Doncaster cut him off, holding up his hands in a placating gesture.

"Maybe that's going too far. You did groundwork, though, didn't you. Hacking. And the Liberate Pōneke Wellington terrorists were training you up to it, weren't they? If you hadn't been caught in that car crash, if the Nix Gen-ens bombings hadn't got your friends caught, you'd be out there, causing mayhem with no one to stop you."

Liberate Pōneke Wellington... Lucas had been part of the group that carried out the bombings? Four years ago. Not long after the crash. Was this the "D-Day" Raymi had mentioned in the dark on the hill? I tried to exchange glances with Lucas, desperate to know that Doncaster was lying, but Lucas wouldn't look at me.

"Lucas. Tell me you didn't..." I trailed off. He still wasn't looking at me.

It was true then.

My chest felt like someone had punched through it. Sure, they'd exposed Gen-ens, but innocent people had died too.

"I tried to stop them!" Lucas burst out, fists clenched at his sides. "Maybe if you'd let me stay undrugged a little longer, no one would have died!"

Doncaster considered him. "Maybe. But you can't live on maybes."

I took a deep breath. Maybe it was true, maybe the bombings would never have happened if Lucas had been there. Or maybe he would have been involved, nixing Gen-ens and murdering people...

No. I couldn't believe that of him, couldn't think that. Doncaster was just trying to throw me off, and I couldn't let him. "It doesn't matter. What matters is that you created the Great Plagues. On purpose."

There was a long silence. The wind whispered through the trees, and I could hardly fault the sim. It sounded exactly like the real thing, none of those crackly compression sounds or narrow tinniness you got from low-pro recordings. Doncaster didn't look like he'd noticed the forest wasn't real, either. He settled himself on the leaves, seeming to grow in confidence. How many other cards did he have up his sleeve?

"Even if I did have some hand in the Plagues – and I'm not saying I did – you need me on your side. Who else would support your Match?"

I'd sort of expected this. If I broke our deal he'd switch us back to an illegal Match. But the Match system was corrupt anyway, wasn't it? If we took him down, we could take that down too.

"I see what you're thinking," he said, eyes boring into me. "But even if you get your Match, that's not the only thing I've done. Mira's diabetic. She'll die without my help."

Without his...

What the hell was diabetic?

Mira looked as confused as I felt.

Doncaster was smiling at her now, in a fatherly sort of way. Patronising. "They had to revise the Matching guidelines because of you and your sister. I took an interest. Usually we'd let nature take its course, but your parents had already lost one child. It didn't seem fair to lose another. And there were a few good Matches in the country that could *almost* eliminate the chances you'd pass it on. Kieran is one of them. Best chemistry match too, I should say. You're lucky."

My blood was roaring in my ears. That they'd let people *die* like this, that Mira was one of them, that she might...

And it was true. My good genes "cancelled out" Mira's bad ones. I glanced at her, but her eyes were locked on Doncaster.

"With a good Match, you won't muddy the gene pool–"

"*Muddy?!*" Mira burst out. Doncaster ignored her.

"...so I set up your chip to manage your insulin levels. Nobody's done insulin management for decades, of course, but the functionality is still there if you know what to code in. You've been diabetic half this year, and you probably didn't even notice."

Mira's hand had gone to her wrist. Her wrist with the dead chip in it.

"Hold on," I said. "You can control it? It's not fatal?"

He shrugged. "It's a simple matter of an imbalance. But there's an expiry date on the code. I'll need to run it again in January."

There it was. The threat.

I'd known Mira might die. She'd told me. But that she could die because the authorities didn't think it was *right* to stop it, that Doncaster was using this to blackmail her, blackmail me–

"You– you–" I didn't have words awful enough to describe him. But his blackmail was working. I didn't want to piss him off.

Mira was very white. Her hand tightened around her wrist, leaving white halos around her fingers.

January. If Doncaster was in a jail cell, could he still do the code? Would the authorities try to stop him? But scratch that, Mira needed a new chip *now*, with Doncaster's insulin code.

Mira could never live outside the cities. She needed their tech to stay alive.

A voice in my ear. Xiao. "Erm, Lucas? Something's happening with the anti-tracking program you started."

Lucas swore softly. I tried not to look at him, or show Doncaster that I'd heard Xiao. We couldn't answer without telling everyone this was a VR sim, but an anti-tracking program glitch was worrying. Xiao was the only one with a chip now, but if they knew to track him, they could find us in a matter of minutes.

"Guys..." Xiao said.

I shook myself. We had to keep going, do as much as we could in the time we had. I'd almost forgotten the world was watching. They'd seen all of this, and Mira's story was just one more nail in the coffin. Maybe someone out there knew how to rig a chip to treat her. Maybe we didn't need Doncaster.

If we could just get him to confess, now, while he was feeling proud of what he'd done... "What about Amy?"

A muscle in Doncaster's cheek clenched.

"Was her life worth all this? If you could go back and do it again, would you do it, knowing you would kill her?"

"Don't talk to me about Amy," Doncaster said, his voice exceedingly soft.

"You didn't mean to do it, did you? You loved her. And you killed her, along with everyone else in the Plagues. Didn't think to give her the cure you had? Couldn't show your hand, let people know you'd had a cure all along? Show you were just waiting until the population numbers were right, so you could say 'thank you, thank you, yes of course I'll rule over you all'."

Doncaster shook his head. "You're delusional."

"I'm not!" I sounded pretty delusional saying that, so I squeezed my eyes shut and tried again. "You killed all those people."

"You really think I'll admit that? When you're probably recording me?"

I swallowed. He was only half-right. He hadn't guessed we were broadcasting live.

"Don't you think you owe it to people? Don't you owe it to Amy? It's the only human thing to do."

He was laughing, chuckles shaking his frail body. He gripped my wrist. "You know the ironic thing, Kieran? All your worry about humanity and fixing things?" He squeezed harder. "If people knew what you are, they'd kill you. You need secrets kept as much as I do."

"That's it," Lucas said, striding over and wrenching Doncaster away from me. "The only talking you do now is telling us how you managed to murder most of the world. Okay?"

"Wait." Of course Doncaster was just baiting me, like he'd baited Lucas and Mira. But Lucas's reaction... "What do you mean, they'd kill me?"

"Kieran–"

"Shut up, Lucas."

"Kieran, you don't–"

"I said, shut up."

Doncaster's eyes crinkled. He pulled out of Lucas's grasp and re-arranged the lapels of his pyjamas. Lucas's lip curled. I could tell he really wanted to kick him.

"*What did you mean*?" I repeated.

"No one's told you, then?" Doncaster raised his eyebrows. "I would have thought... or maybe you might have guessed, smart boy that you are. You're a Gen-en, Kieran."

The world seemed to tilt.

My heart was eating at my ribs.

"What?" I said, very quietly. The breath wouldn't come out for me to speak louder.

"You were genetically engineered," Doncaster continued. "By your mother. You had a lung abnormality before you were born, but she fixed it. And did a few more tweaks while she was at it. In for a penny, in for a pound, right? I bet she thought no one would notice."

"You're lying," I said. A fake bird chirruped from the trees above. Of course he was lying. Wasn't he the keeper of the greatest lie of all time?

But... Dad had almost said something, that night in the kitchen. Mum had cut him off.

"I know it must be a shock, but it's really nothing to be ashamed of."

Nothing–

Nothing to be ashamed of?

Doncaster was watching me. "Maybe it's a lot to get your head around. With what they teach you in school these days, I'm not surprised. But I assure you, I'm not lying. Your cousin can tell you, can't you, Lucas?"

I turned slowly to Lucas, ready to swap rolled eyes, but he wouldn't look at me.

"Lucas?" I choked out. "Lucas? It's not true." There was a long pause.

I could hear the birds and the trees and the breaths of every person in the VR. Mira, the air catching in her throat. Doncaster, a little rattly but steady. The long hiss of Lucas's breath as he let it out.

And me. Though I was hardly breathing at all.

"Tell me it's not true."

Lucas looked up into the trees. "There was a list," he said, his voice far away. "A list of suspected Gen-ens the authorities hadn't done anything about. It had a few well-known people on it. Embarrassing. My group... wanted to pick them all off. Make sure the Gen-ens weren't going to kill everyone again." He chewed the inside of his cheek. "You were on the list, Kieran."

The world was coming down around me. This was VR, this was fake, it would disappear the instant Xiao flicked a switch. It would.

"Maybe... it was a mistake?"

He shook his head. "I asked your mum, that last day before the car crash. You're a Gen-en. I'd already taken you off the list, and made sure the authorities wouldn't notice you again. It took quite a bit of hacking." He swallowed. "I'm pretty sure that's how they caught me."

"But of course it didn't stay hacked for long," Doncaster said. "By the time I came across your file a few months ago, there it was in the restricted access information, security freshly strengthened, safe from prying eyes. So you see, some things are better kept quiet. None of this has to get out."

I found myself on my feet, swaying. All this was fake. Everything was fake.

I was fake.

"Kieran–" Lucas began. I shook my head.

"Shut up."

I forced myself to look at Mira. She had both hands over her mouth and her eyes were wide. But she was staring at Doncaster. Not at me.

She wasn't looking at me.

"I–" I stumbled away from Doncaster and Lucas, up the fake path away from everyone. If I went too far I'd hit a wall, but the fake forest looked like it would go on for ever and ever and maybe I could lose myself in it, just lose myself like an Outsider, never go back and have to face anyone ever again, explain myself, prove myself as a person, prove I had emotions, morality, a soul–

Just like the Gen-en at the hospital. And they'd nixed her.

I reached the wall. Where was the door? I turned.

Lucas was standing over Doncaster with a gun.

37
Gen-en

"Lucas, no–" Mira began, but Lucas had already fired. The explosion echoed through the VR suite.

Doncaster let out a sharp gasp. A patch of deep red spread across his stripy grey pyjama shoulder.

Lucas's arm was stiff, his hand clenched around the gun. Where had he got a gun from? Had he taken it from Doncaster's house? Or had he been carrying it since before then, since he'd taken the supplies from behind the safe house?

I felt hollow, far from everything here, like I was one of the millions of people who were probably watching us right now. Who'd just seen Lucas – Lucas, my cousin – shoot Edward Doncaster. Who'd heard Doncaster say I was a Gen-en.

It didn't seem real. It wasn't real.

"I think I've missed your lungs and your heart, if you have one," Lucas said in a flat voice. I heard the shock crushed beneath – or was I imagining it? Was I really just hoping to see some flash of the old Lucas?

The one who'd never told me about his girlfriend or his hacking or his part in the struggle of Outsiders against city-dwellers. The one who'd known what I was, and had kept it from me.

The one who'd got caught, drugged to oblivion, because he was trying to protect me.

"But I'm not really an expert," Lucas said, in that same flat voice. "Might be fatal. We could get you medical treatment. But I think you know what that will cost."

Doncaster's eyes were scrunched shut and his breath was quick and shallow, but he still hadn't cried out. His teeth edged over his lower lip, digging deep into his skin and leeching it white, and he pressed his hand against the red. His heart was going a mile a minute, rushing the blood through his veins and drawing him closer to death–

Lucas's face flashed into my mind, asking me if there was anyone behind the basement door. *You've got better ears than me.*

Normal people couldn't hear other people's heartbeats. I'd only noticed them occasionally, when I was close to someone and it was quiet or I'd had too much caffeine. But I wasn't normal. Mum was always so touchy about her hearing aids – of course she'd supercharge my hearing if she got the chance.

I squeezed my eyes shut, trying to derail my thoughts.

"You want a confession," Doncaster started, his hoarse voice loud in my ears. I opened my eyes. The fake world was moving, swaying in the roar of my mind, but I didn't think it was a problem with the VR. "I think I'd rather be a martyr," Doncaster said, lips twisting into a grimaced smile. "Shot in the forest by a terrorist, dying–" He sucked in a coarse breath. "Dying far from help, taking my genius and my secrets to the grave."

I choked out a laugh. If only he knew. The police were probably right outside. We were running out of time. And when they came to save him, they'd arrest Lucas for what he'd done, and me for what I am, and everyone else for aiding and abetting...

Wait.

"This isn't the forest," I said. Lucas whipped around to stare at me. I wouldn't meet his eyes.

I cleared my throat. "This is a sim. You're on a live feed to pretty much every corner of the planet. And you just told them all I'm– I'm..."

I couldn't even say it. I closed my eyes and forced out the words. "I'm genetically engineered. You know what that means for me. I'm illegal. I shouldn't exist. If the authorities don't have me nixed or experimented on, terrorists will take me out." I opened my eyes and tried to pour all my confusion, my hurt, my determination into my gaze, trying to communicate all that I was and all that I could be. Maybe I didn't have a soul. Maybe I wasn't a real person. But I felt real.

Doncaster's face was frozen white, from pain or shock I didn't know.

"The Gen-en laws go back to the Plagues. If Gen-ens killed everyone, it proved they were evil. So evil they weren't people at all. But you and I know that Gen-ens had nothing to do with the Plagues." I had him. He couldn't look away. "Right?"

A step towards him. All eyes on me. I was hot, cold, hairs standing up all over my body. If this didn't work, there was no place for me anywhere. "You could save me. You couldn't save Amy, but you can save me. Maybe you don't care about your own life. But I know you can care. That's why you did it, right? Because you cared about the world, and you wanted to see it survive?"

There was a long pause. The world had shrunk to just me and him and the pain clouding his face.

He swallowed and his eyes fluttered shut. His hand clenched in the red blood still seeping from his shoulder. Had I done it?

He licked his lips. He mouthed something, cleared his throat, and began to speak.

"We were destroying the Earth, the climate, the balance of things. There were too many people, too many wars, too much pollution and poverty. Something had to happen. If we hadn't done it, someone else would have."

No one breathed.

"The pandemics of '67 and '70, those were nothing to do with us. Completely natural, as far as I know, just like in the 2020s – viruses mutating and becoming extremely effective killers. But they got me thinking." He was talking quickly now, his voice strained. "And then I found the C38-13-L gene. Two percent of the population had it, spread evenly across the world. Equal for all ethnicities, all religions. If I engineered a virus to target everyone without it, we could solve so many problems. Reset.

"So I did."

Mira made a funny sort of choking sound. I glanced at her and saw the tear-streaks on her cheeks, her lowered eyes.

She thought Gen-ens didn't have true feelings, same as everyone else. Same as I'd thought. But I was a Gen-en and I loved her, and if she could no longer love me...

I was breaking into tiny sharp pieces inside.

The room went blank. The rustling, living bush was gone, and my eyes slowly adjusted to the plain white of the VR studio, the lights dim so they wouldn't interfere with the VR.

There was a thunk. I turned and saw Lucas had dropped the gun to the ground. "We're done."

Doncaster shook his head.

"Do you think you've made the world a better place?" he said. Specks of blood dotted his lips and his breath crackled in his lungs, too loud to be healthy. Though maybe that was just my Gen-en ears again. "Do you really think you have?"

"They're coming for you," came Xiao's shaky whisper. "I couldn't keep the sim going. I'm sorry."

"It doesn't matter anymore," Lucas said. "We have what we wanted. Let them come." He glanced down at Doncaster, his face still flat, clean of expression. "He needs saving."

Doncaster squeezed his eyes shut. His head moved, so subtly I almost missed it, but he shook his head.

"Let me die."

"No," I said. "You can't... you can't just get out of this that easily. The rest of us–"

Hammering. The door shuddered. It was a studio door, not meant for high-level security. They'd be through it in seconds. There was still the back door, but then I heard hard footsteps beyond that door too.

All exits blocked. I guess it was back to my original exit strategy: getting caught.

I glanced at Lucas, but he still wouldn't meet my eyes. Did he think I was an imitation of a person? Playing a part? An imposter?

He'd saved my life four years ago, even knowing what I was. So he must believe there was something more to me than just muscle, blood and bone.

Even if he couldn't look at me now.

The lights went out. I could see only dim shapes in the darkness. And then someone was tugging the back of my hoodie, pulling me down, back, and the floor wasn't where it should be when I flung out my hand to halt my fall, but someone had hold of my shoulders and was lowering and pulling me at the same time.

There was a hole in the floor, and I was in it. I felt the edges slip past my scrabbling fingers and the black dense darkness became even blacker. Hands supported me, guiding me down until my feet hit the floor. Another person – two? – dropped down and something slid shut. A trapdoor.

The dirt milkshake smell was in my nose again. We were back in the basement, somewhere near the hole into the tunnels.

A door crashed open above. The police must have finally broken through, and would be pouring into the VR suite, tasers trained on anything that moved.

"What–" I whispered, pulling away from the hands on my shoulders. In the dark I couldn't see who it was, but I guessed from the breathing and from logic that it was Lucas. "What the hell, Lucas?"

"See, he doesn't even want saving," Raymi muttered.

"Are we getting out of here, or not?" came Mira's voice, from beside Raymi. Thank god.

"Getting out of here," Raymi said, pushing us across the room. She flicked on a tiny torch and held it above us, shadows stretching forward and jumping on walls. We found the laser-cut hole and squeezed through, Lucas, me, Mira, Raymi.

We ran. Lucas turned left at a crossroads, and then a right, through a door (lock already broken), down another tunnel.

A dozen metres in, Lucas staggered and fell against the dank wall.

"I'm fine," he said, brushing me off. "Are they in the tunnel yet?"

I listened past our breaths. I couldn't hear anyone, but I didn't know if I'd be able to. "I don't think so."

"The exit isn't far," Raymi said. "We need to keep moving."

"One minute," Lucas said, hands on his knees as he caught his breath. "Kieran, I'm sorry. I didn't want you to–"

"To know what I am?" I said, voice flat. Like I was the soulless thing everyone expected. Gen-en. *Gen-en.*

"To get hurt!" Lucas said. "I didn't want you to get hurt!"

"You shot Doncaster."

"How else would anyone believe he was the real one? It's like Andrew said, they'd think he was just an actor or a deep fake. If he's actually shot, they can't ignore it."

Andrew. Where was he, arrested? And Xiao was still back in the VR control room, probably in handcuffs. We were just leaving them. Just running, and hiding.

Hiding wasn't going to help anyone.

A distant slam, booted feet.

"They're in the tunnels," I said. "You need to go. You shot Doncaster. They're not going to go easy on you."

Lucas straightened, eyes wide. "What? No, Kieran–"

I took a deep breath. "If I disappear, that's the easy way out for them. They can forget about me. Let everyone else forget about me too. But if I'm there, they can't ignore me. Like you said. If they have to answer to people about what they've done with me, maybe– maybe it can change something. Maybe I can get Mira her dia-whatsit medicine, and they'll free Nīkau and Andrew and Xiao–"

Lucas's hand clutched onto my arm. He was shaking. "And what about you, Kieran? The law says you're not technically a person. They can do what they want to you. The others they have to give a fair trial, but you..."

I almost gave in, then. But I remembered the Gen-en's face in the hospital corridor, the sound of gunfire as the cops shot at her and I did nothing.

"Lucas," Raymi said in a low voice. "If we don't go now..."

The footsteps were getting closer. I pushed Lucas away. "Go. I'll distract them, I'll be all right."

He threw his arms around me, squeezing the air out of my lungs.

"Be careful, little cuz." Our hearts beat together and I squeezed him back. "Have you still got that holosphere? Your mum was trying to tell you something. Maybe it'll help convince everyone else too."

"I've got it. I'll try."

Raymi pulled him away down the tunnel.

I turned to Mira, to say goodbye even if – the thought twisted ice into my heart – even if she couldn't love me anymore. But she'd barely moved. The light from Raymi's torch was fading.

"You think I'm leaving you here by yourself?" she said.

I swallowed. "You haven't looked at me since you found out I'm a Gen-en."

"If you're a Gen-en... they can't all be evil." With an effort, she stared into my eyes. "I want to stay with you."

"Get arrested with me."

"I've never been arrested."

"Mira–"

She kissed me, arms tight around my neck, breath hot against my skin.

And that's how they found us. Torchlight dancing on the walls. Hands around my shoulders, under my arms, pulling me away, faces flashing past, blurred into nothing. They pulled my wrists together behind my back. The sharp bite of steel tightening to hold my hands in place.

Mira smiled, and it was brave, and fierce, and defiant.

38
Future

REPORTERS WERE WAITING FOR us outside the police station, pointing cameras first at Mira's cop car and then at mine. They couldn't see through the windows – I'd watched similar newscasts of mirrored cop cars disappearing into the depths of a police station. Now I was in one of those cop cars, images beaming across the world.

This was what I'd wanted, I told myself as we slid into the dim underground garage, gates clanging shut behind us. They'd recuffed my hands in front and the metal cuffs were cold against my wrists, a red light blinking on the short bar that linked them. The more people knew I was here, the more people would question what was happening. And hopefully I'd planted enough seeds of doubt that the authorities couldn't just smooth things over.

Plus Lucas's stunt with the gun.

Was Doncaster still alive? I hadn't seen anything of him except a smear of blood on the fake leaves. The cops in my car hadn't even given me the time, so I didn't bother asking about Doncaster.

Did I want him to live?

Or not?

He'd given up his secret to save my life.

A yawning chasm opened inside me. *Gen-en*. If people still believed Gen-ens were evil at their soulless core, I was a threat just by existing.

—— · ——

The cell they put me in was better than I expected. Bed, stainless steel toilet, warm. I eyed the air conditioning vent, wondering if I might squeeze through, but I'd have to lose a few dozen kilos and dislocate my shoulders to have any chance. The cell was in a corridor of similar cells and I closed my eyes and listened, trying to hear other people. May as well use my freak hearing, right?

I *could* hear breathing. Two sets. I remembered earlier in the night, hearing Mira's breath around the corner. Was she here?

"Mira?" I called.

"Kieran?" Yes! It was her. At least they'd put us in the same cell block.

"Xiao!" came Xiao's voice.

"Xiao?"

"Yeah. Thought I'd join in, seeing as no one was calling *my* name."

"You all right?"

"Trying not to think about it." He paused. "Are you?"

He would have heard Doncaster's revelations. "Also... trying not to think about it."

"Jessica will rep us," Mira said, her voice certain. How could she still be so determined, so sure in the face of everything that had happened? "She'll make sure they code my chip to manage my health. She'll get us all out. I still have the holosphere, too, that will help."

If they decided the history in it was worth believing.

Mira kept asking for water and her voice got softer as the day wore on. Was this the diabetes? How long did she have?

—— · ——

I woke from broken sleep around eight the next morning. The door was open, and a guard jerked his head for me to get up. A second guard put the handcuffs back on my wrists, and they led me down the hall to a small room with a chair and not much else. One wall was frosted glass, and when they left me the glass cleared. A mirror-image room was on the other side, and Mum was sitting on the chair, hands clenched tight in her lap. Her brow cleared when she saw me.

"Thank god. Have they hurt you? Have they fed you?"

"No. What– I–" I wasn't awake yet. I looked away and tried again. It was easier if I wasn't looking at her. "Is Lucas–"

"Disappeared."

My heart lightened. "Do you know if Andrew–"

"I just spoke to his mother. He's out on bail."

"And Nīkau?"

"Nīkau?" She shook her head. "I don't know a Nīkau."

"He–" No, if she hadn't seen him on newscasts she wouldn't know anything. And I couldn't describe how he'd helped me and Lucas, people were definitely watching us. "Never mind. What about Doncaster? Is he...?"

"He's in the hospital. Stable, they say, but they'll keep him there for a while under guard. Are you–" Her hands clenched tight again. "We don't have long. How are you?"

I laughed but cut myself off, feeling like I might never stop otherwise. "Not great. Mira's sick. They might nix me. And you–you did this. Me. Gen-en."

"Kieran." Her voice cracked on my name. "You would have died without it. I had the opportunity. I thought it was worth the risk. *You* were worth the risk."

"But I–" How could I explain it to her? She didn't have to second-guess her own nature. Fight against her own prejudices. "Doncaster said he wanted to erase the differences between people so they'd stop killing each other. But erasing the differences didn't solve anything. It just made people obsess over new differences. The world hates evil soulless Gen-ens. Hates me. And–" I swallowed. I'd agreed to keep Doncaster's secret so I could be with Mira. Maybe it wasn't just the drugs. Maybe it was my Gen-en heart. "And how do I know they're wrong?"

She looked like she might cry. "I know you, Kieran. You're kind and brave and loyal. Maybe misguided sometimes, but so is everyone. When I decided to do... what I did... I knew there was more to Gen-ens than what they told us. My father told me about a girl my grandfather knew when he was young. She was a Gen-en. The holosphere I gave you, it was hers."

The boy in the pictures. Had he been my great-grandfather?

"You uncovered the lie, Kieran. Things can change. They already are. There are protests happening all around the world – San Francisco, Berlin, Johannesburg, Tokyo, Sydney. Here."

"About what?" I asked. My throat was dry. I hadn't been able to think of what might be happening outside my cell.

"Everything. The lie about Gen-ens. Withholding medicine. Drugging people. Matching and reproduction laws. The rules for PVAFS."

"Outsiders," I said. She nodded.

"Things can change, Kieran. They just need time. And someone to make a stand."

—— · ——

The call on Mira's meds came through by nightfall. Yes, they'd tracked down the code for insulin management and they would do it. Right now it was an emergency exception, but Jessica Riley said they'd be revising a whole lot of legislation in the coming weeks, months and years, and things like diabetes management would become common practice. A nurse put another chip in Mira's arm and I stopped imagining the worst. Jessica had news of Nīkau too – they were holding him pending trial, but treating him well.

The decision on my status came the day after. Nixing was off the table. Until they figured out what to do about Gen-ens, they'd treat me like a human minor.

It was a win.

—— · ——

They broadcast Doncaster's trial, but I didn't get to see it. No screens in cells. The first I knew was when Jessica called me and Mira into the glass-divided interview room.

"The verdict's guilty," Jessica said, as soon as the frosted glass cleared. Mira and I were sitting two metres apart, still handcuffed and chairs bolted to the floor. There was spark in Mira's eyes that hadn't been there last I saw her. "Didn't take long at all, really, with his confession on record and your holosphere's historical context clinching it. I think the court couldn't do anything else, with some of these protests threatening to break into riots. People dechipping themselves. Outsiders leading peace parades into the cities. The authorities are going to have to do a lot to regain trust."

"What does that mean for us?" Mira asked.

"The courts need to decide if your actions were illegal or justified and, if I may say, heroic. They'll push back your trial until there's more agreement on what the law looks like going forward. Same with your mother, Kieran, and Nīkau, Andrew and Xiao."

I hadn't known how tense I'd been until those words. The muscles in my shoulders and neck began to unwind. "What happens now?"

"Everything's pretty chaotic at the moment, but I'm confident I can get you out on bail."

"And our Match?"

I twisted to face Mira. "You still–"

"I meant what I said in that tunnel, Kieran."

"They repealed the percentage rule, replaced it with the old blood-relation rule." Jessica said, smiling. "So now there's nothing against your Match."

Screw the guards. I shot out of my chair and met Mira halfway, looping my cuffs over her head so I could hold her. She did the same to me and we spun in a circle, laughing, and kissed like it was the first time.

—— · ——

Everyone thought I should stay out of town for a while, just until the courts sorted things out and the protests died down. Mira's parents invited me to spend the rest of the summer on the Mākara wind farm, where there were fewer reporters and people to stare. After a sleepless night trying not to relive the crash, I said yes. I needed to face things. And the crash had screwed up my life, but it had begun the unravelling of so many lies. The world was changing because of it.

Andrew stayed over the night before so he could see me off. "I have news," he announced when he came in the door, practically fizzing.

"You're coming too?"

"What? No." He furrowed his brow at me. "Unless you want me to? I don't want to be a third wheel or anything..."

"I was joking." We didn't quite have the easiness we'd had before, but we were getting there. Things took time to heal, Margaret said, and we just had to keep trying. Talk things out when we needed to. I think he'd forgiven me for not telling him about genome categories – at least, he said he had and I was beginning to believe him. "But you'd better visit."

His face cleared. "Of course I'll visit. But guess what."

I grinned. "What?"

Andrew checked around for stray parents or little sisters, then came close, his voice low. "Prajna sent me a message. She saw me on the news and wanted to check I was all right."

"That's great!" I said cautiously, hoping there was more to it. If this was just a few texts, he was way too excited and I didn't want to see him disappointed again.

"Then she called, and we talked and she said she was sorry, and she's been going to the protests against genome categories and everything. She asked if I could forgive her, and if I ever wanted to get back together, she was up for it. I think– I think we might actually have a chance."

"Amazing!" I slapped my hand against his and pulled him in for a hug. "You guys are so good together. Hey! We can go on double dates at the VR suites! Once, like, court goes well. And I'm back from exile."

"Summer exile. Over before you know it."

We spent half the night gaming and talking, falling asleep in the living room in front of the TV. It was almost like old times.

—— · ——

"Are you sure?" Mum said for the twentieth time as I swung my pack on my back the next morning. She'd begun looking me in the eye again few days ago, when I made a weak joke about super hearing. I didn't know if I'd forgiven her yet, but I was on the way to it. Another thing where all the good and the bad was tangled up together – if she hadn't done what she did, I wouldn't have lived. But now I had to live with it, fight back against all the Gen-en myths that were lodged so deep in my head. Not to mention everyone else's Gen-en phobia.

The Mākara minivan was waiting for me, its gruff driver at the wheel. My bike was already on the back.

"I'm sure," I said. "It'll be fun."

Verity gave a snort that could have been a laugh. "You just want some alone time with your *girlfriend.*" Her eyes were sparkling with tears though, so I wrapped her in a tight hug.

"I'll be back soon. You guys can come out and visit, even."

"Cycling day trip," Dad said. "That'll be an adventure, Ver."

I pulled my parents into the hug, and dragged Andrew in too. "It's only a few weeks."

"Stay safe," Mum said. "Don't do anything stupid."

"Me? Stupid?" I gave a watery grin and climbed into the minivan.

—— · ——

I watched for the corner where the crash happened, but there were so many corners and I couldn't be sure which of them it was.

And then we were turning in the gate of the compound, wind turbines towering above us, and Mira was running to meet me, and it didn't matter which corner. It was in the past, and this was my future.

She kissed me before I'd even left the van. It was long and sweet and I hadn't even known how much I'd missed it. Someone wolf-whistled from a window above us.

"Ha!" she said when we broke away, her cheeks pink. Her middle finger was extended towards the wolf-whistler, but her eyes were on me. "No more secrecy. How was the drive?"

"Bearable."

"Good."

"How are the meds?"

She tapped her wrist and made a face. "Don't even notice it's doing anything, so it must be working. I feel way better than I did on New Year's Day."

"Thank god." I wrapped my arms around her and squeezed until she pushed me away, laughing.

—— · ——

My room was in the guest wing, a few minutes' walk from the Sorenssen family apartment. It was small; a single bed beside a window looking over a courtyard, a wardrobe and a desk and chair. The window was open, letting in a breeze and the sound of birdsong. I dumped my things and let Mira drag me to the kitchens, where she picked up a rucksack from the cook. There weren't many people around – most of the workers were out on the wind farm, including Mira's dad – and a few of them looked at me askance as we passed. I tried to ignore it. There were enough smiles on the other people to make me feel I was welcome.

We looked in on Mira's mum in the shared office. I put on my best charm – anything I could do to convince her she'd made the right decision inviting me here.

"Where are you off to?" she asked, eying Mira's cycling shoes.

"It's a surprise," she said. "We'll be back by dinner."

Half a bottle of sunscreen later, we were on our bikes and threading our way down the road, trees reaching overhead to touch and birds flitting from branch to branch. The stream chattered beside us. A kēreru flew past, its wings beating the air.

The stream grew wider until it could only be called a river. It spread across the valley and lapped at the rubble of the old road, a road that now led straight into the water. The dam had never protected this part of Wellington from the ocean. Mira swung up onto a bike track that followed the riverbank, curving between water and trees.

Not long after, the hills opened out and the river became the sea.

White breakers swept around to the left of the narrow beach, driftwood scattered amongst the clumps of seaweed. Rust-riddled iron twisted in drifts of sand – the only remnants of the settlement the sea had taken – beach grasses and sandpipers bringing new life to the ruins. Across the river mouth a few dunes rose beneath hills that were almost cliffs. Sun danced on the water. Seagulls surfed the blustery breeze.

"Mākara Beach," I murmured, drawing to a stop. "It's beautiful."

"Yep," Mira said. She pointed across the river mouth. A tiny figure stood beneath the rockface, and as I watched they dragged a kayak into the water. "There's someone waiting for you."

I recognised him. Lucas. In a second I'd thrown down my bike and was running into the water, feet sliding on the shifting stones. It didn't take him long to kayak across the two hundred metre stretch and as soon as he was close enough I grabbed him in a rough hug. The kayak tipped and he dropped the oar, but he hugged me back just as strong.

"We made it," Lucas said. He'd put on weight. "Only four years late."

"A few detours," I returned.

Mira had saved the oar, and helped drag the kayak up onto the beach. It didn't seem real. Me, Lucas, here. Alive and well.

We caught up over a picnic lunch from Mira's rucksack. Lucas was living with the Horokiwi Outsiders in a new spot up the coast, and seemed to have found a niche fixing their IT gear. I could tell he'd move on eventually, though. Despite their dabble with revenge, the Horokiwi group liked the quiet life and Lucas wanted something more.

"Raymi?" I asked, but he shook his head. Maybe he'd find another Outsider group somewhere. Or maybe one day the cities would open up enough to welcome him back.

Lucas had brought a container of stew from Ruby's kitchen, and set about heating it over a small burner. We ate Mira's strawberries and garlic bread, apples, cheese and crackers, choc mint fudge bars and ginger beer. Ruby had been allowed into the city to see Nīkau, who was being kept on remand pending trial. He looked good, Lucas said, and his lawyer was confident about the trial – Mikale, Adelaide and Jake had been the ringleaders for the dam attack, and Nīkau had only been helping save a life when he stole the antidote for Lucas. Mikale, Adelaide and Jake themselves had disappeared into the bush.

Lucas and I told stories of our adventures in the old days, things I couldn't bear to remember a few weeks ago. Now they were stories shared, stories of good times that might come again.

The sun was far through the sky when he left us, promising to message when he could.

"Happy?" Mira was lying next to me, my arm beneath her head.

I turned and kissed her hair. "Happy. Thank you."

"What are world's best girlfriends for?"

"Oh, so you're claiming that title, are you?"

"I don't see any evidence to refute it." She counted things off on her fingers. "Helped you break your cousin out of hospital, helped you kidnap a national hero, helped you take down the whole damn government, at great cost to my own health. Got arrested with you, jailed with you, freed with you–"

"We don't know how permanent that is," I broke in. She gave me a disbelieving eyebrow.

"With your handsome face? No one's going to lock you away again."

"I feel objectified and labelled."

She laughed and grabbed my chin to kiss me.

The world had changed, was still changing. And we'd had some part in that. Soon I'd go back to school, try to find my place amongst everyone, figure out what I wanted to do with the rest of my life. Deal with people who thought I shouldn't be there. But for now the sun was shining, the waves crashing onto the beach, Lucas had a future, and I was lying here with Mira. Together.

Where I was supposed to be.

Acknowledgements

THIS BOOK HAS BEEN a long time in the making. There are so many people who've played a part in its journey, and I would be very surprised if I manage to capture all their names on this page, but here goes. Deepest everlasting apologies to those I miss...

To all the people who've seen and given comments on different versions of this book, thank you for your insights, your generosity and your time. It's made the book so much stronger, and I very much appreciate it. Thanks to my cover designer too, for a beautiful atmospheric cover.

Thanks to Ms Lippert, who read us many amazing young adult books aloud and ignited my love for YA. To Isobel, for companionable reading at lunchtimes in the library. To the person who wrote a misleading information sheet on how many 300 level credits you needed to graduate with a BA, which led to me taking an emergency summer course on dystopias and reading Brave New World. To all my friends and cousins who have dealt with me foisting my books on them and asking hopefully, are you finished yet? What did you think?

Thanks to Nicola, for reading early versions and all the awesome times together. To Andie, for suggesting we stay up until dawn and watch sunrise over the Remutakas with champagne (and for putting me up while I did my emergency summer course). To Gemma, for fly line discussions and enthusiastic reads of other manuscripts. To all my writing group friends, in London, Sydney and Wellington, for all the productive chats and writing company. Jessica, for being a wonderful writing buddy, critique partner and Canberra guide. Jackie, my amazing cohost, who suggested that maybe Kieran and Mira didn't need quite as many bombshells in their relationship. Monique, for the close read and discussions of the future. Thanks to Mel for so much writing and publishing advice and commiserations, and being the queen of organising get-togethers, and to Emma for being so supportive and such a lovely person.

And finally thank you to my whānau: Mum, who is always willing to read and proofread and accompany me to Seatoun to stare at where a dam might go or take pictures, Dad, who thought I might like Gattaca, loves to debate interesting questions, and is a tech extraordinaire, Diane, for her steadfast support and encouragement, and Declan, for name suggestions and patiently waiting for stories to be finished. Look, I finished this one!

About the author

Sanna Thompson lives in Pōneke Wellington, Aotearoa New Zealand with a cat, some friends, and many books. She once spent a year climbing up and down Brooklyn Hill, the same route Kieran takes home, and loves walking on wild, windy beaches – as long as there's coffee and gelato nearby. The Paradise Generation is her first novel, and was shortlisted for the Storylines Tessa Duder Award in 2022. You can find her at www.sannathompson.com or on Instagram or Twitter (/X) @sannathonz. If you'd like to sign up to Sanna Thompson's newsletter (and/or get a bonus short story from Mira's point of view, "Mira, Alone"), go to linktr.ee/sannathonz.

Made in the USA
Middletown, DE
20 November 2024

64971868R00208